Crimes Collide Vol. 5

A Mystery Short Story Series

Kristine Kathryn Rusch
and Dean Wesley Smith

wmg
PUBLISHING

Crimes Collide, Vol. 5

Published by WMG Publishing

Cover design by Allyson Longueira/WMG Publishing

ISBN-13: 978-1-56146-716-7
ISBN-10: 1-56146-716-2

Due to limitations of space, expanded copyright information can be found on page 527.

Contents

Noir or Dark

Kristine Kathryn Rusch

I began this series of introductions for the volumes of Crimes Collide with an introduction titled "Light or Cozy." And here's the follow-up.

I don't expect you all to read these books in order. I don't even expect you to read them all at the same time. Or to read them all, for that matter, since some have subject matter that might not appeal to you.

Most people prefer light reading. But some of us also read very dark fiction. Dean and I both write very dark fiction at times. And then we pretend we have no idea where those ideas came from.

My dark stories here are very dark. I scan the titles and see that not a one of them would have fit into the "light or cozy" volume. Then I scan Dean's titles and realize the same thing.

When Dean writes dark, his stories are usually short, sharp, and very powerful.

You need to read this volume with the lights on. No reading on your phone in the dark in bed. Make sure every light in the house is blazing and all the doors are locked.

Don't say I didn't warn you....

Ten Stories by Kristine Kathryn Rusch

Cowboy Grace

Kristine Kathryn Rusch

Cowboy Grace

"Every woman tolerates misogyny," Alex said. She slid her empty beer glass across the bar, and tucked a strand of her auburn hair behind her ear. "How much depends on how old she is. The older she is the less she notices it. The more she expects it."

"Bullshit." Carole took a drag on her Virginia Slim, crossed her legs, and adjusted her skirt. "I don't tolerate misogyny."

"Maybe we should define the word," Grace said, moving to the other side of Carole. She wished her friend would realize how much the smoking irritated her. In fact, the entire night was beginning to irritate her. They were all avoiding the topic du jour: the tiny wound on Grace's left breast, stitches gone now, but the skin still raw and sore.

"Mis-ah-jenny." Carole said, as if Grace were stupid. "Hatred of women."

"From the Greek," Alex said. "Misos or hatred and gyne or women."

"Not," Carole said, waving her cigarette as if it were a baton, "misogamy, which is also from the Greek. Hatred of marriage. Hmm. Two male misos wrapped in one."

The bartender, a diminutive woman dressed wearing a red and white cowgirl outfit, complete with fringe and gold buttons, snickered. She set down a napkin in front of Alex and gave her another beer.

"Compliments," she said, "of the men at the booth near the phone."

Alex looked. She always looked. She was tall, busty, and leggy, with a crooked nose thanks to an errant pitch Grace had thrown in the 9th grade, a long chin and eyes the color of wine. Men couldn't get enough of her. When Alex rebuffed them, they slept with Carole and then talked to Grace.

The men in the booth near the phone looked like corporate types on a junket. Matching gray suits, different ties—all in a complimentary shade of pink, red, or cranberry—matching haircuts (long on top, styled on the sides), and differing goofy grins.

"This is a girl bar," Alex said, shoving the glass back at the bartender. "We come here to diss men, not to meet them."

"Good call," Carole said, exhaling smoke into Grace's face. Grace agreed, not with the smoke or the rejection, but because she wanted time with her friends. Without male intervention of any kind.

"Maybe we should take a table," Grace said.

"Maybe." Carole crossed her legs again. Her mini was leather, which meant that night she felt like being on display. "Or maybe we should send drinks to the cutest men we see."

They scanned the bar. Happy Hour at the Oh Kaye Corral didn't change much from Friday to Friday. A jukebox in the corner, playing Patty Loveless. Cocktail waitresses in short skirts and ankle boots with big heels. Tin stars and Wild West art on the walls, unstained wood and checkered tablecloths adding to the effect. One day, when Grace had Alex's courage and Carole's gravely voice, she wanted to walk in, belly up to the bar, slap her hand on its polished surface, and order whiskey straight up. She wanted someone to challenge her. She wanted to pull her six-gun and have a stare-down, then and there. Cowboy Grace, fastest gun in the West. Or at least in Racine on a rainy Friday night.

"I don't see cute," Alex said. "I see married, married, divorced, desperate, single, single, never-been-laid, and married."

Grace watched her make her assessment. Alex's expression never changed. Carole was looking at the men, apparently seeing whether or not she agreed.

Typically, she didn't.

"I dunno," she said, pulling on her cigarette. "Never-Been-Laid's kinda cute."

"So try him," Alex said. "But you'll have your own faithful puppy dog by this time next week, and a proposal of marriage within the month."

Carole grinned and slid off the stool. "Proposal of marriage in two weeks," she said. "I'm that good."

She stubbed out her cigarette, grabbed the tiny leather purse that matched the skirt, adjusted her silk blouse and sashayed her way toward a table in the middle.

Grace finally saw Never-Been-Laid. He had soft brown eyes, and hair that needed trimming. He wore a shirt that accented his narrow shoulders, and he had a laptop open on the round table. He was alone. He had his feet tucked under the chair, crossed at the ankles. He wore dirty tennis shoes with his Gap khakis.

"Cute?" Grace said.

"Shhh," Alex said. "It's a door into the mind of Carole."

"One that should remain closed." Grace moved to Carole's stool. It was still warm. Grace shoved Carole's drink out of her way, grabbed her glass of wine, and coughed. The air still smelled of cigarette smoke.

Carole was leaning over the extra chair, giving Never-Been-Laid a view of her cleavage, and the guys at the booth by the phone a nice look at her ass, which they seemed to appreciate.

"Where the hell did that misogyny comment come from?" Grace asked.

Alex looked at her. "You want to get a booth?"

"Sure. Think Carole can find us?"

"I think Carole's going to be deflowering a computer geek and not caring what we're doing." Alex grabbed her drink, stood, and walked to a booth on the other side of the Corral. Dirty glasses from the last occupants were piled in the center, and the red-and-white checked vinyl tablecloth was sticky.

They moved the glasses on the edge of the table and didn't touch the dollar tip, which had been pressed into a puddle of beer.

Grace set her wine down and slid onto her side. Alex did the same on the other side. Somehow they managed not to touch the tabletop at all.

"You remember my boss?" Alex asked as she adjusted the tiny fake gas lamp that hung on the wall beside the booth.

"Beanie Boy?"

She grinned. "Yeah."

"Never met him."

"Aren't you lucky."

Grace already knew that. She'd heard stories about Beanie Boy for the last year. They had started shortly after he was hired. Alex went to the company Halloween party and was startled to find her boss dressed as one of the Lollipop Kids from the Wizard of Oz, complete with striped shirt, oversized lollipop and propeller beanie.

"Now what did he do?" Grace asked.

"Called me honey."

"Yeah?" Grace asked.

"And sweetie, and doll-face, and sugar."

"Hasn't he been doing that for the last year?"

Alex glared at Grace. "It's getting worse."

"What's he doing, patting you on the butt?"

"If he did, I'd get him for harassment, and he knows it."

She had lowered her voice. Grace could barely hear her over Shania Twain.

"This morning one of our clients came in praising the last report. I wrote it."

"Didn't Beanie Boy give you credit?"

"Of course he did. He said, 'Our little Miss Rogers wrote it. Isn't she a doll?'"

Grace clutched her drink tighter. This didn't matter to her. Her biopsy was benign. She had called Alex and Carole and told them. They'd suggested coming here. So why weren't they offering a toast to her life? Why weren't they celebrating, really celebrating, instead of rerunning the same old conversation in the same old bar in the same old way? "What did the client do?"

"He agreed, of course."

"And?"

"And what?"

"Is that it? Didn't you speak up?"

"How could I? He was praising me, for godssake."

Grace sighed and sipped her beer. Shania Twain's comment was that didn't impress her much. It didn't impress Grace much either, but she knew better than to say anything to Alex.

Grace looked toward the middle of the restaurant. Carole was standing behind Never-Been-Laid, her breasts pressed against his back, her ass on view to the world, her head over his shoulder peering at his computer screen.

Alex didn't follow her gaze like Grace had hoped. "If I were ten years younger, I'd tell Beanie Boy to shove it."

"If you were ten years younger, you wouldn't have a mortgage and a Mazda."

"Dignity shouldn't be cheaper than a paycheck," she said.

"So confront him."

"He doesn't think he's doing anything wrong. He treats all the women like that."

Grace sighed. They'd walked this road before. Job after job, boyfriend after boyfriend. Alex, for all her looks, was like Joe McCarthy protecting the world from the Red Menace: she saw anti-female everywhere, and most of it, she was convinced, was directed at her.

"You don't seem very sympathetic," Alex said.

She wasn't. She never had been. And with all she had been through in the last month, *alone* because her two best friends couldn't bear to talk about the Big C, the lock that was usually on Grace's mouth wasn't working.

"I'm not sympathetic," Grace said. "I'm beginning to think you're a victim in search of a victimizer."

"That's not fair, Grace," Alex said. "We tolerate this stuff because we were raised in an anti-woman society. It's gotten better, but it's not perfect. You tell those Xers stuff like this and they shake their heads. Or the new ones. What're they calling themselves now? Generation Y? They were raised on Title IX. Hell, they pull off their shirts after winning soccer games. Imagine us doing that."

"My cousin got arrested in 1977 in Milwaukee on the day Elvis Presley died for playing volleyball," Grace said. Carole was actually rubbing herself on Never-Been-Laid. His face was the color of the red checks in the tablecloth.

"What?"

Grace turned to Alex. "My cousin. You know, Barbie? She got arrested playing volleyball."

"They didn't let girls play volleyball in Milwaukee?"

"It was 90 degrees, and she was playing with a group of guys. They pulled off their shirts because they were hot and sweating, so she did the same. She got arrested for indecent exposure."

"God," Alex said. "Did she go to jail?"

"Didn't even get her day in court."

"Everyone gets a day in court."

Grace shook her head. "The judge took one look at Barbie, who was really butch in those days, and said, 'I'm sick of you girls coming in here and arguing that you should have equal treatment for things that are clearly unequal. I do not establish Public Decency laws. You may show a bit of breast if you're feeding a child, otherwise you are in violation of—some damn code.' Barbie used to quote the thing chapter and verse."

"Then what?" Alex asked.

"Then she got married, had a kid, and started wearing nail polish. She said it wasn't as much fun to show her breasts legally."

"See?" Alex said. "Misogyny."

Grace shrugged. "Society, Alex. Get used to it."

"That's the point of your story? We've been oppressed for a thousand years and you say, 'Get used to it'?"

"I say Brandi Chastain pulls off her shirt in front of millions—"

"Showing a sports bra."

"—and she doesn't get arrested. I say women head companies all the time. I say things are better now than they were when I was growing up, and I say the only ones who oppress us are ourselves."

"I say you're drunk."

Grace pointed at Carole, who was wet-kissing Never-Been-Laid, her arms wrapped around his neck and her legs wrapped around his waist. "She's drunk. I'm just speaking out."

"You never speak out."

Grace sighed. No one had picked up the glasses and she was tired of looking at that poor drowning dollar bill. There wasn't going to be any celebration. Everything was the same as it always was—at least to Alex and Carole. But Grace wanted something different.

She got up, threw a five next to the dollar, and picked up her purse.

"Tell me if Carole gets laid," Grace said, and left.

Outside Grace stopped and took a deep breath of the humid, exhaust-filled air. She could hear the clang of glasses even in the parking lot and the rhythm of Mary Chapin Carpenter praising passionate kisses. Grace had had only one glass of wine and a lousy time, and she wondered why people said old friends were the best friends. They were supposed to raise toasts to her future, now restored. She'd even said the "b" word and Alex hadn't noticed. It was as if the cancer scare had happened to someone they didn't even know.

Grace was going to be forty years old in three weeks. Her two best friends were probably planning a version of the same party they had held for her when she turned thirty. A male stripper whose sweaty body repulsed her more than aroused her, too many black balloons, and aging jokes that hadn't been original the first time around.

Forty years old, an accountant with her own firm, no close family, no boyfriend, and a resident of the same town her whole life. The only time she left was to visit cousins out east, and for what? Obligation?

There was no joy left, if there'd ever been any joy at all.

She got into her sensible Ford Taurus, bought at a used car lot for well under Blue Book, and drove west.

It wasn't until she reached Janesville that she started to call herself crazy, and it wasn't until she drove into Dubuque that she realized how little tied her to her hometown.

An apartment without even a cat to cozy up to, a business no more successful than a dozen others, and people who still saw her as a teenager wearing granny glasses, braces and hair too long for her face. Grace, who was always there. Grace the steady, Grace the smart. Grace, who helped her friends out of their financial binds, who gave them a shoulder to cry on, and a degree of comfort because their lives weren't as empty as her own.

When she had told Alex and Carole that her mammogram had come back suspicious, they had looked away. When she told them that she had found a lump, they had looked frightened.

I can't imagine life without you, Gracie, Carole had whispered.

Imagine it now, Grace thought.

The dawn was breaking when she reached Cedar Rapids, and she wasn't really tired. But she was practical, had always been practical, and habits of a lifetime didn't change just because she had run away from home at the age of 39.

She got a hotel room and slept for eight hours, got up, had dinner in a nice steak place, went back to the room and slept some more. When she woke up Sunday morning to bells from the Presbyterian Church across the street, she lay on her back and listened for a good minute before she realized they were playing "What a Friend We Have in Jesus." And she smiled then, because Jesus had been a better friend to her in recent years than Alex and Carole ever had.

At least Jesus didn't tell her his problems when she was praying about hers. If Jesus was self-absorbed he wasn't obvious about it. And he didn't seem to care that she hadn't been inside a church since August of 1978.

The room was chintz, the wallpaper and the bedspread matched, and the painting on the wall was chosen for its color not for its technique. Grace sat up and wondered what she was doing here, and thought about going home.

To nothing.

So she got in her car and followed the Interstate, through Des Moines, and Lincoln and Cheyenne, places she had only read about, places she had never seen. How could a woman live for forty years and not see the country of her birth? How could a woman do nothing except what she was supposed to from the day she was born until the day she died?

In Salt Lake City, she stared at the Mormon Tabernacle, all white against an azure sky. She sat in her car and watched a groundskeeper maintain the flowers, and remembered how it felt to take her doctor's call.

. . .

A lot of women have irregular mammograms, particularly at your age. The breast tissue is thicker, and often we get clouds.

Clouds.

There were fluffy clouds in the dry desert sky, but they were white and benign. Just like her lump had turned out to be. But for a hellish month, she had thought about that lump, feeling it when she woke out of a sound sleep, wondering if it presaged the beginning of the end. She had never felt her mortality like this before, not even when her mother, the only parent she had known, had died. Not even when she realized there was no one remaining of the generation that had once stood between her and death.

No one talked about these things. No one let her talk about them either. Not just Alex and Carole, but Michael, her second-in-command at work, or even her doctor, who kept assuring her that she was young and the odds were in her favor.

Young didn't matter if the cancer had spread through the lymph nodes. When she went in for the lumpectomy almost two weeks ago now, she had felt a curious kind of relief, as if the doctor had removed a tick that had burrowed under her skin. When he had called with the news that the lump was benign, she had thanked him calmly and continued with her day, filing corporate tax returns for a consulting firm.

No one had known the way she felt. Not relieved. No. It was more like she had received a reprieve.

The clouds above the Tabernacle helped calm her. She plugged in her cell phone for the first time in days and listened to the voice mail messages, most of them from Michael, growing increasingly worried about where she was.

Have you forgotten the meeting with Boyd's? he'd asked on Monday.

Do you want me to file Charlie's extension? he'd demanded on Tuesday.

Where the hell are you? he cried on Wednesday and she knew, then, that it was okay to call him, that not even the business could bring her home.

Amazing how her training had prepared her for moments like these and she hadn't even known it. She had savings, lots of them, because she hadn't bought a house even though it had been prudent to do so. She had been waiting, apparently, for Mr. Right, or the family her mother had always wanted for her, the family that would never come. Her money was invested properly, and she could live off the interest if she so chose. She had just never chosen to before.

And if she didn't want to be found, she didn't have to be. She knew how to have the interest paid through offshore accounts so that no one could track it. She even knew a quick and almost legal way to change her name. Traceable, but she hadn't committed a crime. She didn't need to hide well, just well enough that a casual search wouldn't produce her.

Not that anyone would start a casual search. Once she sold the business, Michael would forget her and Alex and Carole, even though they would gossip about her at Oh Kaye's every Friday night for the rest of their lives, wouldn't summon the energy to search.

She could almost hear them now: *She met some guy*, Carole would say. *And he killed her*, Alex would add, and then they would argue until last call, unless Carole found some man to entertain her, and Alex someone else to complain to. They would miss Grace only when they screwed up, when they needed a shoulder, when they couldn't stand being on their own. And even then, they probably wouldn't realize what it was they had lost.

Because it amused her, she had driven north to Boise, land of the white collar, to make her cell call to Michael. Her offer to him was simple: cash her out of the business and call it his own. She named a price, he dickered half-heartedly, she refused to negotiate. Within two days, he had wired the money to a blind money market account that she had often stored cash in for the firm.

She let the money sit there while she decided what to do with it. Then she went to Reno to change her name.

Reno had been a surprise. A beautiful city set between mountains like none she had ever seen. The air was dry, the downtown tacky, the people friendly. There were bookstores and slot machines and good restaurants. There were cheap houses and all-night casinos and lots of strange places. There was even history, of the Wild West kind.

For the first time in her life, Grace fell in love.

And to celebrate the occasion, she snuck into a quickie wedding chapel, found the marriage licenses, took one, copied down the name of the chapel, its permit number, and all the other pertinent information, and then returned to her car. There she checked the boxes, saying she had seen the driver's licenses and birth certificates of the people involved, including a fictitious man named Nathan Reinhart, and *viola!* she was married. She had a new name, a document the credit card companies would accept, and a new beginning all at the same time.

Using some of her personal savings, she bought a house with lots of windows and a view of the Sierras. In the mornings, light bathed her kitchen, and in the evenings, it caressed her living room. She had never seen light like this—clean and pure and crisp. She was beginning to understand why artists moved west to paint, why people used to exclaim about the way light changed everything.

The lack of humidity, of dense air pollution, made the air clearer. The elevation brought her closer to the sun.

She felt as if she were seeing everything for the very first time.

And hearing it, too. The house was silent, much more silent than an apartment, and the silence soothed her. She could listen to her television without worrying about the people in the apartment below, or play her stereo full blast without concern about a visit from the super.

There was a freedom to having her own space that she hadn't realized before, a freedom to living the way she wanted to live, without the rules of the past or the expectations she had grown up with.

And among those expectations was the idea that she had to be the strong one, the good one, the one on whose shoulder everyone else cried. She had no friends here, no one who needed her shoulder, and she had no one who expected her to be good.

Only herself.

Of course, in some things she was good. Habits of a lifetime died hard. She began researching the best way to invest Michael's lump sum payment—and while she researched, she left the money alone. She kept her house clean and her lawn, such as it was in this high desert, immaculate. She got a new car and made sure it was spotless.

No one would find fault with her appearances, inside or out.

Not that she had anyone who was looking. She didn't have a boyfriend or a job or a hobby. She didn't have anything except herself.

She found herself drawn to the casinos, with their clinking slot machines, musical come-ons, and bright lights. No matter how high tech the places had become, no matter how clean, how "family-oriented," they still had a shady feel.

Or perhaps that was her upbringing, in a state where gambling had been illegal until she was 25, a state where her father used to play a friendly game of poker—even with his friends—with the curtains drawn.

Sin—no matter how sanitized—still had appeal in the brand-new century.

Of course, she was too sensible to gamble away her savings. The slots lost their appeal quickly, and when she sat down at the blackjack tables, she couldn't get past the feeling that she was frittering her money away for nothing.

But she liked the way the cards fell and how people concentrated—as if their very lives depended on this place—and she was good with numbers. One of the pit bosses mentioned that they were always short of poker dealers, so she took a class offered by one of the casinos. Within two months, she was snapping cards, raking pots, and wearing a uniform that made her feel like Carole on a bad night.

It only took a few weeks for her bosses to realize that Grace was a natural poker dealer. They gave her the busy shifts—Thursday through Sunday nights—and she spent her evenings playing the game of cowboys, fancy men, and whores. Finally, there was a bit of an Old West feel to her life, a bit of excitement, a sense of purpose.

When she got off at midnight, she would be too keyed up to go home. She started bringing a change of clothes to work and, after her shift, she would go to the casino next door. It had a great bar upstairs—filled with brass, Victorian furnishings, and a real hardwood floor. She could get a sandwich and a beer. Finally, she felt like she was becoming the woman she wanted to be.

One night, a year after she had run away from home, a man sidled up next to her. He had long blond hair that curled against his shoulders. His face was tanned and lined, a bit too thin. He looked road-hardened—like a man who'd been outside too much, seen too much, worked in the sun too much. His hands were long, slender, and callused. He wore no rings, and his shirt cuffs were frayed at the edges.

He sat beside her in companionable silence for nearly an hour, while they both stared at CNN on the big screen over the bar, and then he said, "Just once I'd like to go someplace authentic."

His voice was cigarette growly, even though he didn't smoke, and he had a Southern accent that was soft as butter. She guessed Louisiana, but it might have been Tennessee or even Northern Florida. She wasn't good at distinguishing Southern accents yet. She figured she would after another year or so of dealing cards.

"You should go up to Virginia City. There's a bar or two that looks real enough."

He snorted through his nose. "Tourist trap."

She shrugged. She'd thought it interesting—an entire historic city, preserved just like it had been when Mark Twain lived there. "Seems to me if you weren't a tourist there wouldn't be any other reason to go."

He shrugged and picked up a toothpick, rolling it in his fingers. She smiled to herself. A former smoker then, and a fidgeter.

"Reno's better than Vegas, at least," he said. "Casinos aren't family friendly yet."

"Except Circus Circus."

"Always been that way. But the rest. You get a sense that maybe it ain't all legal here."

She looked at him sideways. He was at least her age, his blue eyes sharp in his leathery face. "You like things that aren't legal?"

"Gambling's not something that should be made pretty, you know? It's about money, and money can either make you or destroy you."

She felt herself smile, remember what it was like to paw through receipts and tax returns, to make neat rows of figures about other people's money. "What's the saying?" she asked. "Money is like sex—"

"It doesn't matter unless you don't have any." To her surprise, he laughed. The sound was rich and warm, not at all like she had expected. The smile transformed his face into something almost handsome.

He tapped the toothpick on the polished bar, and asked, "You think that's true?"

She shrugged. "I suppose. Everyone's idea of what's enough differs, though."

"What's yours?" He turned toward her, smile gone now, eyes even sharper than they had been a moment ago. She suddenly felt as if she were on trial.

"My idea of what's enough?" she asked.

He nodded.

"I suppose enough that I can live off the interest in the manner in which I've become accustomed. What's yours?"

A shadow crossed his eyes and he looked away from her. "Long as I've got a roof over my head, clothes on my back, and food in my mouth, I figure I'm rich enough."

"Sounds distinctly unAmerican to me," she said.

He looked at her sideways again. "I guess it does, don't it? Women figure a man should have some sort of ambition."

"Do you?"

"Have ambition?" He bent the toothpick between his fore- and middle fingers. "Of course I do. It just ain't tied in with money, is all."

"I thought money and ambition went together."

"In most men's minds."

"But not yours?"

The toothpick broke. "Not any more," he said.

Three nights later, he sat down at her table. He was wearing a denim shirt with silver snaps and jeans so faded that they looked as if they might shred around him. That, his hair, and his lean look reminded Grace of a movie gunslinger, the kind that cleaned a town up because it had to be done.

"Guess you don't make enough to live off the interest," he said to her as he sat down.

She raised her eyebrows. "Maybe I like people."

"Maybe you like games."

She smiled and dealt the cards. The table was full. She was dealing 3-6 Texas Hold 'Em and most of the players were locals. It was Monday night and they all looked pleased to have an unfamiliar face at the table.

If she had known him better she might have tipped him off. Instead she wanted to see how long his money would last.

He bought in for $100, although she had seen at least five hundred in his wallet. He took the chips, and studied them for a moment.

He had three tells. He fidgeted with his chips when his cards were mediocre and he was thinking of bluffing. He bit his lower lip when he had nothing, and his eyes went dead flat when he had a winning hand.

He lost the first hundred in forty-five minutes, bought back in for another hundred and managed to hold onto it until her shift ended shortly after midnight. He sat through dealer changes and the floating fortunes of his cards. When she returned from her last break, she found herself wondering if his tells were subconscious after all. They seemed deliberately calculated to let the professional poker players around him think that he was a rookie.

She said nothing. She couldn't, really—at least not overtly. The casino got a rake and they didn't allow her to do anything except deal the game. She had no stake in it anyway. She hadn't lied to him that first night. She loved watching people, the way they played their hands, the way the money flowed.

It was like being an accountant, only in real time. She got to see the furrowed brows as the decisions were made, hear the curses as someone pushed back a chair and tossed in that last hand of cards, watch the desperation that often led to the exact wrong play. Only as a poker dealer, she wasn't required to clean up the mess. She didn't have to offer advice or refuse it; she didn't have to worry about tax consequences, about sitting across from someone else's auditor, justifying choices she had no part in making.

When she got off, she changed into her tightest jeans and a summer sweater and went to her favorite bar.

Casino bars were always busy after midnight, even on a Monday. The crowd wasn't there to have a good time but to wind down from one—or to prepare itself for another. She sat at the bar, as she had since she started this routine, and she'd been about to leave when he sat next to her.

"Lose your stake?" she asked.

"I'm up $400."

She looked at him sideways. He didn't seem pleased with the way the night had gone—not the way a casual player would have been. Her gut instinct was right. He was someone who was used to gambling—and winning.

"Buy you another?" he asked.

She shook her head. "One's enough."

He smiled. It made him look less fierce and gave him a rugged sort of appeal. "Everything in moderation?"

"Not always," she said. "At least, not any more."

Somehow they ended up in bed—her bed—and he was better than she imagined his kind of man could be. He had knowledgeable fingers and endless patience. He didn't seem to mind the scar on her breast. Instead he lingered over it, focusing on it as if it were an erogenous zone. His pleasure at the result enhanced hers and when she finally fell asleep, somewhere around dawn, she was more sated than she had ever been.

She awoke to the smell of frying bacon and fresh coffee. Her eyes were filled with sand, but her body had a healthy lethargy.

At least, she thought, *he hadn't left before she awoke.*

At least he hadn't stolen everything in sight.

She still didn't know his name, and wasn't sure she cared. She slipped on a robe and combed her hair with her fingers and walked into her kitchen—the kitchen no one had cooked in but her.

He had on his denims and his hair was tied back with a leather thong. He had found not only her cast iron skillet but the grease cover that she always used when making bacon. A bowl of scrambled eggs steamed on the counter, and a plate of heavily buttered toast sat beside it.

"Sit down, darlin'," he said. "Let me bring it all to you."

She flushed. That was what it felt like he had done the night before, but she said nothing. Her juice glasses were out, and so was her everyday ware, and yet somehow the table looked like it had been set for a *Gourmet* photo spread.

"I certainly didn't expect this," she said.

"It's the least I can do." He put the eggs and toast on the table, then poured her a cup of coffee. Cream and sugar were already out, and in their special containers.

She was slightly uncomfortable that he had figured out her kitchen that quickly and well.

He put the bacon on a paper-towel covered plate, then set that on the table. She hadn't moved, so he beckoned with his hand.

"Go ahead," he said. "It's getting cold."

He sat across from her and helped himself to bacon while she served herself eggs. They were fluffy and light, just like they would have been in a restaurant. She had no idea how he got that consistency. Her home-scrambled eggs were always runny and undercooked.

The morning light bathed the table, giving everything a bright glow. His hair seemed even blonder in the sunlight and his skin darker. He had laugh lines around his mouth, and a bit of blond stubble on his chin.

She watched him eat, those nimble fingers scooping up the remaining egg with a slice of toast, and found herself remembering how those fingers had felt on her skin.

Then she felt his gaze on her, and looked up. His eyes were dead flat for just an instant, and she felt herself grow cold.

"Awful nice house," he said slowly, "for a woman who makes a living dealing cards."

Her first reaction was defense—she wanted to tell him she had other income, and what did he care about a woman who dealt cards, anyway?—but instead, she smiled. "Thank you."

He measured her, as if he expected a different response, then he said, "You're awfully calm considering that you don't even know my name. You don't strike me as the kind of woman who does this often."

His words startled her, but she made sure that the surprise didn't show. She had learned a lot about her own tells while dealing poker, and the experience was coming in handy now.

"You flatter yourself," she said softly.

"Well," he said, reaching into his back pocket, "if there's one thing my job's taught me, it's that people hide information they don't want anyone else to know."

He pulled out his wallet, opened it, and with two fingers removed a business card. He dropped it on the table.

She didn't want to pick the card up. She knew things had already changed between them in a way she didn't entirely understand, but she had a sense from the fleeting expression she had seen on his face that once she picked up the card she could never go back.

She set down her coffee cup and used two fingers to slide the card toward her. It identified him as Travis Delamore, a skip tracer and bail bondsman. Below his name was a phone number with a 414 exchange.

Milwaukee, Wisconsin and the surrounding areas. Precisely the place someone from Racine might call if they wanted to hire a professional.

She slipped the card into the pocket of her robe. "Is sleeping around part of your job?"

"Is embezzling part of yours?" All the warmth had left his face. His expression was unreadable except for the flatness in his eyes. What did he think he knew?

She made herself smile. "Mr. Delamore, if I stole a dime from the casino, I'd be instantly fired. There are cameras everywhere."

"I mean your former job, Ms. Mackie. A lot of money is missing from your office."

"I don't have an office." His use of her former name made her hands clammy. What had Michael done?

"Do you deny that you're Grace Mackie?"

"I don't acknowledge or deny anything. When did this become an inquisition, Mr. Delamore? I thought men liked their sex uncomplicated. You seem to be a unique member of your species."

This time he smiled. "Of course we like our sex uncomplicated. That's why we're having this discussion this morning."

"If we'd had it last night, there wouldn't be a this morning."

"That's my point." He downed the last of his orange juice. "And thank you for the acknowledgement, Ms. Mackie."

"It wasn't an acknowledgement," she said. "I don't like to sleep with men who think me guilty of something."

"Embezzlement," he said gently, using the same tone he had used in bed. This time, it made her bristle.

"I haven't stolen anything."

"New house, new name, new town, mysterious disappearance."

The chill she had felt earlier grew. She stood and wrapped her robe tightly around her waist. "I don't know what you think you know, Mr. Delamore, but I believe it's time for you to leave."

He didn't move. "We're not done."

"Oh, yes, we are."

"It would be a lot easier if you told me where the money was, Grace."

"Do you always get paid for sex, Mr. Delamore?" she asked.

He studied her for a moment. "Don't play games with me, honey."

"Why not?" she asked. "You seem to enjoy them."

He shoved his plate away as if it had offended him. Apparently this morning wasn't going the way he wanted it to either. "I'm just telling you what I know."

"And I'm just asking you to leave. It was fun, Travis. But it certainly wasn't worth this."

He stood and slipped his wallet back into his pocket. "You'll hear from me again."

"This isn't high school," she said, following him to the door. "I won't be offended if you fail to call."

"No," he said as he stepped into the dry desert air. "You probably won't be offended. But you will be curious. This is just the beginning, Grace."

"One person's beginning is another person's ending," she said as she closed and locked the door behind him.

The worst thing she could do, she knew, was panic. So she made herself clean up the kitchen as if she didn't have a care in the world, and she left the curtains open so that he could see if he wanted to. Then she went to the shower, making it a long and hot. She tried to scrub all the traces of him off of her.

For the first time in her life, she felt cheap.

Embezzlement. Something had happened, something Michael was blaming on her. It would be easy enough, she supposed. She had disappeared. That looked suspicious enough. The new name, the new car, the new town, all of that added to the suspicion.

What had Michael done? And why?

She got out of the shower and toweled herself off. She was tempted to call Michael, but she certainly couldn't do it from the house. If she used her cell, the call would be traceable too. And if she went to a pay phone, she would attract even more suspicion. She had to consider that Travis Delamore was following her, spying on her.

In fact, she had to consider that he had been doing that for some time.

She went over all of their conversation, looking for clues, mistakes she might have made. She had told him very little, but he had asked a lot. Strangely—or perhaps not so strangely any more—all of their conversations had been about money.

Carole would have been proud of her. Grace had finally let her libido get the better of her. Alex would have been disgusted, reminding her that men couldn't be trusted.

What could he do to her besides cast suspicion? He was right. Without the money, he had nothing. And she had a job, no criminal record, and no suspicious investments.

But if he continued to follow her, she could go after him. The bartender had seen them leave her favorite bar together. She had an innocent face, she'd been living here for a year, got promoted, was well liked by her employer. Delamore had obviously flirted with her while he played poker the night before, and the casino had cameras.

They probably had records of all the times he had watched her before she noticed him.

It wouldn't take much to make a stalking charge. That would get her an injunction in the least, and it might scare him off.

Then she could find out why he was so sure he had something on her. Then she could find out what it was Michael had done.

———

The newly remodeled ladies room on the third floor of the casino had twenty stalls and a lounge complete with smoking room. It had once been a small restroom, but the reconstruction had taken out the nearby men's room and replaced it with more stalls. The row of pay phones in the middle stayed, as a convenience to the customers.

Delamore wouldn't know that she called from those pay phones. No one would know.

She started using the third floor ladies room on her break and more than once had picked up the receiver on the third phone and dialed most of her old office number. She'd always stop before she hit the last digit, though. Her intuition told her that calling Michael would be wrong.

What if Delamore had a trace on Michael's line? What if the police did?

A week after her encounter with Delamore, a week in which she used the third floor ladies room more times than she could count, she suddenly realized what was wrong. Delamore didn't have anything on her except suspicion. He had clearly found her—that hadn't been hard, since she really hadn't been hiding from anyone—and he had probably checked her bank records for the money he assumed she had embezzled from her former clients. But the money she had gotten from the sale of the business was still in that hidden numbered account—and would stay there.

Her native caution had served her well once again.

She had nothing to hide. It didn't matter what some good-looking skip trace thought. Her life in Racine was in the past. A part of her past that she couldn't avoid, any more than she could avoid the scar on her breast—the scar that Delamore had clearly used to identify her, the bastard. But past was past, and until it hurt her present, she wasn't going to worry about it.

So she stopped making pilgrimages to the third floor women's room, and gradually, her worries over Delamore faded. She didn't see him for a week, and she assumed—wrongly—that it was all over.

———

He sat next to her at the bar as if he had been doing it every day for years. He ordered a whiskey neat, and another "for the lady," just like men in her fantasies used to do. When he looked at her and smiled, she realized that the look didn't reach his eyes.

Maybe it never had.

"Miss me, darlin'?" he asked.

She picked up her purse, took out a five to cover her drink, and started to leave. He grabbed her wrist. His fingers were warm and dry, their touch no longer gentle. A shiver started in her back, but she willed the feeling away.

"Let go of me," she said.

"Now, Gracie, I think you should listen to what I have to say."

"Let go of me," she said in that same measured tone, "or I will scream so loud that everyone in the place will hear."

"Screams don't frighten me, doll."

"Maybe the police do. Believe me, *hon*, I will press charges."

His smile was slow and wide, but that flat look was in his eyes again, the one that told her he had all the cards. "I'm sure they'll be impressed," he said, reaching into his breast pocket with his free hand. "But I do believe a warrant trumps a tight grip on the arm."

He set a piece of paper down on the bar itself. The bartender, wiping away the remains of another customer's mess, glanced her way as if he were keeping an eye on her.

She didn't touch the paper, but she didn't shake Delamore's hand off her arm, either. She wasn't quite sure what to do.

He picked up the paper, shook it open, and she saw the strange bold-faced print of a legal document, her former name in the middle. "Tell you what, Gracie. How about we finish the talk we started the other morning in one of those dark, quiet booths over there?"

She was still staring at the paper, trying to comprehend it. It looked official enough. But then, she'd never seen a warrant for anyone's arrest before. She had only heard of them.

She had never imagined she'd see her own name on one.

She let Delamore lead her to a booth at the far end of the bar. He slid across the plastic, trying to pull her in beside him, but this time, she shook him off. She sat across from him, perched on the seat with her feet in the aisle, purse clutched on her lap. Flee position, Alex used to call it. You Might Be a Loser and I Reserve the Right to Find Someone Else, was Carole's name for it.

"If I bring you back to Wisconsin," he said, "I get a few thousand bucks. What it don't say on my card is that I'm a bounty hunter."

"What an exciting life you must lead," Grace said dryly.

He smiled. The look chilled her. She was beginning to wonder how she had ever found him attractive. "It's got its perks."

It was at that moment she decided she hated him. He would forever refer to her as a perk of the job, not as someone who had given herself to him freely, someone who had enjoyed the moment as much as he had.

All that gentleness in his fingers, all those murmured endearments. Lies.

She hated lies.

"But," he was saying, "I see a way to make a little more money here. I don't think you're a real threat to society. And you're a lot of fun, more fun than I would've expected, given how you lived before you moved here."

The bartender came over, his bar towel over his arm. "Want anything?"

He was speaking to her. He hadn't even looked at Delamore. The bartender was making sure she was all right.

"I don't know yet," she said. "Can you check back in five minutes?"

"Sure thing." This time he did look at Delamore, who grinned at him. The bartender shot him a warning glare.

"Wow," Delamore said as the bartender moved out of earshot. "You have a defender."

"You keep getting off track," Grace said.

Delamore shrugged. "I like talking to you."

"Well, I find talking with you rather dull."

He raised his eyebrows. "You didn't think so a few days ago."

"As I recall," she said, "we didn't do a lot talking."

His smile softened. "That's my memory too."

She clutched her purse tighter. It always looked so glamorous in the movies, finding the right person, having a night of great sex. And even if he rode off into the sunset never to be seen again, everything still had a glow of perfection to it.

Not the bits of sleaze, the hardness in his expression, the sense that what he wanted from her was something she couldn't give.

"You know, the papers said that Michael Holden went into your old office, and put a gun in his mouth and pulled the trigger. Then the police, after finding the body, discovered that most of the money your clients had entrusted to your firm had disappeared."

She couldn't suppress the small whimper of shock that rose in her throat.

Delamore noted it and his eyes brightened. "Now, you tell me what happened."

She had no idea. She had none at all. But she couldn't tell Delamore that. She didn't even know if the story was true.

It sounded true. But Delamore had lied before. For all she knew he was some kind of con man, out to get her because he smelled money.

He was watching her, his eyes glittering. She could barely control her expression. She needed to get away.

She stood, still clutching her purse like a schoolgirl.

"Planning to leave? I wouldn't do that if I were you." His voice had turned cold. A shiver ran down her spine, but she didn't move, just stared down at him unable to turn away.

"One call," he said softly, "and you'll get picked up by the Nevada police. You should sit down and hear what I have to say."

Her hands were shaking. She sat, feeling trapped. He had finally hooked her, even though she hadn't said a word.

He leaned forward. "Now listen to me, darling. I know you got the money. I been working this one a long time, and I dug up the records. Michael closed all those accounts right after you disappeared. That's not a coincidence."

Her mouth was dry. She wanted to swallow, but couldn't.

"'Member our talk about money? One of those first nights, here in this bar?"

She was staring at him, her eyes wide and dry as if she'd been driving and staring at the road for hours. It felt like she had forgotten to blink.

"I told you I don't need much, and that's true. But I'm getting tired of dragging people back to their parole officers or for their court date, or finding husbands who'd skipped out on their families and then getting paid five grand or two grand. Then people question your expenses, like you don't got a right to spend a night in a motel or eat three squares. Or they demand to know why you took so danged long to find someone who'd been hiding so good no cop could find them."

His voice was so soft she had to strain to hear it. In spite of herself, she leaned forward.

"I'm forty-five years old, doll," he said. "And I'm getting tired. You got one pretty little scar. Did you notice all the ones I got? On the job. Yours is the first case in a while where I didn't get a beating." Then he grinned. "At least, not a painful one."

She flushed, and her fingers tightened on the purse. Her hands were beginning to hurt. Part of her, a part she'd never heard from before, wanted to take that purse and club him in the face. But she didn't move. If she moved, she would lose any control she had.

"So," he said, "here's the deal. I like you. I didn't expect to, but I do. You're a pretty little thing, and smart as a whip, and this is probably going to be the only crime you'll ever commit, because you're one of those girls who just knows better, aren't you?"

She held her head rigidly, careful so that he wouldn't take the most subtle movement for a nod.

"And I think you got a damn fine deal here. The house is nice—lots of light—and the town obviously suits you. I met those friends of yours, the ball-buster and the one who thinks she's God's Gift to Men, and I gotta say it's clear why you left."

Her nails dug into the leather. Pain shot through the tender skin at the top of her fingers.

"I really don't wanna ruin your life. It's time I make a change in mine. You give me fifty grand, and I'll bury everything I found about you."

"Fifty thousand dollars?" Her voice was raspy with tension. "For the first payment?"

His eyes sparkled. "One-time deal."

She snorted. She knew better. Blackmailers never worked like that.

"And maybe I'll stick around. Get to know you a little better. I could fall in love with that house myself."

"Could you?" she asked, amazed at the dry tone she'd managed to maintain.

"Sure." He grinned. That had been the look that had made her go weak less than a week ago. Now it sent a chill through her. "You and me, we had something."

"Yeah," she said. "A one-night stand."

He laughed. "It could be more than that, darlin'. It took you long enough, but you might've just found Mr. Right."

"Seems to me you were the one who was searching." She stood. He didn't protest, and she was glad. She had to leave. If she stayed any longer, she'd say something she would regret.

She tucked her purse under her arm. "I assume the drink's on you," she said, and then she walked away.

He didn't follow her—at least not right away. And she drove in circles before going home, watching for his car behind hers, thinking about everything he had said. Thinking about her break, her freedom, the things she had done to create a new life.

The things that now made her look guilty of a crime she hadn't committed.

She didn't sleep, of course. She couldn't. Her mind was too full—and her bed was no longer a private place. He'd been there, and some of him remained, a shadow, a laugh. After an hour of tossing and turning, she moved to the guest room and sat on the edge of the brand new unused mattress, clutching a blanket and thinking.

It was time to find out what had happened. Delamore knew who she was. She couldn't pretend any more. But he wasn't ready to turn her in. That gave her a little time.

She took a shower, made herself a pot of coffee, and a sandwich which she ate slowly. Then she went to her office, sat down in front of her computer and hesitated. The moment she logged on was the moment that all her movements could be traced. The moment she couldn't turn back from.

But she could testify to the conversation she'd had with Delamore, and the bartender would back her up. She wouldn't be able to hide her own identity should the police come for her, and so there was no reason to lie. She would simply say that she was concerned about her former business partner. She wanted to know if any of what Delamore told her was true.

It wouldn't seem like a confession to anyone but him.

She logged on, and used a search engine to find the news.

It didn't take her long. Amazing how many newspapers were online. Michael's death created quite a scandal in Racine, and the pictures of her office—the bloody mess still visible inside—were enough to make the ham on rye that she'd had a few moments ago turn in her stomach.

Michael. He'd been a good accountant. Thorough, exacting. Nervous. Always so nervous, afraid of making any kind of mistake.

Embezzlement? Why would he do that?

But that was what the papers had said. She dug farther, found the follow-up pieces. He'd raised cash, using clients' accounts, to bilk the company of a small fortune.

And Delamore was right. The dates matched up. Michael had stolen from her own clients to pay her for her own business. He had bought the business with stolen money.

She bowed her head, listening to the computer hum, counting her own breaths. She had never once questioned where he had gotten the money. She had figured he'd gotten a loan, had thought that maybe he'd finally learned the value of savings.

Michael. The man who took an advance on his paycheck once every six months. Michael, who had once told her he was too scared to invest on his own.

I wouldn't trust my own judgment, he had said.

Oh, the poor man. He had been right.

The trail did lead to her. The only reason Delamore couldn't point at her exactly was because she had stashed the cash in a blind account. And she hadn't touched it.

Not yet.

She'd been living entirely off her own savings, letting the money from the sale of her business draw interest. The nest egg for the future she hadn't planned yet.

Delamore wanted fifty thousand dollars from her. To give that to him, she'd have to tap the nest egg.

How many times would he make her tap it again? And again? Until it was gone, of course. Into his pocket. And then he'd turn her in.

She wiped her hand on her jeans. It was a nervous movement, meant to calm herself down. She had to think.

If the cops could trace her, they would have. They either didn't have enough on her or hadn't made the leap that Delamore had. And then she had confirmed his leap with the conversation tonight.

She got up and walked away from the computer. She wouldn't let him intrude. He had already taken over her bedroom. She needed to have a space here, in her office, without him.

There was no mention of her in the papers, nothing that suggested she was involved. The police would have contacted the Reno police if they had known where she was. Even if they had hired Delamore to track her, they might still not have been informed about her whereabouts. Delamore wanted money more than he wanted to inform the authorities about where she was.

Grace sat down in the chair near the window. The shade was drawn, but the spot was soothing nonetheless.

The police weren't her problem. Delamore was.

She already knew that he wouldn't be satisfied with one payment. She had to find a way to get rid of him.

She bowed her head. Even though she had done nothing criminal she was thinking like one. How did a woman get rid of a man she didn't want? She could get a court order, she supposed, forcing him to stay away from her. She could refuse to pay him and let the cards fall where they might. Years of legal hassle, maybe even an arrest. She would certainly lose her job. No casino would hire her, and she couldn't fall back on her CPA skills, not after being arrested for embezzlement.

Ignoring him wasn't an option either.

Then, there was the act of desperation. She could kill him. Somehow. She had always thought that murderers weren't methodical enough. Take an intelligent person, have her kill someone in a thoughtful way, and she would be able to get away with the crime.

Everywhere but in her own mind. No matter how hard she tried, no matter how much he threatened her, she couldn't kill Delamore.

There had to be another option. She had to do something. She just wasn't sure what it was.

She went back to the computer and looked at the last article she had downloaded. Michael had stolen from people she had known for years. People who had trusted her, believed in her and her word. People who had thought she had integrity.

She frowned. What must they think of her now? That she was an embezzler too? After all those years of work, did she want that behind her name?

Then again, why should she care about people she would never see again?

But she would see them every time she closed her eyes. Elderly Mrs. Vezzetti and her poodle, trusting Grace to handle her account because her husband, God rest his soul, had convinced her that numbers were too much for her pretty little head. Mr. Heitzkey who couldn't balance a checkbook if his life depended on it. Ms. Andersen, who had taken Grace's advice on ways to legally hide money from the IRS—and who had seemed so excited when it worked.

Grace sighed.

There was only one way to make this right. Only one way to clear her conscience and to clear Delamore out of her life.

She had to turn herself in.

She did some more surfing as she ate breakfast and found discount tickets to Chicago. She had to buy them round-trip from Chicago to Reno (God bless the casinos for their cheap airfare deals) and fly only the Reno to Chicago leg. Later she would buy another set, and not use part of it. Both of those tickets were cheaper than buying a single round-trip ticket out of Reno to Racine.

Grace made the reservation, hoping that Delamore wasn't tracking round trips that started somewhere else, and then she went to work. She claimed a family emergency, got a leave of absence, and hoped it would be enough.

She liked the world she built here. She didn't want to lose it because she hadn't been watching her back.

Twenty-four hours later, she and the car she rented in O'Hare were in Racine. The town hadn't changed. More churches than she saw out west, a few timid billboards for Native American Casinos, a factory outlet mall, and bars everywhere. The streets were grimy with the last of the sand laid down during the winter snow and ice. The trees were just beginning to bud, and the flowers were poking through the rich black dirt.

It felt as if she had gone back in time.

She wondered if she should call Alex and Carole, and then decided against it. What would she say to them, anyway? Instead, she checked into a hotel, unpacked, ate a mediocre room service meal, and slept as if she were dead.

Maybe in this city, she was.

The district attorney's office was smaller than Grace's bathroom. There were four chairs, not enough for her, her lawyer, the three assistant district attorneys and the DA himself. She and her lawyer were allowed to sit, but the assistant DAs hovered around the bookshelves and desk like children who were waiting for their father to finish business. The DA himself sat behind a massive oak desk that dwarfed the tiny room.

Grace's lawyer, Maxine Jones, was from Milwaukee. Grace had done her research before she arrived and found the best defense attorney in Wisconsin. Grace knew that Maxine's services would cost her a lot—but Grace was gambling that she wouldn't need Maxine for more than a few days.

Maxine was a tall, robust woman who favored bright colors. In contrast she wore debutante jewelry—a simple gold chain, tiny diamond earrings—that accented her toffee-colored skin. The entire look made her seem both flamboyant and powerful, combinations that Grace was certain helped Maxine in court.

"My client," Maxine was saying, "came here on her own. You'll have to remember that, Mr. Lindstrom."

Harold Lindstrom, the district attorney, was in his fifties, with thinning gray hair and a runner's thinness. His gaze held no compassion as it fell on Grace.

"Only because a bounty hunter hired by the police department found her," Lindstrom said.

"Yes," Maxine said. "We'll concede that the bounty hunter was the one who informed her of the charges. But that's all. This man hounded her, harassed her, and tried to extort money out of her, money she did not have."

"Then she should have gone to the Reno police," Lindstrom said.

An assistant DA crossed her arms as if this discussion was making her uncomfortable. It was making Grace uncomfortable. Never before had she been discussed as if she weren't there.

"It was easier to come here," Maxine said. "My client has a hunch, which if it's true, will negate the charges you have against her and against Michael Holden."

"Mr. Holden embezzled from his clients with the assistance of Ms. Reinhart."

"No. Mr. Holden followed standard procedure for the accounting firm."

"Embezzlement is standard procedure?" Lindstrom was looking directly at Grace.

Maxine put her manicured hand on Grace's knee, a reminder to remain quiet.

"No. But Mr. Holden, for reasons we don't know, decided to end his life, and since he now worked alone, no one knew where he was keeping the clients' funds. My client," Maxine added, as if she expected Grace to speak, "would like you to drop all charges against her and to charge Mr. Delamore with extortion. In exchange, she will testify against him, and she will also show you where the money is."

"Where she hid it, huh?" Lindstrom said. "No deal."

Maxine leaned forward. "You don't have a crime here. If you don't bargain with us, I'll go straight to the press, and you'll look like a fool. It seems to me that there's an election coming up."

Lindstrom's eyes narrowed. Grace held her breath. Maxine stared at him as if they were all playing a game of chicken. Maybe they were.

"Here's the deal," he said, "if her information checks out, then we'll drop the charges. We can't file against Delamore because the alleged crimes were committed in Nevada."

Maxine's hand left Grace's knee. Maxine templed her fingers and rested their painted tips against her chin. "Then, Harold, we'll simply have to file a suit against the city and the county for siccing him on my client. A multi-million dollar suit. We'll win, too. Because she came forward the moment she learned of a problem. She hasn't been in touch with anyone from here. Her family is dead, and her friends were never close. She had no way of knowing what was happening a thousand miles away until a man you people sent started harassing her."

"You said he's been harassing you for a month," Lindstrom said to Grace. "Why didn't you come forward before now?"

Grace looked at Maxine who nodded.

"Because," Grace said, "he didn't show me any proof of his claims until the night before I flew out. You can ask the bartender at the Silver Dollar. He saw the entire thing."

Lindstrom frowned at Maxine. "We want names and dates."

"You'll get them," Maxine said.

Lindstrom sighed. "All right. Let's hear it."

Grace's heart was pounding. Here was her moment. She suddenly found herself hoping they would all believe her. She had never lied with so much at stake before.

"Go ahead, Grace," Maxine said softly.

Grace nodded. "We had run into some trouble with our escrow service. Minor stuff, mostly rudeness on the part of the company. It was all irritating Michael. Many things were irritating him at that time, but we weren't close, so I didn't attribute it to anything except work."

The entire room had become quiet. She felt slightly lightheaded. She was forgetting to breathe. She forced herself to take a deep breath before continuing.

"In the week that I was leaving, Michael asked me how he could go about transferring everything from one escrow company to another. It required a lot of paperwork, and he didn't trust the company we were with. I thought he should have let them and the new company handle it, but he didn't want to."

She squeezed her hands together, reminded herself not to embellish too much. A simple lie was always best.

"We had accounts we had initially set up for clients in discreet banks. I told Michael to go to one of those banks, place the money in accounts there, and then when the new escrow accounts were established, to transfer the money to them. I warned him not to take longer than a day in the intermediate account."

"We have no record of such an account," the third district attorney said.

Grace nodded. "That's what I figured when I heard that he was being charged with embezzlement. I can give you the names of all the banks and the numbers of the accounts we were assigned. If the money's in one of them, then my name is clear."

"Depending on when the deposit was made," Lindstrom said. "And if the money's all there."

Grace's lightheadedness was growing. She hadn't realized how much effort bluffing took. But she did know she was covered on those details at least.

"You may go through my client's financial records," Maxine said. "All of her money is accounted for."

"Why wouldn't he have transferred the money to the new escrow accounts quickly, like you told him to?" Lindstrom asked.

"I don't know," Grace said.

"Depression is a confusing thing, Harold," Maxine said. "If he's like other people who've gotten very depressed, I'm sure things slipped. I'm sure this wasn't the only thing he failed to do. And you can bet I'd argue that in court."

"Why did you leave Racine so suddenly?" Lindstrom asked. "Your friends say you just vanished one night."

Grace let out a small breath. On this one she could be completely honest. "I had a scare. I thought I had breast cancer. The lumpectomy results came in the day I left. You can check with my doctor. I was planning to go after that—maybe a month or more—but I felt so free, that I just couldn't go back to my work. Something like that changes you, Mr.

Lindstrom."

He grunted as if he didn't believe her. For the first time in the entire discussion, she felt herself get angry. She clenched her fingers so hard that her nails dug into her palms. She wouldn't say any more, just like Maxine had told her to.

"The banks?" Lindstrom asked.

Grace slipped a small leather-bound ledger toward him. She had spent a lot of time drawing that up by hand in different pens. She hoped it would be enough.

"The accounts are identified by numbers only. That's one of the reasons we liked the banks. If he started a new account, I won't know its number."

"If they're in the U.S., then we can get a court order to open them," Lindstrom said.

"Check these numbers first. Most of the accounts were inactive." She had to clutch her fingers together to keep them from trembling.

"All right," Lindstrom said and stood. Maxine and Grace stood as well. "If we discover that you're wrong—about anything—we'll arrest you, Ms. Reinhart. Do you understand?"

Grace nodded.

Maxine smiled. "We're sure you'll see it our way, Harold. But remember your promise. Get that creep away from Grace."

"Right now, your client's the one we're concerned with, Maxine." Lindstrom's cold gaze met Grace's. "I'm sure we'll be in touch."

Grace thought the eight o'clock knock on her hotel room door was room service. She'd ordered another meal from them, unable to face old haunts and old friends. Until she had come back, she had never even been in a hotel in Racine, so she felt as if she weren't anywhere near her old home. Now if she could only get the different local channels on the television set, her own delusion would be complete.

She undid the locks, opened the door, and stepped away so that the waiter could bring his cart/table inside.

Instead, Delamore pulled the door back. She was so surprised to see him that she didn't try to close him out. She scuttled away from him toward the nightstand, and fumbled behind her back for the phone.

His cheeks were red, and his eyes sparkling with fury. His anger was so palpable, she could feel it across the room.

"What kind of game are you playing?" he snapped, slamming the door closed.

She got the phone off the hook without turning around. "No game."

"It is a game. You got away from me, and then you come here, telling them that I've been threatening you."

"You have been threatening me." Her fingers found the bottom button on the phone—which she hoped was "0." If the hotel operator heard this, she'd have to call security.

"Of course I'd been threatening you! It's my job. You didn't want to come back here and I needed to drag you back. Any criminal would see that as a threat."

"Here's what you don't understand," Grace said as calmly as she could. "I'm not a criminal."

"Bullshit." Delamore took a step toward her. She backed up farther and the end table hit her thighs. Behind her she thought she heard a tinny voice ask a muted question. The operator, she hoped.

Grace held up a hand. "Come any closer and I'll scream."

"I haven't done anything to you. I've been trying to catch you."

She frowned. What was he talking about? And then she knew. The police had put a wire on him. The conversation was being taped. And they—he—was hoping that she'd incriminate herself.

"You're threatening me now," she said. "I haven't done anything. I talked to the DA today. I explained my situation and what I think Michael did. He's checking my story now."

"Your lies."

"No," Grace said. "You're the one who's lying, and I have no idea why."

"You bitch." He lowered his voice the angrier he got. Somehow she found that even more threatening.

"Stay away from me."

"Stop the act, Grace," he said. "It's just you and me. And we both know you're not afraid of anything."

Then the door burst open and two hotel security guards came in. Delamore turned and as he did, Grace said, "Oh, thank God. This man came into my room and he's threatening me."

The guards grabbed him. Delamore struggled, but the guards held him tightly. He glared at her. "You're lying again, Grace."

"No," she said and stepped away from the phone. He glanced down at the receiver, on its side on the table, and cursed. Even if he hadn't been wired, she had a witness.

The guards dragged him and Grace sank onto the bed, placing her head in her hands. She waited until the shaking stopped before she called Maxine.

Grace had been right. Delamore had been wearing a wire, and her ability to stay cool while he attacked had preserved her story. That incident, plus the fact that the DA's office had found the money exactly where she had said it would be, in the exact amount that they had been looking for, went a long way toward preserving her credibility. When detectives interviewed Michael's friends one final time, they all agreed he was agitated and depressed, but he would tell no one why. Without the embezzlement explanation, it simply sounded as if he were a miserable man driven to the brink by personal problems.

She had won, at least on that score. Her old clients would get their money back, and they would be off her conscience. And nothing, not even Delamore, would take their place.

Delamore was under arrest, charged with extortion, harassment, and attempting to tamper with a witness. Apparently, he'd faced similar complaints before, but they had never stuck. This time, it looked as if they would.

Grace would have to return to Racine to testify against him. But not for several months. And maybe, Maxine said, not even then. The hope was that Delamore would plea and save everyone the expense of a trial.

So, on her last night in Racine, perhaps forever, Grace got enough courage to call Alex and Carole. She didn't reach either of them; instead she had to leave a message on their voice mail, asking them to meet her at Oh Kaye's one final time.

Grace got there first. The place hadn't changed at all. There was still a jukebox in the corner and cocktail waitresses in short skirts and ankle boots with big heels. Tin stars and Wild West art on the walls, unstained wood and checkered tablecloths adding to the effect. High bar stools and a lot of lonely people.

Grace ignored them. She sashayed to the bar, slapped her hand on it, and ordered whiskey neat. A group of suits at a nearby table ogled her and she turned away.

She was there to diss men not to meet them.

Carole arrived first, black miniskirt, tight crop top, and cigarette in hand. She looked no different. She hugged Grace so hard that Grace thought her ribs would crack.

"Alex had me convinced you were dead."

Grace shook her head. "I was just sleeping around."

Carole grinned. "Fun, huh?"

Grace thought. The night had been fun. The aftermath hadn't been. But her life was certainly more exciting. She didn't know if the tradeoff was worth it.

Alex arrived a moment later. Her auburn hair had grown, and she was wearing boots beneath a long dress. The boots made her look even taller.

She didn't hug Grace.

"What the hell's the idea?" Alex snapped. "You vanished—kapoof! What kind of friend does that?"

In the past, Grace would have stammered something, then told Alex she was exactly right and Grace was wrong. This time, Grace set her whiskey down.

"I told you about my lumpectomy," Grace said. "You didn't care. I was scared. I told you that, and you didn't care. When I found out I didn't have cancer, I called you to celebrate, and you didn't care. Seems to me you vanished first."

Alex's cheeks were red. Carole stubbed her cigarette in an ashtray on the bar's wooden rail.

"Not fair," Alex said.

"That's what I thought," Grace said.

Carole looked from one to the other. Finally, she said, very softly, "I really missed you, Gracie."

"I thought some misogynistic asshole picked you up and killed you," Alex said.

"Could have happened," Grace said. "Maybe it nearly did."

"Here?" Carole asked. "At Oh Kaye's?"

Grace shook her head. "It's a long story. Are you both finally ready to listen to me?"

Carole tugged her miniskirt as if she could make it longer. "I want to hear it."

Alex picked up Grace's whiskey and tossed it back. Then she wiped off her mouth. "What did I tell you, Grace? Women always tolerate misogyny. You should have fought him off."

"I did," Grace said.

Alex's eyes widened. Carole laughed. "Our Gracie has grown up."

"No," Grace said. "I've always been grown-up. You're just noticing now."

"There's a story here," Alex said, slipping her arm through Grace's, "and I think I need to hear it."

"Me, too." Carole put her arm around Grace's shoulder. "Tell us about your adventures. I promise we'll listen."

Grace sighed. She'd love to tell them everything, but if she did, she'd screw up the case against Delamore. "Naw," Grace said. "Let's just have some drinks and talk about girl things."

"You gotta promise to tell us," Alex said.

"Okay," Grace said. "I promise. Now how about some whiskey?"

"Beer," Alex said.

"You see that cute guy over there?" Carole asked, pointing at the suits.

Grace grinned. Already, her adventure was forgotten. Nothing changed here at Oh Kaye's. Nothing except Cowboy Grace, who'd finally bellied up to the bar.

The Wedding Ring

Kristine Kathryn Rusch

The Wedding Ring

i

The smell of coffee woke her. Serena stretched her arm across the soft sheets to find Dylan's side of the bed cold. She eased her eyes open. He'd actually pulled the covers up, and placed them under the pillow.

She smiled. In the five days they'd been married, he hadn't done that before. She had teased him a lot about leaving the bed unmade.

His answer was serious at first: *We're in a hotel, babe. They make the bed for us.*

Then he slowly realized she was joking. *They would make the bed, babe,* he said, *if we ever leave it.*

And finally, he said, *I'll make the bed the minute I know we're not going to use it.*

Oddly, that last memory stabbed her heart. She sat up, covers pulled to her chest. The room wasn't as dark as it had been; light filtered in around the thick curtains.

She blinked. The smell of coffee was strong. She made herself take a deep breath and smile. Dylan was in the other room, with room service waiting for her. He probably hadn't wanted to wake her. He'd done that the last two days, telling her that she needed her strength.

And then he leered.

He had a good leer. She loved that leer, because of the twinkle in his eyes. He was the most handsome man she had ever seen—even after she had taken her beer goggles off.

She hadn't been drunk when she met him, but she hadn't been sober either. She'd been standing in one of the casino's beautifully decorated hallways, just outside the etched glass windows of the most popular nightclub in the place. She was wearing a slinky silver dress she had bought with her surprise slot winnings.

At the behest of the desk clerk when she checked in, she had taken one free pull on the gigantic slot machine in the lobby—and she'd won $10,000 instantly.

She was cautious with her cash, always had been. She had put $5,000 in an account in a major bank here in Vegas, planning to transfer all of it and close the account when she got home. The remaining money was found money that she added to her vacation stash.

And the first thing she had purchased had been a dress so slinky, she felt like another woman.

She drank like one too, a little something every night, hoping it would give her courage—or at least, make this two-week trip a bit more fun. The trip hadn't started as a single-woman adventure. Initially, she had booked it for herself and her boyfriend of long standing, Charles. When Charles ended their relationship three months before they were due to leave, she had kept the trip on the schedule because she felt like she had something to prove.

She called this trip the Liberation Vacation.

Three days in, she'd been feeling more restless than liberated. She was also feeling a bit pathetic. The alcohol helped just a little, but only a little. It led to her dancing by herself in a casino corridor because she wasn't certain she could face the flashing lights and blaring noise and ultimate shocking aloneness of dancing by herself inside that nightclub.

Then Dylan showed up—a blond god in a silk suit.

He was romance-novel gorgeous, broad shoulders, muscular torso, narrow hips, a body which she later learned was as perfect unclothed as it was clothed. His hair was trimmed just enough to be stylish, but not enough to make him look fussy. He had stuffed the tie in the pocket of his jacket, making him a little less perfect.

When he saw her, he had smiled at her, and extended his long-fingered hand. "A woman as pretty as you should never dance alone."

It had been a long time since someone called her pretty. Suddenly, the highlights she'd put in her hair, the weight she'd lost in the build-up to this Liberation Vacation, money she'd spent on the slinky dress she'd probably never wear at home were all worth it.

She took his hand, surprised and pleased to find calluses. He tucked her hand in the crook of his arm, and led her inside that nightclub. They'd danced and drank and laughed, and laughed, and laughed, and by the time they were done, their hands were all over each other.

She'd never been a public kisser, but she had been that night—hell, he could have taken her on the bar if he'd wanted to. In fact, she suggested it. He had said he didn't want them to get arrested at their magical first meeting.

After the nightclub closed, they ended up in his hotel room first, and barely made it through the door before the suit and the slinky dress came off. Combustible sex, of the kind she'd only read about, and then more sex, and some room service, and finally a bit of conversation, in which she learned that he was in Vegas to celebrate his own freedom—only his was a sad little freedom: his father had died two months earlier, and Dylan—he was Dylan Thomas, named for the Welsh poet—had been his father's caretaker for the past two years.

Freedom, and liberation, and the surprising loneliness.

Oh, clearly they had realized they were kindred souls. He was foot-loose now that the estate was settled, and she had to go back to work, and, he said, he loved Denver, had always meant to live there—and he'd give it a try for her. By the end of the day, that "try" had turned into a certainty, and the two of them knew they couldn't live without each other.

The Elvis Chapel was a cliché she wanted to avoid, but they both wanted to marry immediately, thinking it romantic. No plans, no preachers, no haggling over the bests. No china patterns, no wedding invitations, just them—him in his silk suit (which they had to have pressed) and she in her slinky dress, commemorating the moment of meeting.

He bought her roses and she bought him a matching boutonniere.

They picked out expensive rings, with matching ruby stones and thick gold. He paid for hers, and she paid for his, and they clutched the boxes as they left the jewelry store, carefully located near some of the other chapels.

Only one chapel looked like a sedate place. At the edge of the Strip, where the rents were probably still cheap, the building was small and tasteful with soft organ music playing in the front, and a lovely little white and gold backdrop used for photographs.

A substitute preacher married them—the regular guy was on his own honeymoon (*Isn't that romantic?* the substitute asked with a comfortable smile)—and took a dozen photographs taken after Serena and Dylan filled out all of the various paperwork.

Her friends would hate it that she married Dylan so soon after meeting him, but while he paid the preacher, she texted them photos anyway, so they could see her joy as it happened. The photos covered everything: the chapel, Dylan from the side, the back, and then grinning at her as he walked up. The preacher gave them the actual wedding photos and a disk with the images so they could print out more copies.

Afterwards, they went back to Serena's hotel because her winnings had earned her an upgrade to one of the suites, and a conversation with the front desk clerk had gotten them yet another upgrade—a honeymoon suite, complete with champagne, caviar, chocolate-dipped strawberries, and two free room service meals.

Now, she followed the scent of coffee into the living room, after wrapping a robe around herself. The covered room service tray sat on the large table which she and Dylan had used for carnal purposes more than once.

There was no Dylan, and there was no note. She checked the bathroom. She frowned, wondering where he had gotten to, when her image in the mirror stopped her short.

Her lips were swollen, her cheeks scratched by stubble, her gold-streaked hair messy. She looked well and thoroughly satisfied.

She smiled at herself—and then the smile faded as she realized what was missing.

Dylan's toiletries.

He'd spread them across the vanity—the special shampoo for his gorgeous hair, the shaving cream for his ultra-sensitive (and oh, so lovely) skin, even his toothbrush. All missing.

Her heart skipped a beat, and she thought she misremembered where the toiletries had been, but she hadn't. She knew she hadn't.

Maybe he had put them in the half bath near the door—she had teased him enough about his "products," since he actually had more than she did. Maybe he was hiding them because she embarrassed him.

She pulled the robe tighter, and walked across the suite to the half bath near the door.

It looked lovely, with its little flower vase in one corner of the vanity, and the hotel toiletries on the other side. Who knew that the sight of a clean bathroom, beautifully decorated and absolutely perfect, would set her heart racing.

Racing and sinking at the same time.

She walked out of the little bathroom, her hands shaking now. Her body knew what her mind was refusing to acknowledge.

He wasn't here.

He had left.

But that wasn't possible. They loved each other. People who loved each other didn't treat each other like this. They didn't. They just didn't.

She walked quickly through the entire suite, suddenly angry that it was as large as the first apartment she had ever had. Lots of places to hide; lots of places to conceal things.

She looked in closets—empty except for her things. Her slinky little dress hung on a hanger, alone, not near his silk suit. He had said those two things should remain forever together.

Their wedding clothes.

Her dress. Alone.

She swallowed hard, kept looking. His suitcase was gone. His toiletries were gone. His clothes were gone.

The bed was made.

There was no note.

Except...

She stomped to the dining table, and lifted the lid off the room service tray.

One meal. Eggs, lightly scrambled. Toast, dark. A slice of watermelon. An uncut banana for later. And a pastry for dessert.

Just like she liked it.

And no note.

No damn note.

She flung the cover across the room. The cover clanged as it hit the wall, then clattered all the way to the floor. The sound was not satisfying.

Her lower lip trembled at the thought. That word: *Satisfied*. The bastard. The fucking bastard. Literally.

Her eyes teared up, and she took a deep breath.

She went back into the bedroom, and grabbed her phone, clicking it on, and froze.

It had reverted to factory settings. *He* had switched it to factory settings. All of her information was gone.

How had he gotten her password to unlock the phone?

And then she remembered him watching her as she opened her phone. Watching over and over again.

Her fingers shook, but she typed in all her information, then asked the phone to download her information from the cloud.

The phone told her that she did not have a cloud account. In fact, her phone told her she did not have any kind of account, and she had to sign up with a service provider.

She pulled the phone out of its case, saw the little scratch along the back that had been there since another case broke and her keys had defaced the phone's smooth surface.

It was her phone. But it didn't act like her phone.

She took a deep breath. It hitched. She took another, willing herself to remain steady.

Her purse sat on the chair near the window. She opened it. Her wallet was there, and so was the cash. Her driver's license—*I'll have to change that when I get back*, she had said with a laugh the night they married, when she decided to take his name. His name. Jesus. His name.

She refused to let her mind go any farther down that road. She had her driver's license, her credit cards, her insurance card, everything. But she stared at her wallet, afraid it would all bite her in ways she didn't understand.

She couldn't use her phone, but she could use the hotel's phone. In the closet, there was a phone book. She flipped the pages until she found hotels and casinos, kept flipping until she found his hotel, the one she had watched him check out of. But maybe he hadn't. Maybe he—

She called the front desk of that hotel, asked for Dylan Thomas, and waited as the clerk checked.

"I'm sorry, ma'am," the clerk said. "We do not have a guest by that name."

She tried her last name, then a variation of his name, then asked the clerk to see if someone was using the same credit card that Dylan had used when he stayed there about a week ago.

The clerk's tone got frosty. "Ma'am, I'm sorry. We don't give out that information."

"He's missing!" Serena said, her voice suddenly sounding like someone else's. Screechy and terrified and watery, and oh, so devastated. Was she devastated? She didn't want to be devastated. She couldn't be.

She had known him less than a week.

But she had married him.

The bastard.

"Oh, dear, ma'am," the clerk said and now her tone was sympathetic. "I'm afraid legally I can't just give this to someone over the phone, but we will work with the police on this. I hope you find him, ma'am. I'm sorry."

And then the clerk severed the connection.

Serena stared at the receiver as if the phone itself had caused Dylan to disappear. She made herself hang up. Hiccupping sobs threatened, but she wasn't going to allow them out.

She needed breakfast, but not the breakfast he had provided. She went back to the dining room table, grabbed the banana—the only thing that wouldn't have gotten cold or soggy—and then went to the bathroom with the gigantic shower.

She turned the water on scalding, stripped off the robe, and stepped inside, managing to control her mind until she lathered parts only a few other people had seen. Then she remembered the feel of Dylan's long fingers.

And that was when she started to scrub—not just to get the feel of him off her skin, but the memory of him out of her mind.

Forever.

ii

She didn't feel better when she got out of the shower, but she felt different. Raw, aching. Determined.

She toweled off her hair, looked at herself in the mirror, and saw—not the satisfied woman from earlier—but someone new, someone with flushed skin and flat eyes, someone who had an expression of sheer fury, and the look of someone who could do actual damage with that fury.

In the shower, she had come up with a plan.

She needed to call the police first. She had the sinking feeling that Dylan had taken everything from her, so she couldn't rack up charges on the hotel phone.

Once the police were involved, then she would work with the hotel. After she got started on that, she would find out what happened to her phone.

She would check her accounts, and if he cleaned them out, which she expected (God, she was stupid—and no, she wouldn't let that thought loose too much or she'd collapse in a sobbing puddle of uselessness), *if he cleaned them out* (she thought loudly to herself, with emphasis, to control her emotional and unruly brain), she would pawn the damn wedding ring with its lovely stones that still glistened on her finger.

He had left all of her cash—five hundred dollars—which was something. Had he cared for her even a little bit? Or had he forgotten that she had cash?

She wiped her hand over her face. Emotions later. Situation first.

She sat on the hard living room couch, grabbed her mostly useless phone, and hit the emergency button. A keyboard showed up on screen, allowing her to call 911.

She did, and said, "I think I'm the victim of a terrible crime," and refused to burst into tears.

iii

The police showed up fifteen minutes later. Two male officers and a female detective. The detective identified herself as Angela Castillo, part of the Las Vegas Sexual Assault Detail, which made Serena start. She hadn't reported a sexual assault.

She'd reported the marriage, the possible loss of everything, his disappearance, but not—

And then she flushed.

When looked at from a legal perspective, if he had no intention of staying married to her, then—

She excused herself, went to the pristine small bathroom, and threw up.

Castillo stood in the doorway. She was in her forties, in shape, with caramel colored skin and dark eyes that seemed to miss nothing. She waited until Serena had cleaned herself up before saying,

"Come on. Let's talk alone. Where would you be the most comfortable?"

Suddenly Serena wasn't comfortable anywhere. The whole hotel room was the scene of the crime. The whole damn city was the scene of the crime.

Castillo looked at the officers. "Just give us a minute."

"No," Serena said. "We have to find him before he gets away."

"You don't know when he left?" Castillo asked.

Serena shook her head.

"Okay, a description, then, and his name. We can start there."

Serena gave his name, and his description to the officers. "I have a picture on my..." and then her voice trailed off. Her phone had been wiped clean. "Maybe with the papers?"

She had put the wedding certificate in her suitcase. She walked to the closet she'd been using, opened the suitcase, and the documents—which had been in a folder on top—were still there. She hadn't put them in the little pouch underneath where she usually put important information while traveling. She had been proud of that damn marriage certificate. She had looked at it whenever she opened the suitcase.

She pulled out the folder, opened it, saw the certificate remained, but there were no pictures any longer—at least not of him. One of her, the only one alone, *the bride shot,* the preacher had called it. She stood before the gold altar in her slinky dress, clutching the roses. She had looked pretty and happy and hopeful.

Naïve little idiot that she had been.

Serena swallowed. "He took them. All of them. Pictures and everything."

"Let me see." Castillo had slipped on gloves. She reached for the folder.

Castillo didn't look at the photo, but at the marriage certificate. Then she showed it to the officers who were also in the room.

"This isn't a valid marriage license." Castillo looked at the officers. "We're going to need someone from Financial and Property Crimes ASAP. Tell the captain we need—oh, never mind. I'll call it in. You go down to the desk, ask to get copies of all of the security video for this floor for the last week, and this morning's video as well. See if we get a good image of this guy."

The officers nodded, and then walked out of the room.

"Let's sit in the living room." Castillo was holding the folder with its one pathetic photograph, clearly waiting for Serena to make a decision.

Serena nodded, then followed Castillo to that hard couch. A sexual assault victim? But she'd given her consent. Over and over. And the sex had been good. It hadn't been coerced.

But it hadn't been what she thought either. It hadn't been the celebration of two people in love, two people who had found each other despite the odds.

She frowned and rubbed her hands on her knees, feeling an ache throughout her body.

Dylan had violated her. Not sexually, not really. She would have wanted him, even for that one-night stand.

But he had violated her emotionally. Intellectually. Personally.

In every single way that counted.

Now, these revelations were taking her heart and crushing it, one little piece at a time.

iv

The next few days were a blur of interviews, explanations, and bureaucratic horrors. Dylan had emptied her bank accounts, taken cash advances from her credit cards at the hotel casino—where she had identified him as her husband on that giddy first night (and every night thereafter). He had taken an online second mortgage against her house.

Serena's house sitter had stopped a stranger from letting himself in—with Serena's keys—so that he could help himself to her belongings. The stranger had looked nothing like Dylan. *Believe me*, Serena's sitter said. *I would have remembered a handsome blond. This guy was short and dumpy and smelled of onions.*

Dylan had taken the sim card from Serena's phone, replacing the card with another. He hadn't wiped the memory as much as stolen everything about the phone that made it Serena's.

Except he hadn't known about the automatic cloud backup. Once the helpful man at the cellular store had helped Serena reset her phone, the cloud downloaded, with a few extra treasures.

Photographs of Dylan, not the ones in the memory—he had clearly deleted those at night while she slept—but buried in the texts she had sent her friends. She had forgotten about those, and told Castillo about them.

The detective Castillo had brought in from Financial and Property Crimes, a hard-faced woman named Kree, had asked for permission to dig through the phone. The phone was where Dylan had gained most of his access. He had everything of Serena's, from her social security number to her passwords, neatly stored in a little unmarked book which she had shown him, a book she kept in her carry-on (with another copy at home).

He had emptied her accounts the day he left, but the other things—the second mortgage, the new credit cards in her name, the credit lines he had opened with her very stellar credit number—those had all happened while she slept, sated, from their lovemaking.

Castillo had looked at Serena with empathy. Kree had looked at her with hard-edged pity. Serena had the sense before the end of the first day that Kree believed most financial crime victims got exactly what they deserved.

But Kree was efficient and helpful. She got the new credit lines and second mortgage cancelled, got the various banks to absorb all of the losses except the important ones—at least to Serena. The actual cash he had taken from her accounts he had done with her written permission, using the signature she had stored in her phone, and he had done so while she thought she was still married to him.

At Kree's advice, Serena consulted with an attorney (one free hour, thankfully) and the attorney said that withdrawing permission after a major fraud had occurred was often hard. Especially since Serena had been in Dylan's company when the fraud happened. The banks would probably sue on that one, the attorney had said, and while they wouldn't win, they would tie her up in court.

Much as this attorney wanted to represent her, he said, she would be better off writing off the losses and beginning again.

His words were harsh; his manner hadn't been. In fact, he had apologized several times, as if he were personally responsible for Dylan's actions.

Everyone was kind to her, and with the exception of Kree, treated her like Dylan had broken her.

Serena was beginning to like Kree more and more. Kree didn't care about Serena's emotional state. Kree wanted to put Dylan away.

"This con is incredibly organized," Kree said one afternoon when Castillo wasn't in the room. "This Dylan guy had a team. The substitute preacher, the guy at your house. I'm sure there were others. And they targeted you and played you. They've done this before. Just not in Vegas."

"I—I'm the first?"

"Here, it seems," Kree said. "We can't find any evidence of this happening to someone else. I have an associate reaching out to the hotels to see if someone reported something like this to them, but the hotels should call us if they realize that a major fraud ring is working the city."

"Maybe the women involved didn't report it," Serena said, trying not to wrap her arms around her torso. She'd been doing that a lot lately. "It's pretty embarrassing. I mean, who would think—"

"Do you know how many people elope in Vegas with someone they just met?" Kree gave her that flat stare. "Enough so that at any given time, there are at least fifty wedding chapels in this city. Fifty. A good half of the weddings here are between drunks who just met."

"Thanks," Serena muttered, knowing Kree believed Serena fit that description. She didn't want to correct Kree's misperception. Serena hadn't been drunk at her wedding—at least with alcohol.

"That's what's bothering me," Kree said, ignoring Serena's slide into self-pity (which Serena liked; it was enabling her to ignore her slide too). "With this many wedding chapels, and so many lonely whatever-happens-in-Vegas-stays-in-Vegas women coming every single day, we should have encountered this crew before. And we haven't."

"If they're not local, how did they get the chapel?" Serena asked.

"He really was a substitute preacher, hired for two weeks while the regular guy went on vacation," Kree said. "Of course, all of the substitute's information was false. It went deep enough that a cursory background check would have seemed on the up-and-up."

"So everyone there—?"

"The regular organist was sick that night," Kree said. "Severe food poisoning, which she got two days into the substitute preacher's gig."

"You think he did it," Serena said.

Kree nodded. "Like I said. Organized. We're bringing in the FBI on this. They have a crackerjack financial fraud team, and since this ring crossed state lines by going after your Denver house, they'll be handling a lot of the case."

"You're not?" Serena felt like she was losing her lifeline.

For the first time, Kree smiled at her. "I'm sticking on this one, whether the feebies like it or not. What these guys did to you..."

Kree shook her head, then bit her lower lip. Her entire body was rigid with fury.

"What those guys did to you," Kree said after a moment in which she took control of her voice, "that was personal. Getting to know you, *seducing* you. They didn't just steal the identity of a name on a credit card. They took your identity, made you volunteer to get a new name, and let you think you were walking into the sunset with the man of your dreams. They're not in this for the money. They're in it to destroy their marks. *That's* unacceptable. We have to catch them before they do it again."

Serena's throat had gone dry. She had to swallow three times before she could speak.

"They didn't destroy me," she said, but her voice sounded almost like a whisper. Broken. Ruined.

Kree looked at her.

Serena swallowed again. "They *didn't*. I'm right here. And I'm going to destroy them right back."

▼

The first thing Serena did upon return from the police station was move to a different room. The hotel comped it, as if they were responsible for Dylan.

The new room was in a different wing, with different décor. She still had a suite, but it looked nothing like the old suite, and she was grateful for that. She had moved her own suitcase, after the police were done with it, and as she hung up her clothes, making the room one-hundred-percent hers, her fingers ran across the almost-invisible zipper beneath her clothes.

The pouch where she stored her important papers while she was in a hotel room. She always removed them and put them in her purse when she got on a plane, but otherwise she left them here.

She hadn't expected to be robbed by her own husband.

Serena took a deep calming breath, something that still wasn't habit yet, and made herself open the pouch.

The documents for her new money market account—the one she had set up for taxes and incidentals from her win the day she arrived—were still inside. Her fingers lingered over them. She hadn't told Dylan about this account. She had told him that she had saved some of the money for taxes, and they could spend the rest, but she hadn't told him she had started a new account to hold that money separate from everything else.

She would have told him, but it had slipped her mind. *He* had made it slip her mind.

She smiled, feeling the first ray of hope in days.

She grabbed her phone to check the account, then realized she hadn't set up online banking for that account. Instead, she called the bank using its 800-number, that old system which felt so 20th century now.

After she punched in more numbers than she cared to think about, she discovered a piece of information that made her giddy: She still had the full $5,000 of her winnings.

She suddenly didn't feel broke any more.

She certainly had less money than she'd had when she fake-married Dylan, but she wasn't going to live paycheck-to-paycheck, like she had feared.

She let out a shuddery sigh and sank down on a nearby chair. Dylan hadn't taken *everything*, the damn bastard.

That realization gave her an odd feeling of power. He hadn't entirely outsmarted her. He wasn't totally brilliant. He could be defeated.

She could defeat him.

She just had to figure out how.

vi

Her first order of business was to put her life back together. Which sounded easier than it actually was. After the police finished with her, after she found a legal counselor and a financial advisor and a fraud specialist who was going to help her repair the damage that Dylan had done, she had to leave Las Vegas.

She was happy to do so. More than happy.

But her home, a Victorian on a twisted street in historic Denver, didn't feel like home any longer. It felt like it belonged to another woman —and essentially, it did.

Serena sold the house quickly and for a good price. Instead of putting all of the money in the bank in an account someone could break into, she scattered it through a variety of investments, none she tracked on her phone. She bought a luxury condo in downtown Denver, on the upper floors of one of the luxury hotels, figuring if she decided to leave the city, she could rent the damn place out.

The condo looked nothing like her old house. The condo was

modern, with white walls and spectacular city views, stainless steel appliances, and interior bedrooms that had a whiff of hotel design to them. She didn't care. She dumped her old furniture, bought new for the condo, and added some modern art, something the old her would have hated. But she liked the jagged edges and the bright bold colors.

She upgraded her wardrobe too, trendy items, as trendy as her condo, and as brightly colored as the paintings. She took night classes in computers, learning the ins and outs of the internet, occasionally cringing at all of the mistakes she had made with her privacy B.D.

Before Dylan. Before Disaster. Before Deciding to change.

She was going to quit her job soon, but no one knew that except her. She had to struggle to pay attention to the classics. She wasn't a professor anymore. She didn't care if the little idiots learned anything.

Her friends were trying to slow her down. They complained when she sold the house. They complained when she moved. They complained when she cut her hair. They complained when she got new clothes.

When they complained too much, she stopped calling them. She wanted to say she made new friends, but she really didn't. She made new acquaintances, people she could laugh with in the bars near her condo, people whom she watched get drunk while she stayed startlingly sober. She learned to sip her wine—no more guzzling beer, no more mixed drinks, no more nothing—and she learned to watch.

She saw pickpockets, working girls, and escorts. She saw the scammers and the flimflam artists. And she realized just how rare Dylan had been.

Usually women ran his kind of scam—not the marrying part, but the sex part. Using desire to get not just in someone's pants but into their wallets as well. Most of the women did it in one night, and many of them got arrested.

No one, as far as she could tell, ever managed to marry and scam—except those men who had different wives in different states, something she slowly learned was a different pathology altogether.

She made a study of con artists and bar behavior. When she wasn't watching people, she explored the internet, searching for a familiar face, searching for a pattern.

One after another, her counselors fired her. *You don't seem to want to get better*, one said to her.

I didn't know I was ill, Serena said in return.

You have no desire to explore your own healing, another counselor said.

I've repaired my life, Serena answered.

No, the counselor said. *You* changed *your life. That's not the same thing.*

Serena hadn't argued the point, although she could have. *She* hadn't changed her life. Dylan had. From the moment she met him. The fantastic sex (which she still sometimes dreamed about), the fake marriage, the hopes for the future—all came about because she met Dylan. That this particular happily-ever-after ended with the princess getting screwed royally by someone posing as Prince Charming didn't alter the fact that the chance meeting in the corridor outside the nightclub would have changed Serena's life no matter what.

She kept hiring counselors, though, mostly as someone to talk to. On her eighth counselor, she finally figured out how to use the system. She talked sideways about Dylan, about what kind of personality he had to have, about what made him tick.

If she figured out how what kind of person he was, she lied to the counselor, she would heal.

This particular counselor bought the argument for exactly two sessions. The next counselor for three. The next for another two. They argued that her healing had nothing to do with Dylan, and she privately begged to differ.

As they spent the hours she paid for analyzing him, she learned a few things.

She didn't believe the counselors who sympathetically said he had probably been sexually abused as a child or that he had a pathological hatred of women. She'd met a few men who hated women. It always came out sideways.

The counselors she believed were the ones who called him a sociopath. He had the charm and the charisma, the lack of interest in society's rules, and the love of putting something over on others.

He clearly had done that with her.

The problem was that people like Dylan felt no remorse, guilt, or shame. They blamed others when caught. So all of the FBI's work in finding him, all of the work Kree was doing and keeping Serena apprised of, wouldn't devastate Dylan, even if he was arrested. He'd be disappointed, but he'd blame all of them for his situation, not himself.

Sociopaths, one counselor said to Serena, *are all about control*.

And that, that little sentence, that one small idea, reverberated through her head for weeks.

Control. She had ceded control to him, and he had taken control of everything else.

But he had made it a game. From the name, to the sex, to the pretend marriage.

It had all been a game.

And games were all about winners and losers.

After she had that realization, her smiles became real, and her determination became strong.

She dropped the counselors and made finding Dylan her number one priority.

vii

It took nearly two years and a lot of focus. Even then, she wasn't certain she had found the right crew.

She used the information she got from the authorities, but she never gave them any information in return. The FBI had found a pattern—the crew would hit an area, usually with a casino, but not always; usually with a great nightlife, but not always; sometimes with relatively simple marriage license requirements, but not always.

The reports were fewer than reports on most fraud crews, because of the thing that Serena had said: women were often embarrassed to admit they had been taken. Some even hired a divorce attorney only to learn that they hadn't really been married in the first place.

The FBI searched for a pattern, Kree watched for the crew's return to Vegas (while keeping Serena apprised) and Serena employed increasingly more sophisticated facial recognition software as she searched likely areas.

She hooked up with a hacker group online, learned how to get into hotel security cameras, and make traffic cameras near hot spots do her bidding.

The FBI made a map of where the crew had been, and Kree had forwarded it. Serena looked at the pattern and did exactly what the authorities did: she tried to figure out where the crew would go next.

But the authorities had to wait for a crime.

She didn't.

And she had the benefit of knowing not just what Dylan looked like, but how he moved, how he slid through a crowd, how he touched women. She also knew what the substitute preacher looked like.

But that didn't find Dylan for her.

Three patterns did.

In the towns without overnight wedding chapels like Vegas, the substitute preacher set up a website for his marriage services, and attached it, like a barnacle, to the regular county clerk's office site. When engaged couples figured out that they wanted to marry, the website would send them to the preacher to set up his bona fides. It took a little time, but this crew seemed to have nothing but time.

That, combined with the travel pattern the FBI figured out, helped her find the preacher.

But it was Dylan's ego that helped her find him.

He assumed he was smarter than everyone else, prettier, smoother, better educated. In one town, he was Bob Browning. In another, Edward Cummings. And with Serena, he had been Dylan Thomas.

Famous male poets—Robert Browning, e. e. cummings, Dylan Thomas.

If the mark knew the name, like she had, Dylan copped to it—*my parents named me for the poet*. If the mark didn't, no one said a word.

And no one else had noticed, except her.

She kept a list of poet names, and had various online alerts set up so that she could track the arrival/appearance of one of those names in the systems of the hotels in the locales that should've been next on the list.

The crew had a system that the FBI found. The crew would go to one city per state, never more than one in a trip, and never to adjoining states. So after they had left Serena in Las Vegas, they went to Washington State.

They never visited the same state in the same year, but they seemed to have favorite states, Nevada being one of them.

Two years, which meant they were due. And after they left Florida, Serena knew they would start all over again. They always went west to east, never east to west. They would skip California, because they always seemed to skip California, which was leading the FBI to believe that the crew had history there, history that probably meant they didn't want to do anything to alert the California authorities.

The FBI was investigating that angle, or so Kree said, but they had little to go on. Serena didn't care about that angle. She cared about catching the crew in the act.

She had a plan.

And when a blond, exceedingly handsome John Donne checked into the priciest hotel on the Las Vegas strip, she knew she had found him.

viii

Serena did not tell Kree or Castillo that she was returning to Las Vegas. She simply arrived. On the flight from Denver, she watched the hotel's security footage over and over again. She hadn't needed her special illegal facial recognition software to recognize Dylan. She knew every inch of that face, and even after she had cleaned up the security footage, she knew that his appearance hadn't changed at all.

Hers had. She was thin to the point of bony, her hair darker and longer. She no longer fit into the slinky dress (yes, she'd kept it), and her wedding ring (yes, she'd kept that too) spun on her left finger.

She'd wrapped yarn around the back of the ring as if she were a teenager, but after she'd checked into a different megahotel across South Las Vegas Boulevard from Dylan's, she scouted hair boutiques so that she could get hers wedge-cut and lightened. She didn't do it immediately—she didn't want Dylan to recognize her (even though she doubted he would)—but she did buy another slinky dress. It wasn't quite the same as the original, but it was close.

Serena had the same shoes, however. She could reappear as her old self at any point. "Old self" wasn't quite accurate: she had only been that slinky blond self for six days, six marvelous delusional days when she thought the fairy tale would never end.

She had no idea how Dylan picked his marks, although she had a theory. She had won that jackpot at the beginning of her stay two years ago, and babbled to the hotel staff like an idiot about the Liberation Vacation and how it was starting perfectly.

Over the years she (and the FBI and Kree) all doubted that Dylan had a crew member on staff, so that meant that he watched for some lucky hapless woman to reveal her loneliness in a painful and public fashion.

He had to spend his days watching for her.

Serena set up a wireless station inside her hotel room, so she didn't have to use the hotel's creaky old system. And she watched the lobby for a few hours before realizing that Dylan wasn't down there, but someone else was.

A short, dumpy guy who looked like he might actually smell of onions moved around the lobby, monkeying with his phone, sitting in a chair, going in and out of the nearby hotel gift shop. Serena didn't know for certain because she had never seen him before, but she was pretty sure that the man she was watching was the same one who had let himself into her house two years before, using her own keys.

He finally left the lobby about four hours in, and it didn't look like anyone had replaced him. Which meant he'd found the right mark.

She reviewed the footage, wishing she had audio as well as video. People—especially nervous people—revealed too much when they were checking into hotels.

She ended up with three possibles—all not-quite-pudgy blondes who looked both lonely and nervous—and watched the dumpy guy's reaction to them. He kept his eye on one for a tad too long. Serena was going to go with her, until she realized that he wasn't looking at the pudgy lonely woman. He was looking at a willowy blonde who seemed ever-so-slightly angry.

The willowy blonde smiled and laughed as she checked in, but the desk clerk looked a bit uncomfortable, the way people did when they heard too much information about someone they didn't know. Then the blonde held out a sparkling diamond ring, shook it at the clerk, and laughed again.

The clerk shrugged, took out a map, and circled someplace on it.

Serena's breath caught. She would bet her last dollar that the blonde wanted to sell that ring. Not pawn it. Sell it.

The crew wasn't targeting lonely women. They were targeting *angry* women traveling alone. After all, what had Serena and her Liberation Vacation been if not angry? She had just been too repressed to admit it by using words like "anger" and "furious." Instead, she had made jokes about her trip.

Serena hacked into the hotel's system, saw that the blonde—one Nicole Warrington—had checked into a suite that had been booked months before, and knew, knew, she was looking at Dylan's next "wife."

If Serena was still a good little girl, she would have called Kree and Castillo and alerted them. But she wasn't. Kree and Castillo would screw everything up.

If they asked later, Serena would say that she wasn't certain what happened to Dylan after she saw him check in.

And if she was honest with herself, she wondered why he was in the same hotel as the mark.

Or maybe he wasn't. Maybe he had gotten the room as insurance, let the dumpy guy use it, and had also gotten another room at a different hotel. That other room would also be under the name John Donne—if, indeed, he was running the same scam.

She would search for that in the morning. Just like she would try—again—to search wedding chapel "pastors." That was harder. Even though the chapels had online advertising, their websites were mostly static, and their business was in-person, so she couldn't figure out if they had hired someone new or gotten a substitute preacher.

She knew that Kree monitored the original wedding chapel, but Serena doubted the crew would use the same chapel twice.

She stayed in her room, ordered room service, and watched security footage until she saw Nicole Warrington leave her suite in a gorgeous red designer gown that showed every single curve to great advantage.

Nicole Warrington looked like a woman trying to shake off a man any way she possibly could.

For several heart-stopping minutes, Serena worried that Nicole would go to a nightclub outside of the massive hotel/casino complex.

But her worries faded as Nicole marched down to the most expensive nightclub inside the complex. Dylan would have to work quickly to catch this woman, because other men would be lined up.

Serena hoped he would work the corridor again, because seeing what he was doing inside the nightclub would be hard. The place had security, but it also had dim lighting that was punctuated by strobe lights when the music demanded it, and she would have trouble seeing faces.

Nicole Warrington went inside, and Serena didn't see Dylan at all.

She let out a breath, wondering if she had focused on the wrong mark.

She didn't want to miss this opportunity, and she was afraid that she might.

ix

There was only one real exit to the club, which Serena monitored for four hours. While she watched, she worked on a second screen, searching lower-tier hotels for John Donne. She almost missed him. Facial recognition didn't find him, because he wore a ball cap low over his face, and he didn't register as John Donne.

He registered as Jonathon Donne.

The thing that confirmed it for her, though, was as she watched the security footage, she saw him roll the keycard over his fingers, just like a poker player rolled a card. He had done that with their keycard more than once.

She knew now that she was on the clock.

She had started reviewing the front desk footage for the megahotel when Nicole Warrington staggered out of the nightclub. Serena let out a breath. She had forgotten: the mark had to be drunk or at least tipsy before Dylan would approach.

And then he walked out, perfect in a gray suit that shimmered in the soft light. Nicole saw him, laughed, and extended her hand. Then they exchanged a kiss that Serena could almost taste.

At the moment, it looked like Nicole was in charge, not Dylan. He looked like the perfect goofy pickup, the guy who couldn't believe his luck. They kissed again, and she slid her hands under his suit coat.

A hotel security guard tapped him on the shoulder, and clearly told them to get a room.

They laughed, and staggered away. They headed to her room, which surprised Serena. Dylan had convinced Serena to go to his, although she couldn't remember how. Maybe she had balked at bringing him to hers. She probably had, with her old paranoia about being robbed.

Not that anyone was thinking of robbery at that moment, except maybe Dylan. He had his back against the row of mirrors inside the elevator, and Nicole was pressed against him.

Serena had to get up and walk away from the computer, her entire body shaking.

She had just become jealous. This wouldn't work if she were jealous. Dammit, she still had feelings for that man, buried deep, but not as deep as she thought.

Serena made herself breathe. Dylan was not her husband. He wasn't even named Dylan. He was some man, some horrible man, who had just targeted another vulnerable drunken woman.

Serena sat back down and reversed the video just a bit. She froze the frame on Dylan's face and made herself stare at it.

This is the face of a man who exchanges sex for money, she reminded herself, mouthing the words as she thought them. *This is the expression of a man who gets off on using people for his own purposes. The excitement of screwing a mark meant more to him than the sex act itself.*

She let the video play forward now, suddenly afraid she would lose them. But of course, she didn't. They just staggered down the hall to Nicole's room, Nicole shaking her dress a little. Dylan laughed. That made her turn, and they kissed again, the same hot kiss they'd exchanged in the hallway downstairs, the kind that wrapped her around him. He took the keycard from her hand, and opened the door, backing her inside.

Serena caught the image of a red dress floating in the air before the door snaked closed.

Her heart split again. She started to stand, but a thought stopped her.

He had done something. Besides kissing Nicole, that is. He had done something else. Something—

Serena reversed the video, then watched, frame by frame. After Dylan took the keycard from Nicole, while she was wrapped around him, and he was holding her up with one hand, he used the keycard to open the door. And then, as her legs tightened around him, as her dress hiked up, he slipped the keycard in his back pocket.

Cool and calculating.

Serena watched the video one more time to make certain. Yep, he had pocketed the keycard, and he would probably make a copy of it. Serena couldn't ever remember giving him her original key card, and he had gotten one from the desk when they moved to the suite, but a move like this would enable someone else to get into the room when Nicole and Dylan weren't there.

Serena suspected he would make a copy as soon as Nicole was asleep.

That twisting in her heart had disappeared. That little maneuver of his made the last of the old naïve Serena die.

And she was glad of it.

Because she had only a few hours to put her plan into action.

x

First, the haircut. She hurried the hairdresser because she didn't want to get seen in the hallway. At some point, Dylan and Nicole would leave that room—sober, deciding to get married. Dylan seemed to like his women sober when he "married" them.

Serena had to watch carefully for that, because she still wasn't sure which chapel the substitute preacher was in.

While her hair was being cut, she had a full manicure, which she had done on that trip two long years ago as well. It felt odd to pamper herself like this: she hadn't done it in a long time.

It didn't relax her. It made her feel like she was being primed for battle.

She finished, returned to her room, ordered room service, and hunkered down. She knew she wouldn't get a lot of sleep in the next twenty-four hours, and she was okay with that.

She could sleep after she was done with Dylan.

At six a.m., room service knocked on Nicole's door. Dylan answered, opening the door so that the waiter could take the food cart inside. Nicole, wrapped in a fluffy robe, her perfect hair messy, was barely visible.

Dylan looked a lot more put together. He signed the tab for the food, which was odd, since he wasn't yet on the room. Maybe he had signed it to his room, or maybe the hotel didn't care.

Then the room service waiter pushed the cart out, leaving the tray with the food inside. As the waiter turned to head down the hall, the security cameras caught his face full-on.

It was the oniony man from the lobby. Serena gasped, the pieces of the scam coming together. Dylan hadn't done everything while Serena was asleep. He had merely collected the evidence and downloaded it or moved it or changed it. Then he had passed it off to an accomplice.

She and Dylan had room service every single day. She thought it was because they didn't want to get dressed, not because Dylan was feeding information to someone.

When the room service waiter arrived day after day, Serena had never gotten out of bed, too embarrassed to face the waiter. Nicole had gotten out of bed, but she looked a bit preoccupied. Still, Serena wondered if Nicole's presence had dampened Dylan's style.

Serena took a deep breath. Now, she knew the con was underway. Of course, she had known it last night, but she really knew it now. She had evidence to share with Kree, Castillo, and the FBI.

This was where Serena should have been a good girl. She could prevent a lot of heartache for Nicole right here.

But Serena didn't want to prevent a few hours of heartache for one woman. Serena wanted to prevent heartache for an entire slew of women, all of whom would become victims if she didn't step in.

Oh, who was she kidding?

She wanted to destroy Dylan. She had always wanted to destroy Dylan. If she stepped in now, she would miss her chance.

He would get arrested either way; she was going to call the authorities eventually.

She just wanted a little payback first.

xi

Dylan and Nicole finally left the hotel room at one in the afternoon. Nicole was wearing a tasteful white lace dress with matching heels. She glowed, and Serena actually felt for her. Nicole had no idea what was coming.

Dylan wore a black suit, not silk, but tasteful, the kind an upper-middle-class man would bring on a business trip. He looked like a man who had never been married before—nervous, proud, happy.

He held Nicole's hand, then kissed it as the door to the room closed.

Serena could have scripted the next hour. Downstairs by elevator, although Dylan wanted to kiss Nicole, she held him back: that woman wanted to look nice for her wedding photos. Dylan smiled, but Serena saw that his gaze had cooled just a little. He wanted the sexual mastery, not the pretty images.

The couple got out on the third floor of the hotel, which had a bridge to a variety of expensive stores. Serena tracked them to the most exclusive jewelry store in the shopping area. Outside, they clearly argued, but Dylan finally held sway. Serena knew his argument: *You only get married once*, he was saying, the bastard. *We need to do some things right. You'll wear this ring every single day of your life.*

Serena looked at her ring, glistening in the Vegas sunlight pouring in the window. She hadn't worn the ring every single day, but she would be lying if she said she hadn't thought about it—and him—day in and day out.

She made herself focus on the screen. Dylan and Nicole walked into the jewelry store, Dylan's hand possessively on the small of her back. Serena could almost feel that hand on the small of hers.

It took longer than she had expected. She and Dylan had chosen within twenty minutes—eager, Serena thought, to get married and then back to their hotel room. But Nicole clearly wanted to find the perfect ring.

When they finally emerged, Dylan clutching a small bag with the store's logo, he looked a little frazzled. He hadn't enjoyed that last hour at all.

Nicole probably wasn't the kind of woman he could manipulate as easily as he'd manipulated Serena.

Nicole said something, and then he handed her the bag. She put it in her purse, and slipped her arm through his. They walked toward the lobby.

Serena prayed they would get a cab. If they got a cab, she could catch them. Him. The stupid substitute preacher.

She could bring an end to all of it.

She twisted her ring.

As they went through the lobby, Dylan stopped at the valet station, and handed one of the valets some cash. Serena felt her heart sink.

No cab. Somehow Dylan had a car.

Damn.

The couple went outside and waited, until a black SUV pulled up. The valet handed Dylan the keys, Dylan passed out more money, and Serena squinted for the license plate.

She didn't quite see it.

She would have to wait until they returned. No matter where they went, it would only take a few hours at most.

She wouldn't take a nap, but she would rest. It was nearly showtime.

xii

The SUV returned to the hotel at eight p.m., later than she expected. Serena had been going quietly insane. She worried that they were going to check out, that she'd never find them again, that they were onto her.

But the SUV pulled up, and as it stopped, Nicole got out, a huge ring on her left hand glistening in the security camera.

Dylan came around the SUV, tossed his keys to the valet like a rich man would. Then the couple walked into the hotel, their steps perfectly in sync.

They stopped in the lobby, and Serena felt her breath catch. They were supposed to go to the most expensive bar in the place and toast their new marriage. That was what she had done—after Dylan had gotten them the honeymoon suite.

As the hotel staff had moved their belongings.

Serena let out a small breath.

Dylan turned, and walked to the desk—and Serena smiled.

Then she picked up her phone. She waited until Dylan and Nicole were done reserving a larger room, Nicole's high-heeled foot playing with the back of Dylan's leg the entire time. When they were done, they headed toward the bar and restaurant complex, and Serena's smile grew.

She called Castillo first because, technically, it was Castillo's case.

"I'm here in Vegas at a conference," Serena lied, "and I think I just saw Dylan in my hotel."

"Don't go near him," Castillo said. "Where are you?"

Serena told her. Serena did not tell her that Dylan had already married and was heading to the bar.

Castillo could find that out for herself.

"You sit tight," Castillo said. "We'll handle this. And remember, he can't hurt you any more."

She was so used to dealing with sexual assault victims. Serena remembered how her heart twisted when she watched that first kiss between Nicole and Dylan—and how it had taken Serena a while to get past that.

"I know he can't," Serena said, and that much was true. "Please, don't worry about me."

And then she hung up. She stared at the security cameras, saw Dylan and Nicole arguing in the corridor. This marriage wouldn't have lasted, even if it were real.

Dylan shrugged, then grinned, a look that Serena hadn't seen before.

Nicole led him—not to the bar, but to the fanciest restaurant in the place.

Clearly she wanted the full honeymoon package—the gorgeous ring, the fancy hotel suite, the pricey restaurant. She wanted the memories.

And, poor sap, she'd get them.

Serena waited until the couple followed the maître d' deep into the restaurant. Then Serena checked her appearance, added some lipstick, grabbed her purse, and headed downstairs.

xiii

Her heart was pounding—not with fear, but with anticipation. She wanted to do this. She wanted it almost as much as she had wanted Dylan that first night.

Serena strode across the hotel, and into the restaurant area. Men who already had a partner tried not to look at her. Men who were alone all smiled as if her appearance gave them hope she would go somewhere with them. Most women gave her the death stare, the one that told her they thought she looked prettier than they did. Other women openly flirted.

She clutched her purse to her side, and entered the restaurant. It smelled of garlic, roasting beef, and freshly baked bread. The maître d' tried to stop her. She gave him her widest smile.

"I'm meeting someone," she said, and pushed past him.

She saw Nicole first. They had a table in the corner. Nicole sat with her back to the wall, her beauty and happiness reflected in the discreet mirrors added just above the chairs to make the room seem bigger.

Dylan sat across from her, his suit coat open, his collar unbuttoned, and his tie loose. He looked like he had already had good sex. Maybe he had, in the car. Or maybe he got satisfied by a con well played.

He sat up as Serena approached, a frown on his face.

Serena made sure she wore a small smile, not a large one. She didn't want to look like the cat that swallowed the canary until all the feathers were in her mouth.

He had just set his napkin down as if he were about to get out of the chair, when she reached him. She slipped her hands inside his suit, down his chest, feeling its familiarity, so flat and perfect. As she did that, she nibbled his ear, then worked her way down his neck, knowing what it did to him.

He gasped just a little, a sexual sound she had forgotten, and tried to move away, but she held him tightly.

"What are you doing?" Nicole demanded. "What's going on?"

Serena kept Dylan in his seat, pressing her breasts against his back, and unbuttoned the front of his shirt near his belt. He reached for her hands, but she slipped them against his warm skin.

She smiled, keeping her mouth against the fragrant side of Dylan's neck. "So this is the new one, Dylan?"

He started at the name.

"Oh, I'm sorry," Serena said, just a little louder. "I meant John. I forget what name he uses on these little excursions."

Nicole's face had gone white. She was looking at Dylan as if she expected him to say something.

The people at the nearby table were watching as well. A waiter, holding a silver ice bucket with a bottle of champagne inside, stood awkwardly by.

"Let me see the ring," Serena said as if she and Nicole were old friends. "He didn't make you buy it, did he? Sometimes he makes the woman buy, and I think that's so rude."

Dylan shoved at her. "Lady, you're crazy."

"I know, my love," she said, sliding her hands down further.

He grabbed her fingers. She could see his face in the mirror. He looked panicked.

Nicole flushed. "Who *are* you?" she snapped at Serena.

"Oh, sweetie," Serena said. "He didn't explain, did he? I'm his wife. We were married years ago. Your marriage isn't legal. The document you signed isn't one that the State of Nevada recognizes, even if the ceremony were performed by a licensed preacher, which yours wasn't. That's just Dylan's—I mean John's—best friend."

"What?" Nicole asked.

"Oh," Serena said, her voice lowering. "Did you marry today? Am I early? You still had a few days of sex left, didn't you? Dylan likes his women to think it's legal. He says it makes them even hotter."

Serena lifted one of her hands and grabbed Dylan's chin tightly. He tried to open his mouth, but she turned his head toward her and kissed him hard.

She pulled her mouth away just enough to say, "My darling loves screwing women. I'm not always able to keep up with him, so I let him roam. Sometimes he gets a bit...involved—"

"I do not!" Dylan finally got some traction. He shoved her backwards. "You damn bitch! What do you think you're doing?"

Her heart was pounding. She hadn't expected him to get so furious.

He raised an arm and was about to hit her, when the waiter dropped the champagne bucket. It sloshed ice everywhere. One of the other diners stood and grabbed Dylan, who struggled against him, screaming obscenities at Serena.

"I'm done with you, you bitch. You have no right to be here! You're *done*."

Her mouth was dry, but she smiled anyway. "Not really. I'm just beginning. I'm going to follow you everywhere, and meet all of your wives. We'll have quite a coven, we wives of the con man named for a poet. We'll—"

"He's a con man?" Nicole was standing, clutching her purse to her chest. "You know he's a con man?"

Everyone looked at her. Water from the ice bucket was sliding across the floor, getting into her shoes, but she didn't even seem to notice.

"He tried to steal everything from me," Serena said.

"You could have *told* me," Nicole said, her voice thick with tears. "You could've stopped the wedding. You could've—"

"It wasn't legal," Serena said. "You're still single—"

Nicole let out a sob and launched herself across the table, pounding Dylan repeatedly with her fists. "You said you *loved* me, you *bastard*. You said—"

"He always says that." A new voice had entered the conversation. Kree stood behind the maître d, wearing an old brown polyester suit coat, and functional pants. She glared at Serena. "Detective Castillo told you to wait."

"And miss this?" Serena smiled. She felt positively giddy.

"It accomplishes nothing." Kree removed a pair of handcuffs from her belt. She expertly snapped the cuffs on Dylan, then dragged him away from the waiter.

"You have no right," Dylan said. "I've done nothing wrong."

Serena gasped at his audacity, but Nicole raised a high heel and kicked. Dylan turned slightly sideways, getting the point of the heel in his thigh.

His eyes narrowed as he said to Nicole, "You were a hell of a lot more fun to screw. I was looking forward to seeing what else you could do."

Nicole screeched and reached for him. Kree moved him even farther away.

Serena knew better than to say anything to Nicole. Serena recognized her pain. Instead, Serena ran a hand along Dylan's face.

"Oh, darling," she said. "You must be slipping. It really didn't take much to convince her that you're the scum of the earth."

His mouth opened in shock, and for a moment, she saw the real man underneath. Panicked, vulnerable, lost. Then his mouth closed and his face flushed. He pursed his lips, and she realized just in time that he was going to spit at her. She barely managed to dodge.

"How very third grade of you," she said. "A real man would apologize."

"For what? Giving you two the best time you've ever had?" he snapped.

Serena tilted her head. "Oh, Dylan, such ego. You always finished a little too fast for me."

He made a growling sound, and Kree yanked him away from her. Another officer had shown up and was helping her.

Nicole had dissolved into a pile of tears. Two of the female patrons had their arms around her as she sobbed.

"I told you to wait." Castillo was standing near one of the tables, arms crossed.

"You sound like Detective Kree," Serena said. She tilted her head at Nicole. "You have a real victim there. You need to deal with her."

"And not the woman who went all vigilante on us?" Castillo's brown eyes missed nothing. She apparently saw the similar dress, the manicure, the haircut.

"I was just going to warn the new wife," Serena lied, "and I got carried away. I'll be happy to come to the station, though, and press charges."

"Tomorrow," Castillo said. "When I'm less pissed at you."

Serena smiled and picked her way out of the mess. Other officers and some security guards were huddled near the doorway. Dylan was being led away. He seemed small now, hunched, as if he'd lost something.

She almost wished she hadn't called the police. She hadn't had that much fun in years. Imagine what it would have been like to follow him from con to con, breaking it up at the exact right moment, having him look over his shoulder, always expecting her to ruin things.

She had planned this a bit too conservatively. She could have done that, and truly ruined him.

She sighed.

The police and the FBI would get enough information from Nicole to arrest the other team members. They'd find the oniony man and the substitute preacher and anyone else who was involved. The entire con would shut down.

The game was over. Serena had won.

She reached for her wedding ring, and started to slip it off. Then she looked at it, the way that Nicole had looked at hers when she got out of the SUV, with wonder and a bit of surprise that it was on her finger.

What was a wedding ring after all, but a trophy? The symbol of a woman who had truly tamed a man.

She closed her left hand into a fist, feeling stronger. Feeling powerful. Feeling complete for the first time in her entire life.

She hadn't expected this happily ever after when she met Dylan.

But she would take it.

She would take it all.

Family Affair

A Smokey Dalton Story

Kris Nelscott

Family Affair

I knew the day had gone bad when the white woman in the parking lot started to scream. I turned in the seat of my mud-green Ford Fairlane, and watched as Marvella Walker and Valentina Wilson tried to soothe the white woman. But the closer Marvella got to her, the faster the woman backed away, screaming at the top of her lungs.

We were in a diner parking lot in South Beloit, Illinois, just off the interstate. Valentina had driven the woman and her daughter from Madison, Wisconsin, that morning.

The woman was a small thing, with dirty blond hair and a cast on her right arm. Her clothing was frayed. Her little blond daughter—no more than six—circled the women like a wounded puppy. She occasionally looked at my car as if I was at fault.

Maybe I was.

I'm tall, muscular, and dark. The scar that runs from my eye almost to my chin makes me look dangerous to everyone—not just to white people.

Usually I can calm people I've just met with my manner or by using a soft tone. But in this instance, I hadn't even gotten out of the car.

The plan was simple: We were supposed to meet Marvella's cousin, Valentina Wilson, who ran a rape hotline in Madison. The hotline ran along the new Washington D.C. model—women didn't just call; they got personal support and occasional legal advice if they asked for it.

This woman had been brutally raped and beaten by her husband. Even then, the woman didn't want to leave the bastard. Then he had gone after their daughter and the woman finally asked for help.

At least, that was what Valentina said.

Marvella waved her hands in a gesture of disgust and walked toward me. She was tall and majestic. With the brown and gold caftan that she wore over thin brown pants, her tight black Afro, and the hoops on her ears, she looked like one of those statues of African princesses she kept all over her house.

She rapped on the car window. "Val says she can make this work."

She said that with so much sarcasm that her own opinion was clear.

"If she doesn't make it work soon," I said, "we could have some kind of incident on our hands."

People in the nearby diner were peering through the grimy windows. Black and white faces were staring at us, which gave me some comfort, but not a whole lot since there was a gathering of men near the diner's silver door.

They were probably waiting for me to get out of the car and grab the woman. Then they'd come after me.

I could hold off maybe three of them, but I couldn't handle the half dozen or so that I could see. They looked like farmers, beefy white men with sun-reddened faces and arms like steel beams.

My heart pounded. I hated being outside of the city—any city. In the city, I could escape pretty much anything, but out here, near the open highway, where the land rose and fell in gentle undulations caused by the nearby Rock River, I felt exposed.

Valentina was gesturing. The white woman had stopped screaming. The little girl had grabbed her mother's right leg and hung on, not so much, it seemed, for comfort, but to hold her mother steady.

I watched Valentina. She looked nothing like the woman I had met three years ago, about to go to the Grand Nefertiti Ball, a big charity event in Chicago. She had worn a long white gown, just like Marvella and her sister Paulette had, but Valentina came from different stock.

Marvella had looked like I imagined Cleopatra had looked when Julius Caesar first saw her, and Paulette was just as stunning.

But Valentina, tiny and pretty with delicate features, had looked lost in that white dress. The snake bracelets curling up her arms made them look fat, even though they weren't.

They didn't look fat now. They were lean and muscular, like the rest of her. That delicate prettiness was gone. What replaced it was an athleticism that hollowed her cheeks and gave her small frame a wiry toughness that no one in his right mind would mess with.

I knew the reason for the change; she had been raped by a policeman who then continued to pursue her after his crime. Even after his murder by one of the city's largest gangs, she felt she couldn't stay in Chicago.

I understood that, just like I understood the toughness with which she armored herself. But I also missed the delicate woman in the oversized dress, the one who smiled easily and had a strong sense of the ridiculous.

"You know," Marvella said, leaning against the driver's side window, "as much of a fuss as that woman's putting up, I don't think we should take her out of here at all."

I agreed. We were supposed to take her to a charity a group of us had started on the South Side of Chicago. Called Helping Hands, the charity assisted families—mostly women and children — who had no money, no job skills, and no place to go. I found a lot of them squatting in houses that I inspected for Sturdy Investments. Rather than turning them out, I went to Sturdy's CEO and the daughter of its founder, Laura Hathaway —who, not by coincidence, had an on-again, off-again relationship with me.

Laura agreed that we couldn't throw children onto the street, so she put up the initial money and got her rich white society friends to put up even more. Without Laura's society connections, Helping Hands wouldn't exist.

It wasn't designed for people from Wisconsin. We had devised it only for Chicagoans, and mostly for those on the South Side. We had a few white families go through our doors over the years, but not many. We only had a few white volunteers. The white face that most of our clients saw—if they saw one at all—was Laura's, and then only because she liked to periodically drop in on the business and check up on everything herself.

"I mean," Marvella said, "what happens if she changes her mind again halfway between here and Chicago? If she starts screaming from the back seat of your car, the cops will pull us over in no time."

I winced. If the woman claimed she was being taken to Chicago against her will, then there were all kinds of laws we could be accused of breaking, not the least of which was kidnapping.

"Tell Valentina this isn't going to work," I said.

"Not going to tell her. She has her heart set on saving that little girl."

That little girl kept looking at me from the safety of her mother's thigh. I could see why Valentina wanted to save her. The little girl's eyes shone with intelligence, not to mention the fact that she was the only calm one in the trio.

Her mother was crying and shaking her head. Valentina was still talking, but it didn't look like she was going to get anywhere.

"You can't save someone who doesn't want to be saved," I said.

"You tell Val that," Marvella said.

"Bring her over here and I will," I said. "Because in no way am I getting near that woman with the diner crowd watching."

Marvella glanced up at them and frowned. I couldn't quite tell, but it seemed like more bodies were pressed against the glass around the door. One huge white man was now standing beside his pick-up truck, twirling his key ring on his right index finger.

"Crap," Marvella said. "I'll see what I can do."

She walked back to the women. She put a hand on Valentina's shoulder and led her, not gently, away from the woman.

Marvella and Valentina talked for a few minutes. Marvella nodded toward the diner.

Valentina looked up for the first time. Her lips thinned. Then she nodded, just once.

She walked back to the woman and her daughter.

Marvella walked back to me and got in the passenger side.

"Let's go," she said.

"That's it?" I asked.

"Not really," Marvella said. "We need to call Helping Hands and tell them to put a white volunteer at the front desk, not that I think that's going to work."

"Why?" I asked.

"Because Val's convinced she can drive the woman to Chicago all by herself," Marvella said.

I looked at the three of them, still standing in the parking lot. The woman wiped her good hand over her eyes.

"Why would she go with Valentina and not with us?" I asked.

Marvella rolled her eyes. "Valentina has apparently reached honorary white person status. She nearly lost it when seen in the company of her black cousin and the mean-looking black driver. You should have heard the crap that woman spouted about niggers come to kidnap her daughter—"

"I don't need to hear it," I said, waving my hand.

"Me either," Marvella said. "I nearly told the bitch to shove it up her bony little ass, but Val wouldn't let me. She said she's just scared and out of her depth and had we forgotten that Madison is 90% white? I'm thinking maybe she forgot or she should have at least told us so we could've brought your society girlfriend along to make little miss holier-than-thou over there a lot more comfortable."

I let the dig at my society girlfriend go by. Marvella and Laura got along, now, after a lot of wrangling and harsh words over the years. This was just Marvella's way of letting her anger out without aiming it at the woman we had driven an hour and a half to help.

"So let's just go," Marvella said. "We'll pull over somewhere with a pay phone and call Helping Hands, and then our job here is done."

I hesitated for just a moment. The little girl was still watching us. Valentina turned slightly, waved her hand in a shoo motion, and I nodded.

I started the car, turned the wheel, and pulled out of the parking lot, glancing into my rear view mirror to make sure no pick-up truck followed us.

None did.

After twenty minutes, I let out a breath.

After thirty, I knew we were in the clear.

After we had made the call to Helping Hands, I figured we were done with this job.

Of course, I was wrong.

Three months later, Marvella pounded on my apartment door. We lived just across the hall from each other.

"I have a phone call you need to take," she said.

I yelled to my fourteen-year-old son Jim that I would be right back, then crossed the hall. Even though it was December and the landlord had forgotten to turn on the heat in the hallway, Marvella was bare foot. She wore a towel around her hair, and a brown caftan that she clearly used as a robe.

"Since when am I getting calls at your place?" I asked.

"Since I can't talk sense into Val," she said.

I peered at her. I hadn't heard from Valentina since that day in September when she'd delivered the white woman to Helping Hands. After she had completed her mission, she had taken me, Marvella, and Marvella's sister Paulette to dinner. She told us about her life in Madison, which sounded a bit bleak to me, and then drove the three hours back so she wouldn't miss the university extension class that she taught the following morning.

Marvella's apartment had the same layout as mine, but was decorated much differently. Hers was filled with dark, contemporary furniture, and African art. The sculptures covered every surface, faces carved from mahogany and other dark woods. The sculptures were so life-like they seemed to be staring at me.

The phone hung on the wall in Marvella's half kitchen. The receiver rested next to the toaster.

"There she is. You tell her our policy." Marvella waved a hand at the phone. "I have to finish getting dressed."

She vanished down the hallway and slammed her bedroom door, as if I was the one who had made her angry instead of Valentina.

I picked up the receiver. "Valentina?"

"Smokey?" She was one of the few people who called me by my real name. Most people in Chicago knew me as Bill Grimshaw, a cousin to Franklin Grimshaw, one of the co-founders of Helping Hands. My real name is Smokey Dalton, and I'm from Memphis. A case four years ago put me on the run and brought me here, forcing both me and Jimmy to live under an assumed name.

On the night she almost died, Valentina overheard Laura call me Smokey, and she never forgot it. She once told me that Bill didn't suit me and Smokey did. Since Jimmy, Laura, and Franklin all called me Smokey, I never felt the need to correct Valentina.

"Marvella said I'm supposed to talk sense into you," I said, "only she won't tell me what this is about."

"Linda Krag disappeared," Valentina said.

The name didn't ring a bell with me. "Linda Krag?"

"The white woman I took to Helping Hands in September," Valentina said. "I'm sure you remember."

"I do now," I said, and then realizing that sounded a little too harsh, added, "She had that pretty little daughter."

"Yeah," Valentina said. "They've both been gone a week now."

"I thought they were in Chicago," I said.

"They were," she said.

"And you're still in Madison?" I asked.

"Yes," she said. "That's why I'm talking to you. No one told me she was missing until they sent my targeted donation back."

Valentina sent money every month to Helping Hands earmarked only for Linda Krag and her daughter. If the money couldn't be used for Linda Krag, then Helping Hands was duty-bound to return it. The policy was Laura's. She believed that everyone who donated money had a right to say how it would be used.

"So you called to find out what was up," I said.

"And discovered that she had left her apartment a week before. No one will tell me where she went."

"Did she take her daughter with her?" I asked.

"Of course," Valentina said. "She won't go anywhere without Annie."

I sighed. I knew the arguments Marvella had already made because they were the ones I had to make. Helping Hands followed its name exactly: It provided helping hands. If a client no longer wanted help, we couldn't force it on her.

Besides, we had rules. The client received her living expenses for the first month. We paid her rent and utilities and gave her a food budget. In return, we asked that she either apply for work or go to school.

If the client refused to do either, we stopped the support. If she couldn't hold a job, we got her more job training, but if she lost the job because of anger, discipline or a drug problem—and the client wouldn't get help curbing that problem—then we stopped providing assistance.

Linda Krag had been difficult from the start. She almost refused to go into Helping Hands, even though we had found a white volunteer to take her application. Chicago's South Side, filled with black faces, terrified her. Eventually, Valentina talked her into the building. Once there, she agreed to all Helping Hands' terms and actually went to classes to get her GED.

But she hated the apartment that she was assigned. Not because it was bad or in a bad neighborhood, but because she and her daughter were the only whites on the block. She claimed to be terrified, and wanted an apartment in a "normal" neighborhood.

Since we knew of no programs to combat innate bigotry, we searched for—and found—her an apartment in a transitional neighborhood near the University of Chicago. She liked that. She had gotten her GED, applied for college, and found a part-time job, one that didn't tax her still-healing hand. Her daughter went to Head Start half the day.

Last I heard, everyone was happy.

But clients who started as roughly as Linda Krag often didn't make it through the program. They had too many other problems.

I said all of this, and more to Valentina, and as I spoke, she sighed heavily.

"Has anyone thought about her husband?" Valentina asked when I had finished.

I leaned against the wall. A wave of spicy perfume blew toward me from the bedroom. Marvella was not just getting dressed. She was getting dressed up.

"What about her husband?" I asked.

"Maybe he found her."

"Or maybe," I said gently, "she just left."

"She wouldn't," Valentina said. "Her family is dead. She has no friends. That loser isolated her from everyone she knew when he took her to Madison. She wouldn't know how to start a new life."

"Actually," I said, making sure I kept the same tone, "Helping Hands was teaching her how to make a life for herself and her daughter."

"Exactly," Valentina said. "I got a postcard from her daughter Annie two weeks ago. She sounded happy. Linda added a sentence thanking me. She wouldn't just give up. Not now."

"You spoke to her about this?" I asked.

"No," Valentina said. "But leaving now just isn't logical."

Neither was staying with a man who nearly beat her to death, but I wasn't going to argue that point with Valentina.

"Val," I said, "a lot of women do things that aren't logical."

I winced as the words came out of my mouth. I should have said "people," but it was too late to correct myself.

"Women are not illogical creatures," Valentina snapped.

Marvella had come out of the bedroom. She was wearing an orange dress with a matching orange and red scarf tied around her hair. She had heard the last part of this conversation, and she was grinning now.

She knew the mistake I made.

"I didn't mean it that way," I said. "I just meant that people can be irrational."

"Linda's not irrational," Valentina said.

I was already tired of this fight. "You mean the woman who wouldn't get into the car with me and Marvella because she was afraid of black people? That Linda?"

Valentina made a sound halfway between a sigh and a growl. "Smokey, look. You have to trust me on this. I got a real sense of her. It took her a lot of guts to run away from Duane. It took even more to go to Chicago. But she knew it was right for Annie. Linda wasn't going to go back to him. Not ever."

"I didn't say she would," I said. "Maybe she thought she could do better on her own."

"She knew she couldn't," Valentina said. "She was terrified of being on her own. That's why she didn't get into the car with you. She knew she couldn't defend herself and Annie, and you—I'm sorry, Smokey—

but you look like every white person's nightmare. I don't think she'd ever spoken to a black person until she spoke to me. Asking her to go with you and Marvella was one step too many for her. But she did go to Chicago, she did get her GED, she did start over."

"Yeah."

I must have sounded as skeptical as I felt because Valentina added, "You have no idea how hard all of that was for her. She wouldn't be the kind of woman who would do it all over again all on her own. Especially not with Annie."

I sighed. Marvella crossed her arms and raised her eyebrows, as if asking if I was going to finish soon.

"All right," I said. "Let's say I grant you that she wouldn't run off. What then, in your mind, could have happened?"

Marvella rolled her eyes.

"I think the husband found her," Valentina said. "I think she's in trouble, Smokey. Both her and Annie."

"And this is a gut sense," I said.

"Stop patronizing me!"

I almost denied that I was, but then I realized that I would have been lying.

"I need to know if you have facts to back up this assumption," I said.

Valentina didn't answer for nearly a minute. Finally she said, "No."

"So," I said. "It begs the question. How could the husband have found her? Is he particularly bright?"

"I don't know," she said.

"Did you tell anyone where she went?"

"Not even the folks here at the hotline. Only one of the women knew what I was doing, and all she knew was that I was going to take Linda to some of my friends in Chicago."

"So," I said, then winced again. I was even sounding patronizing. "Would she have called this man for any reason?"

"I don't think so," Valentina said. "No."

"Then how could he have found her?"

"I don't know," Valentina said. "I just want you to check on her. You and Marvella have made it really, really clear that Helping Hands doesn't track people who vanish. So how about this? How about I hire you to find her, Smokey. Does that work for you? I have a lot of money. I'll pay your standard rates plus expenses. I can put a check in the mail today."

I almost told her that it wasn't necessary, that I would do this one for free. But I was a little annoyed at her stubbornness, and besides, Jimmy was growing so fast that I couldn't keep him in shoes. My regular work for local black insurance companies and for Sturdy paid the bills, but couldn't cover the added expenses of a growing teenage boy.

"All right," I said, and quoted her my rates. "I'm going to need a few things from you, too. I need some basic things. I need the husband's full name. I need to know where he lives and, if possible, where he works. I need to know where he lived with Linda and Annie."

"Okay," Valentina said.

"But—and this is very important—I don't want you investigating or talking to him. If you can't do the work by phone, using a fake name, I don't want you doing it. Is that clear?"

"I know how to investigate, Smokey," she said with some amusement in her voice.

"Good," I said. "Because the last thing I want is for this nutball to go after you."

"He won't," she said.

But I got the sense, as I hung up the phone, that Valentina Wilson—the new version, the muscular woman I'd seen three months ago—would welcome his attack. She'd welcome it, and happily put him out of commission.

"Well?" Marvella asked.

"Well," I said, "it looks like I have a missing persons case."

She rolled her eyes again. "And I thought you were a tough guy."

"Sometimes," I said, "it's just easier to do what the client wants than it is to convince them they're wrong."

"Is she wrong?" Marvella asked.

"Probably," I said with a sigh. "Probably."

Linda Krag's new apartment was in student housing near the University of Chicago. The neighborhood had once been filled with middle class professors' homes, but now those homes were divided up into apartments, with bicycles parked on the porch and beer cans lying in the lawn.

Those lawns were brown. Winter hadn't arrived yet, despite the chill.

In the early fall, when Linda Krag had seen this place, it had probably looked inviting. Now, with the naked trees stark against the gray skyline, the leaves piled in the street, the battered cars parked haphazardly against the curb, the block looked impoverished and just a little bit dangerous.

Or maybe I was projecting. Linda Krag, white and young, might have felt comfortable here, but I felt out of place, despite the University neighborhood's known color-blindness and vaunted liberalism.

I had the skeleton keys from Helping Hands. Linda's stuff had not been removed from the apartment—she had until the end of the month before her belongings would become part of the charity's donation pile. I doubted anyone had visited this place once everyone realized she was gone.

The apartment was on the second floor. More bikes littered the hallway, and so did several more beer cans. The hall smelled of beer.

Linda's door was closed tightly. There were scrapes near the lock and the wood had been splintered about fist-high. I had no idea if that damage predated Linda's arrival. With student housing, it was almost impossible to tell.

I unlocked the deadbolt and had to shove hard to get the door to open. It had been stuck closed. As I stepped inside, I inspected the side of the door and noted that the wood was warped.

I pushed the door closed, but it bounced back open. The warped wood made it as hard to close as it was to open.

I had seen the apartment she had been given on the South Side. That had been a two bedroom with a full kitchen and stunning living room. I had put up another family there a year or so ago. They had worked their way through the Helping Hands program and had bought their own house last summer.

I couldn't believe she would have left that place for this one.

But people's prejudices made them do all kinds of crazy things.

The apartment smelled sour. A blanket was crumpled at the end of the couch, and a sweater hung off the back of a kitchen chair someone had moved near the window. The kitchen was to my right. The table, with two chairs pushed against it, was beneath a small window with a good view of the house next door.

A full ashtray sat on the tabletop, along with a coloring book and an open —and scattered—box of crayons. Dishes cluttered the sink, which gave off a rotted smell.

More cigarettes floated in the water filling the bowls at the bottom of the sink. A hand towel rested on one of the burners. It was the only thing I moved, using the skeleton keys so that I wouldn't have to touch it.

Then I went through the kitchen into a narrow hallway. The second bedroom was back here. A bed was pushed against the wall. Clothing—pink and small—was scattered all over the floor. More clothes hung on the make-shift clothing rod by the door.

The clutter was every day clutter, not slob-clutter. It looked like the kind of mess a person made when she left in a hurry, meaning to clean up later. It disturbed me that a woman who cared so much about her daughter—a poor woman—would leave most of her daughter's wardrobe behind.

The hair rose on the back of my neck. I didn't want Valentina to be right. If she were right, then we had lost more than a week in searching for this woman.

And a week, in a missing person's case, was a long, long time.

I made myself walk back through the kitchen and down another narrow hallway to the full bedroom. It wasn't much larger than the daughter's room. The full-sized bed left barely enough space between the wall and the side of the bed for me to walk around it.

The bed was unmade. Pillows sideways, blankets thrown back. But the bottom of the blankets—along with the sheets—was tucked in. The tucks were perfect military tucks, something that wouldn't last during weeks of restless sleep.

Linda Krag usually made her bed. She usually made it with great precision.

Her clothing hung in the small closet, separated by color. A pair of shoes was lined neatly against the wall.

The sour smell was stronger here. It didn't smell like dirty dishes, but something else, something that I should have recognized, but couldn't.

I pushed open the bathroom door, and the smell hit me, making my eyes water. Vomit. Old vomit. It lined the edge of the bathtub, the floor beneath the sink, and the toilet itself. It had crusted against the wall.

I made myself go into the room. Another cigarette butt floated in the sloppy toilet water. The bathroom mirror was cracked, and a small handprint—child-sized—marred a white towel still hanging on the rack.

I looked at the handprint, wondering if that delicate little girl had been the source of all this vomit.

But as I pushed against the towel, I realized the handprint was a different color.

The handprint was made of dried blood.

I couldn't find any more answers in Linda Krag's apartment, so I drove home.

I'm sure my neighbors wondered why I hurried out of my car that afternoon, and took the steps to my apartment two at a time.

Jimmy had a half an hour of school left before Franklin picked him and the Grimshaw children up and took them to an after-school program we had started three years ago. If I called Franklin now, I could probably arrange for Jimmy to stay the night.

I wasn't sure I would need all that time, but I figured I had best plan for it.

Linda Krag and her little daughter Annie had been missing for several days. Some would have argued that a few more hours would make no difference, but to me, they would have.

If the woman was in trouble, then every second wasted would be a second closer to her death. Because, if Valentina was right, and Linda Krag had been taken by her husband, that man wouldn't be interested in rebuilding their relationship.

He would punish her.

And he would do it one of several ways. If he was just a man filled with uncontrollable rage, he would beat her until he felt better. But if he was a sadist—and if what Valentina said was true, that Linda Krag's daughter was the most important thing in her life—then he would hurt the daughter to punish the mother.

People who got punched in the stomach hard or repeatedly often vomited, sometimes uncontrollably. I hoped that the amount of vomit in that small bathroom had come from an adult, but there was no way to tell.

I clenched my fists. Then I released the fingers slowly, making myself breathe. I picked up the phone, called Franklin, explained the case—since he was part of Helping Hands too—and asked him to take care of my son for at least the next twenty-four hours.

Then I hung up and set about finding Linda Krag.

Unlike the stuff you see on *Mannix* or *Hawaii 5-0* , detective work is seldom fisticuffs and confessions. Usually it's long and repetitive legwork. I was going to try to cram a week's worth of legwork into a single day.

So I went into my office and made calls.

My office was in the bedroom between mine and Jim's. I decorated it with used office furniture (bought at a bargain when I first moved here), filing cabinets that were nearly full, and a new-fangled answering machine that Laura had bought me. I hadn't taken the thing out of the box yet.

I pushed the box aside, picked up the phone, and called Valentina. She wasn't there, so I left a message, asking if she had found that information for me. I hoped she would call me back while I was still at home.

Then I started a series of calls to area hospitals and doctors' offices. I had found, over the years, that if I put on a slight East Coast accent and spoke a little quicker than I usually did, people gave me information without many questions.

Hospitals, trained to keep some information confidential, were a tougher nut to crack. But my years as an insurance company investigator helped there. If I called Billing and told them I had an unpaid bill from the hospital itself, I usually got full cooperation.

I did this now, saying that I had a bill for my client Linda Krag, without dates of her hospital stay or any listing of her procedure. I couldn't pay the bill unless I had that information.

Billing departments all over the city scrambled to help me. They hand-searched their records. I told them that we had received the bill today, which made us (or more accurately, them) believe that the procedure happened within the past month.

Each call took about fifteen minutes, because the billing person I spoke to did a thorough search. Each call also ended with the same discouraging phrase:

It seemed that Linda Krag had not shown up at any doctor's office or hospital in the Greater Chicago area in the past month. At least, not under that name.

The next thing I did was check the morgues and funeral homes. That was a little easier—with funeral homes, I asked when the Linda Krag funeral was scheduled, and with morgues, I just asked my question in a straightforward manner.

No one had heard of her.

When I finished, I realized I should have asked after her daughter as well—Annie Krag. But the very idea of searching for death records for a child made my stomach twist.

I thumbed through the phone book, wondering if I could run the same hospital scam for the daughter on the same day, when my phone rang.

It was Valentina.

She gave me an address on the east side of Madison, the husband's full name—Duane G. Krag, age 35, and the make and model of his car, a white 1968 Olds with Missouri plates. Up until three weeks ago, he had worked at the Oscar Mayer plant not far from his home.

I didn't like that last detail at all. "Did he give notice or did he just disappear?"

"He finished his shift on Friday and failed to show up on Monday," she said.

"You got this information how?" I asked.

"A few well-placed phone calls," she said. "I know some people here now."

I didn't quite trust her tone. "You didn't go there, right?"

"No," she said. "I have no reason to. Do I?"

"None," I said.

"Besides," she said. "He's been using his phone."

I leaned back in my chair. "How do you know that?"

"One of my volunteers at the hotline also works for the phone company. It's amazing what they can find out about you."

I bet it was.

"Do you have information for me?" she asked.

"I've been to the apartment," I said. "So if she did leave on her own, she left a lot behind."

I wasn't going to tell her about the vomit or the blood. I had no idea what had happened, so I wasn't going to scare Valentina unnecessarily.

"She wouldn't do that, Smokey." That edge of worry had returned to Valentina's voice.

"I tend to agree with you. I'm about to go back to see if her neighbors saw anything unusual."

She was silent on the other end. I wondered if she could tell that I was withholding information from her.

"I hope you find her," she finally said.

"Me, too," I said. "Me, too."

I hadn't lied to Valentina about one thing: My next step was to return to the neighborhood and ask if anyone saw anything unusual. I didn't relish going back to this neighborhood, but I saw no other choice.

It was already dark when I drove back into the neighborhood, which made me even more uncomfortable. As I approached Linda's block, I debated whether or not I wanted to park there or on a nearby street.

I ended up with no choice. Every parking spot for blocks was taken. I finally found a parking place near a bookstore on 57th, and I walked to the apartment building.

I didn't have a date or an exact incident, but I did my best. I stopped student after student, asking if they had seen the woman with the little blond girl who lived just down the block. Most remembered her—there weren't a lot of children on this street—but none had talked to her.

And no one had seen her for at least a week.

By the time I got to her apartment building, I was feeling discouraged. I took the steps up the porch just as a young man came out of the front door wheeling his bicycle.

His red hair brushed the collar of his coat. He smelled faintly of incense and marijuana. His eyes were clear, however.

He started when he saw me.

"What do you want?" he asked.

"I'm here to see Linda," I said. "I'm a friend of hers from Madison."

He studied me for a minute, then he said, "Linda didn't have any friends in Madison."

Finally, someone who knew her.

"Who told you that?" I asked.

"She did," he said.

"Well, that's a little awkward," I said, trying to seem humble. "She lived next door to me and my wife and we talked all the time. We're in Chicago to see family and I was wondering if she and Annie could join everyone for lunch tomorrow. I guess I thought we were better friends than we were."

The boy shrugged. "Maybe I misunderstood her. We only talked a few times. My roommate knew her better."

"Knew her?" I asked, then realized the question sounded sharp, so I did my best to cover. "Did your roommate move?"

"No," the boy said. "Linda and her husband reconciled. He said he was taking them back to Madison. I would've thought you knew that, since you lived next door."

I shook my head. "They haven't been back all month," I lied. "He moved out. I thought they were getting a divorce."

"Yeah, that's what I thought," the boy said. "But my roommate—he's Duane's brother—he said it was a love match and all it would take was some persuading."

I shivered, and it wasn't from the growing chill. Someone had clearly been persuaded, and not in a good way.

"I never thought it was a love match," I said, looking at the door, but deliberately not looking at the upstairs window, as if I didn't know which apartment she had lived in.

"I think the whole thing's kinda weird, myself," the boy said. "I was studying for my econ exam when he came to get her. It didn't sound like a love match to me."

"What do you mean?"

The boy shrugged again. "It's none of my business, really."

And he said it in a way that also meant it was none of mine.

"They fought?"

"Nothing like that. But that little girl sure cried hard. I'd never heard a peep from her before that."

"Was she all right?" I couldn't help the question.

The boy looked at me. He was frowning. "You know, I wondered. So I looked out the window. They all got into his car. He put suitcases into the back and Linda, she was holding her daughter. She saw me looking, and she waved at me. So I knew everything was all right."

I started in surprise. I hadn't expected Linda Krag to think of anyone except herself and her daughter. But she had protected her neighbor. By pretending everything was okay, she made sure he didn't intervene.

"When was this?" I asked.

"A week ago Wednesday. I know because the exam was on Thursday." He grinned. "And of course, I aced it."

"Good for you," I said, and hoped it didn't sound patronizing. Then I thanked him, and went back down the stairs.

There was no point in asking anyone else questions.

Duane's brother had clearly alerted him to Linda's presence, probably on the weekend between the time Duane last punched in for work and the Monday when he hadn't shown up. Duane had come here, tried to talk to her, hit her so hard she threw up or hurt the little girl somehow.

Then, when he realized Linda actually knew people here, he took her and Annie out of the apartment. He drove them somewhere.

But the question was where.

I didn't have the capability to track someone like him, even with his white car and Missouri license plates. Ten days was a long time.

And he could have taken her anywhere.

Except, Valentina told me that he had been using his telephone.

He was in Madison, in his old stomping grounds, and if we were lucky, Linda and Annie were still alive.

I didn't break any speed limits heading to Madison, but I wanted to. I wanted to get there as quickly as I could.

Had he kept her in Chicago, I would have had options. I knew people in the police department, I had friends who worked alongside me and could act as back-up. I even knew people who could have discretely checked on the apartment and let me know he was inside.

The only person I knew in Madison was Valentina. And I didn't want to involve her. But I was beginning to think I wasn't going to have a choice.

Because I couldn't see any good way for this to play out.

Madison was a white town. I couldn't just barge into a white man's apartment and demand that he hand over his wife. I couldn't call the police with my suspicions—and they couldn't do anything anyway. A man was entitled to treat his family anyway he liked. Only when things got "out of hand" and the definition of that phrase varied from police department to police department, could the police step in at all.

So as I drove, I tried to formulate a plan, but I couldn't come up with a good one.

I only hoped that Valentina's friends included someone other than the lady who worked for the phone company.

Because otherwise, I was about to make a difficult situation worse.

Valentina's hotline was housed in an old church near Lake Mendota, not far from either the state capitol building or the University of Wisconsin.

I knew better than to show up unannounced at a hotline run primarily by women who dealt daily with rape. The last thing they needed to see was a muscular, scarred black man pounding on the church door. So I called ahead, leaving Valentina worried, but willing to open the hotline's doors for me.

Three cars were in the parking lot when I showed up around ten. The church looked like it had once been a monstrosity of the Protestant type—some stained windows, but not a lot of iconography. A tasteful cross carved into the brick chimney, but little else besides the building's shape to even suggest it had once been a church.

Valentina was waiting outside, wrapped in a parka that looked two sizes too big for her. She waved as I pulled up, then shifted from foot to foot while I got out of the car.

The minute I stepped outside, I knew why she was dressed so heavily. It was a lot colder here than it was in Chicago. There was also a dusting of snow on the ground, visible under the church's dome light.

Valentina didn't say hello.

"The fact that you're here means something bad is going on, doesn't it, Smokey?"

"Yeah," I said, since there was no reason to lie. "Where can we go to talk about this?"

She led me inside and up a flight of stairs into the former sanctuary. It smelled of freshly cut wood. She flicked a light switch and a dozen overhead lights came on.

Instead of revealing church pews, a choir loft, and an altar, the lights revealed piles of wood, several saws, and some half built walls.

She waved a hand at it. "We need room for women to stay overnight, and after what most of them have been through, we can't ask them to share a room like some kind of church shelter."

"Overnight?" I asked as I stepped over a pile of 2x4s.

"So many won't go home after they've been raped. They won't go to the hospital, and they won't see a friend, particularly if they've been battered. Most don't have money for a hotel room either." She ran a hand through her short hair. "Actually, it was Linda who gave me this idea. She was so afraid of Duane."

She let the words hang. We stopped near stairs that had clearly once led to the altar. Someone had pulled the carpet off them, and one of the stairs to my left had already been dismantled. But we sat on the top step, surveying the work in progress.

"I take it the hotline itself is somewhere else," I said.

"In the basement," she said. "I figured it was best if my volunteers didn't know what was going on."

I nodded. As carefully as I could, I told her what I had learned. I also told her that I had come to find Linda.

"You can't go to that neighborhood at night," Valentina said.

"I can't go period," I said. "No one can walk up to the door of that apartment and ask Duane Krag what he did with his wife and daughter."

Valentina rested her elbows on her knees. To her credit, she didn't say I told you so nor did she reprimand Helping Hands for not searching for Linda sooner.

"What can we do?" she asked.

"We can't do anything," I said. "But I need some information from you. Tell me about those apartments."

She frowned for a moment. Then she said, "They're single story, low income housing."

"Government built?"

"Yes, with Model Cities money," she said, citing one of the many Johnson era programs that Nixon had dismantled in his first term. "They were built to look like row houses, so that each family could feel like they had privacy."

"But they're attached?"

"Yes," she said.

"They're government buildings. They should have fire alarms. Do they?"

She frowned. "It's not something I normally notice, and I was there three months ago, not really paying attention. But the city is pretty anal about making sure every building follows code. This place isn't like Chicago at all. No one can buy off a building inspector."

I nodded, hoping that was the case. "Then the buildings have to have fire alarms. The trick is where."

"I have an idea," she said. "I'll tell you mine, if you tell me yours."

"Done," I said, and then told her what I was planning.

Of course, she wouldn't let me go alone. I should have known that when I arrived outside the hotline building. I had forgotten how stubborn Valentina could be.

"You have to do exactly what I tell you," I said as we drove to the apartment complex.

Madison at night was pretty deserted. On the wide swatch of East

Washington Avenue, I had only seen two other cars. I drove underneath well tended street light after well tended street light, past warehouses and buildings from the turn of the century.

No one could break into one of those buildings without drawing some kind of attention, even though the streets were empty.

"I will do exactly what you say, Smokey," Valentina said with some bemusement. "You don't have to keep repeating that."

"I just don't want you hurt," I said. "If the cops show up, you have to get out. Is that clear?"

"I know a cop to call," she said. "We'll be all right."

I glanced at her. She was staring straight ahead, the light playing across her face. The occasional shadows hid the hollows in her cheeks and she looked a lot more like the woman I had met four years ago.

"Is he one of your contacts?" I asked.

"I have to know everyone from police officers to the best criminal attorneys," she said. "I'm getting quite a list."

I nodded. "Well, they're not going to like what we're about to do."

"Don't like it," she said. "I just don't see any other choice."

Neither did I.

She gave me good directions to the apartment complex. I drove past it once, to see it for myself.

It was already starting to look worn. The hope that the city had placed in its low income housing had faded with the Johnson Administration. But there were still things that made this place unusual.

It had functioning lights over every front door. Each apartment number was clearly marked. The sidewalks in front of each apartment had been shoveled. None of the windows were boarded up, and none had security bars either.

The lights were on in the Krags' living room. Someone had pulled the curtains against the outside, but I could see the flickering shadows of a television set.

Someone was inside.

Which made me sigh with relief.

Just like driving past the building's side, and seeing a giant fire alarm built onto the outside wall.

"Looks like you were right," I said to Valentina.

"It was the only logical place," she said. "I'm going to have to run to pull two alarms."

"It's necessary," I said. "I don't want him to think that we've targeted his building."

"Okay," she said. "Drop me off here. The parking lot is—"

"I'm going to park in front of his apartment," I said.

"He'll see you."

"It's all right," I said. "I know what I'm doing."

Unfortunately, I had snuck into neighborhoods before. I knew how to do it, and do it well.

I dropped Valentina on the corner, then went around the block. She was supposed to wait five minutes before she went anywhere near that first alarm.

I hoped she listened.

As I got ready to turn back onto the Krag's street, I turned off the car's lights and took my foot off the gas. I coasted to a stop in front of his sidewalk, and shut off the ignition.

Then I unscrewed the dome light. I opened the driver's door as quietly as I could, and slipped out, careful not to close the door too tightly.

Staying on the street, I walked around the corner. There was no alarm on this side, but I didn't expect one. The alarm was on the other end of the building, hidden in that alcove between two buildings.

I waited at the front corner of the building, in the shadows so that I could see the street but no one could see me.

Then an alarm clanged. It sounded very far away.

Another followed. The second one was deafening.

Valentina had been right; Madison's low income housing was up to code.

Now we'd see how long it took the fire department to respond to a major fire.

I hoped it was a long time.

People started shouting and screaming. Families came out the front doors, wearing bathrobes and pajamas, barefoot against the cold.

I silently apologized to them.

No one came out of Duane's apartment.

Families, carrying children, holding blankets, turned and looked at their homes. Voices rose in confusion at the lack of smoke and flames.

Valentina ran to my side. No one seemed to notice her in all the chaos.

"Where are they?" she asked.

"No one came out," I said.

"What are we going to do?"

I was about to tell her that I would break in the back, when the door banged open. The little girl came out wearing footie pajamas. Her hair was a rat's nest and she was sobbing.

"Help me! Help me!" she yelled. "My mommy won't come. My mommy won't come."

"Get her to the car," I said as I sprinted for the main door. I didn't want anyone else to answer her summons.

So far, no one had noticed her. They were still talking and yelling and looking in the opposite direction.

Valentina ran at my side. We reached the little girl at the same time.

"Annie," Valentina said, crouching in front of her and putting her hands on the girl's shoulders. "We're going to get your mom out."

"*Get her to the car*," I repeated, then pushed the door open.

The apartment was a jumbled mess—overturned chairs, a ripped couch. The television was on, but no one was watching it.

That sour smell was here too, and it turned my stomach.

I hurried down the corridors, checking the kitchen, then the bathroom, and finally one of the bedrooms. The interior smelled of old blood.

I flicked on the light.

A body was leaning against the wall, a spray of blood behind it, and a pool of blood below. It took me a second to realize that the body did not belong to Linda Krag.

It was a man's body. It had to be Duane.

Sirens started in the distance, very faint, but growing.

I cursed.

A gun was on the bed.

I left it there and checked the other bedroom.

Linda Krag was huddled in her daughter's bed, eyes wide. "Leave me," she said, but I didn't know if she was talking to me or just repeating what she had been saying to her daughter.

I wasn't even sure she had seen me.

I scooped her in my arms. She moaned when I picked her up. I carried her down that hallway. I could feel dried blood against her skin, but I didn't know if it was hers or his. She hadn't showered in days. The stench of her made my eyes water.

The sirens were getting closer.

I hurried out of the building. People were wandering around, searching for the fire. In the distance, I could see flashing red lights.

Valentina was standing beside my car, leaning on the passenger door. Annie was inside the car, in the back seat.

"Open up," I said.

She didn't have to be told twice. She opened the door to the back seat. Annie leaned forward and Valentina shooed her away.

I put Linda inside. She toppled toward her daughter, but I didn't care.

We had to get out of there.

"Get inside," I said to Valentina as I pushed the door closed.

She did. I got in the driver's side, and started the car all in the same move. Then I backed around the corner, so that no one could see my plates. I backed the entire block, then turned right, away from the apartment buildings, heading toward East Washington Avenue.

"Screw in the dome light," I said to Valentina.

She gave me a funny look, visible in the street lights, then did as she was told.

"What are we doing?" she asked.

"I'm dropping you off, then we're going to Chicago."

She leaned over the back seat. "Linda needs medical attention."

"She's not getting it here," I said.

"Smokey," Valentina said.

"You didn't ask me where Duane was," I said.

She looked at me. "Where's Duane?"

"Daddy's dead," Annie said in a very small voice.

"Jesus," Valentina said, looking at me. "What happened?"

"Don't know," I said. "Don't want to know. And this is the last we're going to say about it. Right, Annie?"

"Smokey," Valentina said, reprimanding me for my tone.

"Right, Annie?" I repeated.

"Okay," Annie said.

The capitol dome loomed in the distance. We were only a few miles from the hotline.

"Where are you taking them?" Valentina asked.

"Back to Helping Hands. We'll find them a new apartment," I said. "Can you get into the back seat, and see if Linda will make it all the way to Chicago?"

"I'll make it." Linda whispered the words. "I'm just fine. Thank you."

I was relieved to hear her respond directly to me. But I knew she wasn't just fine. She wasn't protesting my presence like she had the first time I tried to take her to Chicago.

"I'm going with you," Valentina said to me.

"No," I said.

"You need me," she said.

I turned toward her, trying to keep at least part of my gaze on the road. "Maybe you don't understand. I am about to commit a felony. I don't want you involved."

"Don't," Linda said from the back. "We'll be all right."

"If I take you to a Madison hospital," I said to Linda, "they'll arrest you and take Annie. Do you want that?"

"Nooo." The reply was soft, and I wasn't sure if it came from Linda or Annie herself.

"Jesus," Valentina said.

"So," I said to Valentina, "I'm taking you home."

"No," Valentina said. "You need me. They need me. We'll work this out. I'll take a bus home tomorrow."

The truth was, I did need her. I needed her to monitor Linda's condition. I needed her to keep Annie calm.

I needed her to keep an eye out, to make sure we weren't being followed.

"All right," I said. "Let's get the hell out of here."

Three hours and one furtive gas stop later put us in Chicago at four in the morning. I drove immediately to the hospital nearest my house.

Valentina blanched as we pulled into the parking lot. I had driven her there once, saving her life and changing it forever.

Linda had passed out sometime along the drive, but she was breathing evenly. I had Valentina bring Annie inside. I carried Linda.

The emergency staff took her from me, placing her on a cart. In the florescent hospital lights, it became clear that she was bruised everywhere. The cast on her arm from her previous injury was cracked and ruined. And there was dried blood around her mouth and nose.

"What happened?" The emergency room nurse asked me. She was glaring.

"Her husband happened," I said, deciding not to lie about that at least. I lied about the rest, though. "She lives next door to us. I couldn't just leave her there."

"Good thing you didn't," the nurse said, and wheeled her away.

I stayed and filled out the paperwork, using my own apartment building as Linda's address, and making up a last name for her. I figured the hospital would never check, and Helping Hands would cover the bills.

Valentina took Annie to the waiting room while I worked. When I finished, I followed them there.

They were alone in the room. Newspapers were scattered around them. Valentina had used one to cover Annie. Valentina had fallen asleep in the chair by the door, Annie on the couch near her.

I sat down, my heart pounding.

Now I would have to deal with my split-second decision. Obviously Linda couldn't take the beatings any longer, and she had shot Duane in the face. Then she collapsed. Annie hadn't known what to do or maybe was too frightened to move, until the fire alarm forced her out of the building.

They might have been alone with that corpse for a week or more, until the neighbors reported something. Then the police would have come, charged Linda with murder, put Annie in foster care, and no one would have heard of them again.

No one would have cared that Linda had been repeatedly beaten within an inch of her life. Her only hope would have been an insanity plea, which probably would not have worked—especially since the prosecutor would have said that she had run away from Duane before, and she clearly did not want to be with him.

I was giving Helping Hands a hell of a burden—the damaged mother, the terrified child—but I figured we could deal with it. And if someone determined that Linda was no longer fit to care for her child, we would find Annie a good home, a sympathetic home, one that would help her grow and overcome these last few years.

I'd seen that work. It had worked with my son Jimmy.

Annie sighed and twitched in her sleep. The newspaper fell off her, and I picked it up, gently putting it back over her.

Then I looked at her, really looked at her, for the first time since we picked her up.

She had an ugly bruise on her forehead. It was black and purple and it had seeped down to her nose. Something had hit her hard there.

I felt a quick anger at Duane, and then I froze. I looked at her hand, dangling down toward the floor.

Her thumb was bruised too. And there was a pinch mark on her index finger—the kind you got when you didn't know how to properly hold a gun.

My breath caught. The bruises lined up. If she had held the gun on her father, and the gun had gone off, the recoil would have sent her hands backwards, hitting her forehead with enough force to make that bruise.

Daddy's dead, she had said.

And her mother was in Annie's room, not the adults' bedroom.

Hiding?

Letting her daughter defend her?

I shivered just a little. I didn't want to know, and I wasn't going to ask. I had already broken enough laws for these two. I would let the experts from Helping Hands work with them—and I would never mention my suspicions.

I had brought them here—risked at least two felony charges—so that they could stay together.

I wasn't going to be the one to get in the way of that.

Valentina stirred. "How's Linda?" she asked sleepily.

"Badly beaten," I said. "But they think she'll be all right."

"Good." Valentina looked at Annie. "Bastard beat her too. I had someone look at the bruise. She doesn't have a concussion."

"That's a relief," I said.

Valentina was still looking at the sleeping child. "Think they'll be all right?"

"At least now they have a chance," I said.

And no one could ask for more than that.

Christmas Eve at the Exit

A Sweet Young Things Mystery

Kristine Kathryn Rusch

Christmas Eve at the Exit

"Will Santa know how to find us?" Anne-Marie asked as she hopped out of the van.

"Of course he does, honey," Rachel said, just like she'd said every time they'd stopped.

Anne-Marie didn't answer. She slammed the door hard enough to shake the entire vehicle, and hurried across the empty ice-covered parking lot. Somehow she kept her balance and didn't fall, despite the pink tennis shoes she wore. Her red mittens hung off a string threaded through her pink coat. She'd lost three pairs so far, which Rachel figured had to be some kind of quiet rebellion.

Eight hundred, maybe nine hundred, miles to go, she thought to herself. She hadn't been willing to check the GPS. She wasn't sure if it transmitted the van's location.

Even though she had never even seen the van before she removed it from a storage unit in Winnemucca, Nevada. Even though the van, its license plates, and that storage unit weren't in her name. Even though she had taken a taxi to the units from that weird hotel and casino.

She'd left a trail. It was impossible not to. If someone had followed her, they would have figured it out. She had to leave Anne-Marie with the casino-provided babysitting service, which frightened Rachel more than anything. Then the taxi driver kept talking about how unusual it was to have a woman take a cab to a storage unit. He pressed his card into her hand, told her to call him if her ride didn't show up.

I know you're in trouble, little lady, he'd said through teeth broken so long ago the cracks had turned yellow from the cigars he smoked. *So you just call me and I'll make sure you get back to the hotel, no problem.*

She'd thanked him, trying not to cry. She hadn't wanted him to notice her. She hadn't wanted anyone to notice her. She wanted to be invisible, even though she didn't look like she belonged.

She belonged in Boise, with her trendy blue ski parka and $500 athletic shoes, not in small-town Nevada where she was so obviously a tourist that everyone asked her if she needed directions.

In the end, she hadn't needed the cab driver. She used the key she'd been mailed to open the storage unit, then followed the instructions pasted to the van. Three different identities inside, all with three different credit cards, an entire wad of cash, birth certificates for her and Anne-Marie, and directions to their new place.

Plus seven different pre-programmed cell phones, one for each state. They were numbered. Every time Rachel crossed a state border, she was supposed to toss out the phone she had been using, and take the next one. She'd thrown the first away near the Bonneville Salt Flats, heart pounding, and somehow that—not the abandonment of her own car, the use of a new identity, the loss of all her possessions—had finally convinced her there was no turning back.

She still had the feeling she was being followed. She liked to attribute that to the fact that all modern cars looked alike, so the dark blue SUV she saw in Salt Lake might have had nothing to do with the dark blue SUV that cut her off in Rock Springs. Or the beige sedan that seemed to dog her trip from North Platte to Kearney.

She ran a hand through her wedge-cut dark hair. She'd bought and paid for that wedge cut, as per instructions, at a beauty shop in Cheyenne, where the kind sad-eyed woman there also gave her a pencil for her eyebrows—to thicken and darken them—and taught her how to alter the shape of her face with blush, foundation, and the right kind of lipstick.

The wind blew hard here in Omaha, carrying with it a chill she hadn't felt in a decade. Her brand-new ski parka felt too thin despite its state-of-the-art promises. Of course, the radio had been telling her that she was driving into a holiday "polar vortex" that filled the air with cold that could kill in less than an hour.

She was glad for the van, glad for the clothes she wore, glad for the interstate with its protective traffic, but she hoped to be off the road soon. She was afraid for Anne-Marie and afraid for herself, and the weather didn't help matters.

She pulled on her gloves, and carefully followed her daughter inside. The ice was so thick that it added another layer to the parking lot. The lot had been well-tended; the snow from a massive storm two days ago—one that had been ahead of her all the way—was piled alongside the edges of the lot, taking up at least one row of spaces.

Anne-Marie watched her from inside. Her blond hair wisped out of her blue-and-pink cap, her round cheeks were bright red with cold, and her blue eyes twinkled in the Christmas lights framing the glass door. She looked like a child waiting for Santa Claus instead of a little girl who had no idea how much her life had already changed.

Rachel pushed the door open, heard the bing-bong of electronic notification, and saw a twenty-something dark-skinned man behind the desk. His appearance momentarily startled her. She'd lived in Idaho so long that she had forgotten how diverse the rest of the country was.

He looked at her and grinned. The expression softened his face, and made the red-and-green silk scarf around his neck seem appropriate. "I assume this little one belongs to you?"

"She does," Rachel said with a smile that she had to force. She put her hand on Anne-Marie's shoulder and guided her daughter toward the tall front desk, festooned in garlands.

A real Christmas tree took over a corner of the lobby, filling the air with the scent of pine.

"She and I have been discussing Santa," the young man said. His nametag identified him as Luke.

"She and I have as well," Rachel said. "She thinks he won't find her because we're very far from home. I told her that Santa is magic, and can find everyone."

"Yes, he can," Luke said, leaning over a little so that he could see

Anne-Marie on the other side of the desk. "And people like me, we help Santa when he needs it."

Rachel's stomach clenched. She tried not to look frightened by that admission, but it was hard. She wanted to ask Luke who else he would help if need be, but she didn't.

She wanted to seem as normal as she could for a woman who brought her daughter to a chain hotel off I-80 on Christmas Eve.

"What's the largest room you have?" She really couldn't afford it, but it was Christmas, and she wanted the room to be festive somehow.

"We have a choice of everything," Luke said. "We're empty at the moment, although I expect the usual travelers and truckers after ten."

She smiled. His good mood, surprising for a man working on the holiday, was infectious. He smiled back and tapped at the computer keyboard. As he did so, the Christmas lights woven into the garland above him winked off the tiny sparkly red-and-white candy canes in his pierced ears.

"When do you get to go home and celebrate?" she asked as she pulled out her wallet. She was pleased that her hands weren't shaking.

"I'm here all night, ma'am," Luke said, sounding distracted. He was still staring at the screen in front of him.

"Will Santa find you?" Anne-Marie asked, her voice a little shaky.

Rachel braced herself for him to say something disparaging like, *Santa hasn't found me for years, honey*.

Instead, Luke reached to one side of the computer and grabbed a real candy cane. He kept it under the lip of the desk, then looked up at Rachel, a question on his face. She nodded her approval.

His smile became real then and he leaned over the desk again, offering the candy cane to Anne-Marie. Anne-Marie took it like it was the most precious thing she'd ever received.

"Santa doesn't have to find me," he said. "I'm one of Santa's helpers."

Anne-Marie clutched it to her pink coat. "Really?" she asked breathlessly.

"Really," he said.

She backed away a little. "Can I put this on the tree?" she asked Rachel softly.

But Luke heard. "It's okay, hon," he said as he tapped the keyboard some more. "The tree has enough candy canes on it. That one's for you."

Anne-Marie frowned. Rachel smiled at her, encouragingly. The last thing she wanted was for her daughter to be this wary. Had she taught Anne-Marie that? Or had Anne-Marie learned it through observation?

"You can put it on our tree when we get upstairs if you want," Rachel said.

Anne-Marie nodded seriously, and clutched the candy cane to her chest. Luke was looking at Rachel over the computer.

His questioning gaze startled her.

"We've been setting up a small tree at nights in the hotel rooms," she said, feeling as if she were giving him the secrets of her soul.

He grinned. "That's wonderful," he said. "Great thinking."

She braced herself again for more questions, like she'd had at the other hotels. *When will you get to your destination? Are you spending Christmas with your family? Where's your husband, sweet thing?*

But he didn't ask them, and she didn't volunteer. Her heart was beating hard, the wallet in her hand feeling like an accusation. She had to remember which identification she was using. It was hard, because she looked at them all every night.

The instructions told her to change identification only if she felt she needed to, and she wasn't sure what that meant, especially since she felt like she needed to change identification every minute of every day.

"We have a suite," Luke said. "No one's booked it. I think it's late enough that I can give it to you at a lower rate."

The price he quoted to her made her heart pound harder but, she reasoned, she'd planned to pay that much anyway, the moment she walked in the door.

All she could feel was the money going out. She wondered how much of it she would owe later.

But she couldn't think about that. Not yet.

"Credit card?" he asked, extending one hand while the other still tapped on the keyboard in front of him.

Her fingers twitched, and she swallowed hard. Then she pulled out the card on top, checked the name, made sure it matched the driver's license in the front of this wallet, and set the card in Luke's hand. He shifted the card so that it fell between his thumb and index finger—clearly a maneuver of long-standing—and then slid it through the card reader.

He had to be able to hear her heart. Everyone had to. Even Anne-Marie who had moved to the Christmas tree like it held the secrets of the world.

She hadn't asked after her father. She hadn't even asked where they were going.

That wasn't natural, was it?

Rachel didn't know. She'd never done anything like this before.

All Anne-Marie had asked was about Santa Claus, over and over again. That, Rachel believed, *was* normal.

"Your card," Luke said, still without looking up. He was holding it out.

Rachel's breath caught. She expected him to finish that sentence: *Your card...didn't run. Do you have another?*

But he didn't. He was just handing it back to her. He hadn't even asked to see ID.

"Your key," Luke said, holding a little folder with a black credit-card sized square and a room number hand-written inside. "You're on the third floor. Just take the elevator up. Would you like help with your luggage?"

Rachel didn't see anyone who could help, besides Luke himself. She was about to say no when she glanced at Anne-Marie, still staring at the tree.

"Yes," Rachel said. "Yes, please."

The van had a compartment in the back built for the spare tire and for some repair equipment. When Rachel found the vehicle inside the storage unit, she had taken the tire out, and placed it flat on the van's carpet, then added the repair equipment on top of it. Later, at the hotel, she had taken out the bag of Santa presents she had bought before leaving Boise, and placed them inside that little compartment.

Then she'd added the suitcases she'd bought just that afternoon at the local Walmart, plus the new overnight bags. And stepped back to look at her handiwork.

So much new stuff, such a lack of familiarity. Only Anne-Marie's favorite toys remained, mostly because Rachel hadn't had the heart to toss them out.

She'd bought a little tree, too, with the lights already attached.

Even though the two of them were running away, she had vowed that her daughter would have Christmas.

Luke had come out with her, leaving a woman Rachel hadn't seen when she checked in to watch the front desk. And Anne-Marie. The woman was watching Anne-Marie, too. The woman looked tired and stressed, and something in her disheveled blouse and wrinkled skirt screamed shift's end, a fact confirmed by Luke just before he left the lobby.

"It's just a minute, Sherrie," he had said to the woman. "I promise. Then you can go home."

"Always just one more minute," Sherrie had said. "I gotta get to the stores before they close."

"Kmart's open until ten," Luke had said, and in his voice was just a bit of contempt. Because he thought Sherrie should shop at Kmart or because she *did* shop at Kmart?

Rachel couldn't tell, and truly didn't care. She just didn't want the woman to see her—at least not much.

Luke, well, Rachel was taking a chance with him. This was the first time since she left Winnemucca that anyone other than herself and Anne-Marie had seen inside the van.

Anne-Marie was still inside the lobby, holding the candy-cane and staring at the tree. She wouldn't even sit down. She had asked Sherrie if she believed Santa would find them.

"You'd be surprised what Santa can find," Sherrie had said.

Rachel pulled the Santa bag out of the hidden compartment. "Is there any way to put this behind the desk for a few minutes without Anne-Marie seeing it?"

Luke grinned at her. "No wonder you weren't worried about St. Nick. He's already been here. Anything good in there?"

"If you're seven, like pink, and have always longed for at least one more Barbie," Rachel said, rather surprised she could banter. She had thought the ability to banter had left her years ago.

He smiled at her. "She'll remember this trip forever," he said as if that were a good thing.

"Yes," Rachel said. "I suppose she will."

She grabbed the overnight bags and slung them over her shoulders. Then she double-checked to make sure she had the key fob. She grabbed the small tabletop tree before slamming the lift gate shut.

"I'll be down for the bag after my daughter falls asleep. You'll still be here?"

"Of course," Luke said. "You've already had dinner?"

For a moment, she thought he was asking if he could join her. Her stomach clenched. Then she remembered that he had said he was working all night. He was just asking for information.

"No, we haven't yet." Her breath fogged the air as she spoke. "I suppose no one's doing delivery tonight."

"Not tonight." Luke sounded apologetic, as if it were his fault that no one else was working. "But most of the restaurants around here are staying open. And there's a church about three blocks away if you're so inclined."

"I think we're too tired," she said. She *hoped*. She didn't want to leave the room after they'd eaten something. It was just too cold.

As if hearing her thoughts, Luke shivered. "I'm taking this in the back, then I'll meet you."

Without waiting for her to answer, he picked his way across the parking lot, slipping more than she liked.

The wind seemed even colder. Cars still whizzed by on the interstate behind her. The lights from the chain hotels and the chain restaurants that hugged this exit should have seemed festive, but they didn't. They seemed like beacons of a past life.

She didn't look at them, instead making certain she got across the slippery parking lot with her burden.

Luke went in a side door, then came back outside without the bag. He truly was Santa's helper. He grinned, took the tree from her, and opened the main lobby doors.

Anne-Marie turned, eyes wide, as if she were expecting someone else, someone she didn't want to see.

Rachel hated how jumpy her daughter had become.

"You brought the tree!" Anne-Marie said to Luke.

"I did indeed," he said, then looked at Rachel. "Will you need help setting it up?"

Rachel was tempted, but she couldn't quite face having a stranger take her to her room.

"Do you have a bellman's cart?" she asked. "That's all we need."

He nodded as if he understood, then disappeared in the back, tree in hand. Anne-Marie watched it go as if he were never going to bring it back.

"Tough traveling on Christmas, isn't it?" Sherrie said to Rachel.

"People are friendlier," Rachel said, and it was true. People *were* friendlier, particularly when they saw her daughter. They assumed that Rachel was on her way to see relatives, that maybe she got behind or needed an extra bit of help.

She never dissuaded them.

"That friendly will end tonight," Sherrie said. "The folks who show up after nine are generally upset because they can't get to Grandma's house or because they got no one to celebrate with."

Rachel gave her a hard look, hoping she'd quit being negative.

Sherrie didn't seem to notice. "Thank the good Lord for Luke, though. Ever since he came here, I haven't had to work a Christmas Day. He calls it his gift to all of us."

"He doesn't have family?" Rachel asked, despite herself.

This time, Sherrie did look at Anne-Marie. Anne-Marie was leaning toward one of the ornaments, as if she'd never seen anything like it.

Sherrie shook her head. Anne-Marie turned around, as if she expected to hear Sherrie's answer. So Sherrie put on a bright smile.

"He loves New Year's. He takes the days around New Year's off. One year, he flew to New York to watch the ball drop. Said he damn near froze his ball—"

"Crudeness on Christmas is not allowed," Luke said, interrupting her. He was dragging a gold bellman's cart, with the tree set on one side of it.

"Where *are* you going this year?" Sherrie asked, as if she couldn't be dissuaded from anything.

"Miami," Luke said. "Party central. And it's *warm*."

At that word, Rachel shivered. She would give anything to live somewhere warm now, but that wasn't in the cards. She had made her choices, and they were good ones.

Or they would be. Once she got to Detroit.

She set the overnight bags on the cart, careful not to knock the tree off it. Her shoulders ached from carrying the bags, and from the stress of driving.

Hours to go, she reminded herself, hearing her fourth grade teacher intone Robert Frost's most famous poem, just like she always did when she realized she couldn't sleep no matter how exhausted she was.

"There's an in-room Jacuzzi," Luke said softly, loud enough that only she could hear him. "Perfect after a long day. Merry Christmas."

"Thank you," Rachel said. She had done nothing to deserve this man's kindness, and yet he had given it to her.

The one thing she did not regret about traveling at Christmas was exactly what she had said to Sherrie: people *were* friendlier. It was as if a bit of the season had infected them, and gave them just a little bit of joy.

"Come on, Anne-Marie," she said, and Anne-Marie scurried to follow her.

Rachel wheeled the cart to the elevators behind the stairs. Anne-Marie didn't even ask if she could ride it. She had in Cheyenne.

"Is Santa really going to find us?" Anne-Marie asked.

"If you fall asleep," Rachel said as the elevator doors opened. "Just like last year."

She regretted the words the moment she spoke them. Anne-Marie had a look of horror on her face.

Without Daddy, Rachel wanted to add. *You don't have to worry about Daddy*.

But she didn't. She'd mentioned last year, and she couldn't take it back.

"I don't like Christmas," Anne-Marie said as she stepped inside, head down.

Rachel's heart twisted. Little kids weren't supposed to say that. Little kids were supposed to plan all year for Christmas, do special things to get in good with Santa, and be so excited that they couldn't sleep the night before.

They weren't supposed to turn off the Christmas specials, and keep their faces averted during the commercials. Christmas wasn't supposed to make them *sad*.

That emotion was for grownups, especially the ones for whom nostalgia was not enough.

Rachel put her hand on her daughter's fuzzy little cap, and didn't say a single word.

Rachel put the little tree on the round table in the suite's kitchenette. The suite was bigger than anything they had stayed in so far. It seemed like luxury, even though they hadn't been traveling very long. Part of her had already forgotten the wealth in her past life.

She took small presents out of the overnight bag and scattered them under the tree, the first time she had done that. It made Anne-Marie frown.

"I don't got nothing for you, Mommy," she said.

"It's okay, baby," Rachel said. "This trip is for me."

Anne-Marie's lower lip trembled, and Rachel wanted to curse Gil. He'd thrown a fit last year when he realized he hadn't gotten as many presents as Rachel had. Anne-Marie had thought he was blaming her, when he wasn't blaming anyone. He was just being an asshole, his specialty.

"I didn't buy the trip," Anne-Marie said softly.

"I know, sweetie," Rachel said, making sure she sounded cheerful. "But you came with me."

Anne-Marie let out a little sigh, then went to her toy bag, and pulled out the stuffed dog that had become her lifeline. She set it on the bed nearest the kitchen, claiming that bed for her own.

"You hungry?" Rachel asked.

Anne-Marie nodded.

"Then bundle back up," Rachel said. "We have to go outside again."

They couldn't really walk to the nearby restaurants, as much as Rachel wanted to. They had to drive, just because of the severe cold. They waved at Luke on the way out and got into the chilly van.

He had been right; most of the chain restaurants were open. Normally, Rachel would have stopped at a super-large truck stop with six restaurants inside of it, as well as shops and showers. No one noticed the people who came and went from those places.

But she decided not to because Anne-Marie had mentioned gifts. Rachel didn't want her daughter to attempt to buy something for her.

Instead, they stopped at the closest family restaurant chain. They all had a disagreeable sameness to her. They smelled of coffee and grease, even in the evenings. They served pancakes at all hours, and usually had pies that looked a little tired in a glass case near the cash register.

This restaurant had an open floor plan, a busboy wearing an elf hat, a manager wearing a tie covered with reindeer, and a waitress whose brown uniform had no holiday decoration at all.

She waved them to a table, then brought waters and menus before Rachel and Anne-Marie could even get settled. They ordered, got halfway decent food, and some free cookies courtesy of the manager.

Rachel was trying to decide whether she wanted to pay with cash or a credit card when she heard Anne-Marie gasp. Anne-Marie's face had gone a kind of white that Rachel hadn't seen since they left Boise. A look that usually meant Anne-Marie had been doing something she thought her father would disapprove of.

Rachel followed Anne-Marie's gaze, and saw a Santa accepting a menu from the waitress. He wasn't wearing any padding under the suit, so it hung loosely, and his beard hung around his chin, as if he'd loosened it. He looked as tired as Rachel felt.

His appearance must have shocked Anne-Marie, who had only seen fat Santas so far. There had been a lot of them. She'd seen Santas everywhere, from the men manning the Salvation Army buckets by every public building to the men standing outside malls, smoking before they went back to work.

"What's wrong, honey?" she asked Anne-Marie.

Anne-Marie shook her head and then scrunched down, as if she didn't want Santa to see her.

Someday, when Rachel got back on her feet, she'd get her revenge on Gil. She wasn't sure what that revenge would be, but her husband had put the fear of God into their child.

And into her.

Or she wouldn't be running now.

The food she had eaten rolled over in her stomach. It had taken a village to get her out of Boise. Her husband was so rich that she'd never thought she could escape him. But a forbidden phone call to her sister had changed her mind.

Helen had begged her to find a pay phone and call back. Helen had asked that before, and Rachel had refused. But this time, she would listen to anything. Helen had hated Gil from the beginning and warned Rachel not to marry him. Rachel had resented that once. Later, she wondered what Helen had seen.

Still, Helen's pushing had made her uncomfortable. It had also embarrassed Rachel. She felt so stupid. But that day, she had gone past her embarrassment, past her inferiority. She was nearly dead inside. And Anne-Marie's eyes were dying too.

So Rachel had found a pay phone near the ladies room in the back of a very large, very old grocery store. Rachel had felt naked making that call, standing to one side, and watching the employees go by, hoping no one recognized her. She had barely been able to concentrate on her sister's words.

Helen had told her that she knew a group of women who could help her and Anne-Marie, if she only followed instructions.

Rachel needed the help. A shelter couldn't take her in, and she had no money of her own. Plus Gil had more resources than any women's organization.

But Helen had reassured her: The organization—SYT—had an incredible amount of money, and Rachel was exactly the kind of woman they could help.

The cost to Rachel? One year's work at the organization, helping women just like her escape from whatever bad circumstance they were in. It would mean donating time and energy to a rehab project in Detroit, using old design skills that had led Rachel astray in the first place.

Once upon a time in a land faraway, she had been the best interior designer in Idaho. She had helped with projects from Boise to Sun Valley, and that was when she had met the multi-millionaire charmer who would become her husband.

She should have known what a control freak he was right from the beginning. He'd had his fingers in every part of her work on that project. But she had agreed with him—his suggestions were good ones—and she hadn't thought anything was amiss until six months after Anne-Marie's birth, when he'd grabbed Rachel's arm so hard during a disagreement that she'd had bruises for weeks.

She'd always thought women who stayed with men like him were doormats, so she tried to escape on her own. That's when she discovered he had his own private army. He called them security, but they tracked every move she made and everything she did.

They had even asked her why she had used that pay phone on the way to the ladies room, and she had told them it was pretty simple: her cell had died.

They hadn't double-checked. Nor did they check her purchases the next time she went shopping. She'd bought what her sister called a "burner phone" every time she shopped, and she hid them in the purses she had stacked in her closet like extra shoes.

"Mommy, can we go?" Anne-Marie asked.

Rachel nodded. She decided to stop waiting for the waitress to come back with their bill. Instead, she went to the cash register and paid with cash.

The Santa was the only other person in the restaurant. He looked out the window. Then his gaze met hers through the glass. Rachel gave him an uncertain smile, mostly for Anne-Marie's sake, and he nodded at her.

Anne-Marie grabbed her hand, and held tightly.

"Let's make sure you're buttoned up," Rachel said. She hated this kind of cold. It required preparation just to walk from a restaurant to the van.

But she had to get used to it. At least a year in Detroit, rehabbing, and getting her credentials back—under one of her new names.

They stepped outside and she sighed. The cold air burned her lungs. Anne-Marie nearly pulled her to the van, making her slide on the ice.

Everyone was nice here. Maybe she would stay one extra day. She wasn't looking forward to a drive on Christmas. Most places were closed, and this arctic blast made travel so treacherous.

She would call Helen after Anne-Marie fell asleep.

They got into the van and drove the short distance back to the hotel. Luke was still at the front desk. He was watching some religious ceremony on television; it took Rachel a minute to realize it was the service from the Vatican.

She waved at him and mouthed, "I'll be back soon," as she and Anne-Marie headed toward the elevator.

They barely made it to the room, before Anne-Marie decided she needed to get some sleep.

Rachel wished she could sleep. Ever since she'd fled Boise, she'd dozed, but never slept deeply. Every time a hotel room heater clicked on, she bolted awake thinking the sound was someone racking a shotgun.

Gil had threatened to kill her if she ever took Anne-Marie away from him, and she hadn't doubted he could make good on the threat.

But Helen was convinced they could build her a new identity, and that no one would ever find her, if she did the right things. Helen had always worked with women's groups, and this one, SYT (short for Sweet Young Things), seemed more organized and wealthier than anything Rachel had ever imagined.

They had had quite a plan for her, and she'd executed 99.9% of it. The hardest was leaving her Lexus SUV in the parking lot of that hotel-casino in Winnemucca, and pretending that she actually had a drinking problem.

She had hidden whiskey all over her house before she left, disguised to look like tea or juice or a whole variety of things, as if she had been a secret drunk all along.

Helen had promised her that someone would take the SUV, and leave it in the snow on a spur road between Winnemucca and Boise. Tracks would lead away from the SUV, and rescuers would believe that she and Anne-Marie had walked away from the car. There would be a high-profile search, and then nothing, until spring, when someone might find a bit of their clothing and Rachel's purse out in the wilderness.

Rachel thought it all a long-shot, but she'd lived in the west long enough to know that families went missing there all the time. They took the wrong road, got stranded, and had no cell service. Rather than wait for rescue, like they were supposed to, they'd try to hike out, and generally die of exposure.

Everyone would believe the story, particularly after all that alcohol got found in the house.

Everyone, she suspected, except Gil.

But Rachel had to trust Helen. It was her only shot. Anne-Marie's only shot. Because Gil terrorized his daughter. Mostly, he wasn't home, but when he was, just a twitch of his lips could make her turn that horrid shade of white that Rachel had seen in the restaurant.

Anne-Marie was terrified of him. As far as Rachel could tell, only because Rachel was frightened of him. To Rachel's knowledge, he hadn't physically hurt their daughter...yet.

But Rachel had known it was only a matter of time.

She sat near the television, turned so low she could barely hear it, and wished she smoked. Or actually did drink. Just to give herself something to do, something that would relax her.

She was on her own until she got to Detroit. Well, sort of on her own. The woman who had cut her hair in Cheyenne told her it got better. When Rachel asked if she was trading services, the woman had gotten very serious and nodded, finger to her lips.

There are women like us everywhere, she'd said. *We're setting up a network. I know it's hard to trust, but you'll be okay, if you just do what they told you.*

And she had. Everything except the toys. And those, she had searched over and over. She'd even stopped in a spy shop in Laramie, and asked if they had one of those electronic bug-finders.

They did, and she asked if she could see how it worked. She brought in the bag of toys and the man demonstrated, finding nothing. He showed her that it did work with some demo they had, and told her that the toys were tracking free.

She believed him. And she had seen him before Cheyenne, before her hair and appearance changed, before she dumped yet another coat, before she had done anything to make herself look like someone new.

Helen hadn't said she had to avoid stores and things. Just warned her to be careful, and to leave her old life behind. No friends, no phone calls, no gloating e-mails to Gil.

Not that Rachel would have done any of that. She had no real friends, not ones she had contacted since her marriage, and she wasn't about to contact her husband. Her cell was gone, left in the Lexus with her purse and her old identification.

Since she got on the road, she was a different woman, although she still felt the same inside.

A knock on the door made her jump out of her skin. She glanced at Anne-Marie, to see if her daughter had heard it.

She hadn't.

Rachel got up and almost went to the door, thinking it was probably Luke from the desk. Then she wondered if he would just come up with the Santa bag. Wouldn't he wait for her call?

She swallowed hard, heart pounding.

If something feels wrong, Helen had told her, *then it probably is wrong. Your subconscious sees something you don't. Get out of that situation*.

Only there was no way out of here. Except the window, which was probably blocked against opening, not to mention the jump from the third floor, into the damn polar express or whatever the hell that cold was called.

Rachel got up and moved silently away from the kitchen area, finding the house phone. She hit "0" and Luke answered.

"You ready for the presents now?" he asked cheerfully.

"You didn't just knock on my door?" she asked very quietly, and even though she tried to control it, she could hear the fear in her voice.

"No, ma'am—damn. I didn't see him go up there. There's a Santa on security camera. He's outside your door. You expecting someone?"

"No," she said.

"Didn't hire a Santa?"

"No." And now she was chilled. She glanced at her daughter. What had Anne-Marie been trying to tell her?

"Okay." Luke no longer sounded cheerful. He sounded businesslike. "He doesn't belong here. I'll kick him out."

"No," Rachel said. "He might be dangerous."

"A *Santa*?"

"How did he get past you?" she asked. "And how did he know we were here, in this room?"

Luke cursed. "Good point. We don't have security tonight either. I'm going to have to call the cops. You hang tight and don't open that door."

And he hung up before she could tell him no cops. The last thing she wanted was cops.

She reached into the purse she was carrying tonight and took out the stun gun that SYT had left in the van with mace and a few other protective things. Her hand was shaking terribly.

"Open the door, Rachel," said a male voice she didn't recognize. "I'm sure we can find a way to convince your husband that this was all a misunderstanding."

Tears threatened. They'd found her. Gil's army, just like she knew they would.

She didn't go near the door. She turned up the television a little more, so that Anne-Marie wouldn't hear, then crept toward the bathroom, keeping the bathroom wall between her and the little corridor that led to the door.

"I'm thinking we fly back to somewhere near Winnemucca, and I bring you and the little one out of the wilderness, saving your lives. It might mean you need to lick your fingers and stand outside in this cold for fifteen minutes because frostbite would really help the story, but if we do that, Gil won't know a damn thing."

Rachel wanted to ask why he would do that, this mystery Santa, but she didn't. She knew better than to engage. If she engaged, she had already lost.

She held the stun gun like it was a real gun. Helen had told her not to get a real gun, not with Anne-Marie in the van. Because Rachel didn't know how to use it, and Helen said, too many bad things happened around children and guns.

"You're not saying anything," the man continued. "I know you want to."

She peered around the wall. The safety chain was on, and she'd deadbolted the door, plus pushed in that so-called security lock. The only way in was for him to knock the door down, right? Or she had to let him in.

That's why he was talking. He wanted her to let him in.

"Mommy?" Anne-Marie asked.

Rachel put a finger to her lips and then she covered her ears, so that Anne-Marie would too. They used to do that when Gil got home from a long day, angry, and wanting someone to take it out on. Rachel would mime instructions to her daughter: remain quiet and don't listen.

"Is Daddy here?" Anne-Marie whispered, and Rachel heard the fear in her voice.

Rachel shook her head. She then indicated that Anne-Marie should join her, because there was protection against this wall, particularly if the man outside wanted to shoot them.

She didn't know if he did. She wasn't sure what the point of that was. But she knew that sometimes Gil could be irrational, and she had no idea who worked for him, or why they felt it necessary to carry so many weapons.

"We can make this work," the man outside the room said.

Anne-Marie grabbed her dog and her slippers, then tucked in behind her mother. Her daughter's warmth made Rachel feel stronger.

"I bet you're wondering why I'm willing to help you," he said. "I've been thinking about it for the last three days as I watched you drive. It's pretty simple, really: you have a big allowance from that husband of yours. You just give me part of it, under the table, and you'll be free and clear. Back in the arms of your family, safe and sound. You don't want to be on the road like this forever, do you?"

She closed her eyes. Maybe, a few years ago, she would have done that. Maybe. But she'd seen Gil get mad at Anne-Marie too many times. She'd seen him clench his fists and unclench them like he meant to hit her.

And Anne-Marie cringed a lot, even now.

"Open the door, Rachel," the man outside the door said.

God, what would he tell the police? That she had faked her death in Nevada? There were no restraining orders against her husband, no calls to 911, nothing to prove her claims of abuse. There was nothing that would prevent him from flying out here and getting her and Anne-Marie.

Rachel was back where she started, no matter what.

She stood slowly, putting her finger to her lips. She wasn't sure she could shut him up, but she had to try. The stun gun, as Helen had told her, could knock down a man five times her size. And then she could—what? Stab him with a butter knife? Use his gun if he carried one?

This hotel clearly had security video, and if she killed him, it would be recorded.

She shouldn't have listened to Helen. Rachel should have known that this plan would all go to hell.

She was never going to escape Gil, never, no matter who made the promises or how big the network was or how much money they threw at the problem.

It had been a dream all along, and she had let herself believe it.

"Honey," Rachel said to Anne-Marie, knowing that she would be damning her daughter too. "I'm going to—"

Sirens. They got louder and then they cut off. But red-and-blue lights reflected in the windows.

At least the police arrived before she could do something stupid. Before she even tried to hurt this unknown man. Not that it would have helped.

Now he was going to the police station, and he'd give them her identity, and—

"I thought you said someone was in the hall," a new male voice said outside her room.

"I did." That voice belonged to Luke. "I'll show you on the security feed. Send your guys out looking. He couldn't have gone far. Some weirdo in a Santa suit. He was menacing my guests."

And then they walked off, still talking.

Rachel's heart kept pounding. Slowly she sank back down, keeping a death grip on the stun gun. After a few more minutes of silence, she put her fingers to her lips again, then quietly, in a crouch, made her way to her purse.

She took out Nebraska's phone, and hit the pre-programmed number.

"Hi," she said breathlessly. "I'm Rachel—"

"I know who you are," said an unfamiliar female voice on the other end of the line. "What's happened?"

Rachel told her, in a low voice, then turned away, adding, "He's seen the van. He knows who we are. He knows where we are. I just wanted to say thanks, but I'm going to have to go home now. Because there's nothing anyone can do—"

"You stay put," the woman said. "I'll have someone meet you in fifteen minutes. We'll have a new vehicle for you and a safe place to stay."

"But how can you get here so fast?"

"Omaha, right?" the woman asked. "Thank God you listened and didn't stop in a small town. Then it might've taken hours for us to reach you. But you're okay there. It might take twenty minutes, seeing it's Christmas Eve, but no more than that. You stay on the line with me while you wait, okay?"

"Okay," Rachel said.

She heard the tapping of a keyboard, some voices, and someone say, "We got it."

Then she glanced at Anne-Marie.

"It was Santa," Anne-Marie said like an accusation.

Not *like* an accusation. It was an accusation.

Rachel nodded.

"He was *everywhere,*" Anne-Marie said.

Rachel closed her eyes for just a minute. Like that stupid song. *He sees you...*

And she had seen him. In truck stops and cafes, smoking outside a gas station in Rawlins. She'd thought him a different Santa every time.

Santa was everywhere this season.

It was the perfect disguise.

The house phone rang and she almost tossed the stun gun into the air. She made herself set it down.

"What's that?" the woman on the other end of the burner cell asked.

"The hotel phone," Rachel said.

It stopped ringing.

"Have you talked to anyone?" the woman asked.

"I called the guy at the desk," Rachel said. "When someone knocked on my door. I wanted to see if it was housekeeping or something."

"Then call the desk," the woman said. "Tell him you're all right. You are all right, aren't you?"

If she didn't think about her elevated blood pressure, then maybe she was. "Yes," Rachel said.

She picked up the hotel phone, and hit "0" again. "Sorry, I—"

"It's all right," Luke said. "The police scared him off. I'm the one who should apologize. They couldn't find him, but at least he's not outside the door. They'll talk to you if you want."

"No," she said. "It's okay."

He hadn't been caught. She didn't know if that was good news or bad.

"Tell him that Candy Mills is coming for you," the woman's voice said on the burner cell. "Tell him it's okay to let Candy come see you."

Rachel told Luke that, even though it felt odd.

"I think I see her pulling in," he said. "I'll send her right up."

Then he hung up.

"I don't know anyone named Candy Mills," Rachel said, and she would remember. The name was weird.

"I'm texting a photo and the passphrase now," the woman said. "She'll give you the passphrase. You'll recognize her from the photo."

"Okay," Rachel said.

"And I'll be on the phone to hear everything."

The cell vibrated in her hand. Rachel looked at it. A middle-aged woman with a weathered face smiled tentatively at the camera.

There was a knock on the door. "Rachel?"

This time, it was a woman's voice.

She said, "There's an awful lot of Sweet Young Things on the road."

The passphrase.

And the moment of truth.

Rachel walked to the door, then peered through the peephole. A woman wearing a heavy jacket let down the hood, revealing a version of that weathered face from the photo.

Rachel crossed her fingers, regretting the fact that she'd left the stun gun behind. She opened the door slowly, keeping the security chain on.

"Candy Mills," the woman said.

"Rachel," Rachel said because she for the life of her couldn't remember her fake name. "And this is Anne-Marie."

She turned to point out her daughter, and her breath caught.

Anne-Marie was standing behind them, pointing the stun gun at the woman. She looked fierce. Her hands didn't tremble at all.

But Rachel's did. She nearly dropped the cell. The woman on the line was asking what was going on.

"Give me the gun, Anne-Marie," Rachel said quietly.

"We don't know her," Anne-Marie said.

"I know, honey, but it's okay," Rachel said.

"Do you know Santa?" Anne-Marie asked the woman.

The woman looked confused. She glanced at Rachel, who drew in her breath slowly. She couldn't help. She didn't dare help. But she tried to convey that the usual answer was the wrong answer.

"I've never met him," the woman said after a moment.

Anne-Marie considered that. Then she set the gun down. Rachel hurried toward it.

The woman closed the door. Rachel picked up the stun gun and put it in her purse. Then she wrapped her arms around Anne-Marie. Anne-Marie clung to her.

"We're going to get you out of here," the woman said. "You'll spend the holiday at my house. It's not much, but it'll do. Christmas put a kink in our plans. But by the 26th, we should have a new van for you, and new stuff. You'll have to leave everything behind."

"Except Anne-Marie's toys," Rachel said. "I checked them. They don't have a tracker."

She thought about the Santa bag at the front desk. Maybe they could pick those up on the way out, and she could thank Luke.

The woman—Candy Mills, if that was her real name—frowned. "I'll double-check. I have some equipment."

She didn't seem too concerned.

"Will he find us again?" Rachel figured it was okay to ask. Anne-Marie had been asking for the entire trip.

"No," Candy Mills said. "We think if there was a tracker, it was on the van. We'll know for sure tomorrow. You said he followed from Winnemucca, right?"

"He had a whole plan," Rachel said.

"Well, we'll take care of that now. He shouldn't be hard to find." She glanced at the tree, gave it a once-over that looked a bit sad.

"You sure you can protect us?" Rachel asked.

Candy Mills smiled, which made her seem younger and friendlier. "Yes," she said. "We've helped a lot of women escape situations worse than yours."

"What if he called Gil and told him where we were?"

"That's why we're going somewhere else. He had no idea where you were headed, right? You never told anyone, right?" Candy Mills sounded a bit intense, as if she wanted to make sure.

"I never said a word," Rachel said. Not even to Anne-Marie.

"I'm signing off now," said the voice on the cell. "You're in good hands."

And before Rachel could say thank you, the woman on the other end of the line hung up.

Rachel swallowed. She didn't want to admit it, but she was happy to have help, even for a day or two.

She felt less alone.

Candy Mills looked at Anne-Marie. "Get your stuff. We're going to go."

Anne-Marie hugged her dog to her chest. She didn't move. "Will Santa know how to find us?"

Candy Mills looked at Rachel, smart enough to realize these questions weren't what they seemed.

"No, honey," Rachel said. "Santa will never find us again."

The sentence made her heart hurt. Somehow, she was going to have to give her daughter Christmas magic again. But not this year.

This year, she was giving her daughter freedom. A real life. A life away from Gil.

"Good," Anne-Marie said, and reached for her clothes. "I hope I never see him again."

"Oh, honey," Rachel said, knowing that wish was impossible. "I hope so too."

Unknown Baby Girl

Kristine Kathryn Rusch

Unknown Baby Girl

The bones were tiny. Carolyn eased them out of the old insulation, her gloved fingers brushing against newsprint and decaying fabric. She was wedged into a crawlspace, her legs hanging out, feet brushing against the basement wall. It was hot and close, and even through her breathing mask, she could smell mold.

"Coming back," she yelled, knowing her voice would sound muffled to Linda, her assistant. In an area this small, she had to let Linda know she was moving, or she might accidentally kick her.

Carolyn cupped the bones between her hands. With them, she caught a bit of insulation, the newsprint, and some rotted material. Linda put her hands on Carolyn's legs, and guided her down. When Carolyn reached the edge, she wriggled backwards, careful to keep her balance even though her hands were full.

She didn't realize, until the light from her helmet met the light from Linda's in the glare of the single bulb the family had kept in the large rambling old basement, that the bones she held belonged to a small child.

—

Tiny bones were part of her work. The walls of houses, particularly old houses, were filled with bones and burrows and nests. Most of the bones belonged to mice or rats, but Carolyn had found a few cats and more than her share of raccoons. She'd encountered a litter of puppies abandoned by their mother and, on one of the scariest afternoons of her new life, a live possum.

The bones she now cradled had once been a living breathing child. She could tell that from the shape of the skull, the size of the pelvis (female), and the thickness of the bones. This wasn't a stillborn baby. This child had been a few months old when someone had buried it in the crawlspace.

Linda poked at the ribs. "This isn't a cat," she said, and that was when Carolyn looked up.

Of course, Linda didn't know. Linda had installed insulation her entire working career. She'd started out as a secretary to the jobs manager, and then had moved into the field, first as a volunteer, and then as an installer. She'd had to prove herself, like most women did in non-traditional professions, and what she had proven was that she could do better than most of the guys. Her size helped—she fit into the tiny spaces that most men couldn't breach—but so did her sense of precision.

Linda could install more bats per hour than anyone on the team.

She was assisting Carolyn only because Carolyn couldn't convince her to stay home. At the moment, Linda couldn't fit into any crawl spaces. She was five months pregnant with her first child, and she didn't seem to realize that she should be back at the desk. No matter how much Carolyn or Linda's doctor or her friends argued that she shouldn't be around the old insulation or the mold or the asbestos that filled the houses where the team worked, Linda refused to take time off.

Carolyn glanced at Linda's bulging belly, and then closed her eyes, not sure she wanted to say anything. But there was no way to keep this quiet.

"It's a baby, isn't it?" Linda asked.

Carolyn opened her eyes. Linda's eyes, covered in goggles, peered at her over the breathing mask that Carolyn made her wear to every job.

"Yeah," Carolyn said.

"We have to report this, don't we?" Linda asked.

Carolyn nodded.

"Christ on a crutch," Linda said with some annoyance. "Why would anyone hire us if they'd hidden a baby in the crawl space?"

So much for maternal sensitivity. Carolyn sighed and set the tiny bones on top of an open plank.

"I don't know," she said, "but I suspect this child has been here for a long, long time."

It took the local police a long, long time to come. Carolyn found some chairs behind the rusted wringer washer. She brought them out, dusted them off, and made Linda sit down.

Then Carolyn poked at the bones, knowing she'd already ruined the crime scene.

They were brittle and yellow with age. Some of the smaller bones were missing. She wasn't sure if that meant an animal got at the corpse or if a baby that young didn't have fully formed finger bones or if some of the tiniest bones had already decayed.

When she'd worked homicide in Los Angeles, most of the corpses she saw were fresh. She'd worked some old deaths—skeletons found at building sites, or in the trunks of junkyard cars—but those had remained unsolved, mostly from lack of evidence.

She wasn't sure that evidence lacked here. The baby had been wrapped in either a garment or a blanket—one piece that stuck to her gloves had a tiny golden duck on it, a baby design if she'd ever seen one—and the newspaper seemed part of the package. She didn't move the newsprint—it was fragile enough—but she'd seen more of it under her helmet lamp inside the crawl space.

The question she had was whether the newspaper predated the insulation that Carolyn had found the baby in, since newspaper was often used as insulation in early 20th century Oregon homes, or if someone had wrapped the poor infant in her blanket, then in a newspaper like yesterday's discarded fish.

Carolyn shuddered, and swallowed hard. She felt panic rise in her, like it used to do in those last days at the LAPD, and she willed it away.

"Bothers you, doesn't it?" Linda said from her chair. She clutched her cell phone in her gloved hand, staring at the little window as if it were providing her with entertainment.

"Doesn't it bother you?" Carolyn asked, her hand brushing against her own stomach. She could almost feel the scars through her gloves and thick shirt—small, like cat scratches, barely deserving the name scar at all.

She had to remember, the doctor had told her, that even though her outsides had had minor surgery, her insides had suffered major trauma.

Trauma. An ectopic pregnancy that had almost killed her, a botched emergency room rescue that caused a fallopian tube to rupture, and a miracle that had somehow allowed her to survive it all.

"You work this job long enough, you see every kind of bone possible," Linda was saying.

Carolyn blinked, coming back to the conversation. "You've seen human bones before?"

"Not baby bones," Linda said. "Just a skull, sitting in the corner of what had once been a walk-in closet. Gave me a start, let me tell you."

Carolyn moved away from those tiny bones. She made herself sit down, stop tampering, remember that she no longer ran crime scenes. She installed insulation because it calmed her. She was building something, not digging into causes already lost.

"A skull?" Carolyn said, tugging on the legs of her jeans. This part of the basement was small and dark. She longed to take off her helmet, but knew she didn't dare. She had no idea what kind of particles she carried on her person.

The company had protocols for work with the old insulation, the dangerous kind, and if Carolyn violated those protocols and then got sick, worker's comp wouldn't cover her.

"Yeah, a skull." Linda leaned back, splayed her legs a little, like Carolyn's sister had done midway through her pregnancies. "We called the cops, did the waiting-around thing, and it turns out it had a rusted bolt in its base."

"A bolt?" Now Linda had Carolyn's attention.

Linda nodded. "Remember how med schools used to use real cadavers. Turns out the skull came from one of those doctor's skeletons, the kind they kept in their offices. The university had put the thing in storage and this prof's son had taken the head as a kind of souvenir. He hid it in the back of his closet, then forgot about it. When his folks died, and he sold the house, he got reminded real fast."

"Must have been scary for him," Carolyn said, thinking how she might have conducted that investigation.

"A little bit. It took some convincing to show that he hadn't desecrated a corpse."

"Still," Carolyn said, "he stole it."

"The university wasn't going to press charges. They didn't want anyone to remember how they'd desecrated corpses, back in the day."

Carolyn smiled, then felt the smile fade. She looked at the tiny bones, the intact but unfinished skull. If she thought about it, she could recall her training—at what age did the soft spot close up? Six months? Whatever it was, this child hadn't made that milestone.

"Wish they'd get here." Carolyn was hot and she wanted to move. If she couldn't work, she wanted out of this basement, with the stench of mold and decay.

"They always think we're overreacting," Linda said. "We had one guy—your predecessor—who called in every squirrel bone he ever found."

"Lovely," Carolyn muttered.

"Don't worry," Linda said. "The town's not that big. Cops here don't have much to do."

That was one of the reasons Carolyn had moved to Skinner City. The murder rate was glacial, particularly compared with Los Angeles, and so was the crime rate. Most of the crimes were meth-related—petty theft, a little arson, and a lot of drug-dealing. With one of the state's major universities in the center of town, the cops also had to deal with rape and underage drinking violations, a lot of traffic problems, and a little computer crime.

"Hullo!" a voice shouted from the top of the stairs. "Anyone there?"

"Down here," Linda shouted back. Boots struck the rotting wood as the cops came down, and Carolyn felt her shoulders tense. Cops even walked different from everyone else. Sweat ran down her spine, settling in the small of her back. She felt a little woozy and she had to remind herself to breathe.

Post-traumatic stress, she reminded herself, using the mantra of her last and best therapist. *It'll be with you forever, but it doesn't have to control you. Just know it for what it is, a sense memory, and remember that you're safe now. You'll always be safe.*

Maybe not always, she knew. But she was safe enough.

Even when tiny abandoned corpses reminded her of the life she had left.

The cops were detectives, which surprised her. Carolyn would have thought that beat cops would come first, confirm that they weren't dealing with squirrel bones, and then send for the detective unit. But Linda had turned out to be right: crime was low in Skinner City, and the detectives showed up mostly out of curiosity and a lack of something new to do.

They were a team—Detective Brauder, a fifty-something silver-haired looker straight out of central casting, and his partner, Detective Moin, a thirty-something redhead with freckles and a cowlick. They were both tall men with broad-shoulders, and surprised as they seemed to find two women in the basement installing (actually, at this stage, removing) insulation, they didn't comment on it.

Brauder poked at the bones just like Carolyn had. Then he looked at her with surprise. "It is an infant."

She got the sense he'd wanted squirrel bones. She recognized his mood; something bad had happened today and he had the need to yell at someone for being stupid. He couldn't yell at whomever had caused the mood. He'd come here hoping to yell at her.

"I think it's been here at least ten years," she said, "maybe more."

Now Moin looked at her with surprise. It was a comical expression on his youngish face. His ears stuck out like Alfred E. Newman's. She could almost picture him on a *Mad Magazine* cover with "What? Me Worry?" written in large letters along the bottom.

"Yeah," he said., not attempting to hide his sarcasm. "Like you can tell that."

Brauder held up a hand, silencing his partner as effectively as if they were going into a building expecting to be fired upon. "What makes you say that?" he asked in a tone that let Carolyn know he had the same suspicions.

Now he wanted to know why she was so good at figuring out the age of infant skeletons—or if, perhaps, she had placed the baby there herself ten years before.

"Carolyn was a cop once," Linda said, shifting on the chair. Both men looked at her as if they were seeing her for the first time. And maybe they were. She had placed a hand along her belly like pregnant women did, calling attention to that bulge.

"Should you even be here?" Moin asked her.

"God, I hate that question," she said. "No, I probably shouldn't, but this is my job and my insides are probably already filled with crap and I really can't afford to take the next four months off. Any more personal questions you'd like to ask?"

"Sorry," he said, leaning away.

"You were a cop," Brauder asked, impressing Carolyn with his focus. It was as if the exchange between Moin and Linda hadn't even happened.

"In Los Angeles," she said. "In a previous life."

"What division?" he asked.

She had to swallow before answering him. "Homicide."

He nodded. "Then tell me what else you know."

He meant about the bones. If she told him what she knew about investigations, about murders, about the dark side of life, they'd be here for two full days.

"The child is not a newborn," Carolyn said. "I'm guessing she's a few months old."

"She?" Moin asked.

Carolyn stood and walked to the bones, as if Moin were a rookie detective on her squad. Linda watched in fascination. Carolyn kept her hand above the tiny skeleton, but pointed to the pelvis.

"Even at this age, you can see the differences in the pelvic area," she said. "It's not as obvious, but to the trained eye...."

Her voice trailed off. Brauder looked at her with compassion.

"LA's a tough beat," he said.

She nodded.

"Saw a lot of this?"

You wouldn't believe, she almost said, but didn't. Instead, she said, "Not babies buried in walls."

Brauder nodded as if reminding himself to get back to business. "Where'd you find her?"

Carolyn pointed to the hole she'd just come out of. It was about eighteen inches wide, and not quite that high. Brauder squinted at it. "You fit in there?"

"Me and my helmet," she said as jauntily as she could.

"There's no way we're going to get inside that," Moin said.

Linda grinned at him. "That's why we get the big bucks."

She sounded gleeful, as if she had something over on him. Carolyn suppressed a sigh. This was why Linda usually worked with only a few other members of Cartwright's Energy Savers. She was combative and held a grudge.

"That's why you took it out?" Brauder asked Carolyn.

"I had to look at it in real light. The bones are so small, I thought they might be animal bones," she said.

"Even with the skull?" Moin asked. He was getting belligerent now. Linda wasn't helping.

"Small animals have skulls," Linda snapped.

"It's hard to see when you have stuff pressing you from all sides. I'd been removing insulation and sometimes particles float." Carolyn tried to give him a reassuring smile before she remembered that she was wearing her mask.

She and Linda probably looked like space creatures, with their miner's helmets (a luxury most installers didn't have), their masks, and their goggles. Carolyn had her goggles around her neck (she hated them) but Linda still wore hers, as if she'd forgotten she had them on.

"Is this stuff dangerous?" Moin was fingering some of the pink fiberglass insulation someone had installed improperly in the 1970s. It peeked out of the edge of the hole that Carolyn had crawled into.

"That's spun glass," Brauder said. "You could cut yourself."

Carolyn didn't bother to correct him. Moin could hurt himself a dozen ways down here, just by being careless.

Moin snatched his hand away.

"I took as much of the surrounding material as I could," Carolyn said to Brauder. "I held it like a tray and brought it back. That's why she's on insulation and newsprint."

He sighed. "We're going to have to get crime techs down here. It'll take a while."

He said that last for her benefit, even though Carolyn knew how understaffed the Skinner City police department was. She had investigated it before she left L.A., thinking she'd move from one police job to another. But when she realized that the pay was one-quarter what she got in Los Angeles and the department had one-one hundredth the manpower, she knew she'd work twice as hard with less recompense. Sure, she wouldn't be working homicides any more—until someone realized she had twenty times the experience of anyone else on the force—and then she'd be back to where she had started.

Besides, the last and best shrink reminded her that she was more likely to suffer incidents of PTSD on a police job than in almost any other kind of work.

"It's okay," Carolyn said. "We can always work the attic."

"What's the job?" Moin asked, still looking at Linda.

"We take out the old insulation," she said slowly as if he was the dumbest person she'd ever met, "and put in the new."

"They're not remodeling this place?" Moin touched the ceiling. It was very close to the top of his head.

"They are," Carolyn answered, before Linda could insult him again. "But only on the public areas. Basement and attic will remain unfinished."

"That's why the first floor is so torn up," Brauder said, and there was a touch of sarcasm in his tone as well. Maybe he didn't like his partner all that much. Or maybe he just didn't like answering silly questions.

"We're saving the easy jobs for last," Carolyn said. "Upstairs all we have to do is put in the insulation and then the contractor's close up the walls."

"I'm helping with that part," Linda said, glaring at Moin as if he were there, trying to stop her.

"Aren't you people worried about getting sued?" he asked Carolyn.

"I signed a release," Linda said before Carolyn could reply. "You really are a nosy bastard, aren't you?"

"I'm here to protect the public trust," Moin said. "Seems to me you're harming it."

"My baby, my public," Linda said.

Brauder smiled then turned away, but not before Carolyn had seen it.

"We're going to close this off down here," he said. "I think you should knock off for the day."

"We don't get paid by the hour," Carolyn said. "We get paid by the bat—"

"Bat?" Moin asked.

She waved a hand at the new rectangles of insulation piled near the carcass of an old toilet.

"We haven't even started to install," Linda said. "We leave now, we get nothing."

"Sorry," Brauder said as Moin added, "You didn't have to call us."

"Yes, we did." This time, Carolyn glared at him. "Murder is murder, whether it happened yesterday or ten years ago."

"Or a hundred years ago," Moin muttered, touching the cobweb hanging in the nearest corner.

"Or a hundred years ago," Brauder answered firmly.

So that was the problem. Moin didn't think cold cases were worth his time.

"I doubt the baby's that old," Carolyn said. "But if she was put here any time in the last seventy years, the killer could still be alive."

This time, Linda shuddered. That hand over her belly widened, as if she were protecting the new life within. For all her hardness, Linda did care about the pregnancy. She'd had dozens of tests, all looking for potential birth defects, and she ate healthy.

She really couldn't afford the time away. She was a single mother. She wasn't sure how she was going to care for the baby after it was born; she couldn't afford day care, and she had no family close by.

"What's the point of arresting someone after seventy years?" Moin muttered. "He already got away with it."

"Get upstairs," Brauder snapped.

Moin flushed, and then hurried up the steps. Brauder ran a hand through his thick silver hair, which fell back into place as if he hadn't disturbed it at all.

"See what I have to contend with here?" Brauder asked.

"How'd he make detective?" Carolyn asked.

Brauder shook his head. "Drugs. It's all anyone knows in this town. Drugs and felony burglary. Apparently it's instant gratification."

"Well," Linda said, "if you find the bastard, I don't care how old he is, I'll make sure he suffered enough for all the years of prison he missed."

Then she stood, rubbed the small of her back, and then added, "Gotta pee."

She headed up the stairs, taking them much more slowly than Moin had.

Brauder watched her go. Then he smiled—a real, thousand-watt Hollywood kind of smile. "You know," he said, "I think she'd do exactly what she says."

"Pee?" Carolyn asked.

"No," Brauder said. "If we catch the bastard, I think she'd take him apart."

Carolyn looked at the small bones, looking even more fragile in the dim light.

"Might be better than a trial," she said, and realized that she'd slipped back into an old, dangerous way of thinking.

By the time Carolyn was thirty-five, she had two-hundred-and-fifty righteous collars. Fifty of those were murder cases, most of which were pled down. She also had one-hundred not-so-righteous collars, and about fifty screwed-up arrests. Twenty-five of the screwed-up cases made it to trial, only to be tossed because she was getting more and more violent as time went on.

Frustration, her last and best shrink said. Carolyn's frustration with the entire criminal justice system was coming out in slaps and hits, in "accidental" shoves against a doorframe, in radically too-tight handcuffs and the occasional kick to the groin.

These criminals weren't going to get convicted and if they did, they'd get five years on something that should've cost them life. Half of her informants got killed, and the rest had children who went on to a life of crime, even though she tried to find those kids halfway houses or after-school programs or space in drug rehab centers.

Frustration was too small a word for it all. Anger was too imprecise. Fury, maybe, or rage might've suited her mood better. And when she found herself kicking open the door to a crackhouse and aiming a gun at a naked, filth-covered two-year-old who immediately started to scream, she turned around and walked away.

Away from the pension, away from the fifteen years she'd toiled getting her detective's shield, away from the friends that she'd already abandoned and the house she'd remodeled from the inside out. When she walked, she discovered the job had been the only thing holding her.

The job and the rage.

When those were gone, she'd slip into weeks-long depression or she'd see a skank pulling a gun on a group of skateboarders, only to realize a few minutes later that it was just another kid holding an iPod.

The department shrink wouldn't let her finish her resignation, telling her she'd get over it, reminding her that she could have a desk job if she wanted just to keep the pension. The next shrink, a skinny little man who'd probably never seen a gun in his life, actually diagnosed the PTSD, but wanted to prescribe a regimen of drugs whose side effects frightened her more than the daytime hallucinations.

It was the third shrink—the last and best shrink—whom she discovered in Oregon after she'd already moved away, who actually helped her recover. A new career, physical labor, and a safe place to vent that rage—in her shrink's office—helped even more.

She wasn't over it, not by a long ways, but she was better. Maybe better than she'd ever been.

Carolyn didn't say any of that to Brauder. He might have understood. When she finally came upstairs, into the torn-up kitchen of the old house, Moin looked at her like she was crazy.

She used to think she was. Not for turning in her shield, but for breaking under the pressure.

The last and best shrink had finally made her list all her successes and all her failures as a cop. Then the shrink had had her list all the times the successes resulted in the proper conviction.

The numbers on that second list were terrifyingly small.

Anyone'd be angry, the shrink said. *Rage is the right reaction to all you've been through.*

And somehow, that simple sentence had been acknowledgement enough.

The rage was easing.

Or it had been, until she found the bones.

The Weatherly job, which was what she, Linda, and everyone else at CES called the house where the bones had been found, was supposed to last all week. With crime scene techs scheduled and a dead body, however tiny, on the premises, much of that week was shot.

Linda drove the truck back to the warehouse. Carolyn had already called the problem in. While Linda parked, Carolyn went inside to check the board, to see if there were other, shorter jobs she and Linda could do while the police investigated the old crime scene.

The office always smelled like expensive coffee. Carolyn couldn't get used to it, any more than she could get used to the comfortable chairs behind all the desks.

She didn't love it here, but she liked it, and that was more than she could say about any part of her previous work.

After she'd cleaned her gear and put it in her locker, she put her clothes in the industrial washer that they kept in the women's locker room. Then she showered, making sure she washed her hair, removing any trace of old insulation. She dressed and came back out just as Linda was entering the locker room.

"I don't see nothing on the board," Linda said as she passed.

"I'll see what I can find," Carolyn said and walked into the main office.

Warren Cartwright was leaning on the receptionist's desk, arms crossed. He was a lean man in his forties. His hair was a bit too long and his mustache too 1970s, but he looked good in a Marlboro Man sort of way.

"A word," he said, as Carolyn walked over to the assignments board.

She sighed. She wondered if he was angry that they were going to be behind on the Weatherly job. She really didn't care about Cartwright's anger—he was a volatile man, but a fair one. She'd worked with real volatile people in the past, and Cartwright didn't compare to any of them.

He led her into his office and closed the door. His office had a view of the warehouse floor. Posters plastered to the wall touted the designs of several environmentally safe insulation products, and a handful of city beautification awards—given because of the company's stellar environmental record—covered the space behind his desk.

He sat down and waved a hand at the upholstered chair near his own personal cappuccino machine.

"I'm not going to give you a second assignment," he said.

Carolyn felt her face heat. She needed the work—not for the money, but for the distraction. She still wasn't ready to spend a lot of time entertaining herself. She really didn't know how.

"Why not?" she asked when she could trust her voice.

"Linda," he said. "I've taken down the jobs on the board. I'm sending her home on half-pay. I looked at it. It's cheaper to pay her half time than it is to pay for some deformed baby for the rest of my life."

His words made Carolyn flush even more. That whisper of rage she'd felt when she found the skeleton returned. She tamped it down as best she could.

"Why don't you just tell her that? I can still use the job."

"She still sees herself as your supervisor," he said.

Linda had trained her when she first arrived. Linda had shown her all kinds of tricks, from ways to wriggle into a crawlspace without dislodging her helmet to ways of removing old insulation without breaking it apart.

"Tell her she's not," Carolyn snapped.

Cartwright laughed. "You tell her something she doesn't want to hear."

Carolyn sighed.

"We're not giving her a job, and then on Friday, a guy I hired to play company physician will give her an exam and order her off her feet."

"Is he a real doctor?" Carolyn asked, thinking of other liabilities.

"Yep. He's even a ladies' doc." Cartwright was refreshingly old-fashioned at times. "But he knows I got this problem, and he's going to do me this favor."

"What does he get out of it?" Carolyn asked.

"My company at every single team match play tournament he wants to sign us up for." Cartwright sighed. He'd once been a local golf legend, and had even gone pro for a while. But the rigors of the golf tour, even at its lowest level, took too big a chunk out of his self-esteem.

To play as someone's ringer was quite a sacrifice for him.

"You're worried about her," Carolyn said.

"Of course I am," he said. "She's too dumb to take care of herself. Someone's got to do it for her."

"And when the baby comes?" Carolyn asked.

He looked at his hands. "We still got four months to figure that out."

Carolyn sighed.

"In the meantime," he said, "I'll make sure you get paid for the next few days. Just play it cool, okay? Act a little bothered, whatever it takes to get Linda to go home."

Beneath his light tan, he was pale. He had circles under his eyes. Carolyn wasn't sure what the cause of the strain was—whether it was Linda, the company, or both—but whatever it was, it was dragging him down.

"You don't have to pay me," she said. "I got enough to cover me."

More than enough, actually. She'd sold her Los Angeles home for ten times what she'd paid for it, and bought a home in Skinner City for less than the original price of her LA place.

She added, "Just make sure I got work next week, okay?"

"Figure the Weatherly job on Monday. I'll call the contractor, tell him what's going on. I'll give you a new partner, too."

"I can do Weatherly alone," Carolyn said.

"I'm sure you can. But I'm already bending enough regulations around here. I'm not bending that one."

Then he picked up the phone, and started to dial. She didn't move. He gave her a pointed look, and she stood. As she let herself out, she heard him telling the contractor that someone had died in the Weatherly house.

The promise was easier to keep than she thought it would be. Linda was tired and wanted to go home. Apparently that little skeleton had gotten to her more than she wanted to admit.

It had gotten to Carolyn too, but she had already known that. She decided she was going to spend some time digging. Her rationale was simple: she doubted Brauder and Moin had the ability to close a case this old.

But she knew, under the surface, that her rationale was wrong. Moin probably couldn't close a cold case but Brauder could. He seemed more competent than a lot of the guys she'd worked with in LA.

Brauder and Moin probably even had the time to close it, which they wouldn't have, if the skeleton had turned up in LA. But she would wager they didn't have the desire to close it.

Neither of them had stared at those little bones as long as she had. Nor had either of them held that tiny frame in their hands. The skeleton had almost felt alive to her in that moment—a fragile thing that could dissolve into nothing if she moved wrong. When she'd wriggled out of the crawlspace, she'd balanced herself precariously just to protect the tiny corpse she'd been holding.

It was her crawlspace.

Her case.

Her baby, deep down inside.

She started with the county records, doing her own title search. The Weatherly job was the correct name for the place: A young couple named Weatherly had bought the house late last year, hired an architect, and began the remodeling.

Before that, the house had been owned by a family named Rollenston, who'd had it for forty years. They bought the house from the original owners, a family named Wolffe.

The house had been built in 1900, earlier than she'd thought, given the condition of the insulation and walls. Several additions were made in the 1920s, and one in the 1970s, which she'd spotted immediately, mostly because of that horrible pink insulation.

The original parcel of Wolffe land covered most of the neighborhood. Two blocks had been sold in the early 1930s, as the Depression was really hitting Oregon. Another block was sold in 1938 but none of it was developed until after the war.

By then, the Wolffe mansion, as it was called, still dominated more than an acre of downtown land, and some pictures the assessors office had made it seem like an island in a sea of trees.

Those trees were sold for lumber in the 1950s, and then the remaining land went in pieces after Jonathon Wolffe died. The family divided it all, selling parcel after parcel, until only the house was left.

Zoning did not allow for multifamily dwellings in that neighborhood, so the house sat until someone was willing to spring for (and live in) the entire mansion. Apparently the Rollenston's had some money in the 1960s and tried to make the place a show palace before rehabbing old houses was fashionable.

They only succeeded in making it livable, and then for only a few years. The house Carolyn had first seen, before any of the wallboard had been torn down, was in a later state of decay. Decay happened quicker in Oregon than California because of the damp climate, but still. It took some serious neglect to damage the house that badly.

She took her notes, and moved locations, this time going to the public library for their local resources and their computers.

The library was small by Los Angeles standards—only a city block wide, and two stories high. It had taken twenty years for the city to pass enough referendums to make the library this big, and while the new building was beautifully designed, it still looked more like a series of on-campus classrooms to her than a library for an entire community.

The parking lot was full, though, which always surprised her. A lot of people used the place despite its inadequacies.

After she found a parking space (near the dumpster, as far from the main door as she could get), she walked down the narrow sidewalk through the immaculate landscaping. She had only come here a few times, found waiting lists so long for the books she wanted, that she decided buying was easier. She had a computer at home, but she didn't want to have records of this search.

She didn't want to do what would have been police business in LA on her precious—and private—home computer.

The computer wing of the library was on the second floor. She walked up, the only person doing so. Everyone else took the escalator even though it was only a single flight. Immediately she was greeted by signs, telling her the regulations, reminding her she only got an hour if there was a waiting list for the machines (after which she could sign up again for another hour), and warning her she could be arrested if she used the computers to download pornography.

People dotted the space, mostly elderly types using a free internet account to write e-mail. A few younger people sat in the very back, struggling with the microfiche machines—probably doing some sort of school assignment.

She went to the desk, and got her assignment, a computer near the restrooms, not far from the newspaper reading room.

She'd start with whatever was online, and then she'd go to the harder-to-use items if she needed to, like newspapers on microfiche and books on the city history. What she was looking for first was an overview, of the city, of the Wolffes, and of the Rollenstons.

The city overview was easy to find. Skinner City had been founded in the mid-19th century as a trading town because it was right on the river. It was named for its founder, Samson Skinner, who built a small cabin near the river's low point, and ferried people across in a skiff that he carved out of logs. Gradually, loggers and fur traders and Gold Rush survivors made their way to the little village he'd founded, along with families that had made the trek across the Oregon Trail.

By the late 19th century, Skinner City had become the second largest in Oregon, and the seat of much of its wealth. The Wolffes were one of the city's most prominent families. Jeremiah Wolffe had family money and he used it to start a bank. At first, it was a convenience money lending operation, mostly for people with irregular work or irregular pay, like loggers and some of the traders. But he made so much on the usury fees—and the laws were changing—so he modified his industry into the First Bank of Skinner City.

He built his house with the proceeds. He raised a family there, and left the house to his eldest son, Jonathon. The daughters were married off with huge dowries in "society weddings" according to the local history website that Carolyn had found. Jonathon Wolffe expanded the bank to Eugene, Corvallis and other nearby towns, and made even more money.

And then the stock market collapse hit. Jonathon Wolffe had apparently leveraged the bank's assets to the hilt as he had tried to grow the company. The businesses went bankrupt, and he lost most of his personal wealth.

Somehow he kept the house, but the Wolffes were never the same after that. According to the website, they went into a steep decline and never recovered.

Carolyn couldn't find anything more specific than that, but she had found more than she expected from combing the web. She had just started looking up the Rollenston's and found only an obituary of the last Rollenston, the widow who, along with her husband, had purchased the house in the 1960s.

Her children lived out of state. She had spent her declining years alone in that house, maintaining an award-winning garden up until her last two years. Outside, apparently, the place looked perfect. But inside...

Someone came up behind Carolyn, and she resisted the urge to blank the screen. The library had the right to monitor—after all, it was their computer.

But she still jumped when a hand rested on her shoulder.

"Researching." Detective Brauder wasn't asking a question. He spoke like he expected to find her here. He pulled over a chair from the nearby, unused computer, and peered at the screen.

"You know," he said, "none of this matters until we know the age of the skeleton."

She logged off even though she didn't have to, then looked at him. His eyes twinkled, and he didn't seem at all put out that she had been snooping on his case.

"You've been researching too," she said.

"Yep. I was right over there—" he nodded toward the microfiche "—when you came in."

"You could've told me earlier that you were looking this stuff up," she said.

"Two pairs of eyes are better than one," he said.

"What about Moin?" she asked.

He snorted. "Moin? You want to know about Moin?"

"I suspect I already do. Showboater, likes flashy cases, likes getting his name in the paper, prefers not to do legwork. How'm I so far?"

"Batting 100," Brauder said. "I'm supposed to settle him down. I'm just waiting until he screws up or gets transferred."

"Didn't you tell him that solving a cold case sometimes gets more coverage than current cases?"

"Not here," Brauder said. "Most cases get a lot of coverage. We're tiny, remember?"

"Not tiny exactly," she aid. "The second-largest city in Oregon."

"If you don't count Eugene-Springfield as one place," he said.

"Which most people do."

They grinned at each other, and she felt giddy, like a schoolgirl. She hadn't felt like that in years.

She made herself look away. Their conversation didn't seem to bother anyone. All the other patrons were either staring at the computer screens or reading magazines, books, or newspapers at nearby tables. No one seemed to whisper any more, not even her. Modern libraries apparently weren't as sacred as the ones she'd grown up in.

"You find anything promising?" she asked him.

"Hell," he said. "I'm overwhelmed by it all. There's so much information on that house that I could write a book about the damned thing."

"Which is why you're going to wait for the tests," she said.

"The forensic anthropologist at the U of O should be able to give us a preliminary date for those bones," he said. "After that, it's anybody's guess."

"What about the newspapers?" she asked.

He frowned.

"You were looking up the newspapers that the baby'd been found in. Did you find anything?"

His gaze met hers, and she could tell she'd surprised him. "How'd you know that?"

"You were working in microfiche. I didn't recognize you from the back. I thought you were with the students. So, since you were doing microfiche, I'm assuming you looked up the family history just like I did, and I'm assuming you probably knew the city history, so you got more done. You figured the best place to start with all this overwhelming information was a full examination of the papers we found in the crawl-space, just to see if there was something in them, something of importance."

"Jeez," he said. "You're good. How'd they let you get away?"

That shuddery feeling came back, and she had to fight to keep her hand away from the scars on her abdomen. She swallowed hard, unable to answer him.

He nodded, as if he understood. His hand found her shoulder again, and this time, she didn't jump.

"Chicago," he said.

It took a moment for the word to register. Then it seemed like she had missed part of the conversation.

"Chicago?"

He nodded. "From 1975 to 1995. Even worked the South Side for a while. That's like working Watts."

"I know," she said, finally understanding him. "You left."

"I fled." He smiled, but his gaze didn't meet hers. "This is my eighth homicide case since signing on with Skinner City. Two were drug-related and easily solved. Four were domestics. One was serial. That was the only case that took any time at all."

"Did you catch him?" she asked.

Brauder nodded. He was looking at the computer screen, but he clearly didn't see it. He saw whatever horrors the serial had reintroduced for him, horrors that he probably wished he could get out of his mind.

"Why do you stay?" she asked.

He squeezed her shoulder and then stood. The faraway expression remained on his face, but he looked at her as he smiled.

"I can't install insulation," he said.

"Neither could I when I first got here," she said.

"And look where it's led," he said, and tapped the screen. "Right back where you started."

"I'm nowhere near where I started." She knew she sounded defensive, but she couldn't help it. "I actually have the time to spend in the library."

He let go of her shoulder. "And not even on your own case."

She braced herself for the Don't Get Involved lecture. But it didn't come.

Instead, he said, "You had dinner yet?"

She looked at his rugged face, the world-weary eyes, and knew she should say no. She didn't need to get this close to her old habits.

"Not yet," she said, and let him help her to her feet.

They went to an Italian restaurant that wasn't mediocre like most of Skinner City's high-end food. The staff seemed to know Brauder, and Carolyn got the sense he came here every night.

They didn't talk about the case. They shared cop stories and her stomach didn't even twist. They talked about moving from a major city to a place that called itself a city because it was so small no one else would recognize its city-ness otherwise. They talked about the differences between Oregon and Illinois, Oregon and California.

And finally, over the best tiramisu she'd had in years, she said, "How come you're not warning me off this case?"

His smile faded, and he set down the coffee cup he'd been holding. "You mean give you the old meddling private detective speech?"

"Yeah," she said.

"You're not meddling."

"I pulled the skeleton out of its cubby," she said.

"And we wouldn't've found it otherwise."

"Some would call that tampering with evidence."

"I suppose," he said. "But you didn't. Any other insulation installer would've done the same."

She nodded, conceding that point to him.

"And," he added, grabbing his fork and cutting a piece from her tiramisu, as if they were old friends, "you're not a private detective. Are you?"

She laughed. "If you know my opinion of private dicks, you wouldn't ask."

"I think the nickname is enough," he said, grinning.

"You have to know that if I went back to investigating, I'd do it with justice on my side."

"Justice," he said, as if he caught her use of the word just as she did. She had meant to say "the law," but the law didn't always provide justice. In fact, as her last and best shrink said, in her cases, the law rarely provided justice at all. "You think people can still get justice?"

"No," she said quietly. "That's why I do what I do."

"I don't see the connection," he said.

"I make sure they stay warm in the winter," she said, "and cool in the summer. I help people save a little money on their electric bills every year. I take care of very small things, so I don't have to think about the big ones."

He studied her for a minute. "Well," he said, his tone as subdued as hers had been. "I still do believe in justice. And that's why I'll take your help."

"Any help'll do, huh?" She meant the sentence to be light, but it came out bitter.

"If any help would do," he said, "I'd give the research part to Moin."

"Instead, you're going to let him handle the cameras."

He smiled. This was a real smile, and it softened his face, made him seem less chiseled. "Let's hope there are cameras, because that means we've solved it."

We. As in him and her. As in their case. She didn't object because there was no reason to. It was their case.

Brauder called her the next day as if she were his partner instead of Moin. The forensic anthropologist had a timeline.

The bones were old, preserved in that basement environment. The anthropologist would have to call in an expert in human skeletal systems, someone who actually dated very old bones, but the U of O guy hazarded a guess.

He said sometime between 1920 and the mid-1970s. When Brauder pressed for the reason for the dates, the anthropologist had given him a one-word answer. *Lead*.

"Lead?" Carolyn asked. She'd met Brauder in one of those fancy Starbucks wannabe places near the library.

"He tested a small segment of bone to see if there was anything unusual about the composition. Apparently exposure to all kinds of chemicals shows up and stays in the bones."

She had known that once. She might even have known about the lead. It wasn't something she paid much attention to. Everyone who grew up in that time period had an elevated lead content in their bones.

"Not lead poisoning, then," she said.

"Not enough to kill the kid or make her nuts or whatever lead poisoning does," Brauder said. "Just enough to confirm that this baby wasn't born after 1980."

"Even if she was born in that house and ate lead chips or whatever," Carolyn said, trying to understand.

"She was too young to get chips on her own," Brauder said. "He says this is just the result of exposure."

Carolyn got up. She had to walk to think. She went back to the counter, ordered as regular a coffee as you could get in these places, because ordering a normal coffee drove the so-called baristas crazy, got it, put sugar in it, and carried it back to the table.

Brauder was balancing his chair on its two back legs. He looked comfortable, as if being on an edge were his natural state.

"Okay," Carolyn said as she sat down. "Let's say I accept this 'expert'" —and she was beginning to doubt he was one, but then, she was used to the best in the field, not the folks who moonlighted for the police department because they were the only people available—"how did he pinpoint 1920? If I remember right, paint was lead-based back to DaVinci."

"I don't know about DaVinci," Brauder said, rocking his chair ever so slightly. "But I do know that lead paint's been around longer than this town. So I asked."

Carolyn's coffee was too hot to sip. She grabbed the plastic water glass she'd gotten earlier at the sugar table and poured melting ice into the cup. "And?"

"And he said that bones older than 1920 would've disintegrated. He suspects that bones from 1920 wouldn't be around either in that environment, but he didn't know for sure, so the back end of his estimate is pretty iffy. I tried to pin him down, but he wouldn't pin. He's sticking with 1920 to the mid-seventies."

"Not 1980," Carolyn said.

"No," Brauder said. "There was something else, some other chemical whose name I literally can't remember that was banned earlier that's also in the body. That's why he's saying mid-seventies at the latest, although he wouldn't rule out sixties either."

"Jeez," Carolyn said, deliberately making herself sound like a hick. "You'd think this expert of yours could be a little more precise."

Brauder grinned. "We get what we pay for."

"He *volunteered*?" she asked.

"He wants to move away from the university. He needs credentials more than money."

Carolyn sighed. "No wonder his estimate is so vague. There's less chance of being wrong."

Brauder shrugged. "It helps, though. It takes the last twenty-five to thirty years out of the equation."

"Which doesn't quite rule out the Rollenstons," Carolyn said.

"Not quite," Brauder said, "but they had sons, not daughters, and those boys were under ten."

"So?" Carolyn asked.

"So there's no record of the Rollenstons having a child in the ten years we cover here."

"Home birth, maybe," Carolyn said.

"Maybe," Brauder said, "but it wasn't that common in the sixties. In those days, women had to go to the hospital. Home births came back in the late 1960s, along with midwifery, and that was with the younger set, not with already established middle-class women."

Carolyn sipped her coffee. This time it was cool enough to taste. She frowned just a little. Real coffee in these places, without the milk or the fizz or the sugar, tasted burned.

"Okay," she said. "You're thinking it's not the Rollenstons themselves. It's not the boys or their girlfriends because the boys were too young at the time. A babysitter?"

"I don't think the death is that modern," he said.

"Because of the newspaper article?" she asked.

"Because of that blanket," he said. "It looked 1940s to me."

"I thought it was a baby garment," she said, and frowned. He was right. The duck did have a pre-1950s look.

"Whatever," he said. "The papers might be insulation. They were really old. But that garment..."

"Maybe a hand-me-down?" she asked.

"Maybe," he said. "But I don't think so."

"You have a suspect," she said.

He shook his head. "I have a theory."

"Give," she said.

"I think a baby would be missed," he said.

She grabbed the hot paper cup, letting the heat sink into her fingers. Missed, even when they didn't become viable. Missed like missed opportunities, like potential ghosts, futures that never were, lives not quite lived.

"You think someone knows about this," she said.

He shook his head. "The baby was in a crawlspace, not in a grave."

"So?" she said.

"So we don't have harsh winters here. No need to put something in the basement because the ground is frozen."

She frowned. That hadn't even occurred to her. The product of being an LA homicide detective versus a Chicago one.

Then her brain clicked. She understood where he was going.

"Even if the baby had been born at home," she said, "someone would have noticed if it was missing."

He smiled as if she were a particularly bright student.

"So you're looking for a period when the house was mostly empty."

"Yeah," he said.

"We know that it was mostly empty after the boys left in the Rollenston family," Carolyn said, "but that's too late. So we're looking at the Wolffes."

He brought his chair forward with a snap. His knees banged the table, making the move seem more awkward than he probably intended.

"My research wasn't complete enough," she said. "All I know is that the son of the original owners held the house in 1929 and started selling off pieces in the 1930s."

"To the disgust of his sisters," Brauder said, "but they couldn't do anything."

"Was he married?" she asked. "I never saw anything about a wedding."

"Yeah," Brauder said. "His wife died in 1920. Giving birth to a daughter."

"A daughter," Carolyn said, "who would've been in her teens in the 1930s."

"Alone in the house with a father who was losing everything."

"Wait," Carolyn said. "I thought the Wolffes owned the house until the mid-1960s."

"They did," Brauder said. "Daddy remarried in 1939. The new bride had some cash. And was fertile enough to give him two sons."

"What about the daughter?" Carolyn asked.

"Joined up in early 1942. Served overseas in one of those female military units they're always talking about on the *Discovery Channel*. She came back decorated. Some kind of above-and-beyond thing. Never married, though."

Carolyn sighed. "And the boys?"

"Military school for one in the 1950s."

"And the other?" Carolyn asked.

"College in New York. He never came back."

"Leaving his parents alone in the house," Carolyn said.

"Until the Rollenstons bought it."

"But the new wife would've been too old to have children," Carolyn said.

"Maybe," he said.

Carolyn swirled the coffee in her cup. The stuff tasted too awful to drink and she wasn't going to get milk or add sugar.

"We have two time periods, then," she said. "The mid-1930s and the late 1950s to early 1960s. The later period seems more likely to me, even if she was at the end of her fertile years."

"She sold the house the minute the old man died. The boys didn't seem to care. The New York son never even came home for the funeral."

Carolyn frowned at Brauder. "Now how did you learn that?" she asked.

He grinned. "You haven't learned about small towns yet, have you?"

"This is a small *city*," she reminded him.

"Same difference," he said. "But the thing is, someone always remembers the juicy stuff."

"You already asked about a disappearing baby."

"And got nothing," he said. "but I did get the funeral story and the remarriage, and the unhappy sons."

"What happened to the one in the military academy?" Carolyn asked.

Brauder's smile faded. "Vietnam."

Carolyn set her cup down. "Did he come home?"

"You could say that," Brauder said, "but he left the better part of himself in those jungles."

"The gossips told you that too?" she asked.

"Didn't have to," Brauder said, and grabbed his own coffee cup, as if he were seeking comfort. "I've met him several times. I just didn't know it."

"How could you not know it?" Carolyn asked.

"People who live under the Eighth Avenue Bridge usually don't give you their last name when you roust them to homeless shelters on cold nights."

"My God," Carolyn said. "I suppose he's the last Wolffe left."

"No," Brauder said. "His brother's still alive."

"And wants nothing to do with him."

"No," Brauder said gently. "He wants nothing to do with anyone."

She raised her eyes to his. "PTSD."

"Spoken like a vet," he said quietly.

"Of a different kind of war," she said.

He nodded, twirling his cup between his fingers. He couldn't say anything after that, she knew, not without confessing to his own nightmares. And cops didn't do that, particularly cops still on the job.

"So what's the plan, coach?" she asked.

He raised his head. His eyes held more compassion than she liked. If he said something about her last statement, she'd leave. Hell, if he touched her, she'd leave. She hadn't signed on to this little investigation to get healed. She'd signed on because she was curious and had a few days off.

"The plan," he said, "is simple, but time-consuming. First we do a little DNA testing, and while we wait, we mine this town for gossip."

"No one's going to talk to me," Carolyn said. "I don't have a badge and I'm too new."

"We can fix the badge part," he said.

She shook her head. "How long does DNA testing take in this state?"

"Months," he said, "unless you know somebody."

"And you know somebody."

"I know a lot of somebodys," he said. "We'll have it in a few days."

"How *CSI* of you," she said, trying to hide her disappointment. A few days was nearing the end of her voluntary layoff. She really wouldn't be able to help as much when she went back to work. "So I'm off for a few days."

"Don't back out on me now," he said. "I still need you."

"For what?" she asked. "Assaulting little old ladies on the street, demanding gossip?"

"Reading the society papers," he said. "Remember those?"

"Yeah," she said. "I also remember that they didn't publish negative news."

"That's right," he said. "But they did publish the comings and goings of the town's most prominent women."

Carolyn let out a small laugh. This was the kind of work she would have passed off on a lower pay grade. Of course, at the moment she was a lower pay grade. She got nothing from this but satisfaction.

"You want me to find emptiness," she said.

"You got it. Nine to twelve months of no news," he said.

"That's if the Wolffes were still prominent enough to hit the society pages in the 1950s," she said.

"They would be. And I want you to look through the entire period. As well as any nuisance suits or missing servants."

Carolyn frowned. "You think the father impregnated someone who worked at the house? Why wouldn't she just take care of it herself?"

"Abortion laws—"

"I'm not talking about abortion," Carolyn said. "There were all kinds of homes for pregnant women to wait out a birth. And a lot of women just married someone else..."

She let her voice trail off. The society pages again. In a town this small, all births got recorded in the paper, just like the deaths did.

"That's a lot of cross-referencing," she said, "particularly if you want me to go back to 1920."

"It is," he said. "Which is why I think you should start with the 1960s and work backwards."

"While you talk to the little old ladies," Carolyn said.

"I've found that men are the worse gossips when it comes to this sort of thing," he said.

"Babies?" Carolyn snorted. "You've got to be kidding."

"Rich guys getting their comeuppance, losing their fortunes, getting their just desserts." Brauder's eyes twinkled. "The Wolffes were prominent long enough that they had to have made a lot of enemies, who would have rejoiced at every little tidbit of the long, slow decline."

"Why don't you just ask the homeless Wolffe?" Carolyn asked.

"His name is David," Brauder said. "And I plan to at the same time as I get him to offer up a bit of his DNA."

Library research, Carolyn found, was a lot more stimulating than she thought it would be. It also was a lot more dangerous. Not in the PTSD way nor in the old habits way, not even in a life-and-death kind of way.

It was dangerous because of all the side roads she could take. Other news stories catching her eye, ads that reminded her how different the world she'd been born into was from the world she lived in now.

She could almost believe that people were more naïve then, that the world was a safer place. Then she looked at the front pages, saw the beginnings of the Vietnam War, the Cuban Missile Crisis, and Kennedy's assassination, and realized that nostalgia was a trap. That world was no safer.

Births and deaths were her main focus, but she kept an eye out for the occasional catty remark, the emptiness that Brauder had been talking about. She found that she could work for hours without standing up, and she finally had to set a timer on her watch, just so that she would walk around.

Her mind got lost in the 1960s, and she was just edging into the 1950s when her cell phone buzzed against her hip. She unhooked the phone from its clip, staring at the display. She had expected a call from Brauder, but this one was from Linda.

Carolyn answered, whispered, "Hold on," even though no one seemed to care about talking loudly in this library, and headed to the stairwell. Reception was poorer here, but she felt like she could speak freely.

"Sorry," she said. "I'm in the library."

Linda didn't even ask why. "Cartwright's sending me home. Half pay. How the hell am I supposed to survive on half pay?"

"You've got savings," Carolyn said because they'd already had that discussion.

"That's for the baby's birth," Linda said, "not for some stupid bed rest."

"Who ordered bed rest?" Carolyn said, truly surprised.

"No one," Linda said. "It's just that he made me see some doctor, says he's worried about me."

"We're all worried about you," Carolyn said. "This is no job for a pregnant woman."

"Like you can talk," Linda snapped. "You worked."

Carolyn felt her breath catch. She had told Linda about her pregnancy a long time ago.

"I worked," Carolyn said after she recovered her breath. "And see where that got me."

"You said the job had nothing to do with the loss. You said the people on the job saved you," Linda said.

They did save her. Her partner had taken her to emergency over her own protests. No one could've saved the baby—which really wasn't a baby yet. Just a mass of cells growing in her fallopian tube, not even in her womb.

That unlucky accident had nothing to do with her police work. The fact that she had nearly passed out twice, had felt vaguely ill for more than a month, and had done nothing about it, just reported to work every day like she had no value otherwise, did have something to do with the job.

Maybe if she had gone in early, maybe if she had seen an ob/gyn when the symptoms first appeared, then she might have saved her body. She'd still be fertile. She wouldn't've nearly died.

She wouldn't have had time for all the worries, the fears, and the memories to catch up to her.

"And they did save you, right?" Linda said.

Carolyn blinked. The stairwell was cold. A small window over the landing let in some real light, but not enough to counteract the fluorescent.

"It's not the same," she said.

"Everyone says that," Linda said. "They never mean it. They mean *do what the doctor tells you, Linda*, like he knows what he's doing."

"He knows more than we do," Carolyn said.

"So you're on his side now?" Linda snapped.

"I've always been on his side. You need to take care of yourself. You need to get away from the chemicals."

"I've been in them for fifteen years. A few months isn't going to make a difference."

"You're not a developing fetus," Carolyn said. "It might make all the difference in the world."

The silence on the other end lasted so long that Carolyn would have thought Linda hung up, if it weren't for the slight hum in the line.

Finally, Linda said, "I don't want to go home. I don't exist when I'm at home."

Carolyn gripped the phone so tightly that her hand hurt. She remembered that feeling, that always-keep-moving feeling, which her last and best shrink said was not a precursor to the PTSD, but the mark of someone who never learned how to be alone.

"So go to the library. Go to a movie. Read up on babies. Take a class."

"The doc said I should rest."

"Rest out of the house," Carolyn said. "He didn't order you to your bed, did he?"

"No," Linda said. "Just to stay off my feet as much as possible. I'll turn into a balloon."

"You're supposed to turn into a balloon," Carolyn said. "You're pregnant."

Again, the long silence. Carolyn looked through the glass diamonds in the metal doors. No one had taken her microfiche chair. In fact, she was the only one on the microfiche machines today. Perhaps because school wasn't out yet.

"Hell," Carolyn said, "I'll take you to three movies a week, if you promise not to whine about being out of the loop."

"Two movies and I get to whine."

"Three," Carolyn said, "starting Monday."

Linda sighed. "Will Cartwright hire me back?"

"I thought he didn't lay you off. You said something about half pay."

"What'm I gonna do, Carolyn? I'm all alone here."

Carolyn knew better than to mention the baby's father. The baby's father had fled the moment he heard about the pregnancy. He didn't want to pay for the child, and he didn't want to pay for an abortion either. He disappeared, and although Carolyn offered to track him down, she was glad when Linda told her not to.

"You're not alone," Carolyn said. "You got me."

"You can't baby-sit. You work all day. And you can't afford to pay for things."

"I can help you find a good daycare. I can contribute a little. I'm not hurting."

Linda sniffled. "You'd do that?"

"Only if you stay home, like Cartwright said."

"I thought you said I could rest out of the house," Linda said.

"I did." Carolyn smiled. "You know what I mean."

"First movie on Monday," Linda said. "I pick."

"No whining," Carolyn said.

"As long as you don't complain about the movie even if it stinks."

"Deal," Carolyn said, and hung up. She went back inside. Her seat had cooled, but the image on the screen remained the same, a hand-drawn lingerie ad from 1959, which made the woman look like she was about to go into battle.

Carolyn sighed and started through the papers again. But her mind was on Linda. The loneliness, the fear. Carolyn had felt that much. She'd guessed about her own pregnancy and to her everlasting regret, she'd never seen anyone about it.

But she didn't want to talk about the baby's father, not even then. She hadn't known who the father was. There were a lot of candidates. In her quest to stay away from her apartment and not think about her job, she'd found a lot of men willing to help.

Half of them she never knew by name.

She almost didn't notice when the phone buzzed again. And this time, it was Brauder. He left a text message, asking her to meet him at his favorite Italian restaurant for dinner.

Even though he didn't specify the restaurant by name, she knew which restaurant he meant. And she was a little disappointed in herself to note that she looked forward to the dinner all afternoon.

Carolyn was early. The waiter who escorted her to her table called her "Mr. Brauder's lady," and she let him make that assumption. Better than telling him they were here to talk about crime scenes and dead children and ancient history.

The restaurant was busy but not packed. People lined the walls, each table enough distant from the other that they didn't seem like they were sharing dinner with strangers. Carolyn appreciated that. She also appreciated the low lighting, which took some of the flaws that age was adding to her features and softened them.

Brauder came in a few minutes after she did. He looked tired and his usually perfect hair was out-of-place. His suit was a little mussed, as if he had changed coats but hadn't looked into a mirror. When he saw her, he gave her a distracted smile.

"Long day?" she asked.

"Domestic," he said. "It'll be on the late news."

"How many dead?" she asked.

He shook his head. "Only one."

"The wife," she said.

He nodded.

"How many children?"

"Four," he said. "The oldest got out and called 911. Saved everyone but his mom."

"Christ," she said. She stopped the waiter and ordered wine. It wasn't a solution, but it would help. "I'm sorry."

"Don't be." Brauder raised his head, ran a hand through that gorgeous hair, and sighed. "It'll be a pleasure to put that bastard through the wringer."

"Shouldn't you be doing that tonight?"

"No need. He's lawyered up. We're going to use statements, the neighbors who're happy to talk, and the family to put him away. After he sweats a little."

She remembered those. She remembered the feeling, the sick exhaustion and the unhappiness mixed with elation that a criminal—a violent, horrible individual—would finally be off the streets.

The waiter brought the wine, and Brauder ordered for both of them, something in Italian that wasn't on the menu. Usually Carolyn hated it when a date did that, but she didn't see this as a date, and besides, she had a hunch he was ordering comfort food, without much regard to her.

"So," he said, "Got DNA results back."

"On the cold case? That's awfully quick," she said.

"Told you I knew someone," he said.

"Who must be a miracle worker."

"We had familial DNA to compare it to," he said, "which cut some time off the lab work. They didn't have to run it through CODIS or anything."

So David Wolffe had given up some saliva. Apparently he wasn't worried about the baby's identity. Or maybe he just didn't care.

"And," Brauder said, "it matched. The baby's a Wolffe."

Carolyn let out a small sigh. She was glad they had guessed correctly.

"Is it David's child?" she asked.

Brauder shook his head. "Not enough points in common. But this is a sibling maybe or a cousin. I've got it on the report, but it's not all in my head any more. I had a distraction this afternoon."

She remembered when she called things like a domestic homicide which had clearly included a hostage situation a distraction. It was amazing Brauder remembered as much as he had.

"Did you bring the report?" she asked.

"Forgot it," he said

She nodded.

"I can show you tomorrow."

"Did David know anything about a lost baby?" she asked.

Brauder blinked, then frowned.

"You didn't ask," she said.

The waiter dropped off some garlic bread. Brauder took a piece. His hand was shaking.

"He thought I was talking about Vietnam," Brauder said. "He told me most of the babies were lost."

Carolyn winced, then changed the subject. She knew better than to press any more. Dinner was mostly silent, with Brauder reviewing his day, and Carolyn trying to figure out ways to distract him.

She paid the bill, and then drove him home. His house, a neat bungalow on Skinner City's east side, looked as lonely as her LA home used to. She almost turned around and took him to her house, but thought the better of it.

She liked him, but she wasn't ready to bring that kind of energy into the house. She still needed her privacy.

And he needed some sleep.

When he called her the following afternoon to thank her, she was ready for him. Before Brauder could say anything, she said, "The child's a niece, isn't she?"

"I didn't tell you that last night, did I? I thought I said cousin."

"You did," she said. "But I figure niece."

She told him her reasoning. For the child to have been a Wolffe and a sibling, Jonathon Wolffe would have had to have had another child in the 1930s and kept it in the house. But to be a cousin would've been harder, since the daughters of the original owner had moved out before 1920, and they would have had to come back, with child, to leave that baby in the crawlspace.

The child had to be either his brother's daughter or the older sister's child.

Then Carolyn told Brauder that she had found the gap they'd been looking for. She'd skipped around in her research to the 1930s.

"The girl who stayed," he said. "The one whose mother died in childbirth."

"Her name was Belle," Carolyn said. "She was supposed to have a great coming out. A debut, they called it in those days. Her father called it off, said he didn't have the money."

"That's not a gap," Brauder said.

"It is when in every other interview, Jonathon Wolffe claimed they had no money problems at all."

"This was before he married the heiress?" Brauder asked.

"Three years before," Carolyn said, "and his daughter disappeared for two of those years. She had her picture taken at the society wedding, looking sad and sallow and fatter than she had in earlier pictures."

"This is the girl who joined up in World War II, right?" he asked.

"Yeah," Carolyn said, "and after she returned, the papers always referred to her as Wolffe's eccentric daughter."

"Because of her war service," Brauder said.

"Because," Carolyn said, "she seemed more than a little off."

In those days, "more than a little off" didn't make the papers. Families tried to hide their eccentric aunts and cousins and daughters. But Belle Wolffe's behavior was so off that no one protected her, not even her father.

She wrote letters to the editor, denouncing everything from the war to the mayor. She took trips and came home early. She tried teaching at the local college and got fired for slapping one of the students.

Then the news about her stopped. No one mentioned her after the oldest Wolffe boy was born. She wasn't in the photographs, and she didn't show up in her father's obituary—Carolyn went back and checked.

It wasn't that Belle Wolffe had died. She wasn't mentioned at all, as if she hadn't existed, as if she hadn't even been a member of the family.

So Carolyn did a little investigating of her own. It didn't take much searching to find that Belle Wolffe was still alive and living in Oregon.

The surprise was that she had been nearby all along.

Belle Wolffe lived in a house she'd owned since 1947 in nearby Simon's Grove. Simon's Grove was now part of Skinner City, but once upon a time, it had been a faraway place, a separate town that people from Skinner City never went to.

The house records were easy to find; they showed that Belle's father Jonathon had initially bought the property and then deeded it to her.

Brauder found David Wolffe, the homeless son, one last time. It seemed he did remember his "dotty" sister Belle and how she'd been banished from the family shortly before his older brother was born.

That made Carolyn as curious as it made Brauder. He picked her up from the county building, where she'd been digging in the records, seeing if she could find anything official on Belle Wolffe.

Nothing had turned up outside of the deed to the house. What little else Carolyn had found, she had found on-line, doing a search from a web café because she had known she'd have to use a non-restrictive server.

Belle Wolffe had a government military pension—not enough to live on, in Carolyn's opinion, but then Carolyn hadn't owned a house outright until this year. Belle also got social security and Medicare and interest income from a trust that her father had set up for her about the time he bought the house.

Carolyn told Brauder all of this as they drove to Simon's Grove.

"Someone knew," Carolyn said.

"We're getting ahead of ourselves," Brauder said.

Carolyn looked at him sideways. He drove with one hand balanced on the base of the steering wheel, the other resting on the door handle as if he expected to jump out at any moment. His mouth was set in a thin line.

He believed the same thing she did, he just didn't want to say it. Not yet. He didn't want to jinx the interview.

She didn't push it. She knew better than to discuss the case any farther. They'd interview the old woman and then they'd come to some kind of conclusion.

Whether they'd find a resolution would be another matter altogether.

The house was a small bungalow, made from a converted carriage house down the road from a nearby Victorian mansion. The mansion was long gone, a victim of Skinner City's expansion and someone's greed for land, but the carriage house remained. The 1940s remodel did little to hide its humble origins.

It sat in the middle of a grove of ancient trees, with trunks so large that Carolyn couldn't put her arms around them. The trees towered over the place and probably made it dark inside.

A white picket fence, newly painted, separated the house from the road. On the other side of the fence, a path wound its way through a thick garden. The house was at the end of the path, the arched doorway dark and forbidding.

Almost like a house out of a fairy tale.

Carolyn suppressed a shudder as she got out of the car. This was too isolated for her. Much as she appreciated her space, she didn't want this kind. The privacy here was so complete no one would know if the house had an occupant at all. And if something had happened to that occupant, no one would know for a very, very long time.

"The gate's latched," Brauder said as he reached over one of the pickets and unhooked it. The gate didn't squeak as he pushed it open. It was amazingly well kept up.

The entire yard was, which surprised Carolyn. She had expected a neglected house, but anything that an eighty-five-year-old woman could reach seemed to be in immaculate condition.

Brauder looked large on the path, like a giant entering fairyland.

Carolyn followed, noting the scents of roses mixing with lilacs and rich loam. Oregon smells, which were still a tad too rich for her California nose.

Brauder had to stand on the lower step, then crouch to knock on the door. The arch was too low. If he'd stood on the stoop, he would have hit his head.

"Just leave it on the porch," a woman said through a powerful intercom.

Brauder looked for it, then as Carolyn was about to point it out, he found it, plastered against the wall—a 1970s addition that looked old and out of place.

"Sorry to disturb you, ma'am. I'm Detective Brauder with the Skinner City police."

There was a clunk as if someone had shut off the intercom. Carolyn frowned, wondering if the old woman would just leave them standing here. Then a small opening appeared in the center of the door—a large peephole, the round fist-sized kind, the kind put on mansions in the late 19th century, not on remodeled carriage houses in the 1940s.

"Prove it," the woman said.

Brauder removed his badge and held it up to the circle. Carolyn mentally applauded the woman for her toughness. A lot of other people would simply have opened the door.

The peephole slammed closed, followed by the sound of deadbolts opening. Finally, the door opened.

The woman behind it hadn't bent with age. She stood very straight. She had broad shoulders and wore a pants suit that had gone out of style fifty years before. That she still fit into it seemed like something Carolyn wanted to applaud.

The woman's face was wrinkled, but not outrageously so, and her hair was steel gray, pulled away from her features into a tight bun. Her eyes glittered with annoyance and her mouth, in a permanent downturn, seemed to turn down even farther.

"What do you want?" she snapped.

"Are you Belle Wolffe?" Brauder asked.

"Yes," the woman said.

"May we come in?" Brauder said. "This isn't something to be discussed on the porch."

She looked at him, then at Carolyn. Her lips pursed just a little as if they were forming the word no, but instead she said, "All right."

Brauder had to duck as he followed Belle inside. Carolyn followed, feeling like an afterthought. She closed the door, not surprised to find the house as dark as she imagined.

The walls had no photographs or artwork, but the table near the door was covered with lilacs, obviously taken from the garden. More flowers lined the route that led into the living room, some potted plants and others clearly plucked stood in tall vases. The effect was stunning and chaotic; somehow Belle had managed to continue her garden inside as well as out.

The living room was barely as big as Carolyn's bedroom, but the arched ceiling and open beams made it seem larger. An overstuffed chair sat by the fireplace, with books piled beside the table. A couch, wrapped in a yellowing plastic, looked dusty and unused. There was no television, but a radio console—the kind that had been expensive furniture in the 1930s—stood where the television should have been. Classical music from the local NPR station poured out of the speakers.

"As you can see," Belle said, nodding at her couch, "I don't usually have visitors."

"We won't take much of your time." Brauder folded his hands in front of him.

Belle sighed. "Sit down, then."

Brauder eyed the couch as if it might bite him, then walked over to it. Carolyn matched his step, careful not to kick over a series of potted violets that looked like starts being nurtured in the humid warmth.

She resisted the urge to dust off the plastic before she sat. The plastic crackled, just like she remembered from similar set-ups in her childhood, and particles from hair to dander to dirt rose up around her.

Brauder sat down beside her, but remained perched on the edge of the couch, as if he were afraid of hurting it.

"Ma'am," he said, "did you—"

"It's miss," Belle said.

"Um, Miss," he said, clearly thrown. "are you familiar with the house at 75 River Lane?"

"Familiar?" Belle said. "I was born there."

"How long did you live there?" he asked.

Her eyes narrowed. "Why? Did something happen to it?"

"It's being remodeled," Carolyn said. "Have you seen it?"

"How could I?" Belle asked. "I don't drive."

"In the remodeling," Brauder said, "we made a discovery."

He seemed to have his feet under him again. Belle had shaken him initially, but now he seemed to know how to handle her.

Carolyn let him. She watched Belle instead.

Belle had literally frozen. She didn't even ask what kind of discovery. She just waited.

"We found a baby's corpse," Brauder said.

He didn't even say skeleton. Corpse was a better word, Carolyn thought. It brought a clearer image, probably brought back some of the past.

Belle remained frozen, except for her eyes, which darted from Brauder to Carolyn and back again.

Not enough to prove guilt, but enough for any good investigator to know he was on the right track.

"The child died in the 1930s," Brauder said, even though he had no real proof of that. Only Carolyn's guesses and the vague report of an inadequate forensic anthropologist. "It was a few months old."

Belle's lips moved ever so slightly, but she didn't say anything.

"We had the child—a girl—tested. She's a Wolffe."

"How could you know that?" Belle snapped.

"DNA," Brauder said. "Your brother David let us test him. The child is clearly part of your family."

Belle's eyes narrowed. "So?"

"So," Brauder said, "we were wondering if you knew what had happened to the child and how it got into the crawlspace of the house?"

"I don't know anything," Belle said.

Brauder glanced at Carolyn, silently asking her to speak. She realized then that he wanted her there as a softening agent, one woman to another.

"Perhaps your father had a girlfriend," Carolyn said. "Or maybe his second wife..."

"I don't know anything," Belle said again.

"It was the thirties," Carolyn said. "The Depression. Times were hard."

"Times were impossible," Belle snapped, "especially if you were pretending to be rich."

"Like your father was," Carolyn said. "He wanted you to marry for money, didn't he?"

"He did that just fine on his own," Belle said.

"Years after the baby," Brauder said, and Carolyn could have kicked him. This woman needed that softer approach. He'd just blown it.

"I don't know anything about a baby," Belle said with such firmness that she had to be lying. Her lack of shock proved that.

"Your brother says you weren't allowed in the house after they were born."

"My brother?" Belle asked. "David said that?"

"Yes," Brauder said.

"How would he know?" she asked. "We've never met."

"Your father gave you this house to keep you away from his family, didn't he?"

"He gave me this house so that I wouldn't bother his nasty little wife," Belle said. "I embarrassed all of them."

"Because you didn't like her?"

"Because I served in the war," Belle said.

"They were embarrassed by that?" Carolyn asked with shock that she actually felt.

Belle gave her a level stare, one that implied that Carolyn was incredibly stupid. "I have more medals than all the men in my family combined," she said. "That bothered them."

Carolyn nodded. "Fragile male egos."

"Don't try to kiss up to me," Belle said. "I don't 'bond.' And I don't like to be played. I know nothing about a baby. Your visit here is wasted."

Her words were so sharp, spoken in a tone so pointed, that they actually seemed harsher than they were.

Brauder was about to speak, but Carolyn was afraid he'd antagonize

Belle more. "We came to identify that baby," she said before he could get his sentence out.

"I told you, I don't know anything." Belle stood. She was clearly going to usher them to the door.

"We'd like you to take a DNA test," Carolyn said. "That way we can figure out how the child is related to your family."

"Get out," Belle said. "And make sure none of your kind ever comes back."

"None of your kind," Brauder said as he got into the car. "That's a phrase I've never heard before."

"She is tough," Carolyn said.

Brauder glanced at her. "You sound like you liked her."

"Hell, no," Carolyn said. "She's cold and empty and it's probably good she lives alone."

"But?" Brauder said as he started the ignition.

"She's interesting," Carolyn said. "I have a hunch that much solitude would drive me batty."

"How do you know it didn't do the same to her?" Brauder asked.

They went back to the station. Brauder had Carolyn join him in an evidence room. A tech vacuumed their clothes for lint and hair. Belle Wolffe had lived alone for a long time. By her own admission, she didn't have visitors. Any DNA found in the house would be hers and hers only.

Brauder wasn't sure it was the kind of evidence that would hold up in court but Carolyn knew without him saying a word that court was a distant, if not impossible, option. They didn't know how the child had died, let alone exactly when it had died.

All they could hope for was an identification, and maybe, a confession.

The identification came from the lab a week later. The child was Belle's daughter.

The confession was the oblique kind.

When Brauder picked Carolyn up the day after she'd completed her part of the Weatherly job, he took her to Belle's little house. And there they found the door unlocked, and a stench that warned them about what they'd find.

It still didn't prepare Carolyn for Belle stretched out on that couch, the plastic removed.

She wore a black pantsuit and matching shoes that looked like they hadn't been worn before. Her hair was down, which somehow made her look older—although that could have been the way her flesh had sunken in on itself or that bit of foam that had dried around her mouth and nose.

Her hands were folded on her chest, the way an undertaker would place them, and in them, she clutched a single rose.

She'd been there so long the rose was dead too.

"She did this after we left," Brauder said quietly.

Carolyn nodded. They'd found pills in the back, or something equally lethal, something that would give her this quiet death.

"I still don't get it," Brauder said. "Why would she kill a child?"

Carolyn shrugged. "She told us. The times weren't hard. They were impossible."

"You think the baby just died?" Brauder asked. "Starved or something?"

"Your forensic anthropologist would've found that. We'd've seen it too. Bones of starvation victims aren't the same as bones from well fed individuals." Carolyn spoke softly as she stared into that sunken face.

"You think she couldn't take it any more," Brauder said, and Carolyn wasn't sure if he was referring to the baby or the knowledge that she might have to pay a price for something she'd done seventy years before.

"I think her father wanted her to marry for money," Carolyn said. "You know, we blame her for what happened. But what if her father took his wrath out on that baby, the one thing that stood in the way of their dreams?"

"There's no sign that he was violent," Brauder said.

Carolyn gave him a sideways look. "There's plenty of signs. What you'd call negative evidence. One son who moved away as soon as he could, another who refuses to acknowledge his family, even when it would benefit him. A daughter forced to live in exile because no one approved of her. A daughter who had been, according to the military, some kind of hero."

Brauder looked at Carolyn over the body of the only person who knew the answers they had been searching for.

"David is a decorated war veteran too," he said. "Look where that's gotten him."

"Ironically," Carolyn said, "I have a hunch the place it'll get him is right here."

She turned out to be right. After the probate was finished, which was relatively short given the fact that Belle had no debts at all and no other relatives besides her brothers, the house became theirs. The older brother signed it over to David. Carolyn doubted he would maintain the garden. She wondered if he could handle the responsibility.

But she had a hunch that the previous owner of the little bungalow had suffered her own kind of PTSD. She hoped the new owner might find solace from his there as well.

At least, she wanted to believe that. Just like she wanted to believe they would care about the little corpse who had started this all.

But the brothers told the state to deal with the unknown baby girl. The state told Brauder, and Brauder told Carolyn. She asked if she could pay for a plot in the small cemetery not far from her house.

"Why?" Brauder had asked. He'd become a friend, a friend who might be something more, and she almost told him the real reason.

But she still wasn't willing to part with that kind of information, not even six months after knowing how trustworthy and kind this man was.

Instead, she'd said, "The child needs someone to mourn her."

And he'd nodded. He'd done the paperwork and she bought the grave, ordered the headstone, and chose a simple epitaph:

Baby Girl Wolffe

Safe at Last

Later that spring, as Carolyn watched the undertaker lower the tiny coffin into the grave and listened as the minister she'd found said a few gentle words, she ran her fingers over her own scars, fading cat scratches on the outside, major trauma on the inside. She planted tulips near the headstone, and planned to bring daisies once a week.

Then she went to Linda's to play with the new baby—a girl—and help with whatever her friend needed.

Times were tough. Times were *always* tough.

But, Carolyn had learned, they were only impossible when you faced them alone.

Scars

Kristine Kathryn Rusch

Scars

Her solace: those weekday afternoons before the school got out and the children invaded the pool. For the last two weeks, the weather had been fair. Sunlight streamed in the floor to ceiling windows on the north and south face of the pool area, dappling the water with brilliant yellow light. Rena particularly liked the way the light filtered into the artificial blue depths below the surface. When she swam into such a patch, the water felt warmer, even though it couldn't be.

The pool was part of a rec center only four blocks from her new apartment; a fact that frustrated her more than the apartment itself. The apartment had three small windows facing south and east with barely enough room on the sills for her small collection of malingering plants. The counters were too low, the toilet too high, and the chrome bar in the shower always caught her in the back. More than anything, she hated the apartment's silence, and hoped, at her six-month review, the shrink at the pain center would say she had recovered enough to care for a cat.

By contrast, the pool was never silent. Not even when she was underwater. She heard the rustle of the filters, the splashing of the other lap swimmers, and the rhythmic bubbles caused by her exhaled breath. When she surfaced, she heard voices and laughter; the radio on a rock station she would never play, and the phone, constant and shrill against the echoy boom of the large room itself. She never paid attention to what happened on the decks. The fact that anything happened at all was enough for her.

Saturday, now, Saturday was different. She never went to the pool on Saturday, saving its pleasures for the weekday, and for the pool attendants who were older. The teenagers who guarded the place on the weekends stared at her. They couldn't hide their revulsion. The adults were more skilled at hiding their shock.

But this Saturday her stereo's tuner went on the fritz, sliding past each station she tried to tune in. For a half hour, she got Christian broadcasting mixing exhortations against sins of the flesh with some pretty good soft rock and then that too faded into static. She had seen all the movies on television, and she had no interest in sports. Her neighbors across the street seemed to be out of town: their little girl and mongrel puppy had not been outside all day—an event Rena lived for—the vitality, joy and love those two shared made her happy even while it made her ache.

She could no longer stand the silence. She grabbed her swim bag, and let herself out the front door, promising herself that the stares would not bother her this time, would not ruin her solace.

She walked, as she always did, head down, wincing each time a car whooshed by. Cars still frightened her. It had taken her nearly a month to get enough nerve to take the bus. Before that, she had had Meals on Wheels, and hoped that they never realized she wasn't really a shut-in.

The first hurdle came in the rec center. She stopped at the window and paid for her session. Disability, combined with the insurance and settlement money, left her more than enough to buy a membership, but she enjoyed being anonymous here. In her old life, she would have been greeted by name—she would have known everyone's name—but here she ignored the faces and personal histories as much as possible. The girl at the window was new: a recent survivor of the life-saving course who had that fresh-faced bright-eyed athleticism so appealing in people under twenty-five.

She smiled when she saw Rena, an open, welcoming smile that made Rena cringe. "Good thing you got here now," the girl said. "I was about to leave."

Rena glanced at the clock. Still a half hour before closing, but that late the desk attendants usually left money collection to the lifeguard. "I have time to swim, don't I?" she asked.

"Sure," the girl said. "In district or out?"

In response, Rena put dollar and three quarters on the counter, signifying in-district membership. It took a moment for her to get the last quarter out of her pocket: she was concentrating on that and so the girl's stare caught her off guard. The ribbed pink skin, the scars crisscrossing the back of her hand were the worst of her wounds: she had crisped both hands and most of her arms reaching into the burning car for Robbie.

The doctors were amazed that she had regained almost total use, but how did one tell that to an eighteen-year-old girl who had never left her hometown?

Rena didn't explain. She pushed open the door to the women's locker room and sighed when she heard voices in the shower. The hair dryer was running, and a woman was speaking baby talk in the changing area. A toilet flushed while Rena stood, indecisive: did she go past the showers, past the perfect naked bodies, or around the concrete dividing wall directly into the changing area, past the full length mirror?

She opted for the showers, noting that the women weren't perfect, their elderly bodies ringed with excess weight and tiny lumps of fatty tissue. They were talking to each other, oblivious to their nakedness, something she loved about women over fifty who had somehow learned to accept age with grace, and not to mourn the loss of their youthful figures. She had talked to one of them once: a woman who had just had a pace-maker put in and who still wore a two-piece bathing suit despite the vertical scar that ran to her bottoms.

Six women stood in the changing area—apparently a class had let out —and one little girl who was standing on the bench, holding the handle to the suit wringer, volunteering to get the water out of everyone's suit. Rena kept her gaze averted and walked to the farthest corner. She set her bag on the wooden bench and undressed slowly, hoping no one watched.

She tried not to watch herself. In the space of an evening, she had lost her husband, her child, and the body she had grown up with. Somehow her face had been spared despite the intense blistering heat when the gas can in the trunk ignited as she was pulling open the side door to save an already dead Robbie. Now, every time she saw herself, that night came back in a blaze of orange against a moonlight sky: broken glass raining all around her; the smell of inky smoke, gasoline and burning flesh as vivid as the moment it happened. Only the smell of chlorine diluted it. Only when she breathed into the water did she feel as if she were blowing black smoke out of her lungs forever.

With shaking hands, she pulled out her neon green one-piece suit. The color was hideous, but at least it wasn't black or red or yellow or any mixture of those three. She slipped it on, then wrapped herself in her towel, hiding in its fluffy warmth. She could feel the gazes upon her, but she pretended she didn't care.

She walked past the women with what dignity she could muster, and headed into the pool area. This late in the day, most of the swimmers were gone. Only the middle lane was taken by a man Rena had never seen before. The lifeguard—a tall, reedy thin girl-woman—stood, feet apart, and life stick clutched against her stomach. She watched the swimmer intently as if she could control each breath he took.

Rena hung up her towel, took a kickboard off the stack and climbed in the shallow end. The water was cold, and she realized with a shock that she had forgotten to take the required shower. She shot a quick glance at the lifeguard, as if she were going to get kicked out of the pool for failing to follow the rules, but the lifeguard didn't seem to notice.

The man finished his lap, surfaced and shook the water off his face like a shaggy dog. Rena slipped into the water, hiding her body. He smiled at her and she smiled back, glad he couldn't see how she really looked. His hair was long and dark; it matched the long dark hair on the rest of his body. He put both hands on the side of the pool and levered himself out.

She left her kickboard on the side, then slid underwater completely and pushed off kitty corner for the deep end. She loved the pool when it was empty. She felt almost normal then. Her doctor was so proud of her: when he first saw her after she had moved here, he thought she would never regain full use of her body again. But he had recommended the swimming, saying that non-weight bearing exercise would stretch her scars gradually and, combined with physical therapy, might give her a normal range of movement. After spending the first week in terror of revealing her body, she finally went to the pool and remembered her love for the water. It was that love, not any dedication to health, that gave her what little freedom she had now.

The laps felt easy; she had found a rhythm. She kept her count, eyes open. A child had left a tiny ring on the bottom, and she was half tempted to dive for it, or maybe catch it with her arm. As she made her flip turn and headed for the deep end, she began planning the move. She glanced at the lifeguard, saw her talking to a slender man—a boy really—as tall as the guard herself. Not the right time then. She was still insecure enough that she wanted the lifeguard's eyes on her when she tried something new.

On the sixtieth lap, she heard a whoop echo over the music. Disappointment ran through her. School was out, and the children would take over for rec swim. Then she remembered: no school. It was Saturday. The pool would close soon. The call was probably the lifeguard warning her to get out.

But she only had ten more laps to go. If the lifeguard wanted her out, she would have to touch her to get her attention. Rena swam as fast and as hard as she could. The push felt good. In water, at least, her body obeyed her.

When she was finished, she pulled off her goggles and squinted at the clock. The pool should have closed fifteen minutes before. The lifeguard was going to be mad at her. She sighed. She probably should have paid attention to that call.

She climbed out of the pool, the water dripping off her body, and grabbed her kickboard. The air, which had seemed warm when she got in, now had a chill. Someone had left the door to the Jacuzzi open. She peered through, but no one sat outside. The Jacuzzi was silent. She came back in and headed for the pile of kickboards.

Rena didn't see the blood until she stepped in it. It was warm and thick, not cool and thin like pool water. She set her kickboard on the pile and swallowed—hard—thinking perhaps she was having one of her nightmares in the daylight. But no. The body was real. The lifeguard lay flat on her back, left hand in the water, eyes open and unseeing, blood draining from one long slash across her throat.

It took the police five minutes to arrive. While she waited, Rena huddled by the phone in the pool office. She shivered in the cool air. She had retained enough presence of mind to touch nothing—she didn't even pick her towel off its peg. Each second felt like an hour. She stared at the clock, concentrating on the movement of the hands, forcing herself to think of nothing but that.

Her psychologist would have been proud of her: no screaming fits, no flashbacks, no post-traumatic shock. She had stayed calm. She wasn't letting herself think about what had happened while she was happily doing her laps.

The sound of a car's wheels crunching gravel in the parking lot frayed her nerves even more. She stiffened, barely allowing herself to breathe. Outside the engine shuddered to a halt. Car doors opened and released a burst of static from the police radio. Then the first door slammed, followed quickly by the other.

She should have gotten up, but she half expected them to die in the parking lot. As if the murderer were still out there, waiting, not attacking her because she was invisible to him. But footsteps rang on the tile floor, the sound echoing over the now-calm water.

"Hello?"

The sound made her jump, even though she expected it. She tried to answer, found her voice stuck in her throat. She swallowed, then managed: "Over here."

As the footsteps approached, she gripped the plastic seat of the stool. The policeman who peered in was red-headed, freckled and young—no. Not young. Boyish. But his eyes had a maturity that she recognized. He was in his thirties, like she was, only time had improved on his features instead of ruined them.

His gaze was flat as he took her in. She cringed even more, not used to such scrutiny, but unwilling to look away. He grabbed her towel from the peg and tossed it at her.

"You look cold," he said.

She wrapped the towel around herself and nodded. The terrycloth was plush, warm, and soft against her skin. She had very little feeling in her hands and arms, but the rest of her scars, left by a hundred pieces of broken glass, had nerve endings intact.

"She's—by the lifeguard station," Rena said.

"I know." His voice was gentle. "My partner's with her."

Rena let out the air she had been holding. She could feel the terror, nibbling at her edges, threatening to overwhelm her.

"Did you see what happened?" he asked.

She shook her head, swallowed. "I was swimming." Then heard how odd that sounded. Swimming while a woman died.

"And you saw nothing?"

She shifted under the towel. A tingling formed inside her: energy, building up. "I heard a yell. I thought she wanted me to get out of the pool. I—" She looked away. "I wanted to finish my laps."

He leaned against the door, his thumbs hooked on the pockets of his jeans. He wasn't wearing a uniform; she hadn't noticed until that moment. His blue chambray shirt and faded denim gave her a degree of comfort. "Were you the only one in the pool?"

"There was a man in the dressing room, I think. He had just got out. And...." She frowned, an image she couldn't quite reach flitting through her mind. "Someone. I thought I saw someone. But I don't remember."

Two more cars pulled up. At the sound of their engines the shakiness she had kept inside moved out. Her entire body trembled.

"You need to get dressed," he said.

She glanced at the locker room door. "Don't you need to look for evidence?"

His smile was rueful. "You watch a lot of crime shows."

She shrugged.

"I'll take you home. You can change there. Then we'll need you at the station to make a statement."

She bit her lower lip to keep her teeth from chattering. It took all of her strength to force out the words: "Am I under arrest?"

"Not right now," he said.

Rena had never had a guest in her apartment. For the first time, she saw it through someone else's eyes. The obsessive neatness of a single person's life: the coffee table with one book overturned to the correct page; the television remote next to the only dented spot on the couch; the absence of knickknacks, crocheted pillows, photographs—anything that would have made a house a home. She had had a home with Dennis and Robbie; she couldn't bear to be in it after they were gone.

"I'll just be a minute," she said.

She fled the living room without looking over her shoulder for the detective's reaction. In the car he had told her his name, Joel Bellin, as if they were meeting on the street instead of over a dead body. She was the one who had insisted on "detective." She didn't want to forget his words. "Not right now" meant that she would be charged later. And she didn't want to be too comfortable with the man who charged her.

The bedroom door had no lock, but the bathroom's did. She grabbed a shirt and a pair of jeans, and set them on the laundry hamper. She was so cold and shaken that she couldn't forgo the shower. Still she had to check the lock twice before she felt safe enough to take off her suit.

The water warmed her, and made the trembling stop. She got dressed quickly and, except for her wet hair, curling around her shoulders, and the faint scent of chlorine, she felt as if she had never been to the pool. It took a minute for her fingers to grab the bathroom lock, but when she did, she let herself out.

He was still in the living room where she had left him. He stood in front of her only bookshelf, scanning the titles. There was a bit of her in the house after all. Shelf after shelf of historical novels and science fiction. Books that took her away from here, but never even pretended to unite men and women or even to examine families.

He stared at her for a moment, taking in the clothes, and then he said, "You know I'm going to ask about it eventually. You may as well tell me."

The directness was new. No one had been as blunt before. She felt heat in her cheeks. "Car accident," she said.

"You alone in the car?"

She shook her head.

"Anyone else survive?" he asked.

Orange against the black of the night: the gagging stench of smoke. Her eyes watered, remembering.

"I'm sorry," he said, and the words sounded sincere.

"It was years ago." She picked up her purse, gripping the strap carefully, and slung it over her shoulder.

"Not that many," he said.

She met his gaze. "Enough," she said, ending the conversation.

Even the police station looked clean in this town. She would have thought it safe if not for the bullet proof glass over every window. Bellin led her through the back tunnels, painted white to hide the concrete architects thought so important in the late sixties. The air had a processed smell, lacking only the stale odor of cigarette smoke to make it feel like the office building she used to work in when she lived in the Midwest. But this was the West. No one smoked in public here.

Voices echoed down the hallway first, mixed with ringing phones, and the blare of a radio. She straightened, bracing herself, and Bellin glanced at her, then looked away. She hated the way he saw everything yet said nothing. Either he should comment or stop looking.

He pushed open the double doors and suddenly she was enveloped in the cacophony. The conversations didn't stop when she entered. People sitting on desks, behind desks, interviewing other people, some in uniform, some not. Two women stood by the coffee machine stirring Sweet 'N Low into steaming chipped mugs. A man, feet propped on his desk, phone cradled between his shoulder and ear, looked at her face, then her hands, then at Bellin, apparently realizing that her injuries were not current, not today's problem.

"This the suspect?" A woman whose voice had the rich, deep timbre of a natural contralto asked.

Rena jumped. Suspect. She hadn't expected it so soon.

Bellin took her elbow, sliding his hand under her forearm, and braced her palm. Her curved fingers, their deep scars, the pink skin, flared like neon in the room. She couldn't look up at the woman who spoke.

"How much range of movement you got, honey?" the woman asked.

Rena tried to grab Bellin's forefinger, wincing as the skin pulled. She could make a tight fist, but it was work. She could move her fingers out of the fist easily, but she couldn't straighten the fingers at all.

"You're right," the woman said. "No way. Not holding and stabbing at the same time."

Finally Rena brought her head up. The woman was short and stocky, but her heaviness was in her muscular shoulders, her powerful arms. Her skin was the color of good coffee and her dark hair hung straight over her ears.

"I'd like to take a statement from you," the woman said.

"Am I a suspect?" Rena asked. She would find a lawyer if she had to. She could afford it. The money sat in four different accounts, untouched. Blood money. Some actuary's estimate of the price of human lives.

"No," Bellin said. He let go of her arm, and it fell to her side, still warm from his touch. "I'll drive you back when you're done."

"Thanks," she said, but he had already turned away, picking up papers from a cluttered desk between them. She felt bereft without him: she had been using him as a lifeline since he appeared at the pool.

"I'm Detective McCary," the woman said. "Must have been pretty frightening, coming out of that pool."

"I didn't see her at first," Rena said.

McCary led her into a small room with no windows. The concrete hadn't been painted here, and the room had a chill that felt as if it would never go away. Metal folding chairs surrounded a Formica table with a tape recorder built into top. McCary produced a cassette from her pocket. "You mind if I record?"

Rena shook her head. She stated her name and address as McCary asked her to do, then retold the story, detail by detail.

"And you saw no one?" McCary asked.

Rena frowned. That tantalizing sensation at the corner of her memory had returned. No one? "I saw—someone." Almost. She almost had him. "It was so brief. I was doing laps, not thinking about it." She bit her lower lip, ashamed of the next admission. "I work so hard now at ignoring people. Like maybe they won't see me if I don't see them."

"Because of the hands?" McCary asked.

Rena swallowed. "The whole body. All but my face."

"But people don't see that. And your face is striking. Model pretty."

Rena closed her eyes against the words. Dennis's words, "model pretty," as if she could have been something other than a secretary, a wife, a mother.

"Sorry," McCary said. "Didn't mean to upset you."

"The whole thing is upsetting, isn't it?" Rena said as she opened her eyes and shivered. Her hair wasn't quite dry yet and the chill was sinking in.

Then—suddenly—the memory came: a slender man, a boy really, with a teenager's thinness, talking to her, gesturing. Rena had seen him before. In the Jacuzzi outside. He had come out of swim team practice to look at her, his eyes dark and cold as he stared. He had mumbled something under his breath, something she had to work hard at not hearing, before going inside, and laughing with his friends.

"He was young. I saw him once before. I think he's on the swim team."

"Can you identify him?"

That face, long bones, not fully grown yet. An uneven beard and lips too full for a boy. And those eyes.

She nodded.

"Good," McCary said. "We'll get the entire team in for a line-up."

Rena heard the dismissal. She reached out, almost touched McCary's hand, then stopped before she could bring herself to do so. McCary watched, brows furrowed.

"The girl," Rena said. "Who was she?"

"I thought you knew," McCary said. "You been going to the pool for months."

"Not on Saturday," Rena said.

"Ah," McCary said, and she appeared to make a mental note, as if the information went into a file somewhere in her head. "She was the head cheerleader at the high school. Her father works at the university. Her mother is one of those charity wives."

"Her name?" Rena's tone was insistent, but she kept her head bowed, submissive, so she wouldn't seem too demanding. She just thought it proper that she would know who the girl was, who had died, on such a beautiful afternoon.

"Candace Walker." McCary smiled, and there was sadness around her eyes. "She hated to be called Candy. I always got the feeling she was waiting to be on her own so that she could change her name."

"You knew her then," Rena said.

"She went to school with my daughter. They had the same homeroom." And more, McCary's tone said. But Rena wasn't going to press. It really wasn't her business, this relationship between high school girls, now or forever.

"It must be hard for you," Rena said.

McCary studied her for a moment. "Death is always hard," she said.

Bellin drove her home. His insistence. She had tried to take the bus, but he had objected. "You need to be gentle with yourself," he had said.

They didn't talk all the way across town. The radio interrupted the silence with occasional bursts of static. When he pulled up to her apartment, he stopped the car slowly. She fumbled with the latch and, for the second time that day, he touched her. He put a hand on her shoulder.

She didn't want to think about how long it had been since someone touched her voluntarily, with no medical purpose in mind.

"He saw you, you know," Bellin said.

She nodded, unable to look at him.

"Does he know who you are?"

"No." Her voice sounded soft, even to her.

"Does he know where you live?"

"No."

"Can he find out?"

Slowly she brought her head up, tilting her chin as her mother had once taught her for a different arrogance altogether. An arrogance that was designed for a more flirtatious age, where women had fewer rights, and so had to use their attitudes to scare men away. "I'm not the kind of woman people remember."

"You're precisely the kind of person he would remember."

"But he thinks I'm beneath contempt."

"You've spoken to him?"

"Once." She flushed. The boy's words fluttered at the edge of her consciousness. If she concentrated, she would be able to hear them.

She had blocked the words for a reason. She pushed them away.

"And?"

"He doesn't believe I'm human." The sentence made her flinch. It was only one of several he had said; the only one she would allow herself to remember.

Bellin brought his hand up again, then clenched his fist as if uncertain about how to treat her. But he didn't say "I'm sorry," nor did he back down. "Is your name on file at the rec center?"

"I'm not a member. I always pay in cash. I prefer it if people don't know who I am." She spoke in a rush, with an anger she hadn't realized she was holding until that moment. All this stress. A girl was dead—murdered—and Rena wanted no part of it. She wanted to hide in her apartment, to find a book and disappear in someone else's world—forever.

He reached into his pocket and pulled out a card. Then he grabbed a pen off the dash, scrawled on the back of the card and handed it to her. "My home phone. I want you to call me if there's trouble."

"I'll call nine-one-one," she said.

"Take it anyway."

And because she could think of no way to argue, she did. Then she tugged on the door handle and pushed the heavy door open. She was glad the neighbors weren't home. What would they think seeing the scarred woman getting out of a police car?

After she got out, she nodded to him, not sure what to say. Gratitude was inappropriate—gratitude for what? taking her away from her world?—and goodbyes seemed trite. So she said nothing. As she pushed the car door closed, he raised his hand in a half wave. She nodded, then turned her back, hurrying to the apartment because she knew he wouldn't leave until she was safely inside.

But when she got inside, she almost turned around and asked him to join her. Instead, she leaned on the door and scanned the apartment for changes. Nothing was out of place. The empty feeling was a familiar one. She had felt it each night since she had moved to Oregon, a painful reminder that she had no one to come home to, no one to talk with, no one who cared. If she allowed it, the feeling would turn into a full blown panic of the kind she hadn't experienced since the Midwest, in those awful days when she had finally been released from the hospital, when the attorneys and the doctors and the insurance agents somehow thought she could live in the same home where her husband laughed and her child played, and she had been happy for much too brief a time.

In the middle of the night, she awoke in pitch blackness, her bed warm and her feet still cold. Her heart was pounding. She had dreamed that the boy/man was with her. He told her she wasn't worth killing, that she wasn't worth noticing at all, that people like her didn't really exist. In his left hand, he held a glass shard—tinted glass, the kind that came from car windows—and he brought it slowly, lovingly to her face. When its point touched the fold of skin beneath her left eye, she screamed and forced herself awake.

With a shaking hand, she turned on the lamp by the bedside. She touched her face, feeling its smoothness, the only comfort she had. The room was silent. Only the hum of the refrigerator to remind her of civilization. She got out of bed, and staggered into the bathroom, the stiffness in her joints making her realize how deep the panic went. She flicked on the light and peered into the mirror. Nothing marred her cheek. No scars on her face, but the hands that touched her skin were unfamiliar to her. In her dreams, her hands were unmarked, as smooth as her face.

The panic welled, like a bubble: if he wanted to find her, he could. Everyone would remember her—the scarred lady. He would wait outside her window and then let himself in, carrying a knife—a glass shard—big orange flames against the night sky.

She found herself standing over her jeans, clutching Bellin's card in her hands. She stared at his scrawl—he crossed his sevens in the European method—and slowly set the card back down. *If there's trouble*, he had said. But nightmares weren't trouble. They were expected, especially after someone had witnessed a murder.

The Sunday morning paper had Candace Walker's high school graduation photo on page one. Rena unrolled the paper on her kitchen table and pressed the sides down while staring at the dead girl's face.

Rena's fingers brushed the side of her plate, sticky with honey. The scent of her half-eaten English muffin mingled with the aroma of the Coffee Corner's French Roast special. But her appetite was gone.

For a moment, Rena stared at the photo. It was a graduation picture. The photographer had given Candace a sensual grace she hadn't had at the pool. The soft lighting and the scooped neckline of the dress made Candace look as if she were about to be kissed instead of photographed for a yearbook.

Rena ran her fingers along the neckline. The ink felt soft, smeary, and left her fingertips black. She took a deep breath and read, studying each line, looking for her name.

But the police had been careful. The article focused on the murder and the discovery of the body, but did not mention any witnesses. A few of the things Rena had told them were reported to the paper by a police spokesperson, but none of the important details were present. No mention of Rena or the boy or the cause of death. But an entire paragraph devoted to the fact the rec center would be closed until further notice.

She sighed and absently picked up her coffee mug. It slid through her fingers, catching on her thumb, and spilling on Candace's photograph. Rena blotted it with her napkin, apologizing to Candace under her breath. Then realized it didn't matter at all.

Candace wouldn't notice anything again.

The shrill cry of the phone made Rena freeze. Her breath knotted in her throat. The cry came again—not muffled as it was when she heard the neighbor's phone—but clear and pure. Hers. Who would call her on a Sunday? The only calls she received were salespeople and the clinic reminding her of her appointments.

Carefully, she set her coffee mug down and walked into the living room. The phone was on the end table near her spot on the couch. She pressed the speaker button to answer. It was always easier than picking up the handset.

"Yes?" She sounded vulnerable. A woman alone. She suspected all her callers knew just from the tone of her voice.

"Rena? It's Joel Bellin."

The detective. She pressed a hand over her heart. She had recognized his voice the moment he had spoken her name. "Yes?" she said again.

He cleared his throat. "We, ah, we have rounded up the members of the swim team, and will have a line-up this afternoon. I'd like to bring you in to look at them, if you don't mind."

The boy's eyes hard and cold, filled with something more than contempt. Something like hate. She had assumed it was because she was damaged. Perhaps it had been something else. "No, I don't mind," she said, but the fear came back, beating against her stomach like the wings of a trapped bird.

"I'll be there in an hour," he said.

"I'll be here," she said, and hit the button, severing the connection.

She stood over the phone for the longest time, wishing that she could leave the apartment, go anywhere. Swim. But she wouldn't be able to go the rec center now. Maybe never again. She had never revisited the site of the accident, sometimes going blocks out of her way to avoid it, finally moving halfway across the country to escape it. She certainly couldn't return to the site of a murder.

Rena went back into the kitchen and picked up her mug. Candace Walker's hopeful face, wrinkled from the spilled coffee, haunted her. Almost unwillingly, she read the girl's biography. Short, dry facts: good student who planned to attend the University of Oregon in the fall, survived by her parents, grandparents, and a younger brother. The obituary was longer than Robbie's had been—what does a reporter say about a five-year-old boy? He hadn't been to school yet. He had learned to walk at eight months, to read by the age of three. Accomplishments, but not the kind that made a résumé. He had laughed a lot, and his hugs were fierce. He had had a little boy smell of sunshine and peanut butter.

She was gripping the mug so tightly the scars on her hand pulled. Odd she had never mourned Dennis like she mourned Robbie, even though she had loved her husband dearly. But he had lived, and he had told her more than once that he did not fear death.

But her son. Her son. He had been her hope. Her future. Her immortality. A bundle of smiles, and tears, and wonder. Newspaper articles never captured the essence of someone's being. What happened to

Robbie's joy and Candace's strength? And who would remember them when their loved ones were gone?

The damp concrete smell permeated the observation room. Four chairs were lined up behind the one-way mirror, and through it, was a room little wider than a hallway where, for the last half hour, men and boys had paraded in front of her, holding numbers to their chests as if they were prizes in a raffle.

Bellin sat beside her so close that she could feel the warmth of his arm next to hers. McCary stood behind them, hands on her hips, frowning at the scene below. The room was cold: the air-conditioning on high. Rena wished she had coffee, tea, something hot to keep her hands warm.

None of the people in the line-up bore more than a casual resemblance to the boy she had seen. All were tall, thin and athletic. All had dark hair and narrow features. But none of them had the eyes or the cruel cut to the lip. After the third group, she found herself questioning her own memory. She closed her eyes for a moment, and his image rose again in her mind, and she knew she had not seen him. Then she asked them to continue again.

Finally the room below was empty. Bellin sighed and leaned back. "That's it," he said.

"That's it?" she repeated, knowing it sounded stupid but unable to help herself. She had thought it would be so easy. "Was that the entire swim team?"

"Plus," he said.

"Maybe he was just someone associated with the team," McCary said.

Rena shook her head. Of that she was certain. "They don't allow anyone but the swim team in the pool area during practice. Even when people show up early for a meet, they have to stay in the bleachers." They had to have missed someone. Had to.

"We used the coach's year roster, and asked him to add names on it if he had to. He didn't. This is the team," Bellin said.

"Are you sure the boy was on the team?" McCary asked.

"I don't know." Rena pressed her hands to her forehead. "He was there one afternoon when the team was there. He wouldn't have been in the pool area if he weren't on the team."

"But you were," Bellin said.

She shook her head. "I was in the Jacuzzi. They let people stay in the Jacuzzi all day."

"He was there then," Bellin said, more to McCary than to Rena. "Someone else is bound to remember him."

A headache had built behind Rena's eyes. She wanted the boy caught. She wanted to go back to her pool, to her quiet, dull life. "Are they protecting him?"

"I don't know," Bellin said.

"I should have brought Sasha's yearbook," McCary said. "Do you mind if I bring it by tonight?"

Rena smiled weakly. "I have nothing better to do."

Rena made a pot of coffee and paced nervously, straightening as she moved. She found it more difficult to have an expected guest than an unexpected guest. She had spent the last half hour wondering what McCary would think of the apartment.

Her stereo still didn't tune properly, so the only music came from the clock radio she kept in the kitchen. The music sounded so tinny that she had shut it off. She almost turned on the television before she realized that any sound would be intrusive.

The kitchen smelled of French Roast and chocolate chip cookies. She hadn't baked since Robbie died. The pain shrink would probably say it was good that she was reverting to old habits, but she wasn't so sure. She would have rather had a swim at the rec center, followed by an evening alone with a book. Anything but this.

At the hum of a car pulling up, she froze. Then the car door slammed, and she hovered near her front door like a girl about to meet a blind date. When the bell rang, she had to count to ten before pulling the door open so that she wouldn't seem too eager.

Detective Bellin stood before her, his white shirt open at the collar, his hair loose and curling around his forehead, the yearbook held casually against his thigh. "Detective McCary couldn't make it," he said. "Problems at home."

Rena swallowed back an odd disappointment. She liked McCary, hoped that they would be able to talk about more than murder over the coffee and cookies she had made. "Nothing serious, I hope," she said.

He shrugged. "Her daughter hasn't been doing too well since the murder. It doesn't help to have a mom who is a cop."

"I would think it would," Rena said. "Protection and all."

"Who protects a cop's family," he asked. "while the cop is protecting the city?"

She had no answer to that except to stand away from the door and let him in. He wore a different pair of faded jeans with cowboy boots peeking out beneath. His hair was still damp on the ends. He had been home to change before he came to see her.

"Smells good in here," he said.

"I made some cookies. Chocolate chip. You want some?"

"And coffee," he said. "The good stuff." He smiled and it wiped away all the lines, the hurts, the age hidden in his face. For the first time, she noticed him as a handsome man, and the realization made her step away.

"I have cups out in the kitchen. I figured we could look at the table—"

"Good idea." He waited for her to lead him in there, even though he knew the way. She went immediately to the counter, and plastic wrap covering the cookies. Her hands were shaking so badly she could hardly move them. But he didn't offer to help and for that she was grateful. She didn't want to seem weak in front of him. She didn't want to seem weak in front of anyone.

"You didn't have to come out here," she said. "I could have come to the station."

"I know."

She crinkled the plastic wrap and tossed it in the garbage under the sink. Then she leaned against the counter, unable to look at him.

"You don't have to take care of me," she said.

She wasn't sure how she wanted him to answer. A quick denial would have confirmed her suspicions, and no one answered an accusation like hers with the truth. His silence, though, was unexpected.

The clatter of mugs on the Formica was the only sound in the room. She gripped the handle of the coffee pot firmly, hoping that her hand wouldn't slip and make her regret her words. The coffee poured smoothly, its rich steam coating her face. She took his mug to him, cradling it in both hands, and setting it gently before him.

"Is that what you think I'm doing?" he said, placing her back on the defensive.

She put the sugar and cream in front of him, then returned to the counter for the cookies. The fragile plate felt awkward in her hands, but she didn't drop it. She set it down carefully, and got her own mug before joining him.

Without saying a word, she grabbed the yearbook from the chair he had placed it on, and put it beside her mug. The yearbook was covered in pale blue leather with the school's emblem and name embossed in gold. The effect was a washed-out, clearly unprofessional choice of some hapless yearbook staff. The scent of well-tooled leather and fresh ink mixed with the coffee. She opened to the index, scanned until she found the page with the swim team, and stared at the picture.

She had seen all of those faces. Young boys with their scrawny bodies looking defiantly at the camera. They wore red briefs as swim suits, a color that made most of them appear even more pale and sickly. All of the boys had been scattered through the afternoon's line up. She read the caption underneath and realized that the whole team was in the shot. How odd. She really had thought she understood the rules about pool attendance.

"Not there?" Bellin asked.

"He's not in the official photograph," she said. She studied the others on the page: the boys hovering over the pool; a boy in goggles with his head shaved coming out of the water; a series of slightly arched bodies caught in the opening dive. He wasn't in any of them.

She closed the book and started over, looking at the whole thing page by page, trying to ignore the loopy unformed writing of the students to McCary's daughter: the banal sentiments that the girl probably treasured. Rena stopped only when she saw Candace Walker's signature at the end of a long page of writing which covered several school photos.

To the First Runner Up: Got to work a little harder, friend. Don't want to go through life always a bridesmaid. Seriously, thanks for covering. Couldn't've done it without you. Too bad you're not going to State. I can use the competition. —Candace

"Charming, huh?" Bellin said.

Rena nodded. She remembered that bitchy friendliness which wasn't really friendly at all. She had probably participated in it willingly when she had been in high school, and she still saw it at the pool among the girls' swim team. "What does she mean by covering?"

"I don't know," Bellin said, "and neither does McCary. Her daughter says it has to do with missing cheerleading practice, but McCary's not sure. She's working on it."

"Anyone thought to get Candace's yearbook?" Rena asked.

He smiled and took a cookie off the plate, as if her suggestion pleased him. "No," he said, and took a bite, making a production out of enjoying that first small taste. She ignored him and went back to the book.

Nothing for pages. She thought it odd that all yearbooks looked the same. The fashions changed, but the faces never did. It was almost as if she were looking at pictures of her friends in 1990s garb. About twenty pages from the end, she stopped and frowned at a photograph in the corner of the girls' swim team page. Bellin had gotten up to get himself another mug of coffee. She took the moment of privacy to stare at the face, eyes burning at her as they had that afternoon in the Jacuzzi.

"That's him," she said, and pointed. She wouldn't put her finger on the page. To touch his photograph seemed too personal and closer than she ever wanted to get to him again.

Bellin stood behind her, his head just above her shoulder, his hands spread on the table around her, as if he were protecting her back while staring at the picture. "Different color trunks," he said.

And he was right. The boy, uncredited in the photograph, was standing beside the diving board, talking with someone hidden by the metal rails. His trunks were blue and fit so snugly that she could see the bulge outlined by the light. He had been caught in a moment of distraction, as the only person credited in the photo—a girl—did a cannonball off the high dive, her hair streaming above her head.

"Another team?" she asked.

"Could be," he said. "At least we know what he looks like now." He patted her on the shoulder. "We'll find him."

"Good." His words took a tension she didn't even know she carried out of her body. She glanced at him, then returned her attention to the book, determined to see if the boy appeared in the last few pages. He did not.

When she finished, she slid the yearbook back at him. "What else do you need from me? You want me to testify?"

"Later." He had returned to his chair, leaving her back cold. His hands were wrapped around his steaming coffee mug, and most of the cookies were gone from the plate. "Another line-up, though. You are planning to stay in town?"

His question had been routine, not intrusive. She made herself speak lightly. "Have nowhere else to go."

He nodded, then his gaze met hers. He studied her for a moment, his eyes moving as they took in her face. Finally he said, "I don't think you need taking care of, you know. I think you're one of the strongest women I've ever met." Then he grinned as if to take the intimacy from his words. He grabbed another cookie and waved it at her. "Thanks for dinner."

"That's dinner?" she asked, but he was already in the living room, and pretending he didn't hear. She took the yearbook to him, and watched as he let himself out. The drama was over. The diversion in a life of sameness was gone. She was now a woman cursed with another nightmare, and a vague sense of loss.

Rena knew she was dreaming because she still had a sense of her body, curled on its left side, warm and snug in her queen-sized bed. But part of the warmth came from the Jacuzzi outside the swimming pool at the rec center, the swirling water caressing her tired limbs. In the dream, it was February—cold, drizzly February, her favorite time in the hot water. She sat with her back to the pool, and lifted her face to the rain, her body warm and her head cool. Only there did she really feel alive.

She didn't hear the door, but the splash made her look up. A boy, teenage thin with corded muscles running along his arms, and his chest, had dropped a black practice brick into the hot tub. His dark eyes glittered as he looked at her, his full lips twisted into a smirk.

Think anyone wants to look at you, bitch?

The words reverberated in her head. She felt the warm bed, and willed herself to open her eyes. But she couldn't. She had to hear this, to remember, to see if he had given her a clue.

I should really cut your face to match, so that you never go out in public. Freaks like you are too ugly to live.

He left the hot tub, turned his back as he headed for the glass door. She placed her feet on the brick and thought of picking it up, of hurling it at him, and then he stopped as if he had read her mind.

Don't ever show your deformed self around me again, bitch. You got that?

She didn't move. Her entire body was trembling, but she didn't move. He pulled open the door, letting out the sound of a splash and the roar of the crowd. Then the door closed, leaving her in silence, with the memory of his words.

The rain streamed down her face, at once hot and cold, fresh and salty. She sat out there until she grew lightheaded from the heat. Then she grabbed her towel, and walked around the building to enter from the front so that she wouldn't see him, wouldn't hear his deep voice ever again.

But it echoed in her dreams. Her dreams. This time she struggled and surfaced, her breath catching in her throat. If he had hated her so much, why hadn't he hurt her? Although he had threatened to cut her.

The darkness seemed to carry his face. Slender, menacing, it formed and reformed on the ceiling, against the windows, over the night stand. With a shaking hand, she turned on the light and basked in its warm glow. Her bedroom, done in neutrals, the off-white walls unadorned, seemed reassuringly familiar. He was only a dream, but the dream was as close as sleep.

She got up and went into the kitchen, her feet cold on the tile floor. The kitchen still smelled faintly of cookies and coffees, reassuring smells, morning smells, family smells. She sank in her chair, and put her face in her scarred hands. Her life would never be normal. She had to accept that, had to accept accidents that destroyed everything she loved, and viciousness that tainted places where she felt safe.

A dream image passed before her closed eyelids: a cheering crowd. She brought her head up. It had been a meet that day. He didn't belong to the local team. He had been part of the visiting team, hence the different trunks. And if she tried, she could probably remember the day, and find out who he really was.

Excitement rose in her chest and she had to pace to keep from feeling overwhelmed. February gray—an early meet, before Valentine's Day because the roses on the back fence which had bloomed on Valentine's Day weren't even budding yet.

Two weeks of newspapers. Something to do. If she found nothing, she wouldn't contact Bellin or waste his time. But if she found something...

If she found something, she might be able to show that young punk that even freaks had a right to live.

The public library was a single-story red brick building that took up less than half a city block. The branch libraries in the Midwest were double the size of this town's only library. She had always dismissed it, thinking a place this tiny wasn't worth her time. Since she had extra money and nothing to spend it on, she bought books at the local chain stores where turnover was so great no one had a chance to remember her.

So when she walked through the door, she was unprepared for the smell of processed air, dust and old books. A wave of nostalgia crashed over her, quicker than she could stop, and for a moment, Robbie's hand was in her own, and Robbie's voice rose over the din, asking for the story lady, and her own rose with his, shushing him, reminding him that libraries were quiet places.

She had to lean against the hardcover fiction shelf (A-Ca) before catching her breath, half wishing for the ghostly presence to remain, and half wishing she would never hear from him again. The loneliness she felt after his visits was almost more than she could bear.

But she had a mission, a purpose for the first time in months. She swallowed hard, and made herself stand, going forward when all she wanted to do was run.

No one had noticed her. Even though it was a Monday afternoon, the library was full. Adults filled the chairs near the tables, browsed the shelves, stood in line in front of the desk. Two women briskly stamped books, then ran them through the demagnetizing machine, while one elderly woman assigned library cards. Rena pushed her hair off her face. She asked the elderly woman where the microfiche was, and had to follow a wrinkled finger to the eastern back corner.

Someone had replaced the card catalogue, probably to save space, and patrons were lined up to use the only available computer terminal. She passed the stacks of phone books and current magazines, to disappear in a tiny musty room that smelled of oil and dust. Four microfiche machines sat in the corner. One had a hand-lettered sign that read *Out of Order*.

She looked in the drawer for the local paper, and found that her memory served: the first half of the year was already on fiche, which made sense in a library this small. She wound the brittle film through the old-fashioned machine, wondering why no one had bothered to computerize this, and turned the knob until she reached the sports section for the first part of February.

It didn't take her long to find the meet. The paper had it all. A list of the students who worked on the meet in the small announcement on Thursday, and local coverage on Friday. A photograph accompanied Friday's story, and she caught a glimpse of his blurry back, made recognizable by the fact that he was heading out the glass doors to the Jacuzzi. To harass her.

He was from Seavy Village, a coastal town. The team's members were listed, and only one lost his race, by a mere two-tenths of a second. The loser's name was John Garnsey.

Two-tenths of a second. It all made a sad, pathetic kind of sense to her now. She put the heel of her hand against her eyes, and closed them. Two-tenths of a second. The time it took to skip the median and crash into oncoming traffic. The time it took to say, "I'm sorry," to the only survivor, burned, covered in glass and unable to cry because there was no fluid left in her body. The time it took to smell bourbon on the breath.

She gave a shaky little sigh, and went outside. The air was cool and the sun hidden behind a cloud. The bus wasn't due for fifteen minutes. She leaned against the bus stand, and wished she could think of nothing.

Rena explained it to Bellin on the phone while she sat on her comfortable couch, the receiver cradled between her shoulder and ear. She called him because she could not face him. Her voice remained calm, but her body shook as she told him her theory.

It seemed both obvious and hideous now. Candace Walker had run the timer on John Garnsey's race. She had clocked him two tenths of a second shy. And in his righteous self-centeredness, he had believed that she erred. For he couldn't believe that he would fail. Someone else had to be to blame.

The loss must have cost him something. Reputation. The respect of his teammates. Something. Enough to cause him to come back and check the lifeguard board. Enough to make him return a third time, and kill her, not caring that Rena was in the pool because Rena wasn't human.

She choked out the last phrase, the part about not being human, and then said nothing. The silence echoed on the phone lines, and for a moment, she thought Bellin didn't believe her. Then he said, "Excellent work. I'll tell McCary and we'll contact the authorities in Seavy Village."

His praise shook her more than the crime did. She clasped her hands tightly together, running her thumbs along her scars to keep herself focused.

"Detective?" she said, her voice calm again. "I'd like to see him when you bring him in."

"You will," Bellin said. "We'll need to do another line-up."

They put him in the third set of men and boys, second from the end. Rena sat in the hard plastic chair and leaned toward the one-way glass, clutching the neck of her sweater with one hand, the edge of the chair with the other.

John Garnsey appeared to be staring right at her. He wore a Beastie

Boys T-shirt and tight blue jeans, and held his number just above his belt buckle as if he were ashamed to hold it.

Think anyone wants to look at you, bitch?

She took a deep breath to wipe the sound of his voice from her memory. As she did, she saw him in a quick, sideways, chlorine-filled glance, gesturing as he argued with Candace Walker on the last afternoon of her life.

"That's him," she said. "Number two."

"You sure?" Bellin asked, his tone cautious.

She turned, wondering why he doubted her. Both he and McCary were watching her, their expressions flat and unreadable. She glanced back at the boy. She held his life in her hands, like she had once held Robbie's. Only she had grabbed Robbie too late.

Freaks like you are too ugly to live.

She shivered. Once. The air-conditioning was too high. Even the sweater she had brought to compensate didn't help. "That's him," she said again. "I'm sure."

Beside her, Bellin exhaled. "Looks like we got a case," he said to McCary.

She nodded, then reached forward and squeezed Rena's hand. "Good work," she whispered. Then she stood. "I'll take care of this," she said to Bellin, and left the observation booth.

Rena was shaking. Her fingernails had turned blue. "Tell me," she said, still staring at the boy's face, "that he dated her. Tell me that she two-timed him or that she beat up his sister."

Bellin put his hands on his knees as if he were bracing himself to speak. "He had never lost a race before." His words were soft. "At least not in high school. Lost once in junior high and came charging out of the water at the timer, but the coach held him back. He was smaller then."

The car was hot, hot, too hot as she reached for Robbie. His eyes were open, his mouth filled with blood. Dennis was still in the driver's seat, twisted toward the back as, in the last moment of his life, he too tried to save his son. Rena took a quick gasp of burning air, a sharp "hah!" as her heart snapped—

From below, Garnsey stared at the wall as if he saw her, as if he knew she was accusing him.

"Does he know what he did? Does he understand?"

And as the paramedics pulled her away from the fireball, the glass rain, she saw a form lurch toward her in the red-gold light. His suit was silk and rumpled, his hair mussed where he had run his hand through it. "I'm sorry, lady," he said, the bourbon on his breath so strong she nearly gagged. "But you shoulda steered outta the way..."

"People like him," Bellin said, "don't believe anyone else exists."

She put her hand over her heart as if she could ease the ache. Her palm was warm, but not warm enough. Never warm enough.

"We'll need you to testify," Bellin said.

Then she looked at him, really looked at him. The fluorescent light took the youth from his face and accented the tiny white scars on his chin and cheek. The crows feet near his eyes were deep, and the area around his mouth showed that he would be wearing sorrow lines as he grew older.

"I'll testify," she said. She could be strong for that.

One by one, the men filed out of the room below. Garnsey had an athlete's gait, a confidence that belied the emptiness beneath it. She didn't understand it; if she could face a drunken man who had slaughtered her family, if she could live every day alone with only scars and memories, then how could that boy kill over the loss of a single race?

"How do you do it?" she asked. "How do you face the world every day, knowing that there are people like that boy in it?"

Bellin stood and placed his hand on her shoulder. She could see his face reflected in the glass, a wavery ghost over an empty room. "It's hard," he said. "But I find my hope when I meet people like you."

The warmth of his hand had penetrated her sweater, like a small, hot sun sending its heat to damaged places within. She leaned her unscarred cheek against his work-roughened knuckles. Time to start taking risks again, to step out of the shadow of a lurching, drunken man in a rumpled silk suit.

"I owe you a real dinner, Detective," she said.

"Joel," he said, reminding her of the warmth he had shown that first afternoon, warmth that she hadn't realized until now had saved her.

"Joel," she said, and smiled.

Combat Medic

Kris Nelscott

Combat Medic

The whap-whap-whap of helicopter rotors invaded her dreams. Eagle blinked awake, and the sound remained. Sikorsky getting close.

Incoming. Wounded.

Her breath caught and her entire body tensed. She threw back covers (soft, woven blanket—um, what?) and swung her legs off the bunk, banging her feet on the floor. The bunk was shorter than she expected, but she didn't have time to think about that.

She groped for her fatigues, couldn't find them within easy reach, grabbed a loose T-shirt and jeans (civilian clothes? Where'd they come from?), slid them on, found bunched-up dirty socks, pulled on two, and then her boots, familiar and comfortable.

She tripped heading for the door, listening for the other nurses, hearing only the drumbeat of rotors, closer, closer, closer, almost as fast as her heartbeat. Stepped through the door, expecting it to bang back as she emerged into the harsh sunlight.

Instead—

Living room, green sofa, blanket on top, large 16-inch TV, her only splurge, canted coffee table with a bong in plain sight, magazines slightly out of order, pale sunlight through the thin curtains.

She took a breath, inhaled the greasy odor of last night's hamburger lingering in the air—even though the cast-iron skillet had been wiped and replaced in the cabinet, dinner plate scrubbed and back on the shelf.

As usual, the galley kitchen, attached to the living room, was the cleanest room in the house.

But the whap-whap-whap grew closer. No incoming, no wounded.

She was home, Berkeley, not Nam, been home for two years, dammit, the dreams should have been over, but they weren't, no matter how much pot she smoked before bed (self-medicating, Eagle, not good, you know that).

But this was the first time—the very first, *ever*—that the sound stayed after the dream had ended. She'd awakened hundreds of times with the stench of truck exhaust mixed with burned skin trapped in her nose, hearing 'copters, bringing in wounded, bringing the dead, and she'd always run forward, always headed toward the crisis, and here, in Berkeley, she always stopped in the kitchen.

Usually the hum of the refrigerator grounded her but she couldn't hear that right now.

Helicopter. Sikorsky, she knew it was a Sikorsky, and most of the wounded, at least from her dreams, came in Hueys, right off the battlefield (if you want to call that goddamn jungle a *field*), so why had she been dreaming about a Sikorsky...?

She ran a hand down her shirt, reflexive, nervous movement, then realized the shirt was stiff with blood. She looked down, saw the rounded top of a peace symbol peaking out of dried black blood.

Blinked, shivered, remembered five days before—

Stumbling down the stairs to the street. Kids screaming, cops everywhere, in riot gear—Jesus Fucking Christ, riot gear, on Dwight, what the hell?

Little explosions in the distance, and the smell—gun powder, a hint of ash at the back of her throat. Brain registers gas masks, on the faces of the cops.

Gas masks.

She moves, and rifles swivel toward her, and for a minute, the screaming fades, except for one voice: Help! Help! He's been shot! Oh, dear God! He's been shot! *and it galvanizes her into action.*

She turns, retreats up the stairs—not to hide like her neighbors, but to get her bag, and the gas mask from the gear she never quite managed to return. She slaps it on, feeling like an alien herself as the world browns from the mask's goggles, then back to the street, and through the chaos, the clouds of tear gas rolling toward her, the shiny guns, the scared cops, she can still hear the voice:

Help! Help! Please, someone help!

At the corner of Telegraph and Dwight, a girl maybe 19, seven years and an entire century younger than Eagle, crouches over a man (boy?), legs splayed, left hand fluttering helplessly. The girl's the one screaming, and Eagle crouches beside her. The girl starts. Eagle realizes the girl's reacted badly to the mask.

"Calm the fuck down," Eagle says, voice echoey and odd through the filter. "I'm a nurse. You need my help."

The girl tears up—whether it's the gas blowing toward them or the relief, Eagle doesn't know, doesn't care. She's not about to give up her mask to this girl. She needs to deal with the boy.

A blood trail on the sidewalk—he'd been hit in the street. Eagle moves his shirt slightly, sees a gaping gunshot wound on the left—open on his torso, so he was hit in the back.

"What the hell?" she asks out loud, and the girl says, "We were just protesting the park. They took over the park..."

And it takes Eagle a minute to realize the girl's talking about the damn parking lot that the hippies have been turning into a green space not too far from her apartment.

Realizes it doesn't matter, realizes that the cops are in no mood to call an ambulance, realizes this kid needs assistance, and digs in, right there, streetside, like she'd done a thousand times in Nam. Hands moving, concentrating only on the next step, not worrying about the guns or the floating clouds of chemicals.

Thinks for a half second of moving him to her apartment, worries he won't make it, treats him right there—triage, really, just making sure he doesn't bleed out, wishing she was three people—one to call for an ambulance with some fucking authority, one to help her close up this wound, and one to yell at the goddamn police: I didn't patch up kids in Nam so you could shoot more kids in fucking Berkeley. What the hell are you thinking? What the bloody hell?

But she is one person, just one. Former Captain June Eagleton, former in theory, but there is no theory, not a single one, because you don't retire, not when you live in a battle zone. Not when you have skills. Not when someone's dying near your doorstep—

Battle zone. She had forgotten which battle zone she was in. She was in the People's Republic of Berkeley, moved here for school (thank you, GI Bill), dropped out, stayed for the cheap rent and the even cheaper dope (helps her sleep. Yet another theory. Helps her sleep), and now, a goddamn Sikorsky hovered outside her window, making her deaf.

The building was shaking and she pulled the curtain back just enough to see the 'copter bank and head toward campus. Again. Campus.

What the hell would a 'copter like that—military grade—be doing over the campus? She ran to the other side of the apartment, with a sideways view of Telegraph and UC Berkeley in time to see the 'copter discharge white gas. It looked like CS gas, an entire load of it, dumped on campus—God, like Nam. Just like Nam. Only then the VC got gassed, civilians too, but Jesus, they were the enemy not people in the center of a goddamn city, an American city.

Her brain was racing. She whirled, grabbed the gas mask again, put it on, then stripped off the bloody shirt and jeans, promising herself again that she'd wash them or toss them or do *something* with them, thought about putting on her fatigues so the cops in the street (there had to be cops in the street, right?) would know she wasn't a student, but if the cops were anything like the group she saw five days ago, anything like the baby-faced National Guard troops who pitched tents in the park yesterday, they weren't going to care that she served.

They were going to think she was a traitor to it all, if they even believe that a woman could serve. How many times was she forced to explain the fatigues, the uniform, the pride she still feels (and feels guilty about).

So she slipped on an old denim shirt, ripped jeans, grabbed her bag and headed into the street for the second time in five days, off to save lives in her own country.

If she even got the chance.

She burst out of her building, made herself stop and look up, trying to get a sense of what direction the wind was blowing. Clothes, drying on a balcony, rippled slightly, and a white flag with Che Guevara's face on it flapped in the breeze.

An easterly breeze.

Shit.

She bolted up the street, screaming at pedestrians to get out, get out, they're dumping gas on the city, and everyone looked at her in fright. Damn mask.

She didn't have time to stop, to tell them more. She hoped they would be smart enough to leave the neighborhood, but she wasn't sure they were. She didn't even recognize most of them.

It was May and students were still here, and she made it a point not to get to know them. She already knew too many people, and son of a bitch, they were weighing on her heart.

A block and a half, that was all she had to cover, and it felt like a fucking effort, particularly since she was watching the sidewalk *and* the sky, and imagining wisps of white gas floating toward her.

Or maybe not imagining. She would probably be able to smell the gas when it hit, not even her mask could keep out all of that burned bleach odor—she'd learned that in training, then on the battle-fucking-field, treating village children for godssake, something she never talked about, not to anyone, not ever. She'd have to burn her clothes when this day was over. This wasn't wimpy-ass tear gas. This was military grade heavy shit.

She made it to A Gym of Her Own, saw a class under way through the plate glass window, six women wearing loose-fitting clothes, trying to learn how to block a punch. Pamela Griffin had a mission: she wanted women to learn how to defend themselves, how to fight *back* and while Eagle didn't want to support that mission, she somehow did, providing medical services almost since the gym opened.

She burst through the door, and a dimwit to her right screamed.

Eagle turned slightly to her left away from the useless screaming meemie, heard the gasps, saw women covering their mouths, frightened of her and her mask.

"You've got to get out of here," she said, voice hollow. "They're dumping CS gas on campus. It's blowing this way, and when it gets here, you're going to have serious problems."

"Eagle?" Pammy, muscular and blonde, the all-American girl gone butch, was standing at the edge of a mat, boxing gloves taped around her hands.

"Yes, goddammit," Eagle said, confirming her identity, even though she shouldn't have to. "Now, get out before this shit hits us."

She didn't have to tell them twice. Not after the riots on Thursday. She was amazed there were that many people in the gym, in the neighborhood, considering the entire city was under martial law, and there was a planned vigil for James Rector at noon.

Rector, the only person who'd died. Rector wasn't her kid. Her kid, whom she'd guarded for hours, still lived, from what she could tell. Rector got shot on a roof, lingered for days, died last night.

And now they were having a vigil for him. Organizing at Sproul Plaza on campus.

On campus. Only a few blocks away.

That's what the 'copter was spraying with CS gas. The fucking vigil.

She whirled, looked out the plate glass window, saw tendrils of gas, floating like fingers in the air, and swore.

"Never mind running," she said. "It's too late. Get to the showers. Right now. The showers."

"Why?" someone asked.

"Just do it!" Eagle shuffled them—eight women total—toward the makeshift locker room. Two showers and a damn door that didn't close as tightly as she wanted.

Pammy helped Eagle herd the women toward that locker room. The ones who got there first were peeling off their clothes.

"Forget the clothes," Eagle said. "Just turn on the water and get under it. Try not to breathe."

She tossed towels at them.

"Hold these over your faces," she said, "and keep your eyes closed."

The water wouldn't get rid of all the effects, but it would help. It would keep the worst of the gas off everyone.

She shoved Pammy toward the showers. "You too."

Pammy was good. Pammy was tough, but Pammy had never been in a situation like this one, and it showed. She started, "But—"

"Go!" Eagle shoved her again, then grabbed an armload of towels, and left the room, hoping Pammy would listen.

Eagle ran to the makeshift kitchen, with dirty cups and a few donuts on the sideboard. She flicked on the water, and dumped the towels in the sink. Then she took two soaking wet towels, and shoved them between the bottom of the locker room door and the floor, trying to fill that space.

Her gaze caught the small opening between the door and the jamb, realized she could do nothing about that, not without losing precious time.

Hurried back into the kitchen, grabbed more towels, saw the water slopping over the edge of the sink and didn't care. The ice-cold towels were soaking her clothes, freezing her fingers.

She ran to the back door first, shoved towels against the jamb. The entire building had to be canted, just like her damn coffee table, because none of the doors were level, not a goddamn one.

She grabbed more towels and dirty clothes, anything cloth, and brought them back to the kitchen. She pulled out her towels, shoved the new towels in the sink, broke a coffee cup and didn't have time to remove it. Hoped she wouldn't cut herself, because tear gas in open wounds was not only grounds for infection, but it hurt like fucking hell.

Whirled, ran to the front of the building, grateful there was only the plate glass window now, because other windows would've been other entry points. (Of course if the building was canted, god knew what cracks would let the gas in.)

The street was white, like the famous Bay fog had drifted over the city, only she knew it wasn't fog, and the ocean had nothing to do with this. She shoved towels around all the cracks in the door, knowing it was too late, but having a little gas in this giant space was better than having the entire place fill with gas.

She finished with the door and the window, headed back to the kitchen. The floor was slippery with water and probably damaged and she didn't care. She wrapped her hand in one of the top garments (forest green soaking wet whatever it was) and reached for the entire pile.

She was going to plaster them all over that locker room door, and hope to hell her triage worked.

When she finally finished with the towels and the water and the prep, she stood, heart pounding, in front of that goddamn plate glass window for what seemed like most of her life.

Three National Guard troops frog-marched a crying red-faced boy down the street toward the stupid park. The troops had made camp there on Friday—Governor Reagan's orders. The entire campus area looked like an armed camp because it was.

She never thought she'd see bayonets attached to M1 rifles gleaming in the sunlight, but she had. And she'd seen hard-faced boys, hard-faced men, who for some reason weren't in Nam, standing shoulder to shoulder in that damn park, standing in front of their tents which were in front of the swing sets.

Her stomach twisted. She'd seen a lot in the last five years. Too much. She was too close to this city; too close to this gym; too close to Pammy. Eagle cared too much.

She didn't want to care, and yet, she'd come here first.

No voices sounded behind her. She could hear the thrum of the water, running through the pipes, and faintly, shouts from outside, bull-horns and screams, and the sounds of panic.

She wasn't watching the time; she had no idea how long it took for the gas to disperse.

But it did. It went from a low-lying fog to a brownish gleam to nothing at all, except—she knew from hard experience—crystals on the roads and sidewalks and everything the stupid gas touched.

She'd have to help Pammy find someone to scrub this place with the right cleaners; hell, she'd have to force Pammy to go home.

Eagle sighed, then went back to the kitchen, washed her hands, and shook them dry. Then she opened one of the drawers where the extra T-shirts and loose pants were stored, removed them, holding them gingerly away from her body so she didn't cross contaminate them.

She put them in a brown grocery bag, and rolled the top closed, then carried the bag to the locker room. She pulled the towels off the door, kicked the ones away from the bottom, and opened the door.

The warm water vapor flowed around her, making her start, a sudden fear that she had stepped into gas. But she hadn't.

"Shut off the water!" she shouted. The squeal of faucets, the thunk of pipes, and then the drum of water ended.

The vapor cleared, revealing drenched women, clothes plastered to them, all but Pammy sobbing, faces red, but whether or not those tears were real, Eagle had no idea. It might've been the gas.

At least no one was vomiting or hyperventilating. At least no one was having a truly bad reaction.

"It's over," she said, and shook the bag. "I have clean clothes in here. You are all going to leave your wet clothes here. They will be either washed or destroyed, depending on how bad the gas was in this building."

One of the women started to say something, but Eagle shook the bag at her.

"You will *not* argue with me," she said. "You will wear the new clothes. You will leave this building. You will head home if home is outside of this neighborhood, and if it is not, you will go to high ground for at least two or three hours, until all of the gas dissipates. Is that clear?"

They were staring at her, water dripping off their faces, puddles around their feet.

"*Is that clear?*" she asked again. She sounded like her first captain, a nurse who'd been in the rotation longer than she had, a woman she'd hated back then, a woman whose toughness had probably saved Eagle's life.

"Yes," Pammy said. "It's clear."

Eagle held the bag for one moment longer. "These clothes are dry and relatively uncontaminated. They will *not* touch any surface in here. After you've removed your clothing, you will take clothing from this bag. You will put that clothing on. If it does not fit, you will trade with another woman. You will not at any time set this clothing down. Do you understand?"

"Yes," Pammy said.

This time, Eagle didn't want Pammy to speak for everyone. Eagle turned toward the other women, knowing they didn't see her brown eyes, but reflections in the mask's goggles.

"Do you understand?" she repeated.

Two women said yes. Four nodded. One—the dimwit—stared at Eagle like a scared rabbit.

Eagle decided the dimwit wasn't worth her time. She thrust the bag at Pammy. "Get them dressed and out of this room in less than five minutes. The longer they're in contaminated space, the more likely it is they'll still have a reaction."

She had no idea if that was true, but it sounded true.

She stepped out of the locker room and pulled the door closed. Then she took a deep breath, tasting the filtered air of the mask.

She was shaking. Goddamn son of a bitch, she was shaking.

Adrenaline, she told herself. Just adrenaline.

And knew she lied.

She pulled her mask off only after the last woman left. Eagle had no idea why she waited. They probably all knew who she was, but she wanted the anonymity. She needed it.

She liked to pretend she had nothing to do with this place, although she'd been acting as its medic for more than a year now. Without her, it would close. The city, the state—someone representing The Man—would use laws on the books that were never used against men's gyms. Laws that shut down places where there were too many injuries. Where there was too much hazard. Of course, too much would be decided by the goddamn authorities.

Eagle had a number in her head, but she had no idea if it was right. She'd told Pammy this: If half the women who got injured here went to a hospital or their doctor instead of receiving treatment from Eagle, the entire place would shut down.

Regulations, the authorities would tell Pammy. *Regulations, ma'am. We're sure you understand.*

Pammy stood beside her, her wet blond hair dark and spiked upward, looking like little more than a kid, even though she was more than a decade older than the students who filtered in here.

"Thanks," she said.

Eagle resisted the urge to wipe her face with her hands. She didn't want to contaminate herself either. "I need another bag," she said.

She could have gotten it herself, but she didn't want to. She wanted Pammy to stop thanking her, wanting that mixture of fear and gratitude the others had shown to become a distant memory.

Pammy gave her a sideways grin, as if she understood—and maybe she did; Pammy gave Eagle space, which was more than most people did—and sloshed her way to the kitchen.

The gym was a wreck of wet towels, discarded clothing, and water. Eagle had a friend in the chemistry department who might know how to clean this up, if he could be persuaded to set aside his politics to help a bunch of women.

If *she* could set aside her politics to ask for help. Eagle would have to pretend to be one of those begging females, and she wasn't. He knew that. He'd probably see right through it.

Pammy came back with a brown grocery bag held between the thumb and forefinger of her right hand. *Good girl, Pammy*, Eagle wanted to say, but she didn't because that was patronizing, and she didn't patronize. But she thought it, which was almost bad enough.

"Thanks," she said, taking the bag, opening it, and tossing her mask inside. She took a small sip of air, noted there was no chemical smell. Only the stench of scared women—sweat and some kind of musk she hadn't smelled since her first days in the Evacuation Hospital in Pleiku.

"You'll need a professional to help you clean this place," Eagle said. "Do not use soap and water. It'll revive the gas. You know anyone—some environmental science bleeding heart or a chemist or someone?"

Pammy nodded, that stupid grin still on her face. "Yeah, I know someone."

"Good," Eagle said. "Call him tomorrow—"

"Her," Pammy said.

Fucking irritating bra-burner, Eagle thought, but didn't say. Everything was women this and women that and solidarity bullshit. That was what started this whole mess.

When she had control over her tongue, she said, "Call *her* tomorrow." Too much sarcasm on the *her*, but oh, well. "You go home today."

"I need—"

"No," Eagle said. "You have no idea if this attack is a one-off. Your business is in a fucking war zone, and right now, you get the hell out. When it settles down, you come back and clean up. I'm not going to stick around to save your ass, got that?"

"Yes, ma'am," Pammy said. "Just let me lock up."

She went toward her office before Eagle could correct her. Eagle wasn't waiting for her. Eagle wanted to leave right now.

But Pammy would worry about where Eagle had gone. Pammy would probably end up staying longer if Eagle left first. She strode to the office, saw Pammy grab her fistful of keys (*Keys—the sign of belonging*, Doc Henry had said as they'd flown Stateside), said, "We're going out the back way, so lock up the front door first. And don't forget your closed sign."

Pammy nodded, eyebrows raised in amusement. Good for her, seeing the humor in this fucking situation. Even though Eagle really didn't believe Pammy should see humor in it, or in anything else for that matter.

If Eagle had her way, she would cover that plate glass window in plywood and then board up the building until the National Guard left this area. She'd seen boys playing soldier too many times; she knew how they loved to destroy things until they were actually in a situation where they had to destroy things, and then they realized just how difficult their jobs really were.

Eagle didn't follow Pammy for the lockup. Instead, Eagle waited by the back door, which led into an alley that had a lot more anonymity. She didn't want either of them to step out of an obvious lefty stronghold (*A Gym of Her Own*, indeed. What the hell was Pammy thinking when she named this place?), not with little tin soldiers running around, eager to show their authority to each and every civilian who crossed their path.

Pammy came back, her clothes bagging and damp, her hair even spikier. She held her wallet and her keys, apparently opting to leave her purse here, until she could come back and clean up.

Whatever Eagle thought of this place (and she tried not to), its founder was one smart woman.

"Let's go," Pammy said, the smile gone now. Apparently her walk-through had scrubbed the humor from the situation.

Eagle opened the back door and scanned the alley. Blue-painted brick across the way and the smell of fresh vomit mixed with garbage. The entire neighborhood would probably smell of vomit after this; when an area this big got hit with CS gas, then people with weaker constitutions were bound to have serious reactions.

She turned toward Pammy, nodded, and then walked down the stone half step into the alley proper, careful where she put her feet. Pammy came out behind her, and, because she knew Pammy expected it, Eagle waited as Pammy locked up.

Pammy jingled the keys, then looked at Eagle. Pammy's shoulders slumped. She had built this place, and leaving it during a crisis clearly upset her.

In another life, Eagle would have clapped her on the back and told her everything was going to be Just Fine. But Eagle had seen too much. She knew that Just Fine didn't happen for most people. Hell, Just Fine was just a state, one that lasted maybe a few years if someone was lucky, and then everything went to hell.

As if to punctuate that thought, the sound of someone dry heaving echoed in the alley. Pammy looked at Eagle, but Eagle didn't meet her gaze. Instead, Eagle searched for the source of the sound.

Dented metal garbage cans lined the brick walls. Other doors, some made of rusted metal, were closed against the alley.

Eagle took a cautious step forward, and found a girl huddled between two of the garbage cans. It looked like she'd been trying to throw up in one of the cans; its ribbed metal side had a trail of vomit chunks.

The stench of vomit had grown stronger as Eagle got closer. Eagle crouched and put her hand on the girl's bony shoulder.

The girl looked up, face red, eyes watering so badly that she could hardly keep them open. Her breathing was shallow, jerky, as if her air passages were restricted.

She was having a bad reaction to the CS gas.

"Pammy," Eagle said, her tone not a request. It was a command—*Get your ass over here*—and to her credit, Pammy understood. "We have to get her to a hospital."

The girl shook her head, but Eagle ignored it. People who needed help often refused it, and she'd learned not to give one good goddamn about what they wanted.

Pammy took the bag with the gas mask from Eagle without Eagle even having to ask.

Then Eagle braced herself and pulled the girl up. Eagle would carry her if need be.

The girl was taller than Eagle, and thinner. Something in her shaky posture and her body style told Eagle that she wasn't bracing a girl at all, but a woman full-grown. Maybe one as old as Pammy.

The woman's clothes were coated in gas and vomit and garbage, but Eagle didn't care. Eagle had already decided to burn her clothes.

"Can you walk?" Eagle asked, putting her arm around the woman's waist.

"I...don't..." The final word would be *know*.

Eagle'd done this more than enough. She knew the only way to answer that question was to try. She took a step forward with the woman, and the woman nearly buckled. Eagle tried again, and this time the woman steadied.

Eagle had no idea how fast they could go. It looked like the woman needed treatment immediately, so she might have to—

"I'm going to get my car," Pammy said, startling Eagle. She'd almost forgotten Pammy was there.

"No," Eagle said. Pammy usually parked in one of the lots—hell, before the whole park thing that started this, Pammy would park on the vacant lot. The People's Fucking Park. "We're taking mine."

"Mine's closer," Pammy said, even though that probably wasn't true.

"Mine's a beater," Eagle said. Plus, she knew she could clean fluids out of it. She'd done it before.

Pammy didn't argue, maybe because the woman collapsed. Eagle swept the woman into her arms—she weighed maybe 100 pounds, too thin for her height—and started to run.

They passed five National Guardsmen, carrying M1s like they meant business, heading toward campus. None of the men even noticed Eagle or Pammy; none of them seemed to care that they were two women carrying another.

No one else was on the street, although a few people opened doors, peered out, and then slammed them shut again.

Great helpful people. Lovely neighbors. Exactly who you'd want to live next to on a day like this.

The hell of it was, Eagle usually loved living near mind-your-own business types. But part of her still hoped that those types would help whenever she needed it.

Apparently, she was wrong.

She finally reached her truck, parked half on the so-called lawn in front of her apartment building. The truck was all rust and primer, uglier than shit on the outside, but underneath, it ran like a top. She kept it looking crappy so no one would steal it. She even kept the damn thing unlocked, and no one cared.

"This is yours?" Pammy asked. She had clearly never seen the truck before.

"Go home, Pamela," Eagle said. "I've got this."

Pammy didn't answer. Instead, she tried to open the passenger door. It didn't budge with her first tug—everything on this truck was big and heavy—so she braced her weight before tugging again.

Eagle was grateful; otherwise she would have had to set the woman down to get the door open. Pammy finally got the door open, and Eagle slid the woman along the bench seat. The woman moaned.

"Go home," Eagle said again.

Pammy peered inside the truck, frowning, probably trying to figure out how she could sit inside. After a few seconds of indecision, she said, "I don't think you should take her to Cowell. They'll be dealing with victims there. The attack looked big—"

"Thank you, Doctor Griffin." Eagle reached around Pammy and slammed the truck's door shut. "Go the fuck home."

Pammy frowned at her, then opened her mouth.

"Thanks," Eagle said again, with a sarcastic spin on the word. As she walked around the truck to the driver's side, she said, "For the record, I'm going to the community hospital. Wind's been blowing in the other direction. The CS gas would've dissipated by the time it arrived there."

"That's what this was? CS gas?" Pammy was following her. Eagle ignored her, pulled the key out of her jeans, and jammed it into the ignition. Then Eagle pressed the clutch, put the truck into reverse, and backed out of the parking space so she wouldn't hit Pammy.

The woman on the bench seat reeked of sweat, the sickly sweet smell of the gas, vomit, and maybe, just maybe, of blood. She moaned.

"Hang tight," Eagle said, shoved the truck into first, and barreled out of the tight, close neighborhood, wishing she had enough guts to hit a National Guardsman along the way.

The hospital was a little over a mile away. She swerved through the streets, seeing nothing and no one, except more cops heading toward campus.

When she reached the hospital, she didn't even try to park in patient parking or near the emergency room doors. She figured everything would be taken. Instead, she parked the truck on the street, then scurried around and pulled the woman out by her feet, just like she would have done if she'd been working the ER. Of course then, she'd have had a gurney. In Pleiku, she would've had other team members, stronger arms and stronger backs, but she didn't. She just had herself.

She got the woman half out of the cab, then slipped one arm behind the woman's back and the other under her knees, half-pushing, half-pulling her out the rest of the way. Eagle closed the heavy truck door with her hip, thanking whatever god was listening that she was parked on a slight incline, and that gravity helped the door close all the way.

Eagle carried the woman across the street, amazed at the silence. No helicopter rotors, no shouting, not even sirens from incoming ambulances. Just the shush of traffic one street over and the flapping of the American flag on its metal flagpole.

She looked up at the flag as she crossed, its red, white, and blue bright against the dull white of the six-story building. She used the sidewalk to get to the emergency entrance, the woman's feet brushing against the green shrubs.

Eagle had to turn and shove the doors open with her back—the damn things weren't automated—and she stepped inside to the familiar stench of cleaners losing the battle with the reek of sickness. She could always tell what the ER problems of the day were just by the smells, and today's was tear gas and vomit. Oh, lucky her.

She made it to the desk before someone saw her.

"I need a gurney," she said.

The woman behind the desk looked at Eagle over cat's eye glasses, her black hair lacquered in a beehive. "Sit down and we'll get to you."

"No," Eagle said. "A gurney. Now."

"*Sit down*," the receptionist said again, "or we won't be able to do anything."

Eagle whirled away from the receptionist, careful to keep the injured woman's feet from swinging outward. Eagle's back ached, and her arms couldn't hold the weight much longer.

When she saw the sign that read *Emergency: Authorized Personnel Only*, she pushed that door open with her back as well, and stepped into close quarters filled with voices and panic and the smell of blood. Beeps told her that someone was using equipment somewhere, and a nurse in traditional white looked up, saw Eagle, and said, "You don't belong back here."

"I'm not leaving until she gets a bed," Eagle said.

The nurse nodded, pushed open a curtain, and grabbed a gurney. She wheeled it toward Eagle, who set the woman down gratefully.

"Her breathing's shallow. She needs oxygen, and God knows what else. I'm hoping she hasn't aspirated some vomit, but she might have. Either way, her lungs are closing because of the—"

"We got this," the nurse said, and leaned over the woman. The nurse ran a hand over the woman's face, then elevated her head slightly.

Eagle turned, about to leave, only to find the receptionist standing behind her with a clipboard.

"You jumped the line," the receptionist said.

Ah, the tyranny of bureaucracy. Eagle hated it more now than she had when she was discharged—and she'd hated it a lot then too.

"She needed help, and you were being difficult," Eagle said.

"Still, we need to get her into the proper position—"

"She is." Eagle looked over her shoulder. The woman was being moved to a different hallway. Someone was taking care of it.

Eagle felt her shoulders relax. She wouldn't have to treat the woman herself, which was what she feared.

The receptionist handed Eagle the clipboard. "You will fill out her information. She jumped the line."

Eagle looked up, really looked, at the emergency room. Adults, with the usual sprains and bruises. Someone complaining of chest pain one room over. A little girl, pale, with sunken eyes, clinging to a teddy bear.

Through the open doors, she saw the waiting area, filled with red-faced students, half passed out, some with foam around their mouths.

"Jesus," she said softly.

"There's no need to be vile," the receptionist said.

Eagle bit back a response. She'd known vile. She wasn't vile. The fucking receptionist was.

But the receptionist wasn't in charge. Eagle had never even been to this hospital before, and for the first time, she regretted it. She went deeper into the ER, searching for the nurse in charge, wondering if it was the woman who had helped her.

The receptionist followed, yelling, and finally an orderly stopped them both. "Ma'am, I can't let you—"

Eagle went around him, and found a different nurse, wearing a slightly cleaner uniform, clutching a clipboard.

"You have a problem in your waiting room," Eagle said.

The nurse gave Eagle a withering glance. The receptionist had reached them. "I tried to stop her, but—"

"For some reason," Eagle said, "you are not being told that your waiting room is full of CS gas attack victims, some of whom are unconscious. Don't you check the waiting room periodically?"

"I'm sorry, who are you?" the nurse asked, using exactly the same tone Eagle would have used had she been confronted with this in the middle of a busy day.

"I'm Captain June Eagleton. I just returned Stateside, and I'm appalled at the state of your waiting room. We at least saw our patients in Nam, and politics didn't get in the way."

The nurse looked at Eagle, then at the receptionist. "What's she talking about?"

The receptionist shrugged, but looked terrified.

The nurse glared at Eagle, then hurried toward the waiting room. Eagle followed. The nurse saw the mess in the room, kids leaning against each other, students crying, some unconscious, and turned, angry, ready to confront the receptionist, who hadn't followed them.

Instead, the nurse saw Eagle. "Captain, thank you. Do you have privileges here?"

"No," Eagle said.

"Then I can't use you. I'm sure you understand—"

"I brought in a woman on my own. She's on a gurney in one of the rooms, just as bad as the folks out here."

"Friend?" the nurse asked, not really looking at Eagle. Instead, the nurse was beckoning other employees, switching the actual emergency room from an afternoon of minor illness and broken bones to major trauma response.

"No," Eagle said. "Found her outside my apartment."

"Then give Gertrude what information you can." The nurse shoved open the door and stepped into the waiting room.

A team followed, more nurses, assistants, a candy striper. They flowed around Eagle, and she felt more helpless than she ever had.

She knew how to handle a crisis, knew how to triage, knew how to work with the sick and get everyone into place.

But she didn't know how to wait.

A hand touched her arm. A woman with short brown hair led her out of the traffic pattern and sat her down inside the reception area. The woman with the black beehive and cat's eye glasses was nowhere to be seen.

"Your friend is here?" the woman said, clipboard on her lap.

"She's not my friend," Eagle said for the second time.

"But you brought her in, right? In room B?"

Eagle shrugged. She hadn't seen the room designations.

"Just give me her name, and we'll take it from there," the woman said.

Eagle hadn't even thought to ask for the woman's name. She couldn't say the woman was a Jane Doe. The woman's treatment wouldn't happen, and lying about her name would just make things worse.

Eagle glanced at the waiting room, the nurse organizing the patients, triaging the worst cases, and knew that some of the reception staff would get fired today.

Or not. Civilian hospitals tolerated a lot more crap than military hospitals did. Especially those in the field.

She'd learned that the hard way, when she'd first come back and thought she could supplement her meager savings with a job at San Francisco General.

"Look," Eagle said, standing. "I've done what I can."

She didn't wait for the receptionist to answer. Or the other receptionist to return.

She didn't want to wait for news. The woman would live. That was all that mattered.

Eagle had learned not to worry about what happened to patients after they left her care a long, long time ago.

She walked out of the emergency room, back stiff, body aching, the sounds of triage around her, the yelling, the crying, the soft-spoken gratitude.

She walked down the corridor, knowing no one had followed her, walked until she found the nearest exit, and stepped into the pale sunlight.

She looked toward campus, saw no more helicopters. She was too far away to hear the sounds of the battles up there if, indeed, there still were battles.

She crossed the street, reached her truck, leaned on its side, and closed her eyes. Just for a moment, feeling useless.

Then she opened her eyes, and looked at the hospital. She had training. She had skills. She could go back—

And deal with the goddamn bureaucracy, the situation where a single receptionist could clog an ER, probably for an hour, no more, but enough. Enough to make it worse, enough to make those protesting kids suffer a little longer.

Eagle climbed in the cab of her truck, unsure whether it smelled of old vomit or she did. She leaned her head back for a moment, knowing this was one of those moments, a decision.

Leave the war zone that the People's Republic of Berkeley had become. Find a new place, maybe a new life, maybe a small town where there were no students, no protests, no martial law, National Guard or military bases. Become someone else entirely, former Captain June Eagleton who would run an ER with military precision, who would fucking die of boredom in her very first month.

Pammy would miss her. No one else would. And after a while, Pammy would forget.

And Pammy's women, they'd sprain their wrists or crack a rib, and they wouldn't have Eagle to cover, wouldn't have Eagle to protect them from the ER receptionists. Receptionists who hated protestors. Receptionists who would think that women, in a gym, had no place fighting, and maybe not even a legal right to defend themselves.

A Gym of Her Own would get shut down, and it would be because Eagle wasn't a phone call away.

Small town or phone call. Hiding from the old war or fighting the new.

She hated her choices.

She hated her life.

But it was hers. And it was better than giving lollipops to sniffling children at their annual checkups, pretending she was making a difference.

She started the truck, put it in gear, made a U-turn, and headed back to the war zone.

The only place she had ever made a difference.

Blaming the Arsonist

Kris Nelscott

Blaming the Arsonist

The first hint that an arsonist had infiltrated the tight community around Telegraph happened on the night of January 23, 1969, in the middle of the Third World Liberation protests.

Pammy had nothing to do with the protests. She had attended UC Berkeley ten years before and, like so many others, stayed in the city, working odd jobs and finally, used her business and physical education double majors to open her own gym.

At least, that was what she told anyone who asked. She never mentioned all the real reasons why she opened the gym. Like the night her friend Doris had died during a beating from her boyfriend. Or the afternoon some thug had attacked Pammy's friend Carol as he tried to steal her purse, slamming her head against a brick wall, rendering her speechless for months.

Even with Pammy's training help, neither woman would probably have overpowered her attacker. But Pammy didn't just train women to fight back; she also trained them how to avoid a violent situation in the first place, using the skills her police officer father had taught her back in Philadelphia when he'd seen too many women hurt because they had no idea how to protect themselves.

The night of the fire she had closed up late. She'd been running a self-defense class that most of the attendees hadn't paid for. They were street people—hippies, flower children, little lost souls she'd been collecting since the doors to A Gym of Her Own had opened the summer before.

By the time she stepped outside the gym's front door, the night sky was strangely orange, and ash floated around her.

She looked up and down the street to make sure nothing was burning immediately next to her. Then she made herself lock the gym door, check the deadbolt, and pocket her keys. Calm, her father had told her all those years ago, solved more problems than panic ever would.

She slung her purse over one shoulder, the purse itself against her torso, and headed into the street. That was when she looked up. A fire towered over the neighborhood, a bright orange wall reaching toward the clear night sky.

Her breath caught.

The fire was *huge*, and farther away than she thought. It was north of her, but it couldn't have been north by much.

She ran to Telegraph Avenue, only to find everyone outside of their apartments. They were all looking toward campus.

The smoke was thicker here, the flames visible to her right. She hurried toward Bancroft and the edge of UC Berkeley.

The campus was bathed in that weird orange glow. She couldn't hear sirens—not yet—and she thought that odd too. But she also didn't hear voices raised in a protest chant or bullhorns exhorting people to march forward—and she'd half expected it.

All month, the Third World Liberation Front, a coalition of minority student groups, had been agitating for an ethnic studies college as part of the university. The students weren't like the students in the Free Speech Movement four and a half years before; these students were militant, often wearing military gear, and provoking the campus police with small acts of violence.

As she walked up to Sather Gate, she expected to see a clash between protestors and police. But the students she saw on Sproul Plaza looked as confused as she felt. More poured into the area as each moment passed, and she finally heard sirens, getting closer and closer.

The fire was coming from her right—one of the buildings on South

Drive. That thought galvanized her and she pushed her way through the growing crowd.

She ran uphill toward the Central Campus. The air was filled with smoke. Her eyes stung, and she had to blink hard to see through the haze.

Flames poured out of the roof on Wheeler Hall, one of the older buildings on campus. University security officers were dragging garden hoses up the flat white stairs into the open doors under the arches.

She needed to talk to security: there were hoses inside—fire hoses along with fire axes, near the fire alarm. Didn't those security officers know that?

As she got close, though, someone grabbed her arm.

Professor Dwight Jones pulled her back. "You don't belong in there, Pammy."

He was right. She could feel the heat on her face. She knew about the hoses, but she didn't know how to fight a fire, especially one like this.

The blaze was big and bold, eating the top of the building. She wondered what it was using as fuel. Wheeler Hall was made of granite.

One of the city's fire trucks pulled in behind her.

She whirled, saw firefighters pouring out of the truck, giving instructions, surveying, already working the scene. One of them grabbed a bullhorn and yelled at the crowd to get back.

She backed off, moving to the edge of the crowd. Professor Jones still stood in front, clutching his old-fashioned book bag, the one he had used when she had taken his European Literature class almost a decade before.

"What were they thinking, Pammy?" he asked her.

It took her a moment to realize that Professor Jones believed this was arson.

"You think someone set this," she said.

"No one was using the auditorium," Professor Jones said. "And the flames just whooshed into life. We all heard it. Not quite an explosion, but something—like all the air got sucked out of the building. Yeah, I think someone set it. And not just anyone. Those damn protestors..."

"Did you see them?" she asked, ever her father's daughter.

"I was teaching a class, Pammy," Professor Jones said, as if she was being thick. Maybe she was. "Besides, how do I know who 'they' are. Half the campus is involved in this garbage, trying to tear down everything just because they didn't get all the toys as children. Selfish little bastards. Look what they've done."

His voice was thick, and she realized with surprise that he was close to tears. She looked at him—really looked at him—for the first time in a long time. He had spent his entire career here, and he had seemed old to her ten years ago. He was nearing retirement. The peaceful academic world he'd known had disappeared five years before, and he was clearly still baffled by the changes.

Another fire truck showed up, and then another. Campus security left the building, some still holding garden hoses. Several students gathered around, hands to their mouths.

Firefighters ran past Pammy, up the stone steps, and into the archway. Another truck—a ladder truck—parked on the grass between Wheeler and South Hall. A ladder rose, and with it, curtains of water began spraying the rising flames.

Ash fell thicker now, big globs of black, wet and thick, like ash-rain. Two security guards backed the crowd up, and a few firefighters threatened to set up some kind of rope. Another firefighter was in earnest discussion with one of the campus security officers.

Pammy put her hand against her mouth, her eyes stinging from the smoke, feeling helpless. The campus looked unbelievably bright from the fire and the lights of the fire trucks.

More students and faculty members had arrived, faces yellow and orange in the flames. Young faces, furrowed with concern. Older faces—professors, graduate students—stoic. One young woman was sobbing uncontrollably as she stood near the trees at the edge of the South Drive.

Sparks danced in the air. Smoke was thicker now. It seemed like the firefighters had started to get the flames under control.

Pammy whirled and walked back toward Sather Road. As she moved, she bumped into a group of students who didn't even seem to notice her. She tensed like she always did, hand securely on her purse. The students hurried toward the fire, and she looked up to see a man leaning against a tree.

He wore camouflage. She probably wouldn't have seen him at all if she hadn't been staring straight at him. His face was dirty, his hair long. He wasn't holding books, but that meant nothing. From the snippets of conversation she had heard, a lot of students and professors had left their belongings inside Wheeler as they escaped the flames.

She nodded at him. He half-smiled, as if he couldn't believe someone was greeting him. And then he slipped away in the direction of Strawberry Creek.

If he hadn't gone down the hillside, she wouldn't have thought the moment odd. But she did.

She crossed to the other side of Sather Road—always be practical, always err on the side of precaution—and then kept one eye out, glancing both ways to make sure she wasn't followed as she headed back to Telegraph. She needed to pick up her car.

She wanted to go home.

Pammy didn't learn anything about the fire until Friday.

She came in early that morning, and made some coffee in her private kitchen.

Once upon a time, the back of the gym had been two studio apartments. She had opened them up, using most of the space as the locker room. The two bathrooms came in particularly handy.

But she had separated off one of the kitchens as part of her office, so that she could make her own coffee and keep her own food in a refrigerator. The other small kitchen belonged to the locker room, and made it easier for the women who occasionally slept here to feed themselves and their children.

Pammy tried not to think about how many building codes she was violating. But she always felt like if the City of Berkeley cared about building code violations in this neighborhood, they would have gone door to door. Everyone down here was doing something wrong—and most of them were doing a lot more wrong than she ever could.

She reserved the main part of the building for the gym proper. She had one fighting space, two large mats, and four heavy bags hanging from the low ceiling. She had six smaller bags hanging off poles. Those bags were set about a foot lower than bags in any other gym she'd ever gone to, one of the many things she had changed for the women who came here.

On one wall, she had two racks of clothing—one a rack of T-shirts with the words "A Gym of Her Own" emblazoned across the front, and a matching rack filled with sweatshirts. On the other wall, she had arranged boxing gloves by size, the smaller the better. She also had a lot of tape and extra pairs of women's sneakers, since so many of the women who came here didn't even have the right shoes.

She loved the smells of chalk and sweat that permeated the space. Those smells signified home for her.

She needed that comfort on Fridays.

Her morning class was two hours long. It had no college students at all. The women who came to Friday's class didn't live in the neighborhood. Pammy had no idea how they found her, but they had. The group were housewives from the same part of town who got tired of having coffee together at each other's houses every morning, and decided to "have an adventure."

Initially, six women had come to the class. By Christmas, three remained.

Pammy hadn't really expected any of them to show up after the Wheeler Hall fire, but they did.

They slid in the front door as if they were doing something wrong. Stella D'Arbus was the only one who usually walked tall, but even on this day, she hurried through the door like someone who didn't want to be seen.

Marie Seabolt followed, clutching a bag that Pammy knew from experience contained all of their gym clothes. They stored the clothing with Marie so that the other husbands didn't ask why their wives kept such horrid outfits anywhere near the house. Apparently, Marie's husband didn't care or didn't look in her bags.

LuAnn Amberson was the last person inside. She was so good at slinking that some Fridays Pammy never saw LuAnn enter at all. She had achieved a kind of ghostly invisibility that disturbed Pammy almost as much as the skeletal faces of some of the hippie women.

"I didn't think I'd see you today," Pammy said to them as the door closed behind them.

Stella waved her bejeweled right hand dismissively.

"We're not really here," she said as she stalked to the reception desk that Pammy had set up a few months ago because, she learned, women expected some place to check in.

"We're safe down here, aren't we?" Marie asked with a little too much concern in her voice.

"The protestors haven't left campus so far." Pammy realized she wasn't guaranteeing safety with that statement, but it was the best she could do.

She stepped behind the desk. She had a small cast iron safe on the floor. Stella had been the one who bought it.

I need some place to put my jewelry, she had said as she gave it to Pammy. *If I leave my regular jewelry at home, Roy is going to think that we're headed for divorce court.*

Pammy could never quite follow that logic, even though Marie had tried to explain it to her once. Stella's husband Roy liked seeing his wife sparkling with more jewels than the Queen of England.

It makes him feel important, Marie had said.

The thing was, in this state, Roy *was* important. He was one of the Board of Regents who ran the University of California system.

"But that fire was scary," Marie was saying now. "If those protestors can burn Wheeler Hall, they're going to burn the whole city."

"That fire was a one-time thing," Stella said, pulling off her rings. "Besides, Roy said it's got nothing to do with the protests."

Then her cheeks reddened. She had clearly spoken out of turn.

LuAnn spoke for all of them, albeit in a whisper. "But the chancellor spoke to the papers. He said it was the protestors."

"Papers schmapers." Stella took off her earrings, then reached behind her neck to unclasp a strand of pearls. "Roy says that they're pretty sure that the protestors didn't set the fire. The university thinks it's better though if everyone believes they did."

"They're not going to correct what the chancellor said?" Marie asked, sounding shocked.

"But, that means the real culprit goes free." LuAnn's voice got a little stronger as she stepped toward the desk. She was a slight woman with delicate features and bright intelligent eyes.

Stella looked trapped. She had to be political, even among her friends. Criticizing the chancellor was probably not the best idea.

Pammy set the jewelry, warm from Stella's skin, in the safe.

"The real culprit will get caught," Stella said without conviction. "I mean, they're looking for whoever it was. But they don't think it's those striker-protestor types. They think, from what they found, that it has something to with the movie nights there."

"Movie nights?" Pammy asked as she closed the safe and spun the combination lock.

Stella was still rubbing one of her earlobes. The other earlobe looked red. Her clip-ons must have hurt. "You know how they show old movies to raise money for various causes. One of the rule changes the university made was to say that student organizations that used Wheeler's auditorium couldn't use it to raise money for non-student organizations."

"So, no movies benefitting Meals on Wheels," Pammy said, realizing she was letting her bias slip through, because there probably had never been movies benefitting something like Meals on Wheels.

"Or movies donating money to the anti-war campaign," Stella said.

"Or movies raising funds to re-elect the Governor of California," Marie said with some heat.

Her two friends looked at her, surprised. Pammy wasn't sure what surprised them. She didn't know Marie's politics. Pammy couldn't tell if Marie was angry that no one could raise funds to re-elect the governor or if she was using that as an example to rile up Stella.

"Why would they think that it was the movie thing?" Pammy asked, trying to change the topic just a little.

"Because," Stella said, "Roy says fringe groups were using those movies to get a lot of money."

Pammy didn't see how. They didn't charge much to show the films, and the auditorium had seated less than a thousand people.

"So they're still blaming the protestors," LuAnn said softly.

Marie nodded. Those two had made the connection, even if Stella was oblivious to it.

"No, this is a different group," Stella said, ignoring the undercurrents as she so often did. "I don't think anyone in that movie club was raising money for the Third...Fourth...Liberating...Protestors—whatever they're called. No one is raising money for them."

Pammy's stomach clenched. She hated Stella's attitudes.

"What kind of proof do they have?" Pammy asked again. She realized that she had again broken her private vow to stay out of this, but she couldn't let it go. The images of those flames haunted her ever since she walked to Wheeler Hall.

"Oh, I don't know." Stella frowned at her. "I really didn't care enough to quiz Roy."

Implying that Pammy was quizzing her.

Stella shrugged. "I just asked enough so that I would know if we could come here today, and not enough to make him think I was actually interested."

And she clearly wasn't interested.

"Shall we change, ladies?" she asked her friends, and then marched toward the locker room.

LuAnn stayed behind for just a moment. She bit her lower lip, then frowned at Pammy.

Pammy had learned how to handle LuAnn these last few months. LuAnn was like a feral cat seeking affection. If Pammy waited long enough, then she might get LuAnn to trust her.

"You let people sleep here, right?" LuAnn asked softly. "I mean, that one morning we came early, there were some women leaving..."

Pammy waited. She wasn't sure what LuAnn was asking. Was LuAnn warning her that the women who slept here might try to harm the business?

LuAnn didn't say anything else, so Pammy finally spoke. "Yes, sometimes I let women sleep here, when they have nowhere else to go. It's not permanent, but it helps them."

LuAnn nodded. She opened her mouth to say something else, then Marie peered out of the locker room door.

"Hey, you going to change or what?" she asked.

LuAnn closed her mouth, swallowed, nodded at Pammy like a terrified rabbit, and hurried to the locker room.

Pammy frowned after her, wondering what that was about, and then shrugged. She might never know.

For days, Pammy kept turning over LuAnn's question in her mind, worrying about the protests and the arson, thinking about Marie's comment about burning the whole city.

Pammy knew that was a privileged paranoia speaking, but she also understood that edge Berkeley was walking on, the feeling that at any moment, the entire community could slip into out-and-out war.

The edge got even more slippery during the next week. The demonstrations on campus turned violent as sixty officers from police departments all over the area marched down Bancroft, slapping batons against their palms.

The protestors broke windows and disrupted classes, all the while trying to explain their position—their demands for an education that included everyone, not just the privileged white students.

When Pammy heard that someone threatened Wheeler Hall again—this time on the phone—saying it would burn all the way to the ground, she felt the beginning of fear. And felt no relief when the threat turned out to be a false alarm.

Then she learned about an actual arson attempt at Girton Hall. The flames got doused before they did any damage.

Girton Hall had been designed in 1911 by architect Julia Morgan as a place for the women on campus to go. Pammy loved Girton Hall. Designed by a woman for women, it was ahead of its time.

After she heard the news, Pammy walked over to Piedmont on one of her breaks, heading toward Girton Hall. She wanted to avoid the continuing protests, which mostly happened around Sather Gate and on Sproul Plaza. She figured she could avoid all the disruption if she went around that part of campus.

As she moved through the chill air, she heard faint chants of "Power to the People" even though there were no protestors up here. At the moment, this part of campus was empty.

But she kept seeing someone out of the corner of her eye, almost like she was being flanked. The hair rose on the back of her neck. She didn't want to whirl around because that would tell whoever it was that he had alarmed her. If indeed it was a "he." If indeed "he" was trying to alarm her.

She turned her head slightly to the right. She saw a young man wearing a white sweater over dark pants, carrying books at his side. He walked close to her, then veered off toward the Greek Theater.

Pammy made the same movement to look at her left side, and saw someone slip just behind her. Her heart pounded.

She was making this up; she had to be. No one was targeting her. She was simply upset by the fires, the police presence, and the demonstrators shouting near Sather Gate.

She hurried to Girton Hall. She let herself inside.

On this day, everything felt off. Despite the chill, there was no fire in the red brick fireplace. No smoke floated near the exposed redwood beams on the ceiling.

The interior of the building smelled like old coffee mixed with an undercurrent of something sharp and chemical. The chairs usually set up in the main hall had been placed against the wall. A cleaning crew of students scrubbed the floor with some kind of soapy substance.

No one greeted her, which was also unusual. Pammy walked around the scrubbers and into the small kitchen. There she saw her old friend, Ada Templeton. Ada leaned against one of the counters, clutching coffee to her chest.

"Is it true?" Pammy asked without saying hello. "Did someone try to burn this building down?"

Ada turned. Her shoulder-length hair was black, and had always seemed a bit unrelenting. Now, the strands around her face were turning white, taming the darkness and adding gravity to her features.

"Seven gasoline-filled bottles with rags stuffed in them," she said tightly. "Someone had tried to light the rags, but the flames didn't catch. Or something like that. The fire department says we 'ladies' will all be fine."

She said that last with sarcasm. Obviously, Ada didn't feel fine at all.

Pammy put a hand on Ada's arm. Ada leaned into her, touched her forehead to Pammy's, and then stood upright again.

"I don't recognize this place any more," Ada said softly.

Pammy nodded. She didn't either. It had been a very quiet campus when they were going to school.

"Were you here when it happened?"

Ada shook her head. "I came in after."

She glanced over her shoulder at the main hall, where the scrubbing continued.

"What did they do? Break a window and throw the bottles in here?" Pammy asked. Shattered bottles filled with gasoline would explain that tangy smell she caught underneath the scent of coffee.

"That's the weird part." Ada set her cup down on the counter. "The bottles were placed in here."

"Placed. As in upright?" Pammy asked. "In the *kitchen?*"

That could have been a terrible disaster. It was hard enough to see the kitchen floor on a good day. In the early morning, with the lights down, someone would have kicked the bottles, spreading gasoline everywhere, and probably dying in the process.

Ada shook her head. "In the main hall, near the fireplace. I've been trying to figure out that part. I mean, this building is old and made of wood. If you wanted to burn it down, the last place you'd put gasoline bombs was near the bricked-in fireplace. Maybe put them under the wooden deck, because the rest of this place would go up like a match. Especially with yesterday's wind."

She had a point. There were a dozen other places to ignite those gasoline bombs that would have completely destroyed Girton Hall before anyone could have stopped it.

"Do you think someone was leaving a message?" Pammy asked.

Ada shrugged her shoulders. "If so, I don't understand it. Do they hate us? Or hate the buildings that President Wheeler had had a hand in sixty years ago? After all, he approved Girton Hall, and Wheeler Hall was named after him. Because this really makes no sense."

"You don't think this has something to do with the protests?" Pammy asked.

"I don't see it," Ada said. "The protestors are fighting for minority rights here on campus, and a lot of them are talking about a women's studies program here too. So, if anything, the protestors would be supportive of places like this one, not try to burn us down."

Pammy tapped her thumb against her chin, as she thought about that. There had to be a reason Girton Hall, of all places, was targeted.

"There's a large group who hate the demonstrators," Pammy said. "Maybe they did it."

"If that's the case, then they should have gone after the Third World Liberation Front's headquarters. Or throw bombs at the demonstrators," Ada said. "Not come here. We've done nothing. We haven't even hosted their events. We've been pretty quiet through this whole thing."

Her voice wobbled, and tears filled her eyes.

Then she wiped at her eyes, as if her own tears had made her angry. "I don't get this. I really don't. What have we done to piss people off? We're not involved in any of the politics right now. None of it. What have we done?"

Pammy finally put her arm around her. Ada leaned into her, shaking slightly. She was still wiping at her eyes.

"Sorry," she said softly.

"Me too," Pammy said. She had no idea what else to say.

Ada took a deep breath and gave her a watery smile. "I feel like we should have some of your students stand guard or something."

She might have meant it as a joke, but Pammy wasn't certain. "I do think you'll need someone here around the clock for a while."

Ada nodded. "We already thought of that. The university frowns on it, but I don't care. We're setting up a buddy list of people who are going to stay here at night. We'll have at least two, maybe more."

"Make sure they can handle themselves if something goes wrong," Pammy said.

"We will. You can help if you want."

"I'd prefer not to," Pammy said. "I have my own business to watch over. But I'll fill in if you need me."

"I'll hold you to that." Ada hugged Pammy. "Thanks for coming."

"I wish it were under better circumstances," Pammy said, and slipped out of the kitchen.

She walked around the entire building, both inside and out, before she started back to the gym for the next round of classes.

Ada's comment about placing the bombs under the porch or near the eaves made Pammy go slow, as she checked to make sure all the bottles had been found. She saw some dry rot, and a lot of problems that the university needed to fix, but she didn't see any glass bottles filled with suspicious liquid.

Nor did she see footprints left by someone else walking around the building.

By the end of her tour, she was slightly chilled and more than a little discouraged. She walked out of the trees surrounding the hall to the main path. The protest chants had died down, but she could still hear angry voices floating up from the central campus core.

She rounded a corner, and a man stood in front of her, arms crossed. He looked vaguely familiar. His hair was cropped short and his eyes were narrowed.

"Find what you were looking for, bitch?" he asked.

She braced herself ever so slightly, making sure her weight was properly balanced so that if he reached for her, she could move out of his way and give him a swift kick at the same time.

"Looks like I just did," she said.

He raised his eyebrows. "You were looking for me?"

"If you're the one who tried to harm these women today."

He grinned. "You women think you're so important. Why would I care about you?"

She shrugged. "Why don't you tell me."

His grin disappeared and he took a step toward her. "I can beat the crap out of you."

She smiled at him. "I'd like to see you try."

He leaned back, almost as if she swiped at him.

"So you can go whining to the police?" he asked after a moment.

"I don't whine," she said.

He glared at her. She watched his body language. He had moved off the balls of his feet, and he was leaning slightly sideways. He wasn't going to come at her, not from that position.

"You just wait," he said. "I'll get you."

And then he walked away, shoulders hunched. It wasn't until he quickly disappeared into the trees that she realized he was wearing camouflage.

He was the man she had seen the night of the Wheeler Hall fire. And now he had been lurking at Girton Hall.

She was going to have to talk to the police. She didn't want to, but she felt like she had no choice.

Even though she had gone back inside Girton Hall and had gotten the name of the detective investigating the arson from Ada, Pammy didn't call him. Instead, she went to the police department and filed an official complaint.

She ended up talking to the desk sergeant because he wouldn't send her back to any of the officers working cases. She made him write down the angry man's description, and she made the sergeant register the fact that she had seen this man at two different arson sites.

"Hours after the events," the sergeant said, trying to dismiss her just like she had known he would.

"*During* the event at Wheeler Hall," she said calmly. "And yes, hours after at Girton Hall. But he had no reason to speak to me like that."

"Lady, college boys got no reason to speak to anyone the way they been lately, but they are. Just because someone was rude to you—"

"Normally, I wouldn't tell you," she said. "But in this case, I think it's important. Someone threatened Girton Hall and burned Wheeler Hall's auditorium. Someone is actively using arson to make a point."

"Yeah, the point is that those students are little rich babies who don't understand that they can't always get what they want," the desk sergeant said.

"That might well be the case," Pammy said. "But my father was a career officer with the Philadelphia Police Department, and he taught me to do things right, especially when crimes had been committed. I'm sure you feel the same way, sergeant."

The sergeant looked at her pointedly, then grabbed a complaint form. "You're such a cop, you fill it out." He slid it and a pen toward her.

She took both and smiled sweetly. "Only if you promise you'll give it to the detective handling the case, and you'll make sure the complaint form ends up in the case file."

The sergeant's gaze narrowed. "Which file?"

"I'd say both," she said, "but if you have to choose one file, then I'd say the Wheeler Hall fire, since this man was there while the fire was still burning."

The sergeant made a disgusted noise.

"Just promise me this won't go in the garbage," she said, as she started to fill out the complaint.

"You don't think too highly of us, do you, missy?" he snapped.

She raised her head.

"Actually," she said using the same calm voice she had used with the man near Girton Hall. "I do think highly of you, or I wouldn't have brought the complaint to you. I know you can't act on these two encounters, but I want to make sure you can act if and when this man gets found."

"You're convinced he's setting the fires," the sergeant said.

"I'm not convinced of anything," Pammy said truthfully. "But I do find his behavior odd, and I think that's important in this circumstance."

"Everyone's behavior is odd these days." The sergeant grabbed a manila file folder and walked away from the desk.

She suspected he had done so to get away from her. She didn't care. She filled out the complaint form and waited until the sergeant returned. She handed it to him, resisted the urge to remind him of his promise, and left the precinct, with barely enough time to make it to her next class.

Pammy taught that class and the final class of the day, happy that afternoon's students were among her most experienced. She had two of the students playact an attack with her, and she had to be careful, because she knew she had a lot of aggression to work out.

After everyone left, she wrapped her hands before pulling on her favorite gloves. She pulled the ties tight with her teeth. She knew that she had to prep properly, because she was still so angry she might hurt herself if she wasn't careful.

Working out alone, she had learned, wasn't always the best idea. But she had no choice this evening.

Then someone knocked on the front door, rattling the glass above the knob.

She didn't jump, but her heart started to race. No one came to the gym after hours unless there was a problem.

She hugged her right hand to her chest and used her teeth to untie the glove. She slipped it off, letting it fall to the floor, revealing her wrapped hand. She had just enough flex in her fingers to open the door if she needed to.

She walked toward the door, ready to tell whoever was out there that the gym was closed for the night.

A woman had cupped her hands around her face and was peering inside. It took Pammy a moment to realize that woman was LuAnn.

Pammy managed to unlock the door. Then she used her wrapped hand to beckon LuAnn inside.

LuAnn grabbed the knob and pushed her way in, using that same almost invisible maneuver she used when she came with Stella and Marie.

"Sorry," LuAnn said as she looked at Pammy's hands. "I didn't mean to interrupt."

Pammy ignored the apology. "Are you alone?"

LuAnn nodded, then glanced over her shoulder. "Can we get away from the windows?"

"If you help me get this off," Pammy said, raising her left glove.

LuAnn nodded.

They walked past the main window, and stopped in the shadows. LuAnn's fingers were shaking as she untied the knots.

Then LuAnn tugged the glove off. Pammy unwrapped her hands quickly, and set everything on a nearby table.

Her fingers were red. She'd wrapped them too tightly. She really had been angry. She wiped her sweaty palms on her pants, and nodded toward the office.

LuAnn swallowed, then headed in that direction. Pammy veered slightly off course to make certain the front door was locked and the closed sign blocked the window.

In the time it had taken Pammy to do that, LuAnn walked the length of the gym. She was favoring her right side, and limping slightly. Pammy hurried to catch up. She opened her office door, and LuAnn scurried inside.

"Are you all right?" Pammy asked as she closed the office door.

LuAnn scanned the room, clearly looking for windows. Then she wrapped her arms around her chest.

"LuAnn?" Pammy asked.

"No," LuAnn whispered. "I'm not all right."

She moved toward the back of the office, almost to the wall.

"What happened?" Pammy asked.

LuAnn's eyes met hers.

"I didn't kill him," she said. "I made sure he was breathing when I left. But I didn't call for help, either. I propped him up so he wouldn't choke, like you said people can do when they're unconscious and laying flat. I propped him up. But he was out. And bleeding. He was bleeding."

She swallowed hard, then bit her lower lip.

"I didn't kill him," she repeated.

Pammy let out a small sigh. She had been through this before, but never with a housewife. Usually with a college student or one of the hippie girls, and the scene of whatever had happened was often close by. In those cases, Pammy could see for herself what happened. In this case, she knew she couldn't.

Pammy had learned an order to these things. Take care of the woman first, then worry about the injured man. Figure out what happened, and how to report it. *If* there was any point in reporting it.

"Before we do anything," Pammy said, "tell me why you're limping."

"I'm not limping," LuAnn said.

"You limped in here." Pammy knew that sometimes people in the middle of extreme trauma were unaware of how they behaved. "I watched you. And you're not moving your right arm much."

LuAnn looked down at herself as if she were surprised. She clenched her right hand into a fist, then released it, moving each finger as if she were trying to see whether or not it was broken.

Her knuckles were skinned and bruises had started to form on them. Her thumb had a long bloody scratch that ran the length of it.

"Oh, God," she said, and her knees buckled.

Pammy caught her before she fell. LuAnn's shirt was damp, and she gasped as Pammy wrapped an arm around her.

Pammy helped LuAnn to a nearby chair.

LuAnn sank into it, moaning slightly. Then she took a shuddery breath, and her eyes filled with tears.

She looked up at Pammy. "I thought I was okay. I drove down here just fine."

Which led to the issue of where the car had been parked. Pammy didn't want to worry about that yet.

"Adrenaline," Pammy said. "Let's see what's really going on."

She didn't wait for LuAnn to answer. Instead, she grabbed LuAnn's shirt at the hem, and lifted. Pammy had learned to make that movement slowly. Six months ago, she had done the same thing with one of the street women, and got slapped in the face for her trouble.

LuAnn didn't slap her. Instead, she watched in surprise as the shirt stuck to her skin. LuAnn started to raise her arms like a child, then stopped in obvious pain.

"We'll cut it off if we have to," Pammy said. "Just stay still."

She looked at the mess before her. There was some drying blood, but not as much as Pammy had expected. There seemed to be more blood on the shirt than on LuAnn's skin.

But that skin was clearly bruised, and some of the bruises were so old they were yellow. Fresh bruises covered her stomach and her ribcage.

"I'm going to press softly," Pammy said, using a technique her first boxing coach had taught her. "I want to make sure your ribs are all right."

She touched gently, feeling the length of the ribs. With each movement, LuAnn sucked in air, as if she were holding back screams.

The ribs felt all right, but Pammy was no doctor. And she didn't like the look of the bruises on LuAnn's stomach. The darkness of some of them made Pammy wonder if LuAnn had internal bleeding.

"You spit any blood?" Pammy asked, careful not to look up. Some questions were easier to answer when there was no eye contact.

"Not any more," LuAnn said.

Pammy felt a slight frustration. "When did that stop?"

"Just after I left the house. I lost a tooth. I think it's in the shrubs." Then LuAnn let out an inappropriate giggle. "Fourth tooth this year. I'm going to look like Granny Clampett if he's not careful."

That joke sounded like something LuAnn had said before, and not to her friends. Maybe to the man she was referring to as "he." Pammy wasn't yet making any assumption about who that was.

"But you haven't spit blood since?" Pammy asked, keeping herself focused.

"No," LuAnn said.

"Are you peeing blood? Is there blood in your stool?"

"I don't know." LuAnn was bristling now. The questions had become personal. "I haven't peed since I left."

"Okay." Pammy wasn't going to push this any more. She got up and went to her desk. "I'm going to cut your shirt off. We'll put one of those sweatshirts on you, okay?"

"I can pay," LuAnn said. "I brought cash."

But Pammy hadn't seen her purse. It was probably still in the car. Pammy hoped that LuAnn locked it, because otherwise that purse was long gone.

"You don't need to," Pammy said.

"You can't—"

"Let me do this," Pammy said, keeping her tone even. She cut the shirt in three places, then eased the pieces off LuAnn.

LuAnn's arms bore the mark of fingerprints. Her right arm hung a little crookedly.

Pammy had no idea how LuAnn had driven down here.

"I'm going to get that sweatshirt," Pammy said as she tossed the pieces of bloody shirt in an old grocery bag.

She picked up an ancient towel from the ragbag she kept near the door, and wiped off her hands. They were bloodstained from that shirt. She tossed the towel into the bag too, then rinsed her hands in her office's tiny kitchen sink.

LuAnn wasn't watching any of this. She was looking at her own hands as if she hadn't seen them before.

Pammy let herself out of the room, and hurried across the floor to the sweatshirts. She grabbed one of the larger shirts, and brought it back to the office.

A movement caught the corner of her eye. She stopped, and looked, thinking it might have come from the door.

She peered in that direction and saw nothing, except a blurred version of her own reflection.

She swallowed hard, then rushed back to her office. She set the shirt on her desk, grabbed another rag, wet it with warm water, and handed it to LuAnn.

"Let's get some of the sticky stuff off." Pammy didn't want to use the word "blood," because she wasn't sure what kind of reaction she would get from LuAnn if she did.

LuAnn took it with her right hand. Pammy frowned. She couldn't quite figure out what was wrong with the arm.

LuAnn tried to rub the rag over her skin with that hand, couldn't, and switched the rag to her other hand. She washed gingerly, as if she were afraid to put any pressure on herself at all.

Pammy had never seen that many bruises on a woman. Pammy had seen a man look like that only once, years ago, when she wandered into the gym where her father worked out. A fighter had been beaten nearly to death by another fighter in an illegal match.

Pammy felt a wave of guilt. How often had she asked LuAnn to run or practice defensive moves when LuAnn looked like this under her clothing? What kind of pain had this woman been in?

"I'm going to drive you to the hospital," Pammy said. "We don't have to tell them what happened, but you need to have someone look at—"

"No." This time, LuAnn's voice was strong. Her gaze met Pammy's. "I'm not going to the hospital."

"LuAnn, I'm afraid you might have some injuries I can't see," Pammy said.

"He'll find me," LuAnn said. "And this time, he won't forgive me. I brought money, all my money, and my jewelry, and my bank book. I'm not going back."

"I don't see your purse," Pammy said, trying not to sound panicked. What a treasure trove LuAnn had brought for some of the street kids.

LuAnn unbuckled her pants, revealing a roll of tinfoil wrapped halfway around her hips, and secured with tape.

Pammy had no idea how LuAnn had done that as injured as she was.

"I promised myself," LuAnn said, "if he hit me again, I'd leave. I was all packed up and ready. But I couldn't go upstairs for my suitcase. I kept this in the back of a kitchen drawer just in case. He never looks in kitchen drawers."

"We'll put that in the safe," Pammy said. "We'll take you to the hospital, and make sure you're all right, and then—"

"No," LuAnn said. "I came here because I thought you'd know what to do. I didn't kill him, Pammy."

"I know," Pammy said.

"But I hurt him. Real bad. And he'll never forgive me."

Pammy braced herself. An angry man—husband, probably—would descend on this gym at any point.

"If we take you to San Francisco General—"

"No," LuAnn said. "He'll look there. He'll look everywhere. You don't know him, Pammy."

Pammy didn't know him. She didn't even know his name. And she had learned the hard way to respect a woman who said her man wouldn't give up.

"I hit him like you taught me," LuAnn said. "Chop in the throat, and he choked. And he bent over, and that's when I hit him on the head with the lamp. He landed hard. He was still breathing. I heard it whistling."

"Where did the blood on your shirt come from?" Pammy asked.

LuAnn bit her lower lip. For a moment, Pammy thought LuAnn wouldn't tell her.

Then LuAnn said, "His head. I had to slide him upright. I wasn't strong enough to lift him. I had to sit down, yank him against my chest, and pull. It hurt."

It probably had, particularly given LuAnn's injuries.

Her description clearly wasn't all that had happened. LuAnn hadn't gotten those bruises on her knuckles from hitting a man in the Adam's apple. Nor had she gotten that cut on her thumb that way either.

But Pammy wasn't going to worry about those details yet. She had too many other things to worry about.

Pammy had no idea how long it had taken LuAnn to get here, but Pammy did know that enough time had passed that a man who had suffered serious neck trauma might have his throat swell up completely.

And if he died, then LuAnn would be charged with murder—and Pammy as an accessory.

"I'm going to call a friend," Pammy said. "She has medical training. I want her to look at you. She'll come here, okay?"

"Okay," LuAnn said.

"Can you tell me one thing?" Pammy asked. "This man, will he come here looking for you?"

LuAnn let out that weird giggle again. "He doesn't know about this. I paid with coupon money. He doesn't know I did this."

Coupon money. Pammy had heard LuAnn talk with Marie about that. They had kept the money they saved from cutting coupons in a separate place from their weekly allowance, so they had extra spending money.

All the girls do it, Marie had said, when she had seen Pammy's surprised face. She had thought the housewives all had money. Stella had disabused her of that.

Our husbands *have money,* Stella had said bitterly. *We have allowances.*

Pammy let out a small sigh. At least the angry man—or the angry man's friends—wouldn't show up here quickly. But they might after talking with Stella and Marie.

"This man," Pammy said, "the one who hit you. He's your husband, right?"

LuAnn looked at her with almost comical surprise. "I thought you knew that."

"Just wanted to make sure," Pammy said. "I just needed to make sure."

She left LuAnn alone in the office for a few minutes. Pammy didn't take the tinfoil-wrapped money because she was afraid to remove it from LuAnn's skin.

So Pammy decided to handle problems one at a time, as if they were on a list. And the first thing on that list was the phone.

Pammy grabbed the sign-in sheets she had developed when she realized that her potential students expected some kind of order and accountability. She hoped LuAnn signed her last name on at least one of the sheets, because Pammy had never asked for it.

LuAnn had signed in the week before as *L. Amberson*. Pammy let out a small sigh. Her job just got a bit easier.

She knew the women lived in the Berkeley Hills, so she used the Berkeley phone book she kept beneath the desk and looked up Amberson. She had a choice of five. So she looked up the address for Roy D'Arbus. Stella had said they were all neighbors.

Pammy found an Amberson on the same street. Her heart was pounding again. What she was about to do was something her father would never have approved of, but it was the only thing she could do right now without revealing where LuAnn was.

Pammy called the Berkeley Police Department, and when a male voice answered, she swallowed, made herself sound panicked, and said, "I don't know what's going on, but there's a lot of screaming next door. The door's open, and I thought I saw some big men running in there. I think they're being robbed."

"Where's this, ma'am?" the male voice asked.

Pammy gave him the Amberson address and hung up. The police did not routinely trace calls—it took time and was expensive. She knew that call would fall into the "anonymous tip" category.

She also knew that her suggestion of a robbery and "big men" would lead the police in the wrong direction.

Her palms were sweating again. She rubbed them on her pants, then picked up the phone and dialed another number from memory.

When she heard a "Yeah?" she said, "I need you right now," and hung up.

She knew that the person on the other end of the phone would be here shortly. June Eagleton had never disappointed her.

Eagle, as everyone called her, had stopped in the gym shortly after Pammy had opened it the year before. She doubted that Pammy had the chops to run a gym, and once Pammy proved herself, Eagle said that Pammy needed a medic because if there were too many injuries coming out of this place—even minor ones—doctors would shut her down.

It would be the excuse they want, Eagle said. *Fighting women threaten men.*

She would know. It had taken Pammy months to discover that Eagle had spent years as a combat nurse in Vietnam. She had come home angry and bitter. Generally, she refused to talk about her experiences, but slowly, Pammy got bits of her story. She wasn't sure she would ever get all of it.

Pammy ducked back into the office to check on LuAnn. The bruise on LuAnn's jaw was getting darker.

"Where did you park?" Pammy asked.

"Down the block," LuAnn said. "Not very good either, I think. I don't know."

"Where's your purse?" Pammy asked.

LuAnn shrugged and then winced. "Home somewhere. Why?"

"Just checking," Pammy said. "My medic friend will be here in a minute."

"Okay." LuAnn sounded exhausted. Clearly, shock was setting in.

"I'm going to go wait for her," Pammy said. "It won't be long."

Then she let herself out of the office. She saw movement again near the large window, and hoped it was Eagle. Pammy was clearly on edge. She hated being put in this position, and yet, she knew, that just by opening the gym, she had put herself here.

Then a face appeared in the doorway. Eagle.

Pammy unlocked the door, and opened it.

Eagle stepped inside. She was thin and weathered, and she always looked tired. She was holding a medical bag just like Dr. Kildare did for his TV house calls. Pammy once teased her about that until Eagle froze her with a look. Pammy never made fun of the bag again.

"What happened?" Eagle asked. "I was expecting a class."

Pammy shook her head. "Husband. She won't go to the hospital, afraid he'll find her."

Eagle's mouth twisted. "She's probably right. I'll see what I can do. Office?"

"Yes," Pammy said.

Eagle nodded, and headed back there. This sort of thing had happened enough since the gym opened that they actually had a system in place. Pammy would keep the injured woman in the back, then Eagle would go in alone and introduce herself.

That prevented the woman from begging Pammy to have Eagle leave, and it also gave Eagle a minute to establish trust.

Pammy glanced at the door. She hadn't locked it behind them. She walked to it, and saw movement against the big glass window.

That bothered her enough to open the door and peer outside. The street was empty, but she heard voices on the breeze. More protests probably, or a rally, or something farther up Telegraph.

She also heard The Doors, filtering down from a nearby apartment.

The night was chilly, and smelled of rain—which was so much better than smelling of smoke.

Although she did get a hint of something sharp, and she immediately flashed back on the smell beneath the coffee odor at Girton Hall.

She looked to her left, where she had seen the movement, just as a dark shape tackled her sideways.

She thumped against the sidewalk, felt her elbow hit hard, but she managed to tuck her head so that it didn't slam into the side of the building. Then she brought her legs up and kneed her attacker in the groin. She hoped her attacker was male, and hoped against hope that she had hit her target.

He yelped, confirming she had.

She wrapped her arms around him, rolled him over so that she was on top, and then punched him repeatedly in the face as if he were a punching bag. She could hear his skull knocking on the sidewalk.

His hands came up, then fell to his side, and she leaned back.

He didn't move.

She waited another minute, thinking he might be playing possum, and then she realized that no man could lie this still after being kneed in the balls.

He was out.

She stood, dusted herself off, and was about to go back inside, when she saw three bottles gleaming in the thin light from the doorway of her gym.

She glanced at the man, realizing she hadn't seen him well because he was wearing camouflage and his face had been deliberately smudged.

"You son of a bitch," she muttered.

She hurried inside, grabbed two jump ropes, and brought them back out. She turned him slightly, tied his hands behind his back, then brought his feet up and tied them as well, anchoring them to his hands.

Then she grabbed him by the back of his jacket and, with one hand, dragged him inside.

In the full light, she saw his face.

It was the man who had confronted her at Girton Hall.

"Got you," she said.

Although she wasn't sure what to do with him—or with those bottles.

She had to get them away from her building. And then she needed to call the police.

Who wouldn't believe her.

But she had to try.

Bottles first. They were too dangerous to keep close to the building, but she couldn't easily dispose of them, particularly if she were going to contact the police.

She left the asshole just inside the door, put on some regular cold-weather gloves, and then went back out. She hurried into the alley and grabbed one of the metal garbage cans. She dumped it out, hoping her neighbors would forgive her for the mess, and carried the can to the curb.

She gingerly picked up each bottle and placed it inside the can. All of the bottles had rags in them, and the liquid was leaching out. She didn't know what to do about that, so she didn't do anything. She just hoped no one bent on destruction found the garbage can before the police arrived.

If they arrived.

She tried not to think about that. Sometimes she hated the fact that she was near campus.

She started to go inside when a Mercedes turned into the alley, and stopped.

Stella got out. Her hair, normally sprayed into submission, was wind-blown, and she wore a heavy coat that was too big for her.

"Do you know where LuAnn is?" she asked without saying hello.

"I've got other issues right now," Pammy said, not wanting to reveal LuAnn's location.

Pammy put the lid on the garbage can, and took a deep breath, hating the smell of gasoline that had just wafted over her. She had to use her training: pretending to be calm was often the same as being calm. Deep breaths kept the panic at bay.

Stella grabbed her arm, nearly knocking her off balance. "Pammy, where's LuAnn? She's missing and someone beat her husband to death."

So he had died. Pammy hadn't called soon enough, or maybe he had been dead when LuAnn dragged him across the floor.

"There's blood all over the house, and the police are saying there was a robbery. LuAnn is gone, and so is the car. Please, Pammy. Have you seen her?"

Pammy couldn't tell Stella about LuAnn now. That would get Stella involved after the fact.

"Sorry, Stella," Pammy said, and shook her off. She couldn't quite lie to her.

She pulled open the door, planning to close it before Stella followed her, but Stella moved quicker than expected. She blocked the door and stepped in right behind Pammy.

Then stopped.

"What the hell?" Stella asked, looking down.

The arsonist was still trussed on the floor, still unconscious. All the color had drained from Stella's face.

"What have you done, Pammy?"

"What have I done?" Pammy asked. "What have *I* done? I've protected this place. This idiot was trying to burn it down. I just put three gasoline bombs into that garbage can and I was going to call the police. That's what I was doing when you got here."

The door to the office opened and Eagle leaned out. "Pammy, I—"

She stopped when she saw Stella. Stella's eyes narrowed. She had met Eagle before, and knew that Eagle helped with medical issues.

"When you're done, talk to me," Eagle said, and closed the door.

Stella wasn't ready to let Eagle go that easily. Instead, Stella stalked across the floor, heading toward the office. Pammy wasn't going to get rid of her no matter what.

Pammy sprinted after Stella and caught her just before she reached the door.

"You don't want to go in there," Pammy said.

Stella glared at her. "I sure as hell do."

Her use of profanity shocked Pammy almost as much as her glare. Stella had never behaved like this before.

"Look, you've already seen something you shouldn't. If you open that door, you're involved, and believe me, you don't want to be."

Stella let out a small laugh. "What makes you think I'm not involved?"

"You don't know what's going on," Pammy said. "You have no idea—"

"LuAnn's in there, isn't she?" Stella said. "And she's in bad shape, isn't she?"

Pammy felt her face heat. She didn't want to answer.

Stella leaned in toward her. "He almost beat her to death in July. She came to my house, and he found her, and I chased the evil s.o.b. off with a baseball bat. But he convinced her to come home to him, don't ask me how, and told her to stay away from me. Thank God she didn't listen. Marie and I brought her here, hoping we'd give her some tools to defend herself. That's what she did, isn't it? She hit him back."

Pammy didn't answer.

Stella grabbed the doorknob.

"You open that door," Pammy said, "and you become party to a crime."

"You mean killing Bruce?" Stella asked. "She should have done it years ago. And it seems to me, Miss My-Father-Was-A-Police-Officer that anything LuAnn did tonight would have been in self-defense."

"Yes, it seems that way to you," Pammy said. "But it won't seem that way to any investigating officer. She fled the scene. Most women can't get away with—"

"I know," Stella said flatly. "But you covered that, didn't you? You called in a robbery in progress. Very smart. Now they're searching for the masked man, just like in *The Fugitive*. There's a blood trail, so the police will have an idea where he went. And when they find him, he'll be trussed up on your floor."

Pammy's breath caught. Stella meant to blame the arsonist for Bruce's death?

Pammy shook her head. "No."

"That's why you tied him up, isn't it?"

"I tied him up because he was trying to burn down my gym. Just like he tried to burn down Girton Hall. Just like he burned down Wheeler Hall. You're not going to be able to pin a murder on him."

Stella harrumphed and shoved the door open. Someone let out a small scream from inside.

Pammy pushed her way in.

Eagle looked at them both, her expression impassive. "I taped her ribs. I think they're just bruised. Her breathing sounds fine. Her right humerus is cracked, I think, but her ulna is definitely broken, one of those twisting injuries that you get when someone turns your arm the wrong way. She says she drove here. I have no idea how. I also have no idea how her fingers work. I think she'll need surgery. I want her to have X-rays, but she won't go to any hospital."

LuAnn's face was chalk white, her eyes sunken into her skin.

Stella glanced at Pammy, confused. Suddenly the situation wasn't so simple.

"You wanted to be involved," Pammy said.

Stella let out a breath. Eagle ignored her.

"I can take her to a friend," Eagle said.

"Where?" Stella asked.

Eagle glared at her. "I don't know you. Not really. And I have no idea why Pammy trusts you. So I'm not telling you a goddamn thing, except that this woman was beaten badly and she needs care and she refuses to get it in the Bay Area. I think I can get her out of the Bay Area with a minimum of consequences to her body and to the future use of that arm. And that's all you need to know."

That last was for Pammy. Eagle wanted Pammy to make a decision. She'd been in this situation with Eagle before. Eagle didn't leave an offer on the table for very long.

"All right," Pammy said. "Keep me informed."

"When I can," Eagle said.

Pammy nodded. They'd made that deal before too.

"You have to go out the back," Pammy said.

"I was planning to," Eagle said. She put an arm around LuAnn and helped her to her feet. They staggered out of the office door.

Pammy escorted them, making sure they were nowhere near the arsonist. He was awake now, because she heard him thumping against the floor. Fortunately, he wasn't shouting. He probably figured untying himself was more important than calling for help.

Stella looked in the direction of the sound, but Eagle didn't. She gently got LuAnn to the side exit.

"You need my car?" Pammy asked.

Eagle shook her head once. "No. I'll call you when I know something."

"Well, know this," Pammy said. "Stella tells me that things just got a lot worse."

LuAnn moved slightly. Eagle looked at Pammy and mouthed, *Did he die?*

Pammy nodded.

"Shit," Eagle said. "I'll make sure we'll deal with the information when the time is right. You gotta clean up here."

"I will," Pammy said.

Stella said, "LuAnn?"

LuAnn stopped and looked at her.

"I'm sorry. I should have gotten you out sooner. I—"

"Save it," Eagle said. "Feel guilty on your own time. I gotta get this girl some help."

And then she steered LuAnn out the exit and into the back of the alley.

Pammy shut the door behind them, and leaned on it for just a moment. Her heart was pounding. Her elbow hurt, and for a half second, she couldn't remember why.

"Is she going to be all right?" Stella asked.

"I have no idea," Pammy said. "But she's not going to come back here. And if Eagle has her way, LuAnn won't come back to Berkeley at all."

She didn't tell Stella that LuAnn had money and jewelry with her. If LuAnn wanted to stay away, she could.

It was out of Pammy's hands now.

Almost.

The thumping in the gym got worse. Pammy let out a breath. She knew he hadn't been able to hear or see what they were doing, but the fact that he'd been here for the last of this bothered her.

"What are you going to do with him?" Stella asked.

Pammy sighed. Her head was starting to ache too.

"Call the cops, and hope to Christ they come down here. I have the name of the detective in charge of the Girton Hall investigation. Maybe he'll think a problem near Telegraph is worth responding to."

"You're sure this is the guy who burned Wheeler Auditorium?" Stella asked.

Pammy nodded.

Stella's eyes narrowed. "Well, then," she said, sounding like the old Stella. "I feel like taking a few prisoners myself tonight. And since I can't work on the crisis I want to work on, I can help you."

"No, Stella, let me—"

"You're right, Pammy," Stella said. "The police won't listen to you. But they will listen to Mrs. Roy D'Arbus about something connected to the university. I will call the police. You will clean up your office."

"Let me check on him first," Pammy said, picking up some tape she usually used for people's hands.

She headed to the front of the gym. The man had rolled closer to the window and was trying to prop himself up so that he could attract attention.

She grabbed his shoulder and pulled him back, making him fall.

"You fucking bitch," he said. "You let me go before something happens. You have no right—"

She wrapped the tape around his mouth and pulled so tight his skin stretched. "My father used to say that all arsonists are sick cowards. He was right."

She pushed the man down, and checked the knots on the ropes. Satisfied that they were tight, she walked back to the reception desk where Stella was on the phone with the police.

"What's the address here?" Stella asked.

Pammy gave it to her.

"Yes, he's inside," Stella said into the phone. "We surprised him, and were able to knock him out. He's tied up now. Please, come get him."

She sounded calm, calmer than Pammy felt. Pammy hoped Stella didn't say anything about LuAnn or anything else.

Stella hung up. "They'll be here shortly." She braced herself on the reception desk. "Now, what else can I do? Help you with the office?"

Pammy looked at her, trying to figure out Stella's motives. Which wasn't true. Stella had told Pammy the motive. Pammy just had to choose whether or not to believe her.

Pammy let out a breath. The reasons she didn't want to believe Stella were the pearls and the hairspray and the make-up. The powerful husband and the privileged life.

Judgment based on appearance.

"I'll take care of the office," Pammy said. "You sit somewhere, but make sure you can see our prisoner."

Stella nodded. The word "prisoner" seemed to shock her a little.

Pammy looked inside the office. It wasn't as messy as she had expected. Just a bit of blood, and the bag on the floor with the remains of LuAnn's shirt.

Pammy couldn't put that in the garbage; the cops would find it and wonder what it was. Then she had an idea.

She leaned out the office door. "Do you know what kind of car LuAnn drives?"

Stella nodded. "It's a brand new Buick. I saw it a block from here."

"That's how you knew she was here."

Stella shook her head. "I knew she was here when they said the car was gone. They figured the burglars stole it, but I knew she had come to you. She couldn't come to me after the last time. The time before that, she went to Marie, and Bruce had found her then too. So this time, she would go somewhere that he couldn't find her."

Pammy didn't want to think about what would have happened if LuAnn's husband had survived. Would she have gone back to him and let him beat her again and again until he killed her? Why did some relationships have to end like that, in blood and beatings and one or the other spouse dying? And why was it common enough that she had to ask that question?

"One block which direction?" she asked.

Stella pointed. Pammy nodded, then put on her gloves and grabbed the bag. She let herself out the same side exit that LuAnn and Eagle had used.

The alley was cold and dark. Pammy tried not to think about whether or not the arsonist had an accomplice. She doubted he did. The accomplice would have stepped in already.

She made herself hurry, picking her way across the gravel.

Once she got to the side street, she saw the new Buick parked haphazardly, not anywhere near the curb. The interior light was on, but the doors looked closed.

As she got closer, she realized that the driver's door wasn't shut all the way.

Pammy looked around. For once she was happy there were no working streetlights here. She looked up, saw closed curtains in the nearby apartments, and no one else on the street.

She pulled open the back passenger door, and dumped the pieces of the shirt on the floor. Then she crumpled the bag itself and threw it against the rear window.

The cops would find the blood, think it was LuAnn's and believe the worst.

Pammy almost left the driver's door alone, and then she thought about it.

Fingerprints. The police would take prints from steering wheel and the door handles. Either the police would find LuAnn and her husband's prints and no one else's or find the prints of someone innocent. And that would be as bad as blaming the arsonist.

Pammy rounded the car. She wiped off the driver's door handle inside and out, then wiped down anything LuAnn might've touched on the drive here.

The police would find the lack of fingerprints suspicious enough to continue the robbery story. They would think only criminals would wipe down a car. They would think—correctly—that a wife in the heat of the moment would never have the presence of mind to clean up after herself.

Pammy wiped the front passenger door as well. Then she hurried back to the darkness of the sidewalk, and made herself walk back to the gym.

No cops yet.

She wanted to be there when they arrived. Because Stella would need all the help she could get.

It turned out that Stella didn't need any help at all. She saw the flashing red-and-blue lights as the police approached, and scurried out to her Mercedes. She stood beside it, arms crossed, as the police car pulled up.

As a uniformed officer got out—not the detective after all—Stella walked over to him.

"Thank heavens you're here," she said. "This man attacked my friend, and slipped. Fortunately, it knocked him out. I can't imagine what would have happened if he was able to finish the attack."

Pammy opened her mouth to object to the story, and then she saw the officer's face. He believed it.

The officer moved his head slightly, commanding his partner to join them. Stella showed them the gasoline bottles in the garbage can, and then led the officers to the gym, talking the entire time as if she had been terrified by the whole thing.

Pammy stayed back. She hated pretending to be a helpless female. But she also knew it worked.

And she admired Stella for the line she was walking. She was pretending to be a helpless female who also happened to be the wife of one of the most powerful men in the State of California.

The cops knew they had to treat her well.

They got the arsonist out of the building, and Stella told them she would follow so she could press charges. She stood near her Mercedes as the cops put the arsonist in the back seat of the squad car.

"Let's go," she said to Pammy.

Pammy almost refused. Then she realized just how sideways this could all go. The arsonist could call Pammy a crazy woman, and the earlier police report that she filed would make it seem like she targeted him.

Or Stella might accidentally mention LuAnn.

Pammy made sure the gym was locked, and then she climbed into the

Mercedes. She had never been inside one before. It smelled of leather and money.

She leaned her head against the seat, suddenly realizing what a long night she had had.

"Thank you for the help," she said to Stella.

Stella let out that same small laugh. It seemed to be her default when something struck her as odd.

"It was nice to be able to help at least one woman tonight," she said.

Pammy smiled to herself. "Yes," she said softly. "Yes it was."

After Eagle's call the next day, Pammy never spoke about LuAnn again. Eagle had driven LuAnn to a hospital, and from the sound of it, they had gone to Sacramento to get help, although Pammy didn't know that for certain.

What she did know was that the Berkeley police believed some thugs had taken LuAnn and brutalized her, then killed her, dumping the body somewhere. The police had no suspects, no real leads. Even the car was a dead end.

Pammy also knew that LuAnn had defended herself, just like she said. Stella saw the evidence and talked to the police. All of Bruce Amberson's injuries were consistent with LuAnn's story, which Pammy found to be a relief.

The police couldn't tie the arsonist—whose name was Ryan Cosgrove—to the Wheeler Hall attack or the bottles left at Girton Hall, but they did charge him with assault on Pammy, and attempted arson at the gym.

There was no trial. He plead out, hoping to avoid being transferred downstate. The police had found other reports of fires, dating back more than a decade. Apparently, Cosgrove had used protests to cover his fires for the past two years.

The police said his choices were random, but Pammy didn't think so. The gym and Girton Hall were women-only. And it turned out, some of the major charities getting money from the movie nights in Wheeler Hall were some of the campus feminist groups.

Pammy couldn't prove it, of course. It wasn't her job to prove anything.

Her job was to train women to defend themselves in bad situations. And as Stella talked up Pammy's capture of Cosgrove, women paid attention.

Even though Pammy felt like she had done very little. She had defended herself and her gym, but she had done it reflexively, while worried about LuAnn injured in her office.

LuAnn, who had come to the gym because her friends loved her enough to ask her to.

LuAnn, who had taken the classes seriously.

LuAnn, who had defended herself instead of dying at her husband's hands.

Pammy would have liked that outcome better if no one had died. Pammy would have liked it better if LuAnn had left that man before he nearly beat her to death.

But Pammy couldn't get everything she liked.

So she had to take the small victories—because she knew, at the moment, the world was too brutal for large ones.

War came to Berkeley months later with tear gas and students dying in the streets. And in the quiet afterward, Pammy's business thrived.

Everyone said it was because of the arsonist.

But Pammy knew that it wasn't. Stella told everyone about the arsonist because she couldn't tell them about LuAnn.

Not that it mattered.

Women came. They learned. And maybe, they'd figure out how to escape before someone died.

Like Pammy wished LuAnn had.

Local Knowledge

Kristine Kathryn Rusch

Local Knowledge

The call came in at 11:54 a.m., December 15, 1995. Body found at Tups Tavern, 35 East 35th street. Webb thought the call routine until he arrived.

Tups, frequented by sailors and longshoremen, was on the lakefront. Superior glistened, never freezing over, never covered with snow. But not pretty either, not in this part of town. In this part of town, the massive lake was dark and dirty, not sky blue like it was everywhere else.

Drug deals went down nearby and the local hookers worked dockside. Knifings were common. But this victim hadn't been knifed.

He'd been shot.

Patrols had followed procedure. Two squads, parked at an angle on the broken concrete parking lot, colored the tavern's gray walls red, blue, red, blue. Barflies stood near the open gunmetal doors, drinks in hand, coats draped over their shoulders to protect them against the cold.

They watched Webb as if he were one of them.

Which, in a way, he was.

He slipped between the dented bumpers, thankful he still fit in small places. Fifty crunches, one-armed push-ups, a half-hour run around the football field, all required before he allowed himself to hug a bar stool and drink until his tongue was numb. He always said the exercise let his body perform his job, and the booze kept his mind from dwelling on it.

But he wondered sometimes, especially when he saw himself reflected in those shabby tattered people whose drinks were more important to them than the life drained on the concrete.

He didn't acknowledge them. Instead, he stopped beside the squads and memorized the scene.

Body belonged to a tall middle-aged man, lambswool coat—too rich for this part of town—exit wound a bloody mess in his back. Shoes shiny Italian leather, almost no scuff marks on the soles, dirt caking the right toe and the left heel. Right hand outstretched, slightly sun-wrinkled, white, with a gold ring, large ruby in the center. Salt-and-pepper hair, neatly trimmed, no strands out of place. Face pressed against the ice- and sand-covered concrete, features not visible from above.

Daylight was thin under a thick layer of clouds. Coroner would have to work in artificial light. Webb slipped on a pair of surgical gloves, crouched, and touched the back of the outstretched wrist.

Still warm. Webb glanced up, saw bloodstained holes in the pile of ice-covered snow plowed to the edge of parking lot.

"Anyone know him?" he asked, as he crouched lower, and peered at the man's face. Then he realized he didn't need to ask.

He knew the man. Tom Johanssen, returning home, after thirty-three years.

Tom Johanssen. The first time Webb had seen him, they'd been in high school. Webb was the gangly new kid from Louisiana—a whole country and half a culture away from Northern Wisconsin. Tom was all black hair and smiles, broad shoulders, chiseled features, and smarter than anyone else. Only he didn't flaunt it, just like he didn't flaunt the girls. Boys liked him too, wanted to be in his shadow, and that was the first time, maybe the only time, Webb had ever experienced—had ever fallen under the spell of—true charisma.

Then Tom shattered it all, the entire brilliant future, the golden dreams, by getting Jenna Hastings pregnant. Two days after graduation, they married, and Webb saw Tom only occasionally: buying groceries at the Red Owl; or riding home from work in the big yellow electric company truck. Webb went to college and Tom stayed behind, and it wasn't until five years later that Tom surfaced again, playing lead in a local country band.

Webb had gone to see the band just after he graduated from Mankato State and just before he entered the police academy. Tom stood center stage, black hair curling over his forehead, guitar slung across his shoulder. Girls crowded him as if he were Elvis, and Jenna was nowhere to be seen. Webb had watched mesmerized, and had wondered then if Tom was divorced.

But the divorce came after the scandal, leaving Jenna with four boys and Tom with another mistake on his record. He joined the service, and went to Germany. Married again, became successful, and sent his folks piles of money. Year after year, he promised to come home, the prodigal son, now back in favor.

He never did come home. Not for his grandmother's funeral or his grandfather's. His sister's wedding or his son's.

He never came home.

Until now.

"I'm taking you off the case." Bernard was hunched over his desk, beefy arms covering two separate piles of papers. He was staring at the file in front of him as if his next words were written on it.

Webb leaned against the door, arms crossed. Despite the stuffy heat of Bernard's office, Webb still felt a chill, as if the cold from the death scene had got deep into his bones. "I can be objective."

"Like hell." Bernard caught a thin strand of hair and twirled it over his bald spot. "You went to high school with him. Florence—"

"I went to high school with him, Ethan went to high school with him, and Mike Conner is Jenna's brother-in-law. Stanton's kid married Tom's kids' half sister—and Pete flew Tom out of town in sixty-two. Everybody in this town is connected to Tom somehow. You lived next door to him for six years." Webb's hands, hidden beneath his arms, were clenched into fists. He didn't know why he was fighting for this one so hard.

"I know," Bernard said. "That's why I want to give this one to Darcy."

"Darcy?" Webb tilted his head back so his crown hit the wood. Bernard was watching him, tiny blue eyes lost in his florid face.

Webb had trouble arguing this one. He'd fought for Darcy Danvers. No one had wanted to hire a woman cop, let alone a woman cop from out of town. She'd come in with more ribbons than anyone, more experience with real crime. She was athletic and tough, smartest woman he'd ever met—hell, smartest anyone he'd ever met—and a real street fighter.

"She doesn't know this town," he said, trying not to wince. That had been Bernard's argument against hiring her, the city's argument against keeping her, and the basis of Webb's defense of her five years back.

"She knows it good enough," Bernard said. "She'll follow through where the rest of us won't."

"I'd follow through," Webb said.

"Even on Flo?"

Webb closed his eyes, his sister's face rising before him, not as it was now, but as it had been that night long ago, puffy, tear-streaked, miserable.

"Even on Flo," he said.

But he didn't get a chance. Bernard took him off the case anyway. Webb staggered out of the office, short of breath and dizzy. Too many emotional shocks. First Johanssen, dead, then losing the case. It should have been his. It had to be his, to make up for thirty-three years.

Darcy was standing at her desk, a file of ancient clippings open in her hands. At forty, she was teenager-skinny, her arms long corded muscle, her breasts nearly flat against a trim torso. Her brown hair was cut short, above her ears, and the lines on her face were only visible up close. From a distance, she looked like a fifteen-year-old boy.

"I want to help you," he said.

"No dice." Her voice was cigarette-gravel. Two packs a day, filterless.

Cigarettes for her, booze for him. Somehow they made it through the long, cold winters. "Bernard took you off this case."

"You'll need a local guide."

"I can find one."

"Maybe," he said. "You don't know what Johanssen did."

She closed the file. "Dumped his wife and four kids for a sixteen-year-old groupie who claimed she was nineteen. Took her to Germany, married her without getting a divorce. Second marriage still might not be legal."

"Surface stuff." He took the file from her, glanced down.

It was from another case, a knifing at the same bar, in sixty-two. He tossed the file on the desk.

"There's always knifings at Tups," he said.

"When Tom Johanssen's band was playing?"

"Nobody plays at Tups. Tom Johanssen's band was drinking. Johanssen and Cindy Waters were already on an airplane for Minneapolis."

"How'd you know?"

"Local knowledge," he said. "Still think you don't need me?"

Darcy studied him. Her left eye was gray, her right eye green, a fact that had always intrigued him.

"So," she said slowly. "Where were you when Johanssen got shot?"

"Got a TOD yet?"

"About ten-thirty, give or take. Coroner's not in yet."

Webb shrugged. "In my car. Listening to the scanner and thinking about lunch."

"Alone?"

"In this town, detectives don't have to partner."

She frowned at him. He once told her she was the only partner he wanted. "Can anyone give you an alibi?"

"Does anyone need to?"

The room had gone silent around them. Maybe he'd raised his voice. He didn't know.

"It might help," she said, picking up the file he'd tossed. "Word has it Johanssen screwed your sister."

"Got that wrong," Webb said. "He didn't just screw my sister. He destroyed her."

Webb's sister Florence wasn't pretty. She'd never been pretty, not even as a little girl, but she'd been close. The wrong kind of close. Her features, taken separately, were perfect: oval eyes, long narrow nose with just a hint of an upturn, high cheekbones, and bow-shaped lips. Put together, they looked like she'd been colored by a child with a crayon too fat for the child's hand.

But what made it worse was that she wanted to be pretty. More than she wanted anything else.

She almost achieved it with Johanssen. She'd been twenty-one then, trim, with hair so black it shone blue in the sunlight. Her smiles had come from her heart and she walked with a lightness she would never have again.

Webb used to think she had finally grown into her body until he stumbled on Johanssen, shoeless and shirtless in Flo's bedroom on the middle of a Thursday afternoon. Flo had been in the bathroom. Webb could hear the water running.

Johanssen had grinned, hair tousled, cheeks still flushed, the sheets smelling of sex. *Your sister's one hell of a woman*, he'd said.

Webb had squeezed his fists tight, held them against his sides, not sure he wanted to fight in his parents' home. *You've got one hell of a woman at your place.*

Not for much longer, Johanssen'd said as he slipped on his shirt.

That what you're telling Flo?

Yep.

It'd better be true, Webb had said, *or I'll be coming after you.*

I'm sure you will. Then Johanssen had grabbed his shoes, and slipped out the window, as if he'd done it a thousand times before. And he probably had.

The conversation had echoed in Webb's mind for years afterwards. The beauty of it was that Johanssen had never lied. He'd never promised that he'd take Flo with him when he left. At least not to Webb. And probably not to Flo.

But Johanssen's strange honesty couldn't excuse what he finally did do. He'd chosen Flo because she was needy, and she'd fallen for him so deep that she'd never love anyone again. That would have been enough for Webb, enough to keep Webb searching for Johanssen all those years, but there was more.

Johanssen'd chosen Flo because of her college money. She'd won two science prizes her last year of high school, the only girl in the state to do so at that time, and she'd gotten three grand in awards. That, plus a thousand inheritance from a dead aunt, and savings from four years of full-time work while living at home, brought Flo's savings account to well over $5,000.

In 1962, with that much money, a man could buy a house.

Or go a long way toward disappearing forever.

On the afternoon he left, Johanssen slept with Flo for the last time. Then he'd convinced her to go to the bank, take out all her money and give it to him. He'd buy plane tickets with it, he said, start a new life far away from here, with a new wife. He just never said who that new wife would be. And while Johanssen's band was getting drunk at Tups Tavern, Flo had sat in her parents' living room, in her very best dress, looking as pretty as she would ever get, waiting for a knock that never came.

She'd refused to press charges, said it was her fault, and didn't change her mind no matter how much her family pushed. She kept her job, never tried college, never moved out of the house, and never fell in love again. And whatever chance she had at pretty died that night, along with her heart.

Sometimes Webb thought it was all his fault. He should have beaten up Johanssen in Flo's bedroom and chased the bastard out of her life.

But he hadn't. And that was something thirty years of police work could never change.

One missed moment, one bad call, had ruined his sister's life.

Forever.

Flo still lived in their parents' house. It was a three-bedroom starter home, built post-war, and had a little over 1,000 square feet counting the basement. Their parents had been dead ten years and Flo had yet to buy her own furniture. She still slept in the same room that she'd had all her life.

Webb walked in without knocking. He shut off the television, like he always did, and crossed the empty living room into the kitchen. His sister sat at the wobbly metal table, slapping cards on the faded yellow surface, a cup of cold coffee at her side.

"You've heard," he said.

"Every asshole in town's called me," she said, without looking up. "Thinking I'd be pleased."

"Are you?"

"I don't know yet." Her hands were shaking. He didn't know if that was from the caffeine, the news, or both. He always suspected that she'd harbored a hope about Tom Johanssen, a hope that Johanssen would come back for her, that he'd made a mistake.

Webb went to the counter, grabbed the pot off her Mr. Coffee, and poured the remaining coffee into the sink. Then he tossed out the grounds. The garbage below the sink was overflowing. He'd have to take it out before he left.

He made a new pot of coffee, grabbed a chocolate from the basket on the sideboard, and took his normal seat at the table. Behind him, the Mr. Coffee wheezed. It was at least fifteen years old.

Flo set her cards down and studied her hands. They were so thin that he could see the bones. Her skin was a sallow yellow—she never got any sun—and he doubted that she ate more than enough to keep herself alive.

"What was he doing here?" she asked.

"I don't know."

"How long had he been here?"

"I don't know that either."

"Don't know or won't say, Webster?" Her voice cracked as she spoke, taking some of the force from it. The force, but not the pain.

"Don't know." He ran a hand through his thinning hair. He'd been so worried about her that he hadn't learned the basic facts. A mistake he had never made before. Maybe Bernard had been right.

Maybe Webb didn't belong on the case.

"You always know." She got up, poured the coffee out of her cup, and then stuck her cup between the dripping coffee and the pot.

"They don't want me on this case." His voice was low.

She spilled, cursed, and ripped off a paper towel. Then she paused, leaning over the sink. "Because of me?"

He debated not telling her, but that wasn't fair. Then she'd think he was lying about what he knew.

"Yeah," he said, staring at her cards. Frayed edges, chocolate stains on the back. She played solitaire a lot. "Because of you."

She didn't move. "It shouldn't make a difference, should it, Webster? Thirty-three years ago? That shouldn't affect now, should it?"

"I don't know," he said, pushing away from his mother's kitchen table. "You tell me."

Options. Choices. The facts Webb knew about Tom Johanssen ended about 1970. He'd left a half second before the scandal broke, joined the army, flew Cindy Waters to West Germany, and married her there. After he got out of the military, he'd moved to some wide-open western state, Montana, Idaho, Wyoming, or Utah, and worked for some computer firm. There were rumors of continued scandalous behavior, from affairs to drug abuse to corporate raiding. He made a fortune. Enough for two houses of his own. He paid off his parents' and his grandparents' mortgages, had two more children, flew his older children to Montana-Idaho-Wyoming-Utah once every few years for skiing and the obligatory parental visit.

And not once did he return.

Not once.

Until now.

That was where Webb's investigation had to start. At Johanssen's decision to return to the land of his sins. Never mind that Webb was off the case. Darcy'd still be digging up graves by the time he had answers to the more pressing question.

The secret wasn't in who Johanssen had hurt. Webb suspected that the list probably extended well beyond Midwesterners. The secret lay in what had made him change enough to come home.

If Webb found that, he'd find the killer.

He knew that much as well as he knew his own sister's name.

He had to work fast. Once Bernard caught him, he was out of time, probably with a suspension, badge and gun turned in for good measure. So he laid the attack like a well-planned military maneuver. People first, machines second.

Johanssen's parents still lived on the corner of Maple and Pine in a red-and-white clapboard house that had seemed bigger when Webb was a kid. He had only been to the house a few times, the most memorable a class picnic at the end of his junior year. The house had seemed wrong, even then. Johanssen was too glamorous, too intelligent to come from a house that had no books on the walls, and which had yellow and brown slipcovers all over the furniture. His parents, Gladys and Phil, were so firmly working class that Webb had trouble associating them with their son. As the picnic wore on that bright sunny afternoon, it soon became clear that Johanssen had done the planning, the cooking, and the cleaning to make it all happen. Webb had felt a stab of pity. His own parents would have helped even if they didn't believe in a project, but it was obvious that Johanssen's wouldn't.

Webb grabbed his badge before he got out of the car. He didn't like rooting this deep into his own past. He didn't like the memories and the way they made him feel, as if he were smaller than he really was. In life Johanssen had made him feel that way; he seemed to do the same in death.

The sidewalk leading to the front door was cracked and broken. The concrete steps showed the signs of harsh winter. A fake grass welcome mat that dated from the sixties sat soggily near the stoop. Webb was careful not to step on it as he knocked.

The yellow curtain covering the window nearest the door moved slightly. Then voices echoed, and finally the door opened. The hunched old man staring through the screen was barely recognizable as Phil Johanssen.

"Mr. Johanssen," Webb said, holding up his badge. "I'm Detective Webster Coninck. I've come to talk to you about your son."

"No need to be formal, Webb," Phil Johanssen said, as he pushed open the screen. "I remember you just fine. Sorry to hear about your folks. Gladys always sent a card."

"I know," Webb said. "Flo and I appreciated it."

Flo had gasped each time she saw the word "Johanssen" on the envelope. She had hoped that the cards had come from Tom.

Webb slipped inside. The house smelled of mothballs, liniment, and fried foods. Phil Johanssen still wore his slippers. His blue pants hung on him, and his red-and-black plaid shirt dated from the late seventies.

Gladys stood in the door to the kitchen. She looked much the same, only faded, as if she had been in the sun too long and it had leached the color from her. Her hair, once the exact shade as Tom's, was now laced with gray, and the wrinkles on her face had the effect of dulling it.

"Webster," she said, and her strong alto took him back to his teenage years quicker than anything else ever could. "I was hoping you'd come."

"Mrs. Johanssen," he said. "I'm so sorry about Tom."

She made a small snort and took his hand. Her grip was surprisingly firm. "Come into the kitchen. I haven't had a boy at my table in too long."

The kitchen had been remodeled. It had a window over the sink, and oak cabinets that still gave off a faintly new scent. The countertops were a shiny ceramic, and the stove, refrigerator, and dishwasher were matching white. The table, covered with a vinyl tablecloth, sat against a bay window opening into the backyard. Plants littered the large sill. On the walls around them, Gladys's spoon collection alternated with Phil's pipe collection.

That was the smell Webb missed, the faint odor of pipe smoke clinging to everything.

"He gave smoking up for his health," Gladys said, following Webb's gaze. "But he couldn't give up the pipes."

She sat down beneath the spoon collection. Phil sat in front of the bay window. Webb sat across from her. The chair was covered with a crocheted cushion that didn't fit his body.

"Has anyone else spoken to you?" he asked, careful to keep his voice gentle.

"Just the boys who came to tell us the news," Phil said.

"Like on the TV," Gladys added. Her hands rested on the vinyl cloth, fingers laced together. Her knuckles were white from the tightness of her grip.

So Darcy hadn't been there yet. She would arrive soon.

"So," Webb said, "when did Tom tell you he'd be coming home?"

"Didn't know until them cops showed up," Phil said. "You'd think the boy would call if he was coming home after thirty-three years."

"So you had no idea he was coming?"

"I did." Gladys had her head down, her hands pressed so tight that they were turning red. "He called two days ago. Said he'd be here tonight. I didn't say nothing because I thought he wouldn't come. Like all them other times."

"Dammit, woman." Phil shoved his chair back. "You could have said something."

"The disappointment—"

"Wouldn'ta killed me." He got up, bowed in an odd, formal way to Webb, then left the room.

Gladys's lower lip trembled. She brought her head up. Webb was sorry for thinking that they hadn't cared about Tom's death. They had been trying to put a good face on it.

For company.

"It would have hurt him something awful, Webb. The last time Tom didn't show, Phil went to bed for a week. Didn't want to do that to him this time."

"Have there been other times when Tom said he'd be here and then never shown?"

She nodded, grabbed a tissue from her sleeve and dabbed at her nose. "Every three years like clockwork. He never made it. Not once. And he always felt so bad after that he'd pay to take us out there. But it ain't the same as coming home."

"No, Ma'am, it isn't."

"I don't know why he hated it so bad. It was like the town burned him and he couldn't face it again. I kept telling him that folks'd forgiven him, but he didn't seem to hear. He was a good boy, Webb. You know that."

"He made quite an impression on me," Webb said.

Gladys studied her hands. Her thumbs worked against each other as if she were rubbing pain out of them. "I'm sorry about Florence," she said, her voice a whisper.

He opened his mouth, closed it, unsure what to say. He almost said that it didn't matter, but it did matter. Tom had ruined his sister's life.

"You tell her that money's still here. I got it in an account for her. Remind her."

Webb went rigid. The room spun and he realized he hadn't taken a breath. Gladys looked up, the lines in her face deeper somehow, and he made himself breathe. He couldn't hide his surprise.

"You—?"

But Gladys didn't answer. She pushed her chair away from the table, stood, and walked to the sink. She grabbed a glass from the sideboard and filled it with water. Her reflection in the window was wavy and indistinct.

"He was a good boy, my Tom," she said. "He just forgot sometimes that things have consequences. Like never coming home. His kids would've liked him here, you know? At a game maybe or that play Donnie was in. It'd meant a lot." She took a sip. "Guess it don't matter now."

"Who killed him, Mrs. Johanssen?"

"That's the question isn't it?" She set her glass down, but she didn't turn around. "Not sure I want to find out the answer."

Neither was he. But fear had wrapped itself around his heart, and he had learned long ago to face that fear, to stand it down as if it were a charging dog or rampaging drunk.

He was on this path. Nothing, not even his own fear, would make him leave.

The Johanssens had offered to repay Flo her $5,000, and she had never taken them up on it. They had it in an account in her name, had since 1971.

When Tom sent them the money to pay off their own mortgage.

Webb didn't want to think about how much money was there, what kind of life Flo could have had if she'd only tried.

He drove away from the Johanssens' sick and shaking and wishing for a drink.

Instead he turned onto Hill, drove past the high school, past the duplexes owned by John Johanssen, and stopped at a crudely constructed A-frame on what looked like a vacant lot bordering John Johanssen's property.

Three brothers. Tom, John, and Scott. Scott Johanssen was the youngest, Vietnam vet, five children and no job.

The yard was a mixture of snow and dirt. Toys, half buried in the muck, were colorful reflections in the glare of a powerful porch light. Webb got out of the car, and trudged on the unshoveled path. It was icy and awkward with tramped footprints. Voices echoed from inside the house. Sharp voices, male and female, that cut off abruptly when he knocked.

There was no screen. When the unpainted door eased open, the scents of dirty diapers and dryer lint floated to him on a bed of warm air. A woman stood behind the door, her body thick with the aftermath of a pregnancy, her blouse stained with milk. The toddler in her arms was kicking her in a vain attempt to get down.

"Scott Johanssen, please," Webb said.

"You a cop?" she asked.

He nodded, reaching for his badge. But she didn't wait. She stood aside and yelled, "Dad, another one!" as she let Webb inside.

He stepped into a kitchen filled with old dishes and an overflowing diaper pail. In the center of the room, a weather-scarred picnic table stood, covered with crumbs and an overturned child's juice glass.

"Through there," she said, waving a hand at the A-shaped doorway.

He followed the trail of baby clothes and toys until he reached shag carpeting that might have been brown and might have been orange. This room smelled no better than the other. The furniture was old and brown, the upholstery torn. A TV was crammed against the unfinished wall, a red "mute" across Dan Rather's face.

Scott Johanssen was crammed into a Barcalounger that sagged under his weight. The footrest tilted, obviously broken. Scott was balding but still baby-faced, his round features a fatter, younger version of Phil's.

"Webster Coninck. Why the hell they got you on the case?"

"Dad," the woman said from the doorway.

Scott shrugged, and slapped the remote on a cup-strewn metal table. "Fair question when you remember that Webster here vowed undying hate on my brother thirty-some years ago."

"I came to offer condolences, Scott."

"Yeah, and monkeys'll fly out of my ass."

"Dad," the woman said. "The children...."

"It's my house, Cheri," Scott said. "You don't like how I talk, you and them kids can go back to that asshole husband of yours."

"I'm sorry," she said to Webb, and then disappeared into the kitchen.

Scott peered up at him. "Condolences my ass," he said. "You want to know if I killed him."

"Did you?"

"Should have, for all the times he left Mom and Dad hanging. And them kids. They worship him, you know, and he didn't even have the time of day for 'em. Not even when he flew 'em to Utah. He'd let that slut of his take 'em places, and then he'd show up maybe for supper, maybe for one day of skiing, and that's all they'd talk about. Me and John, we were always there for 'em, but we were never enough. I was a fat bum, and John was too slick. Their dad was perfect because he was mostly a figment of their imaginations. That's what Tom was good at. Making up lies about himself that other people'd believe."

"What kind of lies?" Webb asked, figuring he'd let Scott talk if that was what Scott wanted.

Scott snorted, slid one finger forward and shut off the TV. A whine that Webb hadn't been consciously aware of disappeared. "Lies? You mean like that corporate job that made so damn much money? I called him at work lotsa times, always got him direct. Then I lost the number, called information, and got the receptionist. She said she'd never heard of him. I got—" he grinned "—well, lessay I can be a mean s.o.b. when I wanna, and she put me through to personnel. Said they had a Tom Johanssen in their records. He'd been there and left years ago. That was in 1979, and when I'd ask him about it, Tom'd just laugh and say, 'Scott, there's business and then there's business.' As if I didn't know that. Every grunt ever lived knows that. Just didn't want to hear my brother saying it, you know?"

Webb wasn't sure he did know. He shifted. His feet had left a fresh snow-mud trail on the flattened carpet. "You ever see him on those trips back here?"

Scott narrowed his eyes. "How'd you know about them?"

Webb shrugged. "Amazing what you hear when you're listening."

Scott pushed back on the arms of the chair. The back of the Barcalounger hit the wall.

"I was still drinking," he said. "So it had to be '88, '89, down to Tups. I had just come from Ma's and she was in a fine fix because she thought Tom was coming home. But he never showed. He was good at that too. So I wander into Tups and take my usual spot when who do I see through that stupid glass bead curtain Tup used to have but my brother in one of his fancy suits, talking to some fat asshole I've never seen before or since."

"What happened?" Webb asked.

"I was drinking." Scott picked up the remote, tapped its end against the metal, making a sound like a brush on a snare drum. "So I wasn't thinking, you know? I shouted his name and stumbled back there and by then him and his buddies are gone."

"You sure it was Tom?"

"I was drinking," Scott said. "I wasn't drunk. Besides, he sent me cash money to apologize for being a jerk and asked me not to tell Ma. Told Dad, though. Big mistake. He tried to find Tom, and when he couldn't, he spent near a year in Tups, hoping he'd come back. He never did. Then Tom flew 'em all out on one of them Utah ski trips, and when Dad come home, he didn't want to talk about it any more."

"You know what Tom was doing here?"

"Nope, and I'm sure Dad don't neither. Like I said, Tom was good at making you think one thing when he was doing another."

Webb knew that. He knew that very well. "So what do you think happened to Tom?"

"I think somebody finally got tired of all the lies and used a bullet to shut him up."

"Any idea who that somebody was?"

"Nope." Scott stopped tapping the remote, and pushed a button.

The TV flicked on, so loud that Webb jumped. "I'm sure you're not hurting for suspects though."

The winter darkness that Webb hated had settled by the time he left. The sky was black—no stars, only clouds—and the streetlights made the snow seem white. Black and white with no gray. Not even the world had room for nuance any more.

John Johanssen lived out near Jenna Hastings Johanssen Conner. John's house was a 3,500-square-foot mock Tudor. It stood on a hill with a view of the river valley, the rolling land, the copper water tracing its way to Taconite County. John owned fifteen acres here, and half the town besides. His rents were sky-high and his reputation nasty. But his buildings were never empty, and if Tom hadn't become such a legend, John would have gotten credit for being the rich Johanssen brother.

John's wide, winding driveway had a square snow blower-built wall on each side. The snow was still picture-perfect, icy pure and fresh fallen white. The garage door was down. Webb parked on the far side, careful to leave room for a second car to park beside him. He got out, slammed his car door, and the sound echoed in the winter air. He followed the snow-blown trail to the immaculately shoveled front porch.

He grabbed the carved brass knocker with his bare right hand. The shock of cold ran through his skin and up his arm. He banged once, then waited, scouting for a doorbell.

He didn't need it. John's wife Evvie pulled the door open, and braced the frame with her right hand. She was too-rich thin and wore fresh makeup despite the late hour. "He's not here, Webster," she said.

"I wanted to talk to both of you," Webb said.

Her smile was tired. "You know I can't do that without John."

John had never liked it, not from the day they got married. Any independence Evvie showed somehow reflected on him. Evvie couldn't talk to another man alone. Webb had been on some of the calls as a beat patrolman. John never hit his wife, but the yelling had terrified the neighbors more than once. Webb suspected that was one of the reasons the couple had moved so far out in the country.

Webb didn't argue. He could talk to them together if he needed to. "Where is he?"

"Funeral home. Someone has to make the arrangements." She brushed a strand of unnaturally dark hair from her face. "I've been trying to call the folks in Utah. The numbers don't work, except the home number, and Cindy won't pick up."

"Someone at the station probably notified her."

"Hope so. We shouldn't have to take care of him. He never did his part for this family." Then she shrugged. "Shouldn't have said that, should I? Speaking unkindly of the dead."

"It's not a sin," Webb said.

"At least, not in the world of Tom Johanssen." She sighed. "I'll have John call. I know he wants to talk. This has him shook."

"And you?"

"I'm surprised it didn't happen years ago." She took her hand off the doorframe. "Thanks for understanding, Webb."

"Always have," he said.

She nodded and eased the door closed. It snicked shut, and he stood for a moment, his hand still aching with cold. He'd always liked Evvie. She and John were high school sweethearts, and seemed to have an understanding. But Webb'd always thought John never treated her well enough, despite the house, despite the trips, despite the money. She had no life away from him, and she should have.

At least Webb thought so. But he wasn't sure if that thought came from his own desire to see Evvie alone and have a real conversation, just once, without the guilt.

He sighed, walked off the steps, and back to his car. When he got inside, the porch light switched off.

The home Jenna Hastings made with her second husband, Steve Conner, was one mile and an entire income district away from John Johanssen's. Jenna lived in a small three-bedroom ranch at the base of one of the rolling hills. Her nearest neighbor on the left had a front yard littered with dead appliances and car parts. Her nearest neighbor on the right lost his home in a winter fire fifteen years ago and replaced it with an Airstream because he hadn't been insured. Jenna had tried to make her home nice, with flower boxes outside the window and a fresh coat of paint every year. But the little house still looked like what it was—a starter home for a family that had never moved on.

Webb used to drive out to Jenna's a lot when Steve was still on the force. They'd have barbecues and parties for the department, and Webb'd watch her four Johanssen boys take care of her two Conner girls. Handsome children, all, with the same restless intelligence he'd once seen in Jenna's eyes.

He turned onto the highway leading to the Conner place and was startled to see the road filled with cars. Black-and-whites parked haphazard, their blue and red lights bright splashes against the snow. His mouth was dry, his stomach suddenly queasy. He had purposely had his scanner off, and now he flicked it on, the buzz and crackle of voices uncomfortably loud.

Steve Conner was standing under the outdoor light, coatless, arms wrapped around his torso. He was yelling at one of the patrolmen who stood, head bowed, blocking Steve from the house. Other officers were walking in and out of the open front door. Even from this distance, Webb could see the damp footprints on Jenna's red-and-black rug.

He got out of his car slowly, like a man in a nightmare. The air, frosty cold, didn't touch him. His feet squeaked on the snow and some of it fell over the edge of his shoe, and instantly melted on top of his sock. He scanned each squad until he saw what he was looking for, Jenna's too-white face pressed against the rolled up window, watching as her husband continued to argue with the officer in charge.

All beat officers, no detectives. That made him shaky. He grabbed one of the patrolmen—a woman, actually, Kelly Endicott, who had gone to school with one of Jenna's kids.

"Who ordered this?" he said.

"Headquarters." She shook his arm off.

"Who?"

She shrugged. "No one wanted a name attached."

"What's the charge?" he asked, hoping that he'd stumbled on something else, that this was a mistake that had gotten out of hand.

"Murder, Webb." Endicott's voice was soft. "They found the gun."

He put a hand to his head. It didn't make sense. They had to do firing tests and match-ups and hours of lab work, and even then they couldn't be certain that the gun they had was the one used in the murder. The idea of ballistics, as used on TV detective shows, was as much a fiction as the locked room mystery.

"What'd they find?" he asked.

"Conner's old service revolver, under one of the cars at Tups. It'd been fired. Conner says the gun was stolen one night when he was at Tups."

Webb nodded. "He'd reported it in years ago."

Conner, a gun nut, had made a special petition to keep his weapons. Webb had kidded Conner about losing his revolver. *Hated the force so much you've gone and lost the one thing to remind you of it.*

Webb rubbed his hand over his face. His skin was getting chapped from all the exposure to the frosty air. "How come Jenna and not him?"

"No motive," Endicott said. "He'd never met Johanssen. She had cause, so they say."

"She's had cause for thirty-three years," Webb said. "Didn't mean she'd do it now."

"I don't like it any more than you do, Webb. Seems to me someone just decided how this would fall, and didn't do the backup work." She tugged on her cap. "But what do I know? I'm still considered a rookie."

She walked away from him, back to Conner and the officer he was yelling at. Webb glanced at Jenna. She had gained weight since high school. She had a matronly fullness, the kind of motherly warmth once drawn in ads for Campbell's Chicken Noodle soup. When she saw Webb, she shook her head, and held up her hand as if he shouldn't come near. He shrugged, and she shrugged in return. Then he retraced his steps to the car, got in, and went back to the station to see who'd caused this travesty.

During the winter, after five, the station had a different feel, a dark, gloomy feel, as if no hope could return to the world. Most of the desks were empty, but cops milled around, finishing business, leaning on counters, talking on the phone. Webb hated night activity. In this town, night activity was always sad activity: drug arrests, drinking violations, domestic violence disputes. Later, after midnight, the bar fights and the knifings would happen, but now, the station's business was usually about kids in trouble with nowhere to turn.

The cops couldn't help them either. The best the kids could hope for was to return to the parents who had neglected them in the first place. The worst was juvie, the petty criminal training ground.

Webb slipped inside. The station smelled of chalk dust and old coffee grounds. The concrete walls muted voices, made them sound as distant and less important than the voices on the police scanner.

Darcy sat behind her desk, hands in her short-cropped hair, a cigarette burning to ashes in a tray below the bright glare of the desk lamp. She was staring at the notes in her phone log, cheeks red with a stain Webb had learned to identify as anger.

"What's the idea not showing up at your own collar?" he asked.

She didn't look up. "Wasn't mine. It was Bernard's."

"The gun's not going to hold up."

"You're telling me." She kicked her chair back. Her eyes were full of red. "Serial numbers were scratched off years ago. Bernard claims the notches in the handle make it Steve's. His brother confirms it. But the gun's wiped clean, no prints, and only one shot fired. Johanssen was killed point blank, so the killer has to have powder burns. I'll betcha Jenna Conner doesn't."

"Why her? Why not Steve?"

"Former cop with a brother still on the force?" Darcy snorted. "You tell me, smartass."

"Shouldn't have arrested her at all, then."

"No, they shouldn't have, but they want it wrapped." She pulled a file from beneath her log. "Makes this all worthless."

Webb pulled up a chair. "What is it?"

"Johanssen's arrest record. Longer than my arm, some drug related, all smuggling. No convictions, not even any overnight stays in jail. Big lawyers, big money."

"And you think they bought someone here?"

She shook her head. "I think this town's too wrapped up in its past to know what's going on in its present."

Webb nodded. The analysis made sense. Tom Johanssen betrayed his wife, so she murdered him, first chance she got. What did it matter that she had to wait thirty-three years to do so?

The problem was, the same logic applied to Flo.

He swallowed, not liking the options. "You know about the trips, then."

"Every three years like clockwork," she said. "Supervising international barges with some 'special' loads. A real hands-on kinda guy."

"Drugs?"

She shook her head. "At first, I think. Then contraband. Going in and out. The Utah company was a front for chip smuggling. Disbanded last year just before the Feds caught up to it."

"So you think this was a related hit?"

"I'm sure of it," she said. "He screwed up, let some investigator get too close. That's why the Utah office closed. His friends didn't like it, and they killed him."

"That's not evidence, Darce."

"Evidence." She waved a hand. "Look at the evidence. The hit's professional. There're no prints, no witnesses, no gun ID, and a weapon left at the scene. Someone wanted him, and they knew if they got him here there'd be plenty of other suspects."

"And a police department unused to these kind of cases."

Her smile was tired. She picked up the cigarette, flicked the long trail of ash into the tray, and took a drag. "I didn't say that."

He smiled back. "But you could have."

"I could have."

He sat down in the metal chair beside her desk. The green upholstery had a rip in it that whistled under his weight. "Let me see the file."

She tossed it at him. "This bothers you?"

"The whole thing bothers me. Tom was a bright guy. Why come here to meet a shipment if he knew his people blamed him for the raid last year?"

"Money?"

Webb frowned, remembering Flo's face on the last beautiful day of her life. "He had other ways of getting that."

He opened the file. Many of the sheets inside were old. Arrest records originally done on typewriters and recopied so many times that the dirt dots outnumbered the keystrokes. As usual on the old ones, the photos were missing, removed to put in a mug book or on another, more successful arrest sheet. The fingerprints were dark whorls of unreadable lines.

He flipped. The later arrest records were on a computer printout. Information, but no original arrest sheets. There was reference to an FBI file, and notes from Darcy's conversation with the head of the FBI's case. A reference sheet in the very back also had a DEA file number.

"There's a lot of stuff here, but not a lot of paper," he said.

She nodded. "They've been trying for him for a long time. He knew computers. He could make details disappear."

Webb closed the file and handed it back to her. Just like Tom. Slippery to the end. Never appearing to be the person he actually was.

Webb pulled his gloves out of his coat—and paused, not liking the hunch that had just grabbed him and wouldn't let him go. "Who did the autopsy?"

"Cerino. There wasn't a lot to do since it was an obvious gunshot wound, so she did a prelim to establish time of death. She'll do the rest tomorrow."

"DNA, fluids, fingerprints?"

Darcy was frowning at him. "Why? We have a positive ID"

"Mine?" Webb asked.

"Yours, and his brother's."

"Scott's?"

"John's."

Webb felt oddly lightheaded. Of course. No one wanted to bother his parents. No one *ever* wanted to bother Tom Johanssen's parents. And everyone knew that his brother Scott wouldn't give him the time of day. Even in death.

"Get someone to fingerprint the corpse and check it against the federal database."

"I doubt he's in the base. I said he disappeared things—God." She stamped out the cigarette. "You don't think he disappeared himself, do you?"

"Why not?" Webb asked. "He did it before. He's the only one who would have known there would be other suspects here. I don't care how good a professional hit man is, he doesn't research those kinds of details."

"But the ID—you ID'd him."

"I haven't seen him since 1962."

"But his brother," Darcy started.

Webb held up a finger, then picked up the phone. He listened to the dial tone as he thumbed through Darcy's battered phone book until he found the number he was looking for. He wedged the phone between his shoulder and ear, and dialed.

"Evvie," he said when she picked up the phone. "Webb again. Sorry to bother you. Is John there?"

"No." She sounded small, hesitant. "He's at his folks. You can reach him there."

"I will," Webb said, "but tell me one thing. When was the last time John saw Tom? Did he go on any of those Utah trips?"

"Heavens, no," she said. "John's too proud to let anyone pay his way anywhere. The last time we saw Tom had to be the last time we went West which was in—I don't know—seventy-nine? eighty?—at least fifteen years ago."

"Fifteen years," Webb said. "Thanks."

He set the receiver down. Darcy was staring at him. "No one's that devious," she said.

"You don't know Tom," Webb said.

"But his parents could have identified him," Darcy said.

"He knew they wouldn't," Webb said.

Darcy shook her head. "He couldn't have relied on that."

"Sure he could," Webb said. "He knew how it worked around here. He knew the department. He knew we would call John for the ID. John takes care of the family. And the entire town bends over backwards to protect Tom's parents."

"But his other brother—"

"Hates his guts. Everyone knows that. You want a reliable identification, you call John."

Darcy was frowning. "So how did Tom get the gun?"

"It was stolen from Tup's right? If you look, you'll probably find that Tom was in town at the same time the gun went missing."

"You think he's been planning this that long?"

Webb gave her a bitter smile. "Tom always has a backup plan."

She shook her head once, as if it were all too much for her. "I'll get right on it," she said.

FBI and DEA involvement somehow circumvented the usual state-to-state rigmarole. Darcy had impressed on them the need for immediate action. The fingerprint ID was fast, made even faster because the dead man was from California, a state that fingerprints all its citizens who get driver's licenses. The body belonged to Anthony McGregor, a computer consultant who had left home three days ago. He had told his wife that he was on a buying trip to the Midwest with a new client, a man with a lot of cash and a lot of connections, a man whom McGregor met through a mutual friend, a friend who had once commented on McGregor's vague resemblance to the client. McGregor had hoped the trip would provide an upward shift in the family's fortunes.

Three hours after his death, Anthony McGregor tried to get a direct flight from Minneapolis to Miami. Since he didn't book in advance, he wasn't able to fly direct. He had a layover in New York City, a layover that extended from one hour to four because of ice problems at Kennedy. Two FBI agents and two DEA agents met Anthony McGregor when he disembarked at Dade County Airport. Strangely, Anthony McGregor was two inches taller and fifty pounds heavier than noted on his driver's license. He'd also lost his need for corrective lenses.

"We get him when the FBI's through with him," Darcy said. "The murder's in our jurisdiction."

Webb rubbed his eyes and took a sip of his cold coffee. He'd been up all night. "You get him, Darce."

"He's ours, Webb."

Webb shook his head. "I'm not going to taint this one. You got a clean case."

"You don't taint it," she said. "You solved it."

He smiled at her, liking that loyalty, knowing that sometimes this was where friendship hid—in the purposeful forgetting of important details. "I added local knowledge."

"Crucial local knowledge."

"Nothing more than some interviews would have provided."

"But not within the right amount of time. We solved this while he was still in transit—"

Webb held up his hand, stopped her. "Darce, he screwed my sister, remember?"

"Oh," Darcy sighed. "A jury'd love that."

"Wouldn't they though?"

She took out a pack of cigarettes, tamped it, then reached inside. It was empty. She crumpled it and threw it at the wastebasket, missing as usual. "How bad do you want him?"

"Bad enough," Webb said, "to get out of the way."

"He sure ruined a lot of lives."

"He did that," Webb said. "And some of the lives ruined themselves."

Thirty years of police work. Thirty years, and he finally caught the man he'd been after all along. Webb stepped outside the station into a pale peach-and-orange dawn. The snow reflected the sun, making the whole city and the lake beyond look rosy.

But he couldn't claim credit, and he wasn't sure he wanted to. He wasn't sure he'd be a hero in his sister's eyes.

He sighed, ran his hand through his hair, and felt the stress of the last twenty-four hours in the oily strands. A shower, breakfast at a diner, and then he'd see Flo. He'd have to work on her now. She couldn't live in silent hope any more. She couldn't play the victim any longer. If he were prosecuting, he'd call her as a character witness, and he'd make sure to have her talk about the double-cross, the first double-cross on Tom Johanssen's record.

She'd have to do it with Johanssen sitting across from her, older now, but still handsome, and rich enough to have real smart attorneys at his side. She'd finally have to stop taking responsibility for Tom Johanssen's actions. She'd have to see him as he was.

Just as Webb had had to do.

He'd felt that little stab of betrayal in the police station, when his hunch rose to the forefront of his mind. He'd identified the body. He'd put himself on the line for Tom Johanssen once again. Believing the hype, believing the image, and almost letting the bastard go.

Again.

Webb had lied to Darcy. It wasn't because of the future court case that he'd stepped aside. That was a good superficial reason, but not the true one.

The true one was that he didn't want to see the fallout from Tom Johanssen's latest double-cross. Before the victims had been his wife and kids, and Flo. This time, Johanssen'd set up his whole family, his folks, his brothers, his ex-wife's new husband, and an entire town. He'd used the animus he'd created thirty-three years ago as a smokescreen to cover his flight to a new life.

At the expense of his ex-wife, his children, and one reasonably successful California computer consultant who had the misfortune to resemble Tom Johanssen enough to fool people who hadn't seen him in years.

Local knowledge.

It worked both ways.

Webb got into his car. He felt as if a burden had lifted, as if the dark cloud he'd been living under had finally passed by. He could move on now, maybe even escape the black-and-white winters, find a place with a bit of nuance, a bit of gray.

He turned the car around and headed east, into the light.

Into the warmth.

The Trendy Bar Side of Life

Kristine Kathryn Rusch

The Trendy Bar Side of Life

I tend bar, not in one of those upscale things that serve weird drinks with funny names, where everyone comes after work for a nanosecond while the bar's the hot spot and then move on when someplace else becomes trendy.

Nope. I tend bar in one of the old dives that still exist in neighborhoods, the kind that no sane person would enter without an invitation, and that invitation only comes from the universe. You know, you lose your job, your wife walks out, your friends tell you to stop whining, so you pass the dive bar you'd never think of entering when you're on the trendy bar side of life.

You walk in, see the decrepit unshaven guy sitting at the edge of the bar, a woman nursing a piss-colored beer at a table that hasn't balanced since 1970, and one of those lighted bubbling beer signs for a brand that got discontinued when you were a kid. You doubt the bar's been cleaned since then, either, although none of the surfaces you touch are sticky or dirty or dust-covered. The place is just so old that the dirt and the now-banned cigarette smoke are embedded into the walls.

I've worked in that kind of bar since the night Ronald Reagan got re-elected, the night I decided to chuck it all and walk into one of those bars myself. Only I walked in, wearing a suit with a lace collar, bow-tie untied, and heels so high they looked like fuck-me-shoes instead of what they really were, which was the required business attire of the day.

Yeah, I'm a woman. Yeah, you're excused if you have no idea. Most people don't know until I open my mouth, and some aren't sure even then. They see the shaved head, the muscular fat, the T-shirt with ripped sleeves, and the bicep tattoos and think "man." They ignore the studs outlining the rim of my ears, the delicate chain around my neck that ends in a tear-drop diamond, and the breasts which, granted, are a bit underwhelming, even with the extra fifty pounds I've gained since that horrid night.

This isn't my bar, even though folks think it's my bar. They never see Bancroft, the owner, who, let's be honest, hasn't crossed the threshold since his first AA meeting in 1991. He calls me on the landline when he's coming by (he doesn't have a cell), stops his Hog in the alley near the garbage cans so he can't smell the piss and stale beer from the back door, and makes me hand him the books (on paper), the cash, and the hard drive backup which, in theory, he takes to the accountant, because Lord knows, a man who doesn't like cell phones doesn't like computers either.

Bancroft tells me I can do what I want with the place. I can redecorate. I can expand to the empty storefront next door (which he also owns). I can start making trendy drinks.

He doesn't care, so long as the bar makes money.

I'm afraid if I alter a damn thing, the money will vanish, and if the money vanishes, then I actually have to confront a few things, like why I work in a dive bar in a redneck neighborhood, why I have the same conversations that I've had weekly for thirty years with the same people, and why even I've started to look at strangers with suspicion because, y'know, they don't belong in *this* bar.

Which is how I look at the new guy when he staggers in. Maybe twenty-five, pretty in a sexually ambiguous kinda way, collar open, shirt askew, tie completely gone. He's walking like something hurts, like a woman does when the high heels she's worn all day hurt not just her feet, but her back as well. Only he's not wearing high heels. His dress shoes are stained on top, but the sides shine.

He gingerly climbs onto a bar stool in the very center of the horseshoe bar and if I weren't paying attention to him, I'd assume he was being prissy—worrying that the seat wasn't clean enough for the black silk pants that matched the shiny black silk suit coat.

I slap a bar napkin in front of him, and he jumps. Then he looks at my hand, resting on that bar napkin, as if he's never seen a hand before.

I frown. And, for once, I modulate my tone so I don't sound actively hostile.

"You want something?"

He raises his head, but his eyes don't meet mine. "I don't know. Jesus. A drink."

Normally, I'd say, *You are in a bar, buddy*, but I don't. Instead, I look closer at him. His hair's spikey, and I don't think that's style. Either a bruise is forming along his chin or something has smudged there.

"Ah...beer," he says, then shakes his head. "Um, no. Whiskey. Brandy. Something that burns."

"Beer, whiskey or brandy," I say. "Which do you want?"

"Jack," he says. "Just give me some Jack."

I pour him a Jack Daniels, and set the glass in front of him. He's already torn up the bar napkin. There's dirt under his fingernails.

His *manicured* fingernails.

He leans over the drink like he doesn't recognize it. I get another glass, and fill it with ice water, and set that in front of him, on a coaster this time, with a bar napkin beside it.

He doesn't even look up. I'm not sure he notices.

My own mouth is dry. I look around the bar, to see who's here. The same crowd is here day to day, so sometimes I don't really notice who's in the bar and who's not. And I haven't noticed until now.

Ma Kettle sits in her favorite booth, her gray wig askew, and her sweatshirt food-stained. Her real name is Cora Kattleman, but I think I'm the only one who knows that, and only because she opened her tab with a credit card fifteen years ago. Everyone calls her Ma Kettle at her insistence, and most folks don't even know the reference, a clichéd but popular hillbilly movie character from the 1940s and 50s.

But then, no one thinks about the nicknames. Most of us in this place have one, and we use it instead of our real names. It's easier that way.

Ma Kettle comes in at noon, every day, and sits in her booth. I set the first vodka tonic in front of her, and maybe by the fifth, she'll say hello.

She doesn't talk much, mostly watches the TV, which I have on mute, and stares at nothing.

She hasn't seen the guy.

And no one else is here, although Rick Winters should come in at any moment. His shift ends at 3:30, and he usually rolls in here by 3:35.

Just me, Ma Kettle, and the new guy, who hovers over his drink like he's about to puke.

The sleeve of his suit is split at the shoulder, and the silk in the back looks smudged, like silk does when it has encountered liquid it doesn't like.

I'm shaking, just a little. I've been there. I've literally been there, right here, at this bar, in ripped clothes, aching all over, staring at a drink I don't want, but not sure what else I can do.

Turning point: Last night of my professional life. Last night of my all-important career. Last night of ain't-she-cute.

That's how I know he wasn't in a fight. Oh, he might've fought. But one of those knock-em-down, drag-em-out fights? Naw. Right now, everything's scraped and raw and coming in images. He's not thinking clear, and I don't blame him.

I also don't lean toward him to talk.

Bancroft leaned in that night, thirty-two years ago, and probably scared a decade off of me. I still have nightmares about that moment, and jump whenever Bancroft leans toward me. Not his fault, but he got roped into those images, those memories.

So this afternoon, I slide the ice water toward the new guy and say, "Did you know him?"

The new guy's hand shakes as he grabs the whiskey glass. His knuckles are scraped and his thumb is swollen and it hangs funny. It might be broken.

"Whatever you think you know," he starts in a tone that puts me, a bartender, back into my lower-class place, "it's wrong."

His voice wobbles on the word "wrong," and he swallows hard.

Naw. I'm not wrong. He wants me to be wrong. He doesn't want me to see him at all, and I see too clearly.

Like Bancroft had with me. I'd said to Bancroft, *Piss off, asshole. Let me drink in peace.*

And he'd said, *I don't think you're going to find peace tonight.*

I don't know what to say now. I know what not to say. So I go for short and succinct, flat tone, as if I don't care. And I do care, even though I don't want to.

"You want that thumb to keep working, you'll need to see a doctor," I say. I don't say anything about his private parts, which've got to be just as bruised. Maybe more bruised. Maybe more than bruised.

I don't want to scare him away.

Now his eyes meet mine. They're brown, two shades darker than his skin. They're also watery, and his lower lip is trembling.

"No," he says in a tone that adds, *Back off.*

I shrug, grab the bar rag and toss it over my shoulder. It smells of the vinegar solution we use to wipe down the back area. I walk away, keeping my eye on the guy in the gigantic mirror behind the expensive alcohol.

He starts to pick up the whiskey, grimaces, and keeps the glass on the bar. That thumb is the size of a dying balloon. With his other hand, he grabs the ice water. The glass shakes as he raises it to his lips. Some of the water drips onto his expensive suit.

The door bangs open. The new guy jumps and spills more water. Rick Winters stomps in and slams the door behind himself. That takes some doing, because I got the door on one of those slow swings, just so no one can slam it.

Rick looks older than he should—balding, a growing beer belly, and a whole lotta attitude. He's staving off burnout by spending the afternoons here, but he doesn't have much longer. Every day for the last six months, he's come in mad.

I open a Heineken and set it at his usual spot on the bar, on the left side of the horseshoe, back to the door. He looks at the new guy.

"What's the story?" Rick asks, with an edge.

I shrug. I don't ask for stories. Rick should know that. It's one reason he comes here. The relief bartender, who usually works weekend days, came in for me one afternoon, asked Rick what had him so pissed off, and got to hear the entire story about a five-car pile-up on the Expressway, which started with the sentence, *Fucking drunk drivers*, and ended with, *and of course, the asshole drunk walked away.*

Rick might be a drunk himself, but the minute his fingertips touch a green longneck, he doesn't go near a vehicle. He says 90 percent of the shit he deals with as an EMT occurs because someone who had too much to drink gets behind a wheel or punches the wife or plays with a gun. Rick says he needs to haul his ass to AA, but he's not ready.

He'll be ready when he quits the job. He's not suited. It's not the drunks he objects to. It's all the blood.

Rick's fingers haven't touched the bottle. He's still looking at the new guy. "Pretty messed up."

"Yeah," I say, not willing to add that I'd mentioned a doctor already.

"It's probably none of our damn business," Rick says.

"It usually isn't," I say, and wipe off an imaginary spot on the bar near that Heineken. Ma Kettle pounds her glass on the table—a sign that I haven't been doing my job: I usually anticipate her drinking needs—and then there's a large clatter and bang behind me.

I whirl in time to see the new guy's head slide off the bar. He'd knocked over his water and his whiskey when he passed out. He would've fallen all the way to the floor, but somehow Rick levitates from his place at the end of the bar and runs to the new guy's side, catching him before he bangs his head again on the nearby stool.

"Shit," Rick mutters. "Shit."

At first, I think he's commenting on working after hours, at dealing with some drunk. We'd done it a hundred times, dragging some idiot to a chair where we throw water in his face, pick his pocket for his wallet and address, and call him a ride home.

Then I realize that Rick isn't looking at the guy or where he's dragging the guy to. He's looking at the bar stool.

He picks up the guy as if he weighs nothing, and swings him toward the door. Liquid drips—I'm thinking whiskey, when my brain registers the viscosity.

Blood.

The guy surfaces, looks up, sees Rick holding him, and screams. I've never heard a sound like that, raw and pain-filled, and completely anguished.

"Call Mercy General," Rick says. "Tell them I'm bringing in a guy. I'll radio."

The guy claws at him, moaning now, kicking, trying to get free.

"You got your rig?" I ask. I've only seen it once, that ambulance he drives like it's a tank.

"No, not that it matters. I got a radio in my truck." Then Rick backs him out the door, and the guy screams again.

The sound fades as the door bangs closed.

"Jesus," Ma Kettle says. "High drama."

Then she holds up her glass.

I pour her another vodka tonic, just because it's easier than fighting with her. I carry the vodka tonic around the bar, and head toward her, careful to step over the blood trail.

In one move, I take the old glass and set the new one down on the wet bar napkin. It's a sign of how distraught I am that I haven't brought a new napkin. Automatic movements and all that.

I turn, look at my bar from the customer's point of view. A thin line of blood drips off the new guy's stool. How had I missed that?

I look at the door, see only a blood trail leading out. Either he hadn't been bleeding that bad when he came in, or the blood disappears in the general ambience of the place.

Here's what I can do: I can call the cops, let them treat this place like part of a crime scene, not that it is a crime scene. It's a crime scene aftermath. Technicalities and all that. I can leave it or I can clean up.

The cops'll come here anyway. Mercy General will have to run a rape kit. Rick'll insist on it, and because he's there, he'll file, as an EMT on the scene. Whether or not the new guy presses charges, well, that's up to him.

Considering how he was sitting for so long in so much pain, considering how he didn't want a doctor in the first place, considering that suit, that condescending tone, he's not going to want cops involved. Hell, *women* don't want cops involved, and it's quote-unquote *normal* for a woman to get raped.

Guys, well, they've got even more stigma to overcome. Not just with the cops, but in their own head.

I go to the back, grab the fluids bucket, the oldest mop, and some bleach. At least three times a month, I clean blood off my floor. I'm damn good at it, after thirty years.

I can make anything disappear.

Except the memory of what came before.

That memory never leaves.

"He won!"

Confetti, balloons, hotel grand ballroom doing double-duty—half a party for the Reagan-Bush Re-election Campaign, the other half for Senator Dwight Corbin. Red, white, blue, the posters with their exclamation points and patriotic lettering lining the walls, including the stupid one, the one that always stopped me short—Ronald Wilson Reagan painted to look decades younger despite the wrinkles on his face, almost Norman Rockwell, an American flag behind him, an unrecognizable George H.W. Bush looking off to the side, and the slogan "Bringing American Back!" which always, always made me ask, "Bringing America back to what?"

If I'd been working national campaign instead of state campaign, I'd've advised against the slogan. I mean, after all, hadn't Ronald Reagan been president for four years already? Bringing America back from the brink? Because we felt like we were on the brink: I just didn't trust Mondale to do anything except flap his gums.

I was a great operator back then, a better operator for Reagan than Senator Corbin, although Corbin's campaign shared me once everyone figured out just how well I could handle the press. Didn't need a lot of press for the re-election campaign—they'd send their flunkies in when the President came to town, which ended up being all of three times. Needed lots of press for Corbin because he was young, because he was new, and because he was dumb as rocks.

I wasn't really grooming him for a national senate seat or even governor once he finished with his state term. I was grooming me for the day when women in politics became more than a curiosity or a curious screw-up, like Mondale's Veep Ferraro, whose husband cocked everything up, the way husbands always do.

So, celebrating, drinking, confetti in my hair—hell, confetti everywhere, including my hoo-ha when it was all said and done. I still don't see confetti as anything but evil, even now.

The rest of the memory gets lost in campaign Sousa marches and cheers of "he won!" and laughter, lots of laughter. The laughter bleeds into every-

thing, like clown laughter in a bad horror film, and then the lights get dim, and there's a bed involved, one of those pasty hotel beds in one of those gold upscale rooms, and I'm holding champagne, and then I'm not, and I stand in the bathroom, aching everywhere, pulling confetti out of my hair and wondering if my lips look bruised.

I paste myself back together, adjust the suit coat, leave the stupid bow-tie undone (who thought of bow-ties for women, anyway?), finger comb my blond curls, wash off my face and ignore my shaking hands.

Then I walk out the door, go back before it closes, grab my purse, leave again, and look at the elevator, think: maybe he's in the elevator. Think: maybe people'll wonder why I'm *in the elevator. Think: they'll want me back in the ballroom. Think: screw the ballroom, and walk to the stairs, conscious that I'm limping a little.*

I blame the shoes. Even in my memory, I blame the shoes—too high, too pointed, too tottery. But really, that year, I lived in extra-high-heels, showing off my calves, my thighs, my ass, because you could go miles with the male operatives if you distracted them with some cleavage and a hint of sex.

That's what I was thinking as I walked down the steps. My fault. Cleavage, hint of sex, only a matter of time. Reached the lobby, didn't go out that way, went down one more flight to the parking garage, only it wasn't a parking garage, it was the basement, a nearly empty function space that I hadn't seen, and a door marked exit that I walked through to an alley that meandered like I was, until I found our street, this bar, one drink, and Bancroft saying I don't think you're going to find peace tonight.

But I did. Peace and oblivion, not in bottles, like Bancroft those first six years. But in the work. The mindless work. I cleaned up after him, tended bar when he couldn't, slept in the back room because, hand-to-God, I didn't want to walk outside again, and I didn't, not that I noticed anyway, until someone (Bancroft?) told me the hotel'd gone bankrupt and the building was empty, and it was the last bastion of the Great Downtown, and it was finally, finally going away.

Thought of torching it myself. Instead, meandered up that alley, stared at the broken windows, the steel door, the now-faded glory, thought: Serves you right, you bitch, and wasn't sure if I was talking to the hotel, or to me, or to the world in general.

Then turned around and headed back to the bar, but first, stopped in the barbershop half a block away, and when they wouldn't shave my head, grabbed the electric razor and started it myself. Lots of screaming, lots of Don't do it, honey, *and I was wondering where the hell they were years before, when someone should've screamed (me, maybe?) and someone should've said* Don't do it, honey *(me again?) and someone should've yanked his hand away, like they yanked the razor out of mine. But Gus, the barber, finished the shave, told me to go buy a wig, said,* At least you got one of them perfect skulls, *and I looked in the mirror, liked what I saw, none of that you're-too-cute-to-work-in-politics-sweetheart, not any more. Looked more like a* Star Trek *alien than the girl next door.*

Took another year to get the tattoos. By then, the extra fifty I carried took away the cute as effectively as the hair. Stopped watching the news, stopped voting, stopped thinking about politics at all. Mostly listened to my drunks repeat the same stories over and over, finding comfort in their miserable little lives, happy that those lives weren't mine, happy that I had a place and some usefulness and that sense I belonged, even if daylight had become foreign and the stench of stale beer normal.

I'da kept going too, if the blood didn't remind me, if the blood didn't—

Ah hell, it wasn't the blood. It was the look on the new guy's face, that shell-shocked, not-me-look I'd seen in the mirror too many times, the dirt (blood) under the fingernails, the way he jumped when my hand got too close.

His wallet sits on the bar, drenched in whiskey, and I pick it up, wrap it in a towel, and put it in the safe. And I think about it, through the long normal night, like the wallet's a talisman, thinking, thinking as Ma Kettle expounds drunkenly on her latest theory about toll ways and city streets, as Screwy Marcus and The Donster argue about next year's playoffs, and as five guys, fresh from their weekly basketball game, stop in on their way home.

Rick never comes back though, and I wonder if tonight's the night he finally gets clean. Then I wonder if the new guy died, and Rick couldn't deal. And then I wonder why I should care about either of them.

But the wallet...it calls me and calls me and calls me, and I know I can't keep it forever. I wait until closing, when The Donster does his chivalric thing and offers (like he does every night) to walk Ma Kettle home, and she refuses, and he does it anyway, and they pretend like it's something new.

I lock the door, open the safe, and pull out the wallet.

It's calf leather, black, and stained now, not just from the whiskey, but probably from blood. That doesn't gross me out. After tending bar for thirty-some years, nothing grosses me out, although behaviors often disgust me.

I take the wallet to the office, which has better lighting, and turn on the overhead, along with the gooseneck lamp that probably curved over the desk since the bar's founding. I set the wallet on a wad of paper towels, even though I know I'm going to clean up the desk anyway. Bleach is a marvelous thing.

I flip the wallet open, see gold cards, platinum cards, and at least five hundred dollars cash. Tucked in both sides of the cash flap are business cards, two wads of them, one white and one a light blue. I pull out the business cards first, expecting to see that he had organized a pile of them.

Instead, I see two different cards for the same man: A.D. "Andy" Santiago. One card, the blue one, with somewhat archaic type, lists his job as "consultant," along with an email address and a phone number.

The white card has a red-white-and-blue logo on the front. The logo's for the Jeff Davis For Senate campaign, and I damn near drop the card. I don't like coincidence. Politics and rape and this bar. Thirty years apart, but still.

I glance at the driver's license. Yep. A.D. Santiago is the owner of the wallet, the guy who stumbled into my bar, the man who looked like I had all those years ago.

Only we got him to the hospital. Bancroft never took me.

I make myself cling tighter to the white card, bending it slightly, and I focus on it. I focus on the now. In the lower left, the card reads Andy Santiago, Media Relations, along with a different phone number and a different email address from the other card.

This one's newer, but I would have known that just from the campaign itself. Jeff Davis is in a dead heat with some other candidate whose name I can't recall. The only reason I know Davis's name is because of the billboards plastered on the Expressway, accusing him of living up to his namesake Jefferson Davis, former president of the Confederacy.

Want to go back to 1861? the billboards ask. They have a Confederate flag as a backdrop. *Vote Jeff Davis For Senate.*

Every once in a while, my old calling catches me, and I have thoughts I can't bury. Like who the hell thought that was a good campaign slogan? It doesn't even name the candidate running opposite Jeff Davis, although, in fairness, who would want her name on a billboard like that?

I shake myself from the reverie, know I mentally walked that way because of the shock of seeing that poor A.D. "Andy" Santiago is a political operative just like I was.

And then he ended up here.

I slip both cards into my back pocket, clench my fist to stop my hand from shaking, and dig through the wallet a little more. The address on Santiago's driver's license is eight blocks from here, on a street that was gentrified ten years ago.

The money's coming back to the neighborhood, as I mentioned to Bancroft a while ago. At some point, we're going to have to upscale the bar or sell it. He doesn't want to sell it: Bancroft doesn't like change. But that was when he gave me permission to remodel the place.

Bancroft isn't the only one who doesn't like change.

And I force my mind back to the wallet. I recognize the way my thoughts wander when there's something in front of me that brings up my past. Only now, I want to face it, and I'm finding that as hard as running away from it.

I write the address down, then fold the wallet back up and carry it, wrapped in paper towels back to the bar. I pull out a plastic sandwich bag from the stack I use for leftover garnish, and slip the wallet inside.

Then I sigh. Crunch time.

I can keep it here until someone comes for it. I can take it to the police. Or I can take it to the hospital.

I glance at the ancient clock emblazoned with the Christmas Budweiser Clydesdales in the snow. It's quarter past eleven. We don't stay open past midnight on weeknights: there's no point.

It's past visiting hours at the hospital, not that I want to look in on this guy. But it's still early enough that someone on the staff with half a brain would be there, who would be able to trace the John Doe that Rick Winters brought in.

If Santiago registered as a John Doe. He seemed pretty out of it when Rick carried him out of here, but Santiago had been conscious. He might've used his name.

I slip the wallet in its baggy in the canvas tote I call a purse, grab my leather jacket, toss them both over a chair, and go through my lockup routine. I have to follow the same routine, day in and day out, or I forget something.

When you do the same thing for decades, you zone out as you do it, and I'm no exception. Books balanced. Pour count entered. Cash in the safe in my office, receipts printed and tallied. Computers shut down. Lights dimmed. Bar gleaming.

Purse and jacket over my arm, check to see if the front door's locked. Yep. Make sure the window bars are secure. Yep. Head to the back, set the alarm, let myself out, and lock up.

Alley smells of vomit again, with a bit of piss mixed in. Supposed to rain tonight, so the smell should be gone by morning. I step gingerly past any puddles, note that the garbage is particularly rancid as well, happy that the pickup arrives before I do tomorrow.

I slip my purse over my shoulder, my jacket over the entire thing, keys in hand, heart pounding like it always does—as if I expect some sex-crazed asshole to jump me in the 20 feet between the bar's back door and the parking lot. Me, round and muscled. Me, who took so many self-defense courses that I can lay out a 250-pound drunk with a well-placed shove to the chest. Me, who hasn't had anyone look at her sideways in maybe fifteen years.

But every night, sure as I lock up, I also talk myself down from the panic, remind myself just how safe I am, remind myself that the asshole who changed the course of my life wasn't some random sex-crazed idiot with a hard-on, he was one of the best known politicians in the state, and goddamn if I shouldn't've enjoyed his attentions because, after all, he spent some of his precious time with me.

That's why I'm shaking. He's still well known. Hell, he's better known. And he's not just in the legislature. He's running it.

And he's hoping to fill it with men like Jeff Davis, hoping to bring the world back to 1861. Just because I think the slogan's bad politics for the opposition doesn't mean I think the slogan's wrong.

My vehicle's the last one in the parking lot, just as it always is. Usually, I look at my black F-150 and smile, thinking *Built Ford Tough* because damned if I don't need a vehicle that's tough and protective, since I'm still on my own.

But this night, I scan the perimeter, like I always do, then I unlock the truck and get inside, locking back up immediately. I don't feel safe. I don't feel unsafe. I feel jangly, a little outside my own body, as if I'm not in complete control.

Maybe the fact that I'm not in complete control is how I ended up at Jeff Davis's campaign headquarters. I realized I was driving there halfway down a side street I don't normally drive on.

Campaign headquarters are never on the beaten path. They're not places voters go to. Campaign headquarters are places to keep voters out of.

I expected this one to have one light burning and a few die-hard true believers, all under the age of twenty-five, to be shuffling papers and manning the phones. Shows how 1980s my campaign memories are, because when I pull up, the entire place is lit up. Yellow light, not pasty fluorescents, illuminates everything behind the glass windows, initially designed for a long-dead retail establishment.

Inside, people talk, exchange papers, lots of papers, and stare at computer screens, which adds even more ambient light. And yes, everyone seems to be under twenty-five—and well-dressed. No hoodies and ripped jeans, no T-shirts and old jeans, no jeans at all. Open-collar dress shirts, suit coats on the backs of chairs, matching pants which fit well—and everyone thin, or at least, thinner than the average American.

Enthusiastic, well-dressed, thin—jeez, it looks more like a movie set than an actual campaign headquarters.

I can't help myself. I pull the truck over, park behind a Prius and feel tempted to go all Monster Truck on its ass. I ignore the thought and what it means (okay, yeah, I'm pissed, but I'm generally pissed, so what's it matter?), grab my giant purse and let myself out.

I can't do innocent anymore, although I'm tempted. I almost revert to Girl Operator, the one who died, along with her blond curls and her innocence.

Instead, I square my shoulders and take a deep breath. No Girl Operator. Instead, Bad-Ass Bartender. Or, maybe, Concerned Friend.

As I walk down the sidewalk, I try on Concerned Friend for good measure. Won't work. Everyone in the headquarters knows Andy Santiago, and I don't. Can't do Bad-Ass Bartender either. Don't have my bar, blocking me from the fighting customers. Don't have my baseball bat for minor scuffles. Don't have my gun for major ones.

Just me, short, squat, bald and tattooed. Big, and muscled, and unexpectedly female.

That should surprise the little shits working to take us back to 1861.

I pull open the campaign office door and, of all things, a bell jingles above me. Conversation ceases. Everyone looks up, a sea of white surprised faces. I remember this now from my years in campaign headquarters:

Alert! Stranger in our midst! Reporter? Spy? Civilian? Volunteer?

Only it's nearly midnight. Who the hell comes into a campaign headquarters at midnight?

I let the door bang behind me. No one approaches me, although someone should. There should be some flunky in charge, even this late at night.

Computers hum in the silence. No one moves, as if I've caught them selling drugs or laundering money. I'm not real fond of standing here, either.

So I meet their gazes, slowly, one at a time, acknowledging them. An I-see-you action that I learned in self-defense class. It works with drunks who're acting up all the way across the room.

Once I've met everyone's gaze, I say, "I was told I could find Andy Santiago here."

In the back of the room, two women glance at each other. Another woman stands up. As she draws closer, I see that she's a little older than the others.

"What do you want with Andy?" she asks.

"It's personal," I say.

"Uh-huh," she says in a tone that says I-don't-believe-you.

"He's not at his place," I say, "and he's not answering his cell. So, a friend said to try here."

Those women glance at each other again. Someone titters in the back.

"You think this is funny?" I ask in my driest voice. "I'm looking for someone. I was told you people could help. Can you?"

The woman glares in the direction of the titter. Then she looks back at me. Her makeup has faded on the right side of her face, as if she's been resting her hand there, and the makeup came off.

"Can't help," she says. "He's not part of this campaign any longer."

"Really?" I ask. "Since when? Because he was still handing out your business cards a few days ago."

Her too-red lips thin. "We parted ways this afternoon."

He showed up in my bar this afternoon.

"Over what?" I ask.

"That's personal," she says.

"Huh," I say. "Because he worked for you. So that should be business."

One of the young men in front of me leans back in his chair. His mouth twists sideways. I think maybe he's trying to smile derisively. It's not working.

"We don't have any room for Log Cabin Republicans," he says.

"Jordy," the woman cautions.

He glares at her. "It's true. That's what Jeff—"

"We parted ways," the woman says. "It turns out that Andy's agenda was different from ours."

I smile, and I know my smile works. "Log Cabin Republicans," I say. "Is he a card-carrying member of that particular organization, or are you rocket scientists labeling him that because you just figured out that he's gay?"

"He's not gay," one of the women from the back says.

"Stop," the woman in charge says. "This is no one's business but ours."

The woman in the back stands up. "Andy's not gay—"

"Yeah, right," says the guy in front of me.

"But he believes in equality for everyone. He's been pushing—"

"An agenda that's not consistent with the Davis campaign," the woman in charge says over her. "So we told him to take his services elsewhere."

The woman in the back is looking at me. She's maybe 21, with long blond hair, and the kind of cute that'll get her dismissed in politics.

I should know.

"Two weeks before the election?" I ask. "That's bit odd, isn't it?"

"You're a reporter, aren't you?" the woman in charge asks.

"Actually, no," I say. "I used to do your job, though, a long time ago in a land faraway."

She looks me up and down, making it clear without saying a word that a woman like me could never have run a position of authority in a campaign. Funny, I used to get dismissed because I was little and cute. And now that I'm neither, I get dismissed for being the kind of person who's too militant to ever be taken seriously.

"Well," she says, "be that as it may, Andy's not here, he's not going to be here, he's not ever coming back, and we have no idea how to reach him. So you have no reason to stay here."

"And no reason to vote for Jeff Davis either, apparently, considering how nice and cooperative his staff is."

"It's midnight," she says. "What did you expect?"

"It's midnight," I say, "and someone's concerned about Andy. I would have expected some compassion, and maybe a little help."

No one responds. I look at each of their faces again, as if I'm memorizing them. A number of the staff won't look at me this time. The young woman in the back, the only one who spoke to me, glances at the woman in charge.

She doesn't say anything. She's still glaring at me.

I want to say *Thanks for nothing*, but that sounds childish, even in my head. So I just turn around and leave. I hear someone lock the door behind me.

I know if I turn around, I'll see a few faces pressed against the glass, watching me go.

Strangely, that sense I had, that jittery not-quite-in-control sense is gone. And so is the underlying panic that I usually feel in a strange neighborhood. You'd think it would be worse here, but it's not.

I get in the truck and sigh. I glance at the clock on the dash. Maybe I can get the wallet to someone who knows Andy Santiago at the hospital desk, but I think that's a true maybe. The other maybe is whether or not I should go home—

A knock on the driver's side window startles me. I swallow a scream, then curse myself. I still haven't learned how to scream for help. Eight self-defense classes, and screaming still doesn't come naturally to me.

I turn, and see the face of that young woman, the one who spoke out of turn, looking up at me. She had to reach up to hit the window with the knuckles of her right hand.

She's not wearing a coat. Her arms are wrapped around her torso and she's shifting from foot to foot as if she's cold.

I lower the window, and don't say anything.

"Why do you need to find Andy?" she asks.

"He left his wallet at my place," I say, which is trueish, "and he's not answering his phone," which is probably true as well.

"Oh," she says. "I thought maybe...."

I wait.

Her face scrunches up and she takes a deep breath. "He's okay then?"

"I can't reach him," I say, as if that's an answer. "That's unusual for a man like him."

She sighs a little. Bites her upper lip, glances over her shoulder.

"They walked him out," she says. "Jordy and three other guys. And it didn't look friendly."

I don't interrupt.

"I'm worried about him," she says and her voice breaks. She seems to be telling the truth. She looks over her shoulder again. Then she adds, "I left my stuff in there. I—they'll—would you walk me back?"

Is she kidding me? After she just told me that four men marched Santiago out of the building, and he ended up raped and beaten? Do they think I'm that dumb? Or do they think she's so appealing that she's going to be bait I would fall for?

I have no idea where that thought came from, but as soon as it crossed my mind, it made me angry.

"No," I say.

Her lower lip trembles. She frowns prettily, and I resist the urge to roll my eyes. Bad-Ass Bartender doesn't really exist outside of the bar, apparently.

"Tell you what," I say. "I'll back up, park in front of your headquarters, and watch as you go in. If anything goes wrong—"

"Forget it," she says, voice plumy with tears. "I can handle it myself."

She stomps away, then pauses just for a moment as if marshaling courage. It's that little movement that catches me. I wheel the truck around and park across the street.

She sees me, then turns her head away.

She goes inside the headquarters. Everyone watches her, like they watched me. No one says anything.

They watch her walk to the back, grab her purse, a laptop bag, and a coat, and then the woman stops her near the door.

The girl isn't bait. She's genuinely scared. And I treated her badly.

I look around the neighborhood, then get out of the truck. I shove the keys in my pocket, and walk to the door, keeping my eye on the girl and the woman. They're arguing.

I pull the door open—apparently she left it unlocked—and say, "You fired her for talking to me?"

They all look at me now.

The girl's face is pale. "I quit, actually."

She can't lie to save herself. That's so different from me at that age. I was the queen of liars. That's how I got and kept my job.

"And I'm leaving," the girl says, pulling the laptop bag away from the other woman.

"The laptop is ours," the woman says.

"The laptop is *mine*," the girl says. "My personal laptop. I never ever used yours. I don't like linked networks."

"It has our work product on it," the woman says.

I know where this conversation is going, and I don't like it.

"So hire a lawyer," I say to the woman. Then I extend my arm to the girl. "C'mon. Let's get out of here."

Her look is both startled and grateful.

The Jordy kid stands up. He's taller than me, younger than me, dumber than me. Even though he's not drunk, I probably have fifty IQ points and a whole lotta living on him. And I can put him down with a shove to the chest.

Only he doesn't know that.

"She's not leaving," he says.

"What're you going to do?" I ask. "Hold her hostage?"

I waggle my fingers at the girl, and she runs toward me. I hold the door open, watching everyone, Jordy, the woman, the other workers still at their seats.

The other girl in the back, the one who had exchanged glances with the one heading to my truck, she's gone too. I hope she went out a back exit, and isn't just in the ladies room.

But she's not my problem. I'm neither cop nor superhero.

"You people are something else," I say, then follow the girl outside.

She's standing on the sidewalk, shivering.

"Do you have a car?" I ask, thinking maybe the Prius is hers.

She shakes her head. "I took the bus."

Worse than a Prius, then. A True Believer, who can't afford a vehicle. True Believers go all Ninja Avenger when they lose their cherry and discover their candidate is an ass and a cad. (They're all asses and cads, at minimum. Often they're crooks and egomaniacs too.)

If she has writing skills, she's going to blog.

If she doesn't, she's going to cause other troubles, and the problem is that the woman inside that campaign headquarters knows it.

"I'll drop you," I say to the girl.

She glances at me, then at the people inside. I can almost read her thoughts. She's having two of them. The first: *They're going to think that I'm connected to this woman*. And the other comes from a much younger, much more vulnerable place: *I'm not supposed to get in a car with strangers.*

The girl takes a deep breath, then nods. We cross the street to my truck, and using the remote access, I unlock the door. I'm getting into a car with a stranger, too, something I haven't done in more than thirty years.

Not that my problems have ever come from strangers.

"I'm D," I say after we're both inside the truck. I don't explain that

"D" is short for "Blondie," which was what the patrons used to call me before I got rid of the hair. Then they called me "Baldie," and all I could hear over the noise of the jukebox was the hard "d," so I took on the name.

"Laney," she says, her voice still shaking. She's glancing out the window as if she expects Jordy and his friends to follow us.

I start the truck and put it in gear in one swift movement. "I take it you like Andy."

"He's a lot of fun," she says, "and he's really smart, and he was *right*."

A girl with a crush, it sounds like.

I check the mirrors, and the door to the campaign headquarters. The remaining staff is arguing. I don't see the other girl.

I pull out and start down the road. "How do you know Andy's not gay?"

"I just do," she says. "I mean, he doesn't seem like it, and he wouldn't be, and he's really nice."

I suppress a sigh, wondering how anyone can be as naïve as she is and still function. I remind myself, as I often do at the bar, that it's not my job to educate people. At the bar, it's my job to help them forget their idiocies for a while.

Right now, I don't really have a job, except maybe to get this girl home.

"Where do you live?" I ask.

"They're not going to come for me, are they?" she asks.

I don't ask "who." I know who she means. "You got a roommate?"

She shakes her head.

"Deadbolts?"

She nods.

"Just don't answer your door tonight," I say, knowing it's not a lot of comfort. But I'm not going to be responsible for this kid. "Call the cops if someone's persistent."

She makes a little involuntary sound of panic. I ignore it.

"Address?" I ask again.

She tells me. She lives all the way across town, near the university. Of course.

I wheel the truck in that direction, and wonder what I'm going to do with the information that the girl has given me. Call the cops? Tell Rick? Tell the hospital?

It's really none of my business.

And I'm not the type who makes it my business. I tend bar, for godssake. Nothing is my business.

"Where were you when he left his wallet?" she asks.

I glance at her. I had said he left it at my place. Either she forgot that, or she's trying to figure out why Santiago would be with a woman like me.

We're nowhere near the headquarters now, and something about being alone in the cab of this truck with this girl makes me decide on honesty.

"He came into my bar," I say, my voice flat.

"Bar?" She frowns at me. "I thought—he says—he doesn't drink."

Maybe like Bancroft doesn't drink. Because no non-drinker would order Jack. Although I had pushed him into it. And he hadn't known what would hurt him.

Maybe someone he knew ordered Jack, and he parroted the order.

"He did," I say. "And then he passed out—"

"He drank that much?" she asks.

I wheel onto the Expressway. Not a lot of traffic this late at night, but the billboard is lit up from below. *Want to go back to 1861?*

"No," I say, answering both questions. "He passed out from blood loss."

"He got beat up in your bar?"

"He got beaten up and raped before he got to my bar."

I let the words hang.

She's shaking her head. "No. You can't rape a..." and then she pauses and her breath catches. "No," she says again, only this time, the tone is different. This *no* is a disbelieving no. She saw something, realized something, knew something.

"Where is he?" she asks.

"Mercy General," I say. "We took him there."

"If you know where he is, why did you come to campaign headquarters?" There's anger in her voice now, as if it's all my fault.

Why did I go to the headquarters? It was the sixty-four-thousand-dollar question. I hadn't meant to, but I'm not sure I should say that to this girl.

"I thought maybe I'd find some of his friends there," I lie. "I thought maybe I'd find someone who cared."

She nods, and goes silent. The Expressway seems alien at this time of night, with the halogen streetlights leaving uneven pools of light across the smooth pavement. We'd gone several miles. We were due for another *Want to go back to 1861?* billboard real soon now.

"I care." She says it so softly that I almost didn't hear her over the hum of the tires. "Can we go see him?"

"It's the middle of the night," I say. "Do you know his family?"

She shakes her head. "Who do you think did this?"

"Who do you think did it?" I ask with more charge than I expect.

She turns away, thinking I can't see her. But I can see her reflection in the passenger side window. Her mouth has thinned, her eyes are narrow, and at first, I think she's angry. Then I realize she's holding back tears.

"If I go to the police," she whispers, "I'm done."

"You already quit," I say, recognizing the irony as the words come out of my mouth. I'm pushing her to take action in a situation where I never would.

"No," she says. "I'm done working in politics."

"Maybe," I say. But politics are different now than they were in my day. No one would believe a girl with a complaint thirty years ago, even if she had been bruised and battered and bleeding for days.

Now, people would believe a girl, a sincere girl of the proper background, who saw something, knew something, accused something. And if she stood up, then maybe—

I smile at myself, mentally pat myself on the back and think, *Hello, Girl Operator.* I thought I'd trained her out of me, but she reappears like the undead, filled with naiveté, optimism and hope.

"You want to keep working in politics more than you want to help a friend?" I ask.

"He's not a friend," she says too fast. "He's...."

He was the hope of a friend. A boyfriend. Someone kind to her.

We've reached her neighborhood. I take the first exit off the Expressway. Students sit outside well-lit bars, one hour before last call. My bar hasn't been open to last call since Barak Obama got re-elected, when the rednecks and the bigots were too scared and angry to go home.

I wonder what made Laney want to return to 1861. She fits into my bar—Bancroft's bar—better than I do, and she doesn't even know it.

I wind through a couple of side streets and find the rundown apartment complex where she lives.

She looks at me for a moment, as if she wants to say something. Then she opens the passenger side door.

"Thanks for the lift," she says, as if we're old friends.

She gets out, slams the door, and half-runs, half-walks to the building. She doesn't look both ways to see if anyone is lurking in the shadows. She doesn't look back either.

I watch her fumble with her keys, open the main door, and head inside.

I don't know why I expect her to do the right thing, when the only person in this entire situation who has done the right thing wasn't me. It was Rick. And he did it without hesitation.

I sigh, pull away from the curb, and drive away.

Eventually, I head home, because I can't think of anywhere else to go.

Home isn't much. It's a condo only because I bought the entire building a few years ago, when I realized it was better to control who I had as neighbors than it was to suffer through another loud drunken party two floors below me.

I have the entire top floor, which sounds more impressive than it is. Living room with a view of the street, good-size kitchen with a view of nothing, a dining room that serves as a storehouse for mail that I forget to sort, and a large bedroom complete with TV and reading chair, and two windows, both locked and shaded. I installed air conditioning and a good heating system, and if you came inside with me (which you never would) you'd think that the windows hadn't been opened since the last century, and you'd be right.

Fresh air is for suckers, baby. And people who trust other people.

My kitchen table is always spotless. I hang my purse over one of the chairs, open the fridge, and take out the sub I bought that morning. I usually have something ready when I get home so I don't have to think about food.

I unwrap the sub. The bread's soggy from the oil and vinegar dressing I splurged on, but I don't care. I eat a few bites, listen to the green pepper crunch, let the pepperoni bite my tongue, and start shaking again.

It's hard to eat. My throat has closed up like it did in those first weeks after I met Bancroft. I trained myself to eat after that—too well, some would say—and I force myself to take a few more bites now.

No regression, no regrets. Just move forward.

Only that's not really working for me right now. I know something. Laney knows something. And neither of us have taken any steps forward.

I cut the rest of the sub in half, and put the good half in the fridge for tomorrow—if I can eat tomorrow. I make myself finish the other half, chase it with some cold water, and head to the bedroom.

The queen-sized bed doesn't even look inviting. The entire room seems like a foreign place. I go to my living room, don't turn on any lights, and sit on the couch, surveying the neighborhood.

Or so I tell myself. Part of me knows I'm reverting to the scared woman I'd been thirty years ago.

And part of me doesn't care.

I wake up with my head jammed against the arm and back of the sofa, a crick in my neck so profound that I moan as I move. The light falling into the room is unfamiliar, and I have awakened much earlier than usual.

I get up, and as I make some much-needed coffee, I look at the clock on the microwave. It's 7:30 a.m.

Even though I don't have to be at the bar until eleven, I know I can't go back to sleep. My dreams were filled with confetti and laughter and cries of *He won!* I'm not going back there just to get a few more hours rest.

I shower, dress, manage to shove some Raisin Bran into my mouth, and chase the meal with coffee. Then, without really thinking about it, I let myself out of the condo.

Mercy General is fifteen minutes away on back roads in rush hour traffic. I get there just as visiting hours open.

I'm not sure if I want to see Andy Santiago. My stomach is as twisted as my neck was this morning, the coffee mixing badly with the cereal. I ask for Santiago's room, and receive the number with no fuss.

Apparently, he was able to tell them who he was.

Hospitals have the same smell—the sour scent of sickness overlaid by disinfectant and cafeteria gravy, with a hint of very bad coffee. I take the elevator to the fourteenth floor, wondering what, exactly, I'm about.

But I don't turn around.

His room is halfway down the hall from the elevator. I pass rooms with moaning patients, beeping equipment, and loud televisions. The room number is displayed prominently on the blond wood.

Santiago's door stands open. I slip inside, surprised to see that the room is private. It has a bathroom near the door, and a bed in the center. Windows cover the outside wall, letting in sunlight.

Andy Santiago looks nothing like the man who came into my bar. His face is gray with pain and that bruise on his chin is five times the size it was yesterday afternoon. He's smaller than I thought, and he wears a hospital gown instead of an expensive suit.

"Mr. Santiago?" I sit on the edge of the chair next to his bed. I don't want to tower over him. In my experience, looming is as threatening as leaning in.

He opens one eye and slowly moves his head in my direction.

"You," he says, his voice raspy with disuse.

I nod. I reach into my purse and remove the plastic bag with his wallet.

"I found your wallet." I set it on the nightstand, near the TV remote. That's when I realize the television is off.

"Thank you," he mouths and closes his eyes again.

I wait a minute, just to see if he'll talk to me. I start to get up, feeling very awkward.

You'd think I would know how to talk to someone in a situation like this. You'd think I would know what's right and what's wrong, how to pressure, how to comfort.

But I don't. I don't know any of it.

I don't even say, *I'm sorry for what happened to you*, because even though the words aren't empty, they sound empty.

I walk out of the room, feeling like I should have done more, but not sure what more actually is. I can't tell him to go to the police; I never did. And I can't offer him the comfort of some support group, because I never found them comforting.

I'm most of the way to my truck when I realize that all the things I would offer a friend, all the common-sense things people do for each other in times of crisis, all the ways our society says we should take care of crime and each other, I have done none of them for myself. Ever.

Coffee-flavored acid rises in my gorge and I swallow, hard. I lean on the truck for a moment.

Then I climb inside, and drive to work, two hours early and thirty years too late.

I clean the front top to bottom in those two hours, and I keep cleaning through the slow arrival of the lunch drinkers. Ma Kettle finds her booth around one, and I give her the usual vodka tonic. A twenty-something couple walks in about one-thirty, looks around, and then gives me a sheepish look before leaving again.

I'm amazed they got inside at all.

I'm clock-watching, waiting for Rick. I'm not sure what I want to talk to him about; I just want to talk.

Then, at three-thirty-five, he arrives, like he always has. Only he doesn't bang the door closed and he doesn't seem quite as angry.

He also doesn't sit at his usual spot at the bar.

He glances at everything, as if memorizing it. I've seen this from regulars before. They're saying goodbye.

I head over, but I don't grab the Heineken. I won't, unless he asks.

"Hey," I say. "I took that guy his wallet."

Rick nods. "He's pretty messed up."

"Yeah," I say.

"They used something—bottle, bat, I don't know," he says. "I didn't ask. But he was hemorrhaging. If we hadn't brought him in, he would've died."

Jesus. In my bar. Right in front of me.

"If you hadn't brought him in," I say.

"What?" Rick asks.

"You did it, not me," I say. "If I had been here by myself—"

"You'd've called 911," Rick says. He looks longingly at the bar stool. I can feel him wavering. "Those bastards. He wouldn't tell me who did it."

"Guys he worked with," I say.

"He told you?" Rick asks.

I shake my head. I don't want to tell him about the campaign office—it's too close, too personal, but...

Rick's staring at me. "What, D?"

"Debra," I say, surprising myself. "I'm Debra."

And then I burst into tears.

Oh, I'd love to tell you everything's hunky dory now, and my life is perfect, and that big-name politician isn't sitting like a slug at the statehouse. He is, and my life is still my life, and nothing's hunky dory.

But Rick knew the detective handling Santiago's case, and Rick made me tell the detective about the campaign headquarters and the Log Cabin Republican comments and the sheer hostility.

They found Laney, and it turns out she was scared not just because she figured out what happened. Right after I had said Santiago was raped, just as she was going to tell me with all her naïve passion that raping a man wasn't possible, a memory hit her, and made the sentence die in her throat.

She had seen the bloody dowel Jordy and his friends used, part of a broken towel-rack someone placed near the back to take out with the recycling. She'd seen it, and better yet, she helped the police find it.

Those four guys who used it to teach Andy Santiago a lesson are going to learn some lessons themselves.

If this were one of those happy feel-good alls-well-that-ends-well kinda stories, I'd tell you that Santiago and I have become friends or that we bonded at our support group. I'd tell you this incident derailed the Jeff Davis campaign.

But none of that happened.

I'm still here, still tending bar, still wondering what to do with my afternoons.

Something's different, though. I'm trying to figure out how to update the bar, so that we're not the neighborhood eyesore as the gentrification continues. I've decided that I like what we are—that wayside, that haven, for the folks whose lives are in the crapper.

There're plenty of trendy bars. I don't like them much.

I prefer places where strangers wander in rarely, and when they do, they tend to stick around until they cross back over to the trendy bar side of life.

I imagine that's where Rick is. Or he's in that same place Bancroft is, the one that knows about the reality of dive bars and the camaraderie of people hanging at the end of their ropes.

About a week ago, Santiago came back, he says, because he owes me. But I keep saying he owes Rick. Santiago doesn't owe me anything.

But Santiago does know that I used to do his job, back in the day, the job he doesn't do any more either, and he knows I once sat on the same bar stool with the same disillusionment.

I don't know if that means anything to him. I'm not sure it means much to me.

I do know that, for the time being, he's finding comfort here.

And who can argue with that?

Ten Stories by Dean Wesley Smith

An Obscene Crime Against Passion

Dean Wesley Smith

One

The night James Ward finally confronted his wife for what she truly was started when police car lights flashed outside the large picture window of his suburban home. The drawn cloth curtains kept most of the light out, as well as the closed blinds under the curtains, but he still noticed the blue-red combination.

He couldn't remember the last time he had opened those windows and unless he heard shots out there in the cul-de-sac, he wasn't opening them now. The last baseball games before the All-Star break were being played tonight and he wanted to make sure he caught as many of them as he could.

He glanced around at his two-bedroom ranch-style home from his favorite recliner wondering where Deborah had gone. Over the last few years they had just drifted into doing their own things in their own ways at their own times.

The marriage had become convenient for both of them, passion a thing of the past, as he had expected would happen when they married but had hoped would not happen, as any newlywed hopes.

His life now was working at the insurance agency and watching baseball and doing a little betting on games down at the local casino. And just waiting. He did not expect his wait to end right before the All-Star Break in baseball.

He honestly had no idea what Deborah's interests had become as they drifted apart. She said she did some teaching, but he didn't remember what type or when or where.

And he honestly didn't care. Sad, considering she was his wife.

James was a tall, handsome man, at least many said that, and did some minor exercise to stay in shape. Deborah was just as stunningly beautiful now as the day he met her.

Everyone who saw them together said they made a perfect couple.

If they only knew.

Suddenly, just as the two teams were returning to the field after the seventh inning to finish up the nine-one disaster-of-a-game he had been watching, a loud banging at the front door shook the house.

"Deborah!" he shouted.

No response.

More banging.

"All right, all right," he said, climbing out of his recliner and heading for the door.

On the front porch stood two police officers. One a man, one a woman. The woman cop had a hooker by the arm and the hooker was turned away from the porch light.

He had no idea why cops would bring a hooker to his door at eight in the evening on a weeknight.

The cops were dressed in standard city cop uniforms and the hooker had on a very, very short skirt that barely covered the bottom of her ass, a mesh blouse that you could see through, torn black stockings, and heels so high that they looked more like stilts than shoes.

Women like her often walked along some of the worst streets downtown. He always avoided those areas. He just wasn't interested.

"You James Ward?" the guy asked.

"Yeah," James said.

"You married to Deborah Ward?" the guy asked.

"I am," James said. "Is she all right?"

"She seems to be," the cop said, handing James a small purse. "But might want to get her some help."

"And keep her off the streets," the woman cop said. "Dangerous downtown."

With that, the woman cop turned the hooker around and pushed her toward the door.

The hooker nodded to James and walked past him into the house, taking the small purse out of his hands as she went.

The cops both nodded to James without smiling and turned back toward their car as James stood there, surprised that the night had finally arrived.

It seemed events had transpired to move his life forward.

Finally, he slowly backed into the house and closed the door.

Then he turned around.

Deborah, his wife of five years, dressed like a twenty-dollar streetwalker, stood there, facing him. Her makeup was almost so thick as to crack and her normally wonderful brown hair had been greased back off her face.

"Surprise, huh?" she said, then popped some gum.

He opened his mouth, but said nothing.

Nothing.

"Let me go take a hot shower, get into my normal costume, and then we can talk," she said. "Be a sweetie and fix me a Bloody Mary. All the fixings are in the cabinet above the fridge where you would never look. It was a bitch of a night out there."

With a practiced ease on the extremely tall heels, she turned and headed back toward her closet and bedroom.

All James could do was stand there and watch her ass sway under her tight, short skirt as she went down the hall. That was an amazing costume she was wearing.

Then he went over and turned off the game and headed for the kitchen.

With this, he was going to need a drink as well.

Maybe two. If the night turned out as he hoped it would.

Two

The kitchen of their suburban home was everything Deborah had wanted when they moved in. White modern cabinets, granite countertops, a dark floor, and modern stainless appliances.

The entire house had been remodeled. Some of it to her wants, a lot to his hidden reasons.

On the way to the kitchen he clicked a few hidden switches that would help him with the evening to come.

The kitchen table was custom-made to fit the space and could hold six, but since neither of them had much in the way of friends, that table had usually seated only the two of them. And their formal dining room had never been used.

Just wasn't either of their styles or their natures to have friends.

James hadn't objected to anything she had added in the remodel as long as it made her smile. When they were first married five years ago, he had loved to see her smile.

She had been fun to watch.

And they had made love regularly, in all sorts of ways. He liked that more than he wanted to admit.

That had ended slowly over the first year.

James dug out the glasses, the Bloody Mary mix, the vodka, and even a couple sticks of celery from the fridge he hadn't noticed before. He normally drank beer and didn't much like vegetables.

He put her drink in front of her chair and sat down in his chair and sipped on his drink, stirring it with the celery.

Since he had spent so much time at the casino lately in the sports book, he and Deborah had taken to eating meals on their own.

Now that he thought about it, the only thing they had left in their marriage was this house. Wow, that was sad.

But it felt more like a fact to him than a sadness. He had hoped for something more. Sure.

But it hadn't happened.

Shouldn't he be angry at all this? At her hooking downtown? At her sleeping with who knew how many other men?

A normal husband would.

He tried to think back. He couldn't remember the last time he had gotten angry about anything. It had been a very long time.

He didn't even get that much of a thrill with winning a bet and didn't get angry either with losing. Gambling used to make him feel alive.

Wow, he had become a dead shell in this marriage. How pathetic was that?

He needed new energy, new focus, new everything. Looked like after tonight he was finally going to get it.

After a few minutes, Deborah came out wearing her blue bathrobe and slippers. Her hair was wet and pulled back and her face looked like it had been scrubbed pretty well to get the makeup off.

She didn't even look close to the same woman who had walked through the front door thirty minutes ago. This was the Deborah he had married.

She sat down and took a pretty good drink of her Bloody Mary, then sat back with a sigh.

"Thanks, I needed that."

He nodded and took another drink as well.

Then he looked at her. "How long have you been doing this?"

She laughed. "If you mean being a prostitute, since I was fifteen. I was trained by my mother."

Again his mouth opened and yet not a word came out.

Nothing.

There was just nothing he could say to that as her husband.

Finally, he just shook his head and took another sip of his drink. A normal husband with a normal wife would be furiously angry at all this, at being lied to, at everything.

But he wasn't.

He couldn't be and he actually didn't feel a thing, as she knew would be the case.

She stared at him for a moment, then seemed to finally take pity on him, as he had been hoping for five years she would do.

"Have you ever met a person who just seemed to suck the life out of a room?" she asked.

He nodded. "Numbers of them back in college. There is a guy by the name of Hank in our office that does the same thing at times."

"You ever wonder where that life goes?" she asked.

He looked into her deep brown eyes and could see her question was serious. She was going to finally tell him the truth.

About damned time. Way too late, however.

"You ever heard of vampires?" she asked.

He nodded.

"Vampires in fiction survive from taking the life force, blood, out of others."

He nodded. He had seen his share of bad movies.

"Blood vampires do not exist," she said, matter-of-factly, looking at him and seeming to hold him.

"But energy eating beings do exist," she said. "They are ancient humans that need the energy, the passion, the life force of normal humans to exist. I am one of them. We call ourselves Primals."

The truth was finally out.

Finally.

The cop had been right, she really did need help. Just not the help the cop had intended.

"Have you been wondering why you feel nothing anymore about anything and are not angry right now about your wife being a hooker?"

He nodded, going with her. "That has bothered me."

"I keep you drained of that sort of energy," she said. "It's why you took that dull job, bet on sports without any thrill of winning or worry about losing, and why we stopped having sex a long time ago."

"You keep me drained?" he asked. "Why would you do that?"

"Because for the next fifteen or twenty years, I needed what we Primals call a cow. You, my sweet James, are my cow."

Damn he wanted to get angry, but just nothing came up.

"What exactly is the function of a cow?" he asked.

"I will not age," she said, "so for the next fifteen or so years, until our age difference starts to get noticed, you will supply me with a base level of energy, passion, joy, enough for me to survive for weeks at a time without being around others."

She was taking his joy, his energy, his caring, as he knew she was. As he had known it from the moment he tracked her down and got close to her, let her feel his energy.

"So why are you hooking?" he asked, sipping on his Bloody Mary.

"Once a week I need the boost, the thrill of sex with strangers, the fear that goes with that sex, the passion of men not used to feeling passion."

"You drain them all?" he asked.

"In a matter of speaking," she said, smiling. "Yes. They feel empty, calm, and without guilt when they leave me."

"So why me?" he asked.

He knew the answer. But now that her truth was out in the air between them, he wanted to hear her say it.

She smiled at him. A cold smile as only a Primal can give, but a real smile.

"Because I love you," she said. "And I wanted to spend a couple decades with you."

"Until I die from lack of energy," he said.

She nodded. "Pretty much."

He knew that wasn't going to happen. And it really made him sad to hear her say that. He had hoped for a different result.

"So are you going to keep hooking?" he asked. "That seems like a rather risky thing to continue to do after tonight, now that your name is on file with the police."

He was actually very glad she had slipped up and her name was on file as a hooker. It would make the next things he had to do even easier.

"I was thinking we need to have your brother come live with us," she said. "We have two spare rooms. Maybe he and his wife could both come. That would be fun for me."

He looked at her, knowing exactly what she was planning, but still playing along. "I don't have a brother."

"Of course you don't," she said, laughing. "I'll find us one, maybe a couple, and get us a cover story. It will be far more fun for a few years than walking those streets in those heels."

He just shook his head. So now he was going to share Deborah with two other people.

It seemed time to end this.

He sipped on his Bloody Mary, then looked up at her and smiled. "Ever hear of a group called Libertas?"

Her face drained of the freshly-washed look. Her eyes darted from one side to the other, clearly looking for a way to run.

There was no way.

He had made this house a perfect Primal trap and he had turned on that trap while she was in the shower.

"You didn't answer my question," he said.

"Libertas is a group of hunters that survive on finding and draining Primals such as myself."

She looked at him, really looked at him. "Are you a Libertas?"

"Of course I am," he said, laughing. "When I saw you that first day we met in the supermarket, your arrogance of just brushing men and draining them, I knew I could easily convince you I could be a perfect cow."

Her eyes flashed in anger. But then that anger faded and her skin got pale.

He sipped on his Bloody Mary as she slowly realized what was happening to her. He was draining her energy into the fields surrounding the house. And the house was then feeding him that energy through his chair.

She tried to stand, to run, but it was too late. She didn't have the energy left in her body for even that much.

A couple hundred years ago, he would have had to fight and kill her in a bloody fashion, cutting off her head and everything.

But with the modern science at his disposal, he could build a trap that would pull the energy from her.

A lot better than cutting off her head.

"How did you keep yourself hidden from me?" she asked, her voice weakening.

"Your arrogance," he said. "You never thought to look and I played your cow perfectly, didn't I? When a hunter starts to believe they cannot be beat, then the hunted have a clear advantage."

She could no longer hold up her head and she slumped to the table.

He could see her clear, wonderful skin start to wrinkle and become brittle just as if she were an old woman.

"And just so you know," he said. "I loved you as well. And if you hadn't wanted me to be your cow, we could have had a great and long life together."

She didn't have the energy to say anything, but she did acknowledge that she had heard him by raising a few fingers.

He sat back, sipping his Bloody Mary, letting the energy she had in her body pour through the house and into him. For the first time in years, he again felt alive.

He had won the fight and another Primal would soon be gone from the planet. And that was worth a drink over.

He kept sipping on his Bloody Mary, watching as his wife of five years shrunk up more and more.

She now no longer had the capability to even move.

Her energy that was pouring through the house to him would keep him alive for decades to come. Because just as Primals, Libertas also were immortal. Only they did not feed off the helpless, they fed from Primals.

He had been doing so for more centuries than he wanted to remember.

She never knew in five years that while she was taking surface, human energy from him, he was pulling deeper energy from her. More than likely that was why she had decided to go find others. She didn't get enough from him because he took almost as much from her as she took from him.

It had been a perfect balance.

Many would say a perfect marriage.

Finally, her body broke apart, mostly into dust as the house kept sucking every last bit of life energy from her.

"It was an interesting five years, Deborah," he said, raising his glass in a toast. "I can't say you were a worthy opponent. But for a while there, the sex was great."

And it had been, which should have clued her to what he really was.

Energy between a Primal and a Libertas in sex could be almost explosive, since they fed back and forth off each other, sometimes cycling energy up into mind-blowing events.

They had had a few such events right before and right after they were married, but she considered them only the passion of their newlywed moments.

And she had always considered him nothing more than a cow.

He had known better.

And just as with every time he married a Primal, he had hoped she would love him enough to not turn him into a cow.

But in thousands of years of marriages now, that had never happened.

But someday he would find the Primal of his dreams. And she would not turn him into a cow, not want to turn him into a cow, and he would not end up killing her for her greed.

A fella could only hope.

Across from him, the dust that had been Deborah just slowly settled onto the chair and on the floor.

Every bit of life energy she had was now his.

He finished his drink and went to get the vacuum cleaner.

And to see who had ended up winning that last baseball game.

The Man Who Laughed on a Rainy Night

A Bryant Street Story

Dean Wesley Smith

The Man Who Laughed on a Rainy Night

Bradford Borne stood in the Oregon rain in front of his three-bedroom ranch-style home in the suburbs of Portland. On his right was the flowering plum tree his wife Radella had planted fifteen years before, the year before she died.

Actually, he had planted it on her insistence. She had sat in a lawn chair eating chips while he had done the work.

But now, to protect against the rain, he wore his dark raincoat and a wide-brimmed rain hat, rain pants over his normal tan slacks, and shoe protectors over his brown leather dress shoes. The rain didn't even touch his glasses. He was completely protected from the storm and the chill evening air of late April.

The homes along Bryant Street were silent in the late hours, the blinds pulled on every home, the televisions flickering light to dark and then light again, shadows projected against the windows indicating all his neighbors were in their normal evening zombie state.

The rain also made seeing very far difficult, so he was convinced no one would see him at all. And this time of night on a weeknight, most every one of his neighbors was home in routine. No chance a stray car would pass by tonight.

And the sound of the rain would cover and dampen any sounds he happened to make.

A perfect night to move his dead wife Radella.

Soft ground from the spring rains, no one to see him.

Perfect. Just perfect.

This would be the tenth or maybe eleventh time he had moved Radella in fifteen years. He sometimes couldn't remember.

The first time was because of a sewer issue with the city. Two years after he had buried her the first time, the city needed to run a sewer line to get everyone in the subdivision off their septic tanks. To connect to his home, the new sewer line would run right through where he had buried Radella.

So he dug her up one rainy, muddy night, dealt with the mess, and moved her to the other side of the garage. It had been a long and horrid night.

But as the months went by after that night, he realized he had actually enjoyed the task. He had enjoyed the fear of getting caught, the physical stress and the labor. It had made him feel alive again, something he hadn't felt since the first year of marriage to Radella.

And since the night he had buried her in the first place.

So the following year, again in April, he moved her again, this time to the back corner of his fenced-in backyard, making sure he left no signs at all of anything being disturbed.

He felt so alive after that second time that he ended up meeting a new love of his life.

The official story was that Radella had left, gone back east. He had filed for divorce and faked her signature and was free of her legally. No one really asked about her.

So he married Marilyn that fall and by April Marilyn was going the same way as Radella had gone. Eating, not interested in much of anything but television, yelling at him for every little slight or misstep.

In six months after their marriage, he had become her house slave, the short little man who went to work, earned the money, and then waited on her when he got home.

In late April of that first year of his marriage to Marilyn, she took a five-day trip back to Florida to visit family and he took the opportunity to move Radella again, giving himself that new feeling of life.

By the following April he was almost dead again, his emotions shut down, his caring for life gone.

So on a dark, rainy April night, as Marilyn slept, he smothered her with a plastic bag and buried her in the yard.

He didn't bury her close to Radella. It was a very large backyard with a high wooden fence around it all. Lots and lots of room back there.

Then, when Marilyn's family in Florida asked about her a month later, Bradford had said she had left him with a man named Roger and he knew she was planning on driving to Florida. They didn't seem surprised and said they had never understood what he had seen in her.

He had filed divorce papers and forged her name and they never found her.

And again, no one really ever asked about her. He clearly made poor choices when it came to love.

Or maybe the choice was to marry someone just like that. He could never figure that out.

In late April of that same year, he moved Radella again, trying his best to get some feeling and zest back.

It worked.

So every April, like celebrating an anniversary, he moved Radella one rainy night and Marilyn another.

Neither Marilyn nor Radella had been a light woman on the days of their deaths. Radella had topped over three hundred pounds without clothes and Marilyn had been close to that. Now after all the years wrapped in plastic and tarps, neither woman had gotten lighter.

And Bradford hadn't gotten any younger or stronger.

Bradford was a tiny man by anyone's standards. He owned and ran his own small grocery store just one mile from his home and he had met both Radella and Marilyn when they were still thin.

Radella's death had been different from Marilyn's. He hadn't actually killed her. Not exactly, anyway. One day, as he was serving Radella dinner, she choked on a large bite of steak, medium rare as she liked it, and he sat and watched her die. He didn't feel guilty or sad or anything. In four years she had killed any part of him that showed that kind of emotion.

So he had wrapped her in a large plastic sheet, securing both ends completely. Then wrapped her in another plastic sheet and secured it solidly as well. That evening, actually, was the most he had touched her since their honeymoon.

He left her the next day in the pantry and bought a very heavy tarp and brought it home with him that night. He wrapped her in that and tied it securely with rope.

That night it rained and the digging was easy, and it made him feel alive but he didn't notice until he had had to move her because of the sewer problem.

Now it was April again. It was a dark, rainy night. It was time.

He laughed and took one more look up and down the deserted street. Tonight he would move them both on the same night. How much fun would that be?

He got his shovel and went to where he had buried Radella last year and started to dig, carefully cutting away the sod so he could replace it later. His plan was to move Radella to the back side of the house near the back deck, then move Marilyn into the hole Radella had spent a year in.

He had a tarp beside the hole for the dirt and the rain splattering on the tarp was almost hypnotic.

He was paying no attention at all, just enjoying the feeling of the work and the rain when he suddenly realized he was too deep.

Radella wasn't here.

He was sure he had buried her right there last April. But she wasn't there and a very dead, very heavy woman wrapped in plastic and a tarp didn't just vanish.

He stopped and walked around the large backyard. In fifteen years she had been in eleven places. Or was that just ten. He was getting confused clearly on where in the large backyard she was.

Ahh, well, he would at least move Marilyn tonight.

He finished preparing the hole he had dug, then went over to the end of the wooden fence to the left of his home, near his bedroom window, and started digging, again putting the sod carefully aside and the dirt on another tarp.

And again he got too deep.

Marilyn wasn't there.

For a moment he felt panic, something he hadn't felt in decades. How could he forget where he buried both of his wives?

He once again walked around the backyard trying to jog his memory from last April.

Or was that the April before?

All the Aprils seemed to run together. Had he not been able to find them last April either?

Finally he went and sat in the rain on his back step, letting the water running off his hat calm him.

Then, after a few minutes, he just started to laugh.

Both ex-wives lost. They were here somewhere, he was sure of that, but where was the question.

He sat and just laughed as the rain poured over him, clearing the air, softening the ground, making it a perfect night.

He honestly didn't need to know this year where they were. Next April he would try again to see if he could find them.

Laughing to himself, he went back to work filling in both holes, patting down the sod, cleaning up what dirt had gotten off the tarp by hosing down the lawn in the rain.

When he was all done, you almost couldn't tell any work had been done in those two areas and the rain was starting to ease just slightly.

He cleaned and put away his shovel, cleaned off the tarps and hung them to dry in his tool shed. Then he went in his back door and took off his rain gear.

He felt tired, but alive.

Very much alive.

Alive enough to get through another year.

He started a pot of coffee and stood in the window and watched the rain while it brewed, smiling to himself.

Next April he would find them.

And move them both.

They were out there somewhere.

He was sure of that.

And that was all that mattered.

The Keeper of the Morals

Dean Wesley Smith

One

I nursed the scotch-rocks like it was the last drink I was ever going to have instead of just the first for the night, twirling the glass and the golden liquid on its paper napkin like a kid's toy. More than likely, it was going to be the drink I remembered most in a long line of drinks, followed by picking up some blonde—they were always blondes—and taking her back to my big house in my Porsche for some fast, sloppy sex and then uncomfortable good-byes.

Around me, the party atmosphere of the "Danny's Crib Lounge," combined with the music from too many speakers, kept the noise level just under that of a jet taking off. I had been lucky tonight to find a place at the bar. Usually I ended up standing, drink in hand, pretending to actually talk to someone I mostly couldn't hear.

But tonight was special. That's what my six co-workers from the legal department had told me. I had closed negotiations on one of the company's biggest deals today, opening up a wildlife refuge for my company's oil rigs to go in and drill. Tomorrow, when the news got out, our stock would shoot up, the left-wing environmentalists would cry, I would get a bonus, and then I would go back to work on the next big deal.

But tonight I got to celebrate.

But I didn't feel like celebrating anything.

Thirty-six years old and I had no idea how I had gotten here.

In this bar.

Doing the job I did.

None. Not a clue.

I used to be one of those liberals who would think of the now-me as the devil. I started off using my legal degree to fight to keep wildlife refuges closed up to companies like the one I now worked for. I took the job with my current employer thinking I could stop some of the company practices from within.

Yeah, right.

What the hell had happened to me?

That wasn't a question I asked myself that often these days. I usually just thought about the money, the stock options, and buying a bigger house, even though alone, I rattled around in the one I had like a kid lost in a big, new school.

I had enough money, but I kept thinking I needed more.

Why?

A soft touch on my shoulder made me turn to my right and into the gaze of a beautiful woman with golden hair and large brown eyes.

My stomach twisted as she smiled a perfect smile showing off perfect teeth. I had barely sipped my first drink and this woman looked fantastic.

My type. She fit it perfectly. In looks as well as everything else. Side-by-side, walking down the street, we would look like Ken and Barbie. The perfect American couple. Her features were almost as chiseled as mine.

Could I get any more superficial? There was more to women than just blonde hair and a beautiful face. I used to look past all that surface stuff, looking for a soul mate, but now it seemed, I never did.

Just like I never really looked at what I did at work.

I felt like I knew her, then shook *that* thought away. I always felt like I knew every blonde I ended up with, but never did. Someday I'd have to get some counseling on that, figure out where in my past the blonde search started.

She leaned in real close and indicated she wanted to say something in my ear over the music and noise.

I turned my head just slightly

"James, Bob sent me," she said, her breath on my ear like what I imagined a whisper from an angel might feel like. "He thought you might need a little boost."

I turned to stare at her directly, then shouted into the music. "Bob? My boss?"

She nodded.

Bob, the short, fat bastard, had sent me a hooker. How crude was that? No matter how good-looking this woman was, I just wasn't interested. Even if she was bought and paid for already.

"Tell him thanks, but no thanks," I said into her perfectly formed ear. "I like to find my own dates."

She laughed, and the laugh seemed to cut through the noise like sharp scissors through tissue paper. "Not *that* kind of boost," she said, leaning in close again.

Her breath smelled of faint cloves mixed with vanilla.

"This kind of boost."

She touched me on the shoulder and I closed my eyes as her hand stroked my arm, filling me with the warmest sensation. Man, she could "boost" me any time she wanted.

Suddenly, all my doubts about what I had done were gone, my drive to get the bigger house was back, and my need to get laid by a beautiful blonde hit me like a sledgehammer.

I opened my eyes to thank her and suggest we go somewhere a little less noisy, but she was gone, vanished into the crowd like so much smoke.

"Well, not sure what old Bob was thinking," I said. "That was lame."

I downed the drink, ordered another, and turned on the bar stool to study the crowd, the memory of her already forgotten. I was looking for a companion for the night. After all, I had some celebrating to do.

TWO

I awoke to my alarm the next morning, my head fuzzy from all the scotch and my tongue feeling like I had ran it through sawdust. The sheets on my massive bed still smelled of last night's conquest, a blonde with a chest twice the size of her IQ. She wore a perfume that, after six drinks, had driven me nuts. But this morning, the remains of it smelled like an air-freshener in a men's room urinal.

I vaguely remembered she had left at some point in the middle of the night, calling a cab and taking enough money from me to buy her own cab. I didn't care, it was only money, and after yesterday's closing of the big drilling deal, I was going to be making a lot more of it.

By the time I was through my morning routine and powering toward work in my Porsche, the remains of the scotch hangover were gone and I was looking forward to all the praise I was going to get at work, not counting the bonus. There had better be a damn big bonus.

Then, like a cloud lifting, I remembered the encounter with the woman Bob had sent. My bonus better be a lot bigger than some strange blonde in a bar, making promises and then not even hanging around to follow through. If Bob paid her more than a few bucks, he was going to have to get his money back, that was for sure.

It took me a few more blocks to really put her face back in my mind.

It was as if the scotch had erased it. I prided myself on never forgetting a name or a face. Then what she had said came back. She had promised a "boost." She had touched me and my attitude had changed. Often just the touch of a woman did that to me. Or at least took my focus temporarily away from a problem.

But this time it had felt different, and there was just something about her I couldn't shake. That feeling that I knew her, that same feeling I had with every damn blonde-haired woman I met. That was part of it, sure. But there was more. Bob was going to do some explaining on this one.

As I expected, when I arrived in my office, on the seventh floor of the ten-story corporate headquarters, there was a message waiting with my secretary to join Bob in his office. I usually beat him into work, sometimes by hours, but on days after closing big deals, I gave myself the freedom to just get there when I wanted to. After all, I deserved that luxury for one day. Tomorrow, I would be back working harder than anyone in the place, coming in earlier, staying later, working weekends. It was the only way to get ahead in this business, and I planned on getting very, very far ahead by the time I was done.

Bob was sitting in his big chair, feet up on his desk as I knocked and then entered his office. He was almost as wide as he was tall, and had a face like a troll stuck in the mud. I tried hard to never stand beside him in any function or picture. It would just make him look bad, and making a boss look bad was never a good career move, even though I was after his job. He was number one in the corporation's legal department; I was number two.

"Nice job on closing that deal yesterday," he said. "Stock is going through the roof, and the guys upstairs are taking hundreds of phone calls from every media outlet there is."

"Great," I said, smiling and sitting down across his desk from him. But it didn't feel that great. It was done, I had managed to pull it off; now it was time to move on, get to the next big deal. The fun was in the chase, not in the having.

It was that way with women as well.

And with my cars and houses. What I owned or had at the moment didn't mean anything. All that mattered was what I was trying to get.

"Bonus check coming your way this afternoon, approved from

upstairs," Bob said, smiling a smile that turned his wrinkled face into a mass of sneers. I knew that smile. It was sincere, even though it didn't look it.

"Thanks," I said. "And if you paid that blonde you sent my way last night more than ten bucks, you got taken. She vanished without so much as a kiss good-bye."

He actually jerked, glanced at me, then looked away, as if I had surprised him by remembering her.

"No big deal," Bob said, shifting his gaze to something in an open drawer beside his desk as he sat up.

I'd hit a very sensitive topic for some reason. I knew Bob after the last two years, and I had made it my job to know his moods and actions. I had surprised him.

"Who was she?" I asked, pushing the topic. "She was sure a looker."

He shrugged, which I knew meant he was going to flat out lie to me, or give me a half-truth.

"Just someone I know from personnel," he said. "I just suggested she stop by and see how the celebrating was doing."

"This someone have a name?" I asked.

He laughed and wagged a fat finger at me. "You know the rules on dating someone in the company."

I smiled. "You were the one that sent her, remember?"

"Not to screw your eyes out," Bob said, shaking his head and pretending to laugh. "Now, can we get to work and leave your personal life outside these walls? What little I already know about it scares hell out of me."

I dropped the subject and Bob and I started in on the next project, working to get right-of-ways through some old family farms for a pipcline. But I had no idea of letting the chase for the blonde from personnel go that easily. When I got my teeth into something like this, I never let go until it was finished.

While Bob was off with the higher-ups having a two-drink, two-hour lunch, I told my secretary I was not to be disturbed, then used my company security clearance to access employee records on a secure screen on my computer.

Sometimes certain legal work required me to do just that, so no one would think what I was doing odd if they noticed at all. It didn't take much of a scan of the people who worked in personnel to tell me that part of Bob's story had been a flat out lie. But I didn't doubt she worked for the company. The question was in what department, and why hadn't I seen her before?

I used the fact that I hadn't seen her to eliminate a dozen different departments I worked in and around regularly, depending on the project. But that still left over five hundred personnel photos to go through.

It took me until two in the afternoon.

She wasn't there.

So who was she, and why had Bob been surprised I had remembered her? She was clearly doing a favor of some sort for him. And the way he had acted, knowledge of her was not something Bob was willing to share.

I sat back, put my feet up on my desk, and covered my eyes, trying to sort out all the details like a giant legal puzzle.

I still believed she worked somewhere in the company. That was the way Bob lied, with half-truths, or truths that left out real basic information.

And I believed now that she had been sent to give me something she called a "boost." More than likely some sort of drug or something on her hands. The fog about last night had now completely cleared and I had a very real memory of what her touch had done to me. If it was a drug, I didn't much like that idea at all. I took my share of alcohol, but drugs were not something I did, or ever wanted to do. Too damn scary, and too much chance of messing with my mind. I made my money with my mind. I ruin that and it would be all over.

She had to work here somewhere, but where?

I looked up the official number of employees in the company from the records I had just gone through, then went into the payroll records and asked how many people were drawing official compensation.

Bingo.

The number was different by one.

So somewhere, this company had a secret employee, and I had no doubt that when I found that employee, it would be a beautiful blonde with wonderful brown eyes and a very scary touch.

Three

I had very little time over the next three days to continue the search for my elusive Blonde Booster, as I was starting to call her. But then, on Saturday, Bob didn't come in, and I was pretty much alone in the building. When I worked a Saturday or a Sunday, I was often one of the only few people in the big, ten-story building. I always got a lot done and liked the quiet. Besides, except for drinking at night and searching for blondes to take home, I didn't have a hell of a lot more to my life than work. Kind of sad when I thought about it, but I didn't much think about it that often.

This Saturday I liked the quiet for another reason. I had a quest.

Instead of going out last night, I had actually stayed at home with take-out Chinese food and studied floor plans and office layouts of the entire company building. There were only a few offices not clearly marked, and those would be my first targets.

I arrived at my office around ten, carrying a large mocha coffee and wearing jeans and a sweater. The old suit and tie were just not needed on a Saturday.

I took the floor plans out of my briefcase and spread them over my desk, studying them once again while I sipped the wonderful flavor of my coffee. Somewhere in this building the Blonde Booster might have an office. If she did, I was going to find it. If she worked from home, then I'd go into personnel records next, working through the payroll until I found out where her checks went. Having high-level security clearance sure came in handy sometimes.

I was staring at the map when a soft voice said from the door, "Looking for me?"

I somehow managed to remain fairly contained, and didn't snort any coffee out of my nose, which, considering the surprise I felt, was a miracle.

"Actually, I was," I said.

She was more beautiful than I remembered. Long, blonde hair flowed down over her shoulders, and her eyes were round, her smile real. She wore a baggy sweater and jeans with tennis shoes, but even that dressed down, nothing about her amazing body was really hidden.

She moved over to my desk, glanced down at the floor plans of the big structure, and then pointed with a fantastically perfect finger and short fingernail to one office that wasn't marked. "That's my office."

"That was going to be my second stop," I said. "Do you have a name?"

"Glenda," she said. "For now, just call me Glenda."

I pointed to a chair on the other side of my desk and then sat down as she did, keeping the desk between me and her. No way I wanted to get near that booster touch of hers again. Or at least not right away. I needed some answers first.

"I'm guessing from Bob's reaction that it's a surprise that I remembered you."

"Not really," she said, shrugging. "I can only do so much on the memory fogging aspects. But it really doesn't matter anymore, since I got the last of what you had at the bar the other night."

I didn't much like the sounds of *that*, but she went on before I could ask what exactly I was now missing completely.

"Since I did," she said, holding my gaze, "you're going to be promoted upstairs next week, over Bob and into a VP position in management, and then you would have been told about my presence here anyway."

I had so many questions about all that she had said, I couldn't think of which one to ask first, so instead I just sipped my coffee and stared at her beautiful face. My goal was to be a vice president, then maybe even higher, but I sure hadn't expected it this soon, and not over the top of Bob.

I did a quick run-through of all the questions, then settled on starting with the most basic. "So, what's your official title here?"

"Keeper of the Morals," she said with as straight a face as I had ever seen.

"And your job description?" I asked, trying not to laugh at her.

She looked me right in the eye. "I extract and contain employee personal morals, mostly in the legal and management departments, so that they can work with the full interest of the corporation at heart."

"And just how do you do that?" I asked, remembering what I had been thinking about at the bar, how I had changed, how I had no idea how I had become the person I had become. That memory scared hell out of me suddenly.

And made me angry at the same time. I didn't much like the idea of something being taken from me without my knowledge, especially under orders from Bob.

"Magic," she said. "Every major corporation has someone like me, a person of magic who can, for a fee, do as asked. And I have to admit, my fee is *very* high."

She smiled at that. She clearly enjoyed money as much as I did.

"I'll bet," I said, trying but failing to push all the memories of what I used to think, how I used to feel about the job I now did.

"Remembering your morals, aren't you?" she asked, smiling at me.

"I have to admit I am. And you're starting to scare me, to be honest with you."

She laughed. "Take a deep breath and look at those memories, at how you used to be. You're going to be a vice president of this company, with a big office two more floors up. Do you really care about how you used to feel when you drove that Volkswagen and camped out at music concerts?"

I started to say that I did, then realized she was right. I didn't care. But I didn't care because she had taken that caring from me. She and Bob.

"What did you do to me?" I asked.

"The first day you were here at work, we met. Remember?"

I started to shake my head, then suddenly the memory of her shaking my hand and holding onto it that first day came flooding back. We had spent a wonderful lunch and afternoon together, talking, laughing, touching.

The memory of that fantastic day flooded back over me like a wet dream. "We went back to my place that night, didn't we?"

She nodded.

I remembered now that I felt like I had fallen in love with her in that one short day. How could I have forgotten that? It still felt like I was in love with her now that I remembered. No wonder I kept going home with blondes. I had been looking for Glenda all this time.

I shook my head. I hadn't felt this far off balance in years. I looked into those wonderful eyes and managed to get out my question again. "What *exactly* did you do to me?"

She shrugged. "I used my magic to take your morals, so you could be a better attorney for the company. That's all. Got the last of a vast supply the other night in the bar."

I wanted to shout at her, call her a common thief, but my legal mind just wasn't believing what she was saying. My memories of my actions, of how I used to feel and think, were clear. I used to care about something more than money and a bigger house.

But now that was all I cared about.

That thought hit me like a hammer to the skull, and I knew, without a doubt, she had done just what she said she had done. She had taken all my caring away.

And the moment I accepted that, my mind snapped back to clear thinking and I knew what I had to do.

"I seem to remember that afternoon and evening as being very special, at least to me. You do that with all the lawyers?"

She actually had the decency to blush. "No, only you. You were my first, and the only since. I've been just waiting until this day came, so I could show myself to you again."

I stood and moved around my desk, kneeling at the side of her chair and touching her wonderful soft skin. "You could still care about a man who has had his morals destroyed?"

"I'm pretty sure that not having morals doesn't mean you can't still love," she said, putting her other hand on mine and holding me to her. "And I didn't destroy them. They're just stored, just like all the others."

"You're not kidding, are you?"

"Not kidding," she said softly.

"And you can put them back into people?"

She nodded and said nothing.

I laughed and stood, moving away from her, pacing, thinking. I often did some of my best thinking while pacing. I was angry, in love, and scared to death about what had been done to me. I needed to get those thoughts sorted out so that my next action wouldn't be completely stupid.

All the time I paced she sat silently, watching me.

Finally, I needed a little more information before I went any farther. I turned to her frowning and worried face. "How easy are these morals moved around and put into people?"

She held up what looked like a small fountain pen. "I have yours right in here. I promised myself I would give them back to you if you asked. That's how much I care about you."

That thought suddenly set me back.

"All my morals fit into a pen?" I asked, stunned. "Guess I didn't have that many, huh?"

"Highly compacted," she said. "You had an overabundance of them, to be honest."

"Yeah, I remember that," I said, laughing. "But for the time being, put that away. I don't want to accidentally get them back just yet."

She now looked puzzled, then the pen vanished back into her baggy sweater somehow. Maybe later, if things went the way I was hoping, I'd get to inspect those pockets a little closer.

"One more question," I said. "Who ordered you to take those from me?"

"Bob," she said. "With approval of the president of the company."

I nodded. That was all I needed.

"I think I owe you a long, early lunch, don't you?" I said, smiling at Glenda. "You saved me a lot of searching around the building."

She still looked worried, but I had a hunch if this woman could really do what she said she had done, and liked money as much as I did, then we were going to be very, very happy for a time in the very near future.

I took her by the arm, and like a modern version of Ken and Barbie, dressed down, we headed to lunch.

FOUR

I escorted Glenda to this fantastic, small restaurant where I knew we could talk for hours and not be disturbed. Over chicken slices and strong cups of mocha, we discovered we really liked each other. And that we both had the same goals, to be fantastically wealthy and powerful.

And I came to remember that even with my morals, I had wanted that same goal. Only I had planned on doing really good things with all the money once I got it.

I asked her why she just couldn't magic-up money and she said it didn't work that way. Her talents were more personal based, either giving someone good feelings or taking feelings from them. That's why the company had hired her to help them with the attorneys and management teams.

"Better than what a lot of my type do for money," she said, looking very alluringly at me.

"What's that?"

"Call girls, dating services," she said. "We can *really* make a man feel good."

"I've noticed that."

"I'm not doing anything," she said, laughing.

"I'm kind of wondering why not?"

"Yeah, me too," she said, smiling a smile at me that I would never forget.

With that, we moved to my house, with me breaking far too many speed limits along the way. We barely managed to get inside and to the bed before working as much magic on each other as we could do.

In the euphemistic sense of course.

More directly, we had great sex. Better than great, actually. But I won't go there.

Finally, after who knows how long, we both lay there exhausted. And for the first time, I didn't want this blonde to leave. I wanted her to stay right beside me.

"So, what exactly can you do with my morals?"

Naked, laying there with her golden body facing me, she suddenly become very worried again. No doubt she thought I might ask for them back, and to be honest, I had thought about getting them back into me as quickly as possible. Not much thought, but the idea did sound right. They had been taken, I wanted them back, just like anything else I owned that was taken.

"You said you can put them back, right?"

She nodded.

"Can you put mine, or Bob's, or the president's, or someone in general from the corporate supply into someone else?"

She now looked puzzled, then nodded. "I don't see why not."

"And even though what you give them is not their own morals, they would still work?"

"Sure. I'm sure it would be as if they got their own back."

I kissed her, then said, "How about we use that vast supply you have in storage to sabotage our company's rivals? Think we could do that?"

She blinked once, then twice, as if not really hearing me.

"You and me," I said, stroking the soft skin on her arm. "Working together. You get the morals into some of those decision-makers in other companies, cripple them with good intentions and feelings for the under-dogs, and I'll take advantage of the situation. Together, we can make a fortune and just keep on moving up in the company."

Again she blinked, then she moved into me with her full body and kissed me like I had never been kissed before. Clearly, she liked my idea. I had no doubt that a woman who could steal other's morals for corporate and personal gain would like it.

The rest of that afternoon and evening we did things sexually I had never done before, or thought possible. Amazing how the promise of a lot of money and a little lack of morals can motivate a person. And I'm sure there was some magic involved as well.

Five

Six months later, I moved into my new corner office on the tenth floor, right next to Glenda's and two doors down from the president's office. Given a little time, that office could be mine as well if I wanted it. I didn't want it.

The view out my window was stunning, looking out over the city. I had gone through two levels of vice presidents since my move out of the legal department. My official title was now Executive Vice President in Charge of Corporate Acquisitions. And I had bought enough of the company stock that, if I wanted to, I could have a seat on the Board of Directors.

I didn't want that any more than I wanted to be president. And besides, most of my stock was in special holding corporations very hard to trace back to me.

I just wanted to be rich. Fantastically rich. And I was almost there.

In my top drawer was the pen that held my morals, locked away safely. Glenda had told me how the pen inserter worked and let me keep it just to make sure it didn't get mixed up with all the other morals we were taking from the corporate 'morals pool.'

Over the past six months, Glenda and I spent every night together in my big new mansion. Next month we had decided I was buying a yacht. All of it was in my name, of course.

I had taken care of dear old Bob quickly after moving upstairs. A little planted evidence and a double dose of morals from Glenda sent him scampering. The little bastard was working as a legal aide down in a shelter and living in a studio apartment after his wife had kicked him out. Served the bastard right for stealing from me.

Now, it was time to put the rest of my plan in motion. With one last look at the fantastic view from the office I had worked so hard to get to, I unlocked my drawer and took out the magic pen holding my morals, then tucked it safely in my pocket.

Then I quickly went over my resignation letter. It said what I needed it to say. I had moved nothing into my office that I wanted to keep. There was nothing about this job that I cared about. Nothing to pack. Having no morals could make you feel that way.

All I ever wanted was the chase, the hunt, the excitement of the search, keeping score with the money. I had been that way even before having my morals stolen.

Now, things were going to get really exciting.

After six months, I had convinced myself that I didn't much care about Glenda either. After all, she was the one who took from me what was mine. There would be other blondes I was sure. Granted, Glenda was damn fun in bed, but as she had told me that first afternoon, many witches were good in bed. It came with the magic.

Sally was almost as good as Glenda. I had met Sally two weeks ago, when she joined Glenda and me for a little three-way afternoon fling. And with a little training from me on some of Glenda's special moves, Sally would be almost as good.

I dropped off my resignation letter with the president's secretary. Then dropped off my good-bye letter in Glenda's office. I told her that her things had already been moved out of my house and which storage unit she could find them in. Granted, it was a cold way to end a relationship, but what did she expect from someone who didn't care? She knew what she had gotten into with me. After all, she was the one who took all my caring and stored it in a magic pen.

On the way down to the main entrance, I stopped off in the basement and slipped a tiny, but very powerful device into the main air flow duct. Glenda and I had come up with the device to use on other corporations, and it had worked wonderfully, spreading morals throughout a building in high doses; so high that often before I could schedule a corporate takeover, the company was dissolving into chaos.

This company, in a short time, would be experiencing the same thing. Glenda would be able to stop some of it if she wanted to, but not enough, and I doubted she would even try.

I had six more of the tiny morals bombs in my briefcase.

I made sure I was outside the building before the thing triggered and started giving back all the corporate executives and lawyers their morals. In very high doses.

The next morning I called my six different stock brokers and put in orders to short a large chunk of my corporate stock, buying options on some more and running puts. I had no doubt the stock was going down, and I was going to make a ton of money on the way down.

Six weeks later, I was richer than I had ever imagined as my former company stock hit bottom and was bought up by yet another rival. During those weeks, Glenda had tried to call me twice, but both times Sally answered the phone.

Sally said Glenda was crying, which meant that she too had been dosed. All I could do was shrug. What did Glenda expect, anyway? The sex had been good, she should let it go.

I didn't tell Sally that I dreamed of Glenda every night, and imagined having sex with her when I was with Sally. I figured that given enough time, that would change. But so far it hadn't.

Six

Ten months later, I had bought massive amounts of stock in six other companies, morals-bombed them, and then got even richer as they crashed and I shorted the stock all the way down. I had become a morals terrorist, destroying companies by making them do the right things. I was sure my bleeding-heart liberal self would be proud of me.

By this time, Sally was also a distant memory, just like I had hoped Glenda would become. Now I spent every night back at Danny's Crib, getting drunk and searching for that perfect woman. Blonde, of course.

None of them measured up to Glenda, but I still searched.

Tonight seemed to be no different than any of the others, yet it was. I knew I was done for the moment, the big plan finished, the last stock sold. I was so rich, it seemed almost silly to keep going. But I knew I wanted more.

I swirled my scotch, letting the ice clink against the side. I could feel it through the cold glass, but I couldn't hear the ice over the pounding of the loud music. I was sitting on the same bar stool that I had been on when Glenda had taken the last of my morals.

My world, it seemed, had come full circle. Now, finally tonight, over a year after that night, was as good a time as any to get who I really was back.

I took out the magic pen I had been carrying for the past month. It was time to retrieve what had been taken from me, to become a whole person again.

I was fantastically rich, I could use that money for some of the causes I supported before I took the corporate job. And the old me would be proud of the fact that I had brought seven greedy corporate giants to their knees. I was sure of that.

I took a quick drink of the scotch, set the glass on the napkin, then without another thought, placed the pen against my skin on my palm and triggered it.

It was as if I had a bad cold that suddenly had cleared up. Everything I had done over the past years in my corporate job came flashing back to me like a movie in fast forward.

And then I suddenly realized how many people I had hurt along the way.

I could almost feel their pain.

Bob, Glenda, Sally, a hundred different blondes, and thousands of employees with families and jobs.

I had hurt them all.

And suddenly I knew that. And suddenly I cared.

"Oh, no, what have I done?" I shouted into the loud music.

And with that I broke down right there on the bar.

And I couldn't stop sobbing into my arm. The bartender finally had me escorted outside and I sat in my new Porsche in the parking lot, banging my hands on the steering wheel and shouting at nothing while I sobbed.

I just couldn't stop.

I had hurt so many people. I could almost feel all their pain, understand everything I had put them through. It was like waves washing over me. Every memory, every deed suddenly was real, had real people attached, had real consequences.

I had nothing to live for any more.

I was the lowest of scum.

I had guns, lots of guns, back in my house. Just one with one bullet would end this, take these thoughts, these memories away, these feelings away.

As I reached to start the car, Glenda climbed into the passenger seat. It took me a moment to realize who it was.

"I was wondering how long it would be before you took back your morals."

All I could do was sob that I was sorry. So sorry.

I had never felt so sorry for anything in my entire life. I had loved Glenda, had hurt her.

I didn't deserve to live.

"I know you are sorry," she said, her voice cutting through the massive waves of self-pity and sadness for what I had done.

Her hand touched me, that wonderful hand, and I suddenly started feeling calmer.

"I'll take about half," she said. "Then we can talk. Is that all right with you?"

All I could do was nod. At this point, I needed anything to make this pain go away.

She kept stroking my arm and I calmed down, got a part of my brain back, got some basic control of myself.

Finally, she stopped. I could feel all the remorse and sadness for my actions, but only as background thoughts. My brain was back.

I turned to stare at her. "You knew I would take my morals back?"

"Of course," she said. "From that first moment in your office. I had money in dummy corporations and shorted our company's stock just like you did as it went down. I got almost as rich as you did."

I sat there for a moment, my mouth opening and closing, realizing just how smart Glenda was, how she had played me just as I had played her.

"And the other corporations?" I asked. "You were following me, weren't you?"

"Of course," she said. "I love you, remember? But that didn't stop me from making even more money while you were doing what you were doing."

I could feel the guilt starting to come up again from what morals she had left in me. She could clearly see it as well.

"You need another little bit drained off?"

I nodded, and she touched me again, and like climbing a long staircase, I got closer to thinking even clearer, like coming out of a dark basement into the light of day.

"Thanks," I said. "I would have killed myself if you hadn't come along."

"I know," she said, her voice sad. "No person with as many morals as you had to start with could live with what you've done over the last few years."

"So, after what I did to you, why did you save me?"

"Love," she said. And then she smiled that smile I had come to know so well. "And greed. We make a really great team."

"Yeah, but you'll never trust me again."

She laughed. "I didn't trust you the first time. Any more than you trusted me. But the sex was great. That's good enough to base a pretty good relationship on, don't you think?"

With that, she actually managed to make me laugh a little, which came out like a hiccup.

I turned in the car seat to face her. "Yeah, it was. I must admit, I've missed that. And I've missed you, every day. I was just so damn angry with you for taking something of mine."

"I know," she said. "But this time you wanted me to take them. And you can have them back any time you want."

I held up my hand. "No, let's just leave it at this level for the moment. Small enough to not control my thoughts, but not completely gone."

"That was the level I settled on for myself as well," she said.

I realized, right at that moment, staring into those golden eyes and smiling face, that I never wanted to hurt her in any way again.

"I really do love you," I said.

"I know," she said. "I love you as well."

"So how come I didn't feel that when I had no morals?"

She shrugged. "I have a hunch that without morals, you don't care about anyone else but yourself. And love requires that caring to work for any length of time."

I nodded, deciding I'd just accept that for the moment and think about it later, when all the swirling emotions were a little more under control.

"So what next?" I asked.

She laughed. "Well, I'm blonde."

"Right on that," I said.

"And I have it on good authority you like picking up blondes in this bar here." She pointed to the front door of Danny's Crib.

"Right again," I said, smiling at her.

"So how about you take me back to that obscenely large mansion of yours and show me what tricks you've learned in bed over the last ten months."

"I'd love to," I said. "And you can show me what you've learned."

"Not a thing," she said. "I've just been waiting for you."

Again, I just sat there, my mouth opening and closing like a damn fish out of water. I stared at her, into those wonderful golden eyes, taking in that fantastic smile. And I let myself feel the love for her, the emotions of sadness at what I had done to her, and the fantastic feeling of happiness that she actually wanted me back, and had waited.

It seems we had a lot of real feelings to talk about.

But that could wait. Sex came first.

Lots and lots of sex.

She was a blonde, I had picked her up at Danny's Crib, just like all the others. But I had a feeling, an honest feeling, that this time, she would be the last blonde I ever picked up there.

And it was a feeling I liked.

That Human Fear

A Cold Poker Gang Story

Dean Wesley Smith

That Human Fear

October 26th, 2017

Retired Detective Debra Pickett stood in the shade of a tall rough-stone wall and watched a five-person forensics crew in white protective suits dig up a grave. Not exactly what she had hoped to do before breakfast this morning.

The Las Vegas sun was barely in the sky and already warm for such an early morning in October. Pickett was glad she had worn a light blouse and a wide-brimmed hat. She had brought a jacket thinking it would be cooler, but had left that in the car.

Beside her in the shade was her partner and lover, Retired Detective Ben "Sarge" Carson. He had on what looked like a cowboy hat to shade his eyes and protect his head. He wore a blue dress shirt with the sleeves rolled up and they both had on jeans and tennis shoes.

The grave the crew was working on belonged to a Mildred Case. Mildred had died eight years ago at the ripe old age of ninety-six, outliving three of her five children and her second husband. From what Pickett could tell, Mildred had had over sixty grandchildren and great-grandchildren and great-great-grandchildren at the time of her death.

The funeral had been very large, from what Pickett could tell from the records. But it wasn't Mildred they really wanted to dig up. It was what Pickett and Sarge thought was with Mildred. And it had taken days to get the court order to do this.

Days of nightmares and worry for Pickett.

She just hoped it would be worth it.

The entire thing had started when she and Sarge and Robin were handed a new cold case to work on. All three of them were a team and as retired detectives, had joined the Cold Poker Gang task force to solve cold cases.

Stephanie Donner, twenty-eight, and one of Mildred's granddaughters, had vanished on the same day as they buried her grandmother. The case had gone cold almost instantly.

So when Pickett and Sarge and Robin got the case, the first thing they started looking at was why the timing of the funeral and Stephanie going missing.

From what they could tell, Stephanie didn't even know her grandmother that well. She was an attractive young woman, standing only five-one with a bright smile and long, brown hair. She got top grades while in college and had worked up until the day she vanished as a project manager for a growing tech company.

She often said how much she loved her job.

She had a partner named Jill that she lived with and they had hoped to be married when the laws changed. Stephanie hadn't lived long enough to see that day, sadly.

Over the next few days after getting the case, Pickett and Sarge talked to dozens of co-workers and friends of the couple, without any success or leads. Everything they were told was the same as the original detectives on the case were told eight years before. No one had a motive to harm Stephanie.

The standard response they got was how nice Stephanie really was. That she had kind words for everyone she met.

Stephanie had told her partner that she was going to her grandmother's viewing at the mortuary, go out to lunch with a couple of cousins she hadn't seen in a while, and then go to the funeral before going back to work.

The cousins never saw her at the mortuary, although Stephanie did sign the visitation book, but about a half hour ahead of the people she was going to meet.

No one saw her from that point forward.

It was Sarge at breakfast at the Golden Nugget that suggested that they look into the staff of the funeral home past what the detectives had done eight years earlier.

Robin, Pickett's best friend and former partner when they were active detectives, had liked that idea and did her computer magic. Robin got the list of names from the funeral home and discovered that all but one had been interviewed earlier. The one guy named Angelo Clark had worked at cleaning and on the grounds of the mortuary. Angelo had vanished without a trace.

"Nothing suspicious about that," Pickett had said.

"The police had him as a person of interest as well," Robin said, reading from her screen, "but never found him before the case went cold."

So the only thing that was different in that funeral home that day was Mildred and her large casket. If for some reason something had happened to Stephanie in that short time and she had been put in the casket at her grandmother's feet, it would explain why Stephanie hadn't been found in eight years.

That's when Pickett started having nightmares.

Both Pickett and Sarge and Robin were sure they were right about this, even though they didn't want to be.

And what Pickett was the most afraid of was that they would find Stephanie with evidence that she had been alive when the casket was buried. That had Pickett waking up from nightmares two or three times a night the last three nights. Once she had been screaming so loud, the cats wouldn't even get near her for breakfast the next morning.

Sarge said the idea of being buried alive was his worst nightmare as well, but typical of Sarge, he didn't show that he was bothered by this. Sometimes the man was just steel.

But being buried alive terrified Pickett.

In front of them it looked like the team was getting closer to the casket and getting ready to hook onto it to lift it up out of the hole they had dug. The court order was that if nothing was found, Mildred was to be just reburied at once.

The cemetery they were standing in was one of the most expensive in all of the valley. It actually had real grass combined with some desert plants and tall trees and palms that allowed a little shade. But with the angle of the sun this morning, only the stone wall along one side actually served as shade.

Every grave had a headstone, most ornately carved in some fashion or another. Mildred clearly had had some money to be buried here.

None of her family had decided to show up for digging up their grandmother. Pickett didn't blame them in the slightest. Always better to remember grandma alive than see her body after eight years in the ground.

Pickett had seen pictures of Mildred before she died. She had been a tiny, shrunken old woman with a bright light in her eyes and a slight smile on her face. Pickett had a hunch she would have liked Mildred.

Three minutes later the crew hooked the lift onto the casket and gently pulled it upward.

"Shall we get closer?" Sarge asked.

"No," Pickett said, shaking her head. "Robin had the right idea in staying home. I've seen enough dug-up bodies that I don't need to see this one."

Sarge nodded.

"Besides," Pickett said, "if Stephanie is in there, this gets sent to an active detective as a murder case. And if she isn't in there, we still have an unsolved cold case on our hands."

Sarge again nodded as the casket was set on a platform built to hold it. Then, wearing masks, two of the techs unlocked the large casket and opened both the top and the bottom at the same time.

Both of them instantly stepped back.

The man on the lift turned his head, while the other two techs also took a few paces back from the coffin.

Then the two who had opened the lid closed it at once and once again locked it.

"Looks like we found Stephanie," Sarge said.

"Looks that way," Pickett said as the lead tech started toward them, pulling off his mask.

"Detectives," the tech said. "You were right. We found a body of what looks to be a young woman wrapped around the older woman's feet in the casket. She was not embalmed, so we have to seal up the casket and get it to processing quickly."

"Thank you," Sarge said. "An active homicide detective will be taking over the case."

The tech nodded and turned to go back to his crew.

"Was she alive while in there?" Pickett asked before the tech got two steps. "Could you tell?"

She had to know. Otherwise she would keep having the nightmares.

The tech turned and shook his head. "No signs of any struggle. From the look of the dried blood and caved in skull, I would say she was dead when put in there. But that will be up to the morgue to make the call."

"Thank you," Pickett said, feeling relieved.

The tech nodded and turned away.

Sarge took Pickett's hand and they walked slowly back to Pickett's Grand Cherokee SUV.

They didn't need to talk.

They were done with the case.

They had given closure to the family of Stephanie after eight years of wondering and that was important. It was up to the homicide detectives to make a case against her killer and find him or her.

She and Sarge and Robin were retired. They only worked cold cases for the Cold Poker Gang task force.

And right now, today, Pickett was very glad that was all they did. They didn't have to notify the family, or open a fresh case with all the photos of that casket, or face the scum who had killed Stephanie and stuffed her in her grandmother's casket.

Pickett had done that job for long enough as an active detective.

And this case made her very glad she had retired.

She squeezed Sarge's hand as they reached the car and he smiled.

"Tough to let this one go?" he asked.

"Not in the slightest," she said. "Not in the slightest."

And with that, she drove them back into Las Vegas toward breakfast at the Golden Nugget buffet.

Their routine was to eat breakfast at the Golden Nugget Buffet.

She needed the routine right now.

She needed to feel alive and in control.

And maybe by next week she might be ready for another cold case.

Maybe.

I Killed Adam Chaser

Dean Wesley Smith

One

There are a lot of people like me, and not enough people like me.

I kill people. It's what I do. It's my job, although I do not need the money and seldom accept it.

Unless I make a mistake, which I never do, no one knows that I have killed a person. Or that anyone has been killed, for that matter.

I am a hired contractor for Clean Sweep, a simple company with a simple slogan: We Take Out the Garbage.

Human garbage.

So let me tell you the story about one sack of human garbage named Adam Chaser. It's a heartwarming story of a simple garbage man (me) doing my simple job, and meeting the love of my life in the process.

At least she could have been.

Two

The snow fell in lazy flakes, blowing on a light Portland wind on the day I met Adam and Lori Chaser. The temperature was hovering at freezing, but it didn't feel cold out. The snow wasn't sticking. Twenty days before Christmas and the people of Portland were celebrating the snow in the air as a sign the season was really upon them. They could do that because Portland seldom got snow that actually became a problem.

The meeting was casual, in the elevator on our way up to our respective condos. We nodded, I refrained from looking at Lori.

I had been given my assignment to dispose of Adam five days before while living in a rented condo in Phoenix. I always rented under an assumed name while on a job and never stayed long in any one place.

That name was now gone.

I have no permanent home and my real name and history have long since vanished from any database. I always became the person I needed to be in the city I live in for the job at hand.

In Portland, I became Dan Garton.

I wore my now dark-brown hair short and stylish to match a look of extreme money. I usually wore expensive sweatshirts and expensive jeans, with five hundred dollar loafers around the building, but I also had a closet of silk suits and everything needed to pull that look off as well. Nothing about me said "fake money." I made sure of that.

The condo I rented was located in an upscale fourteen-story building in a Portland district called The Pearl District. The building had high ceilings, a doorman, and stone and wood and art everywhere. It was first class all the way and comfortable in brown and gold tones that only can be found in the Northwest part of the United States.

The neighborhood had lots of coffee shops, high-end decorator stores, and bookstores. It was a district where most everyone walked or took the electric streetcars that crisscrossed the area. I had hired a limo service to take me anywhere I needed to go at any time of the day or night. A limo and driver remained on duty within one minute of my building's front door.

I seldom used them.

Adam and Lori had a condo in the same building three stories below mine. Adam worked in his family business of investing, and he forced Lori to remain at home at his beck and call.

I had many cameras in every area of their condo so that I could watch their every move.

He forced her to do all the cleaning and demanded that the huge three-bedroom condo be spotless at all times. He forced her to cook a major meal for him every evening, but seldom came home to eat it. Instead he spent many evenings with high-end hookers in a bondage club.

As far as in business, Adam had been the force and money behind two major projects that had caused two hundred families to suddenly become homeless in three major cities. His company had also bought up and closed down five family businesses in the last five months, forcing almost six hundred people to lose their jobs.

He loved causing that kind of pain while making more money than he needed.

I could track his business dealings easily by hacking his company's computer network. They seemed to think no one would be interested in them, thus had taken few precautions. I read every e-mail he sent from work and listened in on every meeting through someone's computer in the room.

I was a master at all things electronic and digital.

I stood exactly six-foot tall and worked out every day. Adam was one inch shorter and weighed one hundred pounds more than I did. In the ten years since he had graduated college, he had become a fat slob who thought himself untouchable and enjoyed inflicting pain on others, including his wife.

Somehow, even with all the abuse from her husband, Lori had maintained her looks and weight since she had married him. She managed to exercise two hours a day. She said on her driver's license that she was five seven, but I would say it was closer to five-five. She had a tiny and perfectly-proportioned body and long black hair that when released reached her butt.

She also spent almost two hours per day on her computer, but I could not follow most of what she did on that computer and could not seem to find the connection into it. It seemed she was not online at all. More than likely Adam didn't let her, so she only played games.

But that was what made me understand her and finally figure out who she really was. What gave her away was my inability to get to her computer.

The exercise and the computer and private time in the bathroom were her only time for herself every day.

She seemed to have some Asian descent in her, while Adam seemed pure white slob.

I had also set up surveillance cameras in the hallways, near the front entrance, in the parking garage, along with every room in their condo. The cameras I used were so tiny that they looked more like the point of a pen than a camera.

Imagine a camera and battery the shape of a small finishing nail with no head. I just had to drill a tiny hole into a wall and insert the camera, usually at a height that no one could touch. And in most cases, the tiny shell of the camera matched the paint color.

And if touched by anyone but me, they generated so much heat from their tiny batteries that they melted and fused into the wall.

They transmitted only to my computer, which only I could access.

For the entire month of December and then most of January, I followed Adam and Lori's routines, their habits, everything about both of them. During that time Adam beat Lori five times, never hitting her in the face.

Clearly she was a strong woman, and she took the beatings almost coldly, which often did nothing more than make Adam even madder. He lived to see the pain on his victims.

After almost two months, it became clear that Adam had no sense that anyone might want him dead, and he took no precautions at all. He was as stupid as he was brutal.

He would be an easy target, which bothered me a great deal. Lori could have cleared him from her life easily with her skills. So before I moved to clear his odor from the human race, I needed to know more about Adam's will and who would take over his company and what Lori would end up with after her husband's sudden demise.

So I dug.

I am an expert on all things electronic and am constantly updating both my knowledge and my equipment.

A garbage man like me has an ability to dig and we don't mind the smell of rot that we often find. And with Adam, I found a great deal of rot.

And I discovered, as I suspected, that Lori would end up with nothing from the company or even the condo if he died.

Not one dime.

It was clear she wanted none of it.

I went in search of why she stayed with him through all the abuse. I discovered that her cover story was that both her parents were dead, but she had a brother who had broken his back in a car accident and his only care was what Adam provided the money for.

Otherwise, she had no assets. Nothing.

Of course, she had assets and it took me some careful digging to find them. She was extremely rich.

And the kid with the broken back wasn't her brother. Her family was as long gone as mine.

She supposedly had stayed with Adam, the monster, because of her brother's care. Not an uncommon story. I had seen similar stories many times in my years working as a disposal artist, so it played.

Over the month of February, without leaving a trace in any record, I fixed all that. By March first, Lori would inherit everything. At least the Lori of her cover story.

That inheritance would anchor her something awful. She would not like that one bit.

And I set up a trust fund that would fund on Adam's death for Lori's pretend brother. It all looked as if Adam had done it over a year's time. And all from his own work computer.

Lori would be so angry when she discovered that. But I knew she never would because she had no idea I knew who she really was.

Or why she was putting up with the false life with Adam.

She was good and I had come to like and admire the small, strong woman.

Emotions were often a bad thing for a garbage collector such as myself. I knew that.

I accepted that risk.

But I had to admit, I was enjoying this just a little.

And I really enjoyed watching her in the shower. Especially since she knew I was watching.

THREE

March tenth, Adam Chaser took a long sip of a cup of mocha his assistant had brought for him. His young female assistant lived in the same fear of Adam as Lori pretended she did.

Exactly fourteen minutes after drinking the coffee, Adam Chaser grabbed his chest while in the middle of a meeting. He fell forward onto a big conference table shouting "Heart! "Heart!"

What I had laced in his coffee was untraceable and forced the heart to shut down just as any normal heart attack.

I returned to my apartment before he collapsed so I could watch the show.

They rushed him to an emergency room at a nearby hospital and called Lori to tell her that her husband was there and more than likely wouldn't make it. She smiled as she slowly gathered up her things and headed for the elevator.

I made sure from my computer that the elevator came up to my floor so I could ride down with her.

"Nice day?" I said.

She smiled at me. "It is now. Thanks."

I assumed she meant to thank me about my comment about the weather since I doubted she would blow her cover just yet. And I was only slightly surprised at her calmness. Usually abused wives are upset when the abuser is taken from them and she needed to be playing that part.

I was wrong.

I held the door for her at the lobby and as she walked past she said, "Would you like to take a drive with me? I have to go play the grieving widow. Or you could call your limo service if you would rather do that."

I stood there holding the door to the elevator open, acting slightly surprised. She was showing herself to me before her job was finished.

That could be a fatal mistake.

She stopped two steps out of the elevator and smiled back at me. "Mr. Dan Garton, or whatever your real name is, you aren't the only smart person on the planet. And you are not the only one who works for Clean Sweep."

In all my life I had never exposed my cover to a target. I knew I was her target. I had known it almost from the beginning. I was the garbage that Clean Sweep needed removed. I knew that day would come some day. More than likely this was her play.

After a moment she laughed. "Close your mouth and call your limo. We have some planning to do."

With that she turned and started across the lobby at a fast walk, nodding to the doorman.

I pretended to pull it together and got the limo out front in less than one minute.

I didn't like this play on her part.

After we got into the back of the limo, she flicked a switch to block all listening devices. I had one on me, but clearly she wasn't trusting me at this moment and I wasn't trusting myself, to be honest, because this play on her part made no sense.

"I want to thank you for setting me up with Adam's business," she said, smiling a smile at me that I had not seen before. "I discovered it yesterday, although like you, I assure you I don't need the money. And the paralyzed kid who's going to get the trust fund really isn't my brother. It just gave me a good cover story."

I said nothing, as she would expect.

"After I get through the grieving widow part and the funeral," she said, "I'll explain everything if you feel like staying around. I hope you do, since Clean Sweep and I went through a lot of trouble to set this up."

We were almost at the hospital.

"Check with them if you don't believe me. They want us to work together on a very special case coming up."

I nodded.

Now I got her cover story. And her actions made sense.

The limo dumped her out at the front of the hospital and then took me back to my condo.

I had known for months that each room had at least three of the tiny black dots that were Clean Sweep cameras.

Adam Chaser died at three-ten of massive heart failure, his grieving widow was at his side.

At four I sent the coded message that the garbage was taken out.

A coded message came back telling me to stay in place.

As I expected.

I wanted to contact them directly, but I stayed with what I had been trained.

I stayed in place and waited and watched Lori.

And she watched me.

And for almost a month we both pretended that we were not being watched.

At times, that was very, very difficult. I did not want to hurt her.

I knew for a fact she was looking for a weakness to kill me. Clean Sweep operatives never retired.

We got retired and taken out to the garbage.

FOUR

April twelfth, she made her first and only move.

I knew she had been watching me in the shower as much as I had watched her in her shower. I tried to vary my morning routine, but I always knew she was there watching me.

And I tried to keep her entertained.

And she did the same for me as well.

This morning, as I started to step into the shower, I could smell the simple poison. It was a slow-acting type that absorbed painlessly through the skin and killed in twelve hours. She had more than likely planted the poison in my showerhead when I had left for lunch yesterday.

I had known she had accessed the apartment. I had put my own cameras in my apartment that she did not know about. I did not have one in the bathroom, however.

I tapped a button under a towel rack.

My special cell phone rang.

She would be able to hear that.

I left the shower running and went to answer the phone I had triggered, wrapping myself in a towel as I went.

I had put a scrambled message to be played to me over my phone in standard Clean Sweep instruction format so she could quickly take the code apart.

The code said I had new garbage to take out in Boston.

I went in and shut off the shower, even though I knew the poison was now long flushed through, I didn't feel safe in there. I dressed quickly in my standard travel clothes.

I quickly packed a suitcase, my computer, and then turned and smiled at one of her cameras.

I slowly mouthed the words "It's been fun."

I went out into the hallway, pressed the elevator button, then stood there waiting.

I knew for a moment she would watch me.

When the elevator dinged only a moment later and opened empty, I knew I had her. Her best bet would have been to get on the elevator first.

I stepped onto the elevator, put my suitcase and briefcase with my computer in the elevator, turned and punched the button for the lobby as if I was about to ride the elevator down. Then as the doors started to close, I triggered a camera loop override showing the door closing to her camera.

I ducked out and into the stairwell.

I silently beat the elevator down the three floors.

She was standing there, gun drawn. She was in her blue nightgown, the one that anyone could see through, facing the elevator as the door opened.

She had her legs spread, gun with sound suppressor aimed at the elevator.

She put four shots into the elevator as the door opened before I put three in her. Two center mass, one in the head.

I doubted anyone heard anything, since both of our suppressors were top rate.

She went down into a pile, showing me clearly that she had no underwear on.

I took my briefcase and suitcase off the elevator.

Then I rolled her onto the elevator and tossed my gun with her. It would never be traceable and I had left no prints on it in any fashion.

I had disabled the cameras on this floor near the elevator and in the stairwell, running them into a loop.

I let the door close and the elevator head for the lobby. Lori was going to expose some of her most private parts to those in the lobby when she reached there. She really should have put on some panties this morning.

I went back up to my apartment and opened my computer back up. Then I sent a virus to her computer that would wipe it clean of everything but standard games.

I also sent a self-destruct to all my cameras, melting them into the walls. And her cameras in my apartment as well. Even if someone dug one out, they would never know what it was.

Then I carefully left tracks on her bank accounts that would let anyone decent with a computer track that she had killed her husband for his money and some of her husband's associates wanted the money back.

I left some videos on her computer of her showing her body to some lover who was not seen behind the camera.

I left threatening e-mails from these made-up associates and love notes from her lover. All dated and untraceable to me.

I unpacked my suitcase and hung up my clothes.

Then I spent one full hour checking every detail of my condo for any traps left by the now very dead Mrs. Adam Chaser.

As with everyone in the building, I was questioned by the police, but I watched their investigation through their computers. They had no leads.

I planted a couple of false ones to help them out a little.

A week later, I gave notice on my condo and paid my last bills and had the limo service drop me at the airport.

Dan Garton stepped into a men's rest room and vanished. The camera in that area of the airport just happened to be having a glitch.

Now I still take out the human garbage.

But now I work for myself.

As I said, there are a lot of people like me. And yet, not enough.

Not by a long ways.

Maybe I'll work on that.

Make Myself Just One More

A Mary Jo Assassin Story

Dean Wesley Smith

Make Myself Just One More

Mary Jo stood, staring at the bottle of Smirnoff Vodka in her hand. She had a pitcher of orange juice beside her on the counter, ice was a touch away in the fridge, and a highball glass sat waiting.

She was fairly certain she could have just one more.

She thought she had done everything right.

The granite surface was spotless, the white cabinets wiped down completely, the floor scrubbed.

Not a spot of anything could have survived in this kitchen. She had even opened every door and make sure nothing had dripped down onto a hinge or in a crack. She had sanitized every tiny inch with bleach.

She had put nothing down any sink, but instead used a plastic bucket for the cleaning water. Then outside in the fenced backyard she had washed the bucket out completely in the gravel at the back end of the path to the yard.

Then she had put the bucket in the ground in a new flowerbed she had planted last week. She had punched some holes in the bottom of the bucket, put a new plant in the bucket, and filled the bucket up with dirt completely.

The bucket was covered completely. It was gone.

Then she had turned on the sprinklers that watered the lawn, including the area of the path where she had poured the cleaning water.

She was very good at this sort of thing.

Mary Jo never expected anything to lead back to her and this house, but it made no sense to take any chance when just a little bit of work would solve any problem.

Then she had gone into the guest room, put her blouse, bra, underwear, jeans, shoes and socks in a black trash bag along with all the cloths she had used for the cleaning and set the bag near the back door.

Then she had gone to her own bedroom upstairs in the four-bedroom, two-bath suburban home, taken a shower, making sure she was clean.

Extra sure. Especially her short brown hair.

She had liked this house in the year since she and Bob had gotten married. It kind of fit a part of her that she didn't often get to enjoy. And she could play the perfect housewife role to a science. She was only five-five, had short brown hair that made her look more like a pixie than anything else, and a body style with narrow hips and a small chest that didn't show any of her strength.

She was a member of an ancient order of assassins. She had lived for thousands of years, as everyone in her order tended to do. And she had never grown tired of her job. Ever. In fact, the job had gotten more challenging as technology improved.

She liked that and the money it supplied her to live a lavish lifestyle.

After her shower, she had dressed in a similar white blouse that she had had on earlier, same style of jeans, underwear, everything, including a second pair of sneakers.

With a pair of white gloves on, she took the black bag and put it into the back of her Jeep Cherokee along with a couple bags of normal week's garbage. She had set this routine up a year ago. This was all normal for her, including the white gloves. She had then driven the thirty minutes to the landfill just outside of town.

There she had made sure every bag was tossed over the edge of the dumping area into an area full of other black bags that a bulldozer was moving around and covering in layers of dirt.

She had paid the attendant in cash and he hadn't even noticed her other than to nod hi as he did every week. His attention was focused on the two pickup trucks behind her full of junk.

Now she was back at her house looking at the bottle of vodka and orange juice and wondering if she dared have one more drink.

After all, it had been the first Screwdriver with just a little too much vodka in it that had started all this mess and then cleaning.

Actually, it hadn't been, but it was fun to think that it had.

She loved her drinks, but was very careful in the thick of a job to not drink too much.

As she stood there, staring at the fixings for a drink she felt she wanted but wasn't sure she needed, her cell phone went off.

It was her husband's ring.

She answered it. "Hi, honey."

"Afraid I'm going to be late for dinner," he said. "Got a body."

"Oh, no," she said, making herself take a deep breath. Her husband was the lead homicide detective for the entire city. This call was normal. Over their year of marriage it had happened a good thirty times.

She had been responsible for a few of those bodies, just as she was for the one that had just been found. But he never knew that and never would.

"I'm sorry to hear that," she said. "How about I wait for you and we go out to Murphy's Diner when you are done."

"Might get late," he said.

"I'll snack until you call."

"That would be nice," he said. He told her that he loved her and then hung up.

He was a good man. She had enjoyed the year plus they had been together. The sex had been good, the laugher real. After centuries of living and killing, she had learned to appreciate those times even more.

She glanced at her watch. It was a quarter after four. The timing was spot on the money.

She glanced at the bottle of vodka one more time, then set it aside, put the pitcher of orange juice back in the fridge and the clean glass back in the cabinet.

Maybe after her dinner.

She then took her purse and went out to her Jeep. The third row of seats was always down in her car so she could carry gardening and groceries easily.

She lifted the seat and there was the bag with a rifle in it. Her disguise bag was there as well.

She slipped on her gloves for a moment and did a quick inventory to make sure everything was with the rifle and the disguise bag and she hadn't forgotten anything, then lowered the seats back into place.

Fifteen minutes later she had parked her Jeep in the mall parking lot out of any camera sight. She then, when no one was around, transferred her rifle to the small Ford four-door sedan backseat and locked the car. The car was brown, with plates mostly covered in mud.

The Ford sedan had been stolen by a man she had never met and left for her. She had paid the man ten grand for the car in a drop bag. He hadn't asked questions.

Then, carrying her disguise bag, she went into the mall and into the public restroom as herself. She came out almost forty minutes later, after dozens of other women had come and gone, as a long-haired blonde with a much larger nose and a tan jacket and red tennis shoes.

She walked to her car not drawing any attention to herself, climbed into the brown sedan and fifteen minutes later had it parked on the top of a pine-tree covered hill just to the right of town.

She had turned the car around so she could go straight down the hill she had just come up and be lost in the streets below in thirty seconds, long before anyone below even knew what hit them.

She left the car running and left the disguise bag in the car. She then took her rifle and made sure it was loaded.

It was a deer rifle, a classic bolt-action Roberts with a scope. Actually the rifle was a collector's item that she remembered back sixty years really liking. The thief who had given her the rifle had assured her it was accurate and had been tested.

She tested it on him and he had been right, actually. The thief was still one of her husband's unsolved cases.

She moved to the small stone wall that kept tourists on this hill from tumbling over the edge of a fairly steep cliff down into an old quarry below. This small turn-around often held teens out parking for some first love experiences in a parent's car.

She was so old now, she could barely remember her first sexual experiences. They had not been pleasant, she remembered that much.

The quarry two hundred feet below was abandoned and mostly a playground for neighborhood kids after school and in the summer.

The body of good old Sam lay below her, right where she had dumped it three hours before.

Sam had been handsome in his own right for forty. He lived with his wife Becky three doors down the street from her and stayed home days to work on a novel. Mary Jo had asked him to help her with a wiring issue in her porch light that she had created. She told him it had sparked and she was afraid of a fire starting.

He had fixed it, they had laughed, she had offered him a Screwdriver in payment for his hard work, and then she had stabbed him in the back, perfectly through his heart with a long ice pick as he moved to get ice.

His blood mostly had pooled on the floor around him, but she had still cleaned everything to make sure.

She had sipped her first drink of the day as he lay dead on her kitchen floor.

She loved Screwdrivers. Best drink ever as far as she was concerned.

Killing never did anything for her, one way or the other, and poor old Sam was just bait for her husband who was the real target.

She checked the area in the small clearing around her to make sure no one was nearby that she would also need to kill, then eased up over the edge of the stone wall and looked down.

Sam's body was now covered.

Her husband stood with two other detectives in a tight group near the body, talking.

Good, she would take care of all three at the same time. First her husband, who was her target, the one she was getting paid to kill. She had slept with her target for fourteen months. She thought of it like a cat playing with a mouse.

She studied the scene quickly one more time. By taking out the other two detectives, it would slow down any investigation.

"Goodbye, dear," she said softly. "This is what you get for pissing off the wrong people who have far too much money."

The rifle was loud, but had almost no kick. The echo of her first shot bounced around through the trees and over the surrounding farmlands.

Her husband went to the ground instantly.

She knew the entry wound would be small in his chest, but most of his back would be blown away from the high-velocity rifle as the hollow point bullet expanded on impact and blew him apart.

She quickly took out her husband's best friend and partner with a second shot before anyone even thought to move for cover.

She killed the third detective as he turned to run.

She picked up the three shells, made sure she had left nothing else where she had fired, then put the gun back in the case on the back seat of the car and headed down the road.

She turned away from the police and then worked her way slowly back toward the mall.

She parked the Ford sedan next to her Jeep again. Then transferred the disguise bag and everything into her car and put the rifle back under the back seats.

She climbed into her Jeep and turned on a high-tech scanner she had in her purse that told her if any camera was watching at all.

Nothing, as she had known for this area of the large mall parking lot.

She quickly pulled off her disguise and tossed them into the bag, zipping it up and putting it on the floor behind her driver's seat.

Then she took off the thin, transparent gloves she had been wearing that were embedded with fake fingerprints and stuck those in the pocket of her jeans.

Back at home, Mary Jo put back on the fake fingerprint gloves and pulled out two more black garbage bags full of weekly trash from the kitchen, including a bunch of stuff she had tossed out of the fridge after wiping prints and putting the fake prints on the stuff.

Then she got the rifle from the car and broke it down and put parts in three bags, wearing her fake fingerprint gloves as she did.

Then she took parts of her costume and spread them through the garbage as well. And she made sure that there was nothing in the bags that would lead to her in this home in any fashion.

Then she headed back to the landfill, made some mention to the man taking her money that it was her second trip because she was cleaning house. He didn't care.

And she tossed the three bags over the edge and into the stinking mess of the landfill.

A moment later the large grader covered all three with a layer of dirt.

Mary Jo then went home to wait to play the part of the grieving widow.

Sam's wife would be grieving as well tonight.

She was watching television two hours later when two uniformed cops came to her door.

One was a woman cop who seemed to be almost in tears.

They told Mary Jo the news and she broke down as the two cops expected her to do.

They asked Mary Jo if there was anything they could do and Mary Jo told them she had a sister who would come over and stay with her. She didn't, but the two cops bought it.

Then the woman cop hugged her harder and longer than was necessary and gave Mary Jo her card for anything she needed.

Mary Jo wondered if her good old husband had been getting a little of that on the side. He didn't seem to be the type. But that had sure been a strange hug.

Mary Jo was about to go fix herself that long-overdue second Screwdriver after the two officers left when her alarm bells went off.

Instead, she went to her bedroom and stripped down and climbed in the shower, all the while pretending to be distraught.

Finding nothing attached to her body, she came out and used a scanner she kept hidden in the back of her dresser drawer to check for bugs.

The woman officer had planted one all right, under the back collar of her blouse.

Audio only.

There were no other bugs in the house.

No young rookie cop would do that, especially so quickly after the entire department was tossed into panic mode. Besides, there was no reason to suspect her.

That girl worked for someone outside the department. More than likely the same idiot who had paid Mary Jo to kill her husband and would pay a second half as soon as she reported in to him.

And now he would pay a far higher sum. You didn't try to double cross Mary Jo. Not ever. The idiots who had hired her had no idea the order of assassins even existed.

Keeping up the act of a distraught wife for the bug, she put her blouse back on with her jeans and tennis shoes. Then she put on thin, clear gloves and took from what looked like a perfume bottle a small drop of fluid on a pad. She carefully wrapped the pad in a tiny bag and stuck it in her pocket. It was an odorless, untraceable poison that would kill anyone who touched it within five minutes.

Then she called the young officer. "I want to see my husband."

"I don't think that is such a good idea," the young woman cop said.

Mary Jo nodded. Both of them were right on script.

"I'm coming to the station anyway," Mary Jo said.

Fifteen minutes later, she pulled up out front after pretending to cry most of the way to the station so that anyone listening to the bug wouldn't be shocked.

The young cop met Mary Jo at the big double door. Concrete steps led up into the front desk of the station.

"I don't think this is a good idea," the young cop said. "He was shot and they need to do an autopsy."

Mary Jo had the poison pad in her hand and her hands were covered in the thin gloves. "You may be right. I don't know what I am thinking."

She gave the young cop a hug, rubbing the pad along her neck before backing away.

"I'm sure sorry," Mary Jo said.

"It's understandable," the young cop said.

Suddenly the young cop looked pale and swallowed hard.

Mary Jo took her under her arm and turned to take her up the three steps and into the station. The drug was very fast acting and this woman would be dead in five minutes tops.

As she did, Mary Jo took off the glove and tossed it into a garbage can near the front door full of Burger King cups and food bags. The poison wouldn't last in the air like that for another thirty minutes and the gloves would dissolve in two hours.

"Help!" Mary Jo shouted to the officers inside as she opened the door. "She just collapsed into my arms on the front steps."

Two cops ran to grab the young officer, then a third nodded to Mary Jo and offered his sincere condolences.

Mary Jo broke into sobs, as scheduled for her part of this passion play, and they let her sit in a back office and calm down before having an officer drive her home.

Then Mary Jo killed the bug on her blouse and made sure the rest of her house was clean of all recording and electronic devices.

It was.

She dug out a burner phone from a fake bottom of her purse and dialed a number.

"Yeah," a voice on the other end said.

"Target is dead. The remainder of my fee has tripled because of your attempt at a double cross. If the money is not in the agreed-upon account by this time tomorrow afternoon, you know the consequences."

"You can't threaten me," the voice said.

"I know where you live, where your children sleep, where your wife loves to eat sushi," Mary Jo said. "I am patient, invisible, and you hired me because I get the job done. The job you hired me to do is done. The price is now four times my fee. Please do not fail me."

Then she hung up, put the phone in a baggy and smashed it into tiny pieces.

Then she put some bleach and a few drops of a special solution into the baggy, sealed it, and tossed it into the trashcan outside. The entire thing would be a puddle of goo in the bottom of the can in an hour.

She then took a deep breath.

Finally, it was time.

She took out the pitcher of orange juice, a highball glass, and the vodka. She filled the glass with ice, added a good solid shot of vodka, then filled the rest of the glass with orange juice.

Then she put everything away before sipping the wonderful drink.

Perfect.

Just perfect.

Maybe, just maybe, a little later, she might just have one more.

After all, a grieving widow could be forgiven a drink or two.

The Yellow of the Flickering Past

Dean Wesley Smith

Act One: A Yellow Oil Mess

Sixteen days after I killed her, I took my dead wife to a movie.

She had always loved movies.

Actually I think she loved the memory of movies more than any one film. And she loved the smell of the buttered popcorn you could buy in theaters, even if the butter was actually only a melted yellow oil from big yellow cans. She said it was part of the movie- going experience and that was all that mattered.

On our first date to a movie I laughed when she asked for an "extra large, extra butter, please."

"You know that shit will kill you?" I said as the guy with a thousand pimples pumped the handle of the butter machine like he was huddled over his first Playboy centerfold. Miss July.

"Sure," my date, soon-to-be wife, later-to-be-dead wife, had said. She never once offered me any of her popcorn. That was sort of how we argued from then on.

And we argued a lot.

She asked for the same "Extra large, extra butter" every time we went to a movie. She never missed a movie.

We went to a lot of movies.

Of course, people who saw us at the movies thought we made the perfect couple. "Fit together," they would say, but after I came out of the coma induced by new love and the first year of marriage, I just didn't see why. She was a light blonde, with a large, white-toothed smile, and wide, innocent green eyes. I actually had light brown hair, but I suppose it looked closer to her color because I kept it cut so short. I had dark brown eyes and people said I squinted a lot. I was almost five-six when I wore my good shoes, and even in heels she still wasn't as tall as I was.

Besides that, we argued all the time and I hated movies and didn't eat popcorn, especially with yellow oil.

The last year of our marriage I started daydreaming about the dreaded yellow oil. I figured no human body could digest that stuff, so it must have been building up in her body over the five years and seven days we were together. Maybe even for years before, just waiting for the right circumstances to set it all off in a huge bang. I dreamed she would explode and the police would just nod and say, "Yup. Yellow oil build-up."

But I could never figure out how to set off the explosion. I watched the papers for months hoping to read about another yellow oil explosion, but never did.

I even consented to sex one night that last year, thinking that might set her off. But the thought of her exploding had me so excited that she said I didn't last long enough to even get her hot. Maybe that was why it didn't work.

Sadly, she never did explode, or even melt. The yellow oil didn't kill her.

I did that. I killed her with a curse from a book of Wizard curses I bought at a used bookstore downtown. A big brown book with a guy on the cover wearing a pointed hat and a star-covered robe.

I wish the yellow oil had killed her instead, in a huge, messy wife-explosion. I wouldn't have minded cleaning up the mess.

After my now-dead wife would get her "extra large, extra butter," she used to love the walk down the carpeted halls of the multiplex theater, past the posters of the other movies showing in all the other theaters. She would stop and point out every show she wanted to see, as if I really cared. The last few years I even stopped pretending I did care, but she kept right on pointing them out.

Then, after the pointing-at-the-poster routine was done she would go into the theater and look around in the low light to find just the right, perfect seat. Finding the exact right seat was always treated as one of the most important events in life. I think a good seat meant more to her than Christmas or her mother's birthday.

Once she had found that perfect place, she always whispered to me that she hoped no one would sit in front of her.

I always just nodded and she would settle in, happy, content, wide eyes focused on the blank screen ahead.

On the times when someone did have the nerve to take the seat in front of her, she would make a rude, almost pig-like noise and make us move to new, perfect seats. Which, of course, again took time. And once settled she would again whisper to me that she hoped no one would sit in front of her.

For a popular movie we moved a lot and usually ended up sitting down front. Then I would get a sore neck from looking straight up at the screen. I always felt I was looking up the actor's nose. Nose hair can really distract from the plot of a movie.

I think, more than even the movie, I think my now-dead wife loved the previews of the coming attractions. Something about the possibility of a future trip to the movies held her spellbound like a deer in front of a car's headlights. We never saw a preview of a movie after which she didn't whisper to me that she wanted to see the movie. And didn't it look just wonderful?

The word "wonderful" was always followed by a long sigh. Just once I wish she would have sighed like that after we had sex.

Near the end of the second year of our marriage I started writing letters to the theater begging them, at first, and then demanding, that they not show previews of coming movies. A nasty phone call from the police department made me stop writing.

The theater kept playing the coming attractions.

She kept wanting to see every movie.

Of course, we went to them all.

And they all had coming attractions.

I still get dizzy just thinking about it.

That, and all that yellow oil she ate.

That, and all that yellow of the time.

Act Two:
The Unlawful Christmas Argument

The idea to take my dead wife to a movie was hers, of course. It seemed that my killing her, then wrapping her body in plastic and stuffing it in an old trunk in the basement didn't even slow down her love for movies. I guess I was wrong to expect that it would.

For over two weeks after I killed her I kept saying no. No way in hell was I going to be seen in a movie theater with the ghost of my dead wife. And there were no curses or formulas in my Wizard's book for getting rid of ghosts, so I had to keep listening to her and arguing with her.

And of course, as when we were married, she ended up winning all the arguments. She finally used the old "it's-almost-Christmas" routine and I caved in like a tunnel cut through mud. But I said I would do it on my conditions.

She didn't care about that. But she did say we had to follow the ghost rules. Wizard curses, ghost rules, my conditions. This was going to be a very complicated trip to the movies.

Before I bought the Wizard's book, I didn't know Wizards even existed. And I never expected that I might be one, but since one of the Wizard curses worked for me, I suppose I am. But so far I've not been able to make another curse work. But I'm going to keep practicing, because what Wizards can do is really cool stuff.

Before she died I didn't realize that ghosts had rules, either. But they do. A lot of them. And I discovered the ghost rules are sometimes a little tricky to figure out. For example, there was the main rule about why she was still even around. She said she had her reasons and they were for her to know and me to find out. She said that a lot during our marriage and I never found out a thing.

I didn't expect that now that she was a ghost this time was going to be any different.

As far as going to a movie went, she figured that if I could get her body close enough to the theater, she, her ghost, not her body, could go inside with me and see the movie. For some ghost rule or another she had to stay fairly close to her body, which is why she had been hanging around the house.

She decided I could put her body in the car and then park the car next to the theater. A simple plan, really. Just get a two-plus week-old dead body right up next to a public theater and then leave it for two hours. I laughed at her when she said that was what we needed to do. I flat out said no way.

She kept at me, kept me up all night again with the what-a-wonderful-Christmas-present it would be for her. I tried a Wizard curse on her that was supposed to have turned her into a frog, but she stayed a ghost and kept at me.

I gave in again. About sunrise. Using Christmas in arguments should be outlawed in all marriages, even after death.

We waited until after dark, which really didn't upset her because she hated the cheap, early shows. She always said going to a regular show was much better. I never did figure out what was the difference between a cheap show and a regular show, except the price. Every time I asked her about the difference she just looked at me as if I was stupid and just couldn't see.

At least this time I would only have to buy one ticket.

As I loaded her body into the hatchback, she stood in the driveway to watch for the neighbors and cars on the street. It had only been a few weeks since she had died and the decay and smell wasn't too bad. Or at least I tried to convince myself that it wasn't that bad.

I had her wrapped in three sheets of plastic and taped so tightly shut no air, or anything else for that matter, could get in there. Yet I was sure as I draped her over my shoulder that I could smell a rotten, nose-clogging aroma of decay. Like a dead dog three days beside the road.

She laughed when I mentioned it and told me it was my guilt catching up with me. But I swore I could smell her rotting, right through the plastic bags and all the tape, guilt or no guilt.

It took what seemed like an eternity to get her body settled and the hatch closed. The backs of newer cars just weren't made for holding bodies like the trunks of the cars my parents owned. Those trunks were big. To get her in the Impala hatchback I had to remove the spare. No telling what problems we would have if we had a flat.

She came through the door without opening it and settled into the passenger seat.

"This is going to be so much fun," she said, and I shuddered. She had said those very words before every movie we ever went to, almost like a recording.

Maybe this was my hell. No maybe about it. I was in hell. I was destined to take my dead wife to a movie three times a week for the rest of my life. Maybe I should just kill myself now and get it over with.

If I could only be certain that would end it.

Act Three: A Yellow Tinge

"You won't think it's sweet if we get caught," I said about halfway to the theater after she told me I was being sweet for taking her to a movie. "I get tossed in jail for killing you, and you'll end up haunting the local cemetery."

She shrugged. "Couldn't be much worse than hanging around here with you."

"Now don't start," I said. "This is how you got killed in the first place.

"Don't you dare blame me again for what happened." She had her hands on her hips, the sign she was getting mad. "I'm the one who is dead, remember."

"How can I ever forget?"

Actually, I had never really totally hated her. At least not enough yet to kill her. But I suppose it was building to that. I sure had wished she was dead enough times.

It was her way of arguing that got to me. One afternoon she started in on me. Or, as she tells it, I started in on her. Either way doesn't make much difference. I got so mad I yelled a Wizard curse at her that I had just read that morning. She laughed, so for a special effect I tossed a handful of sparkle dust from the magic shop in her face. I read that Wizards were always using sparkle dust and I guess it worked.

She backed up away from me rubbing her eyes, tripped, and hit her head hard on the edge of the counter as she went down.

I was over her immediately. I didn't like the way her head hitting that counter had sounded. A sick, deep smacking and cracking sound. Granted, I had cursed her dead, but I wasn't sure I really wanted her that way.

Too late. She was already dead. And her ghost was standing above me leaning over her own body.

"Now see what you have done," she had said. Even dead she had started out annoying.

We rode the rest of the way in silence to the theater. I remembered we had done that a lot. Especially the year before she died. Actually, in the two weeks since she died we had gotten along better than ever before. Something about her not expecting sex, I think.

I parked as close as I could to the multiplex theater building and suddenly she was in a good mood again. She clapped her hands together and floated out of the car before I even had it stopped.

"I'm in heaven," she said, moving toward the ticket window.

I shook my head, muttering that she was a long way from heaven, but I certainly wished she would go there soon. I locked the car and checked twice to see if the hatch was shut tight and the blanket over her body was in place.

By the time I had bought my ticket to the show she wanted to see, she was already inside, floating in front of the popcorn counter, looking sad.

I moved up beside her and as softly as I could, without moving my lips, I asked, "What's wrong?"

She pointed at the popcorn.

"You knew you wouldn't be able to eat any?" I whispered.

She shook her head. "No, it's not that. I can pick it up and put it in my mouth." To demonstrate she took a piece from the counter and popped it into her mouth and chewed with her mouth half open. Thank god no one was watching.

"So what's the problem? And since when can you pick up stuff?"

She shrugged. "I've been doing that for days now. But I can't taste the popcorn."

More stupid ghost rules.

I stared at her for a moment and then glanced around the theater lobby to see if anyone was watching. Again we were in luck.

"Maybe I can find a Wizard spell to help you," I said. "Or maybe you'll just get better with practice." I regretted saying that immediately.

"Oh, you think so? Then get an extra large, extra butter. I'll practice all the way through the movie."

I was about to object when this couple moved up behind me and I was forced to get the guy behind the counter's attention and buy an extra large, extra butter popcorn and a small drink.

By the time I found her in the sixth theater down the hall the previews were already starting. I started to say something and she shushed me, just like she used to do when she was alive.

Dead. Alive. Nothing changes.

I balanced the popcorn on the rail between us and she began to eat handfuls, dropping exactly the same amount that she used to do when she was alive, only this time the dropped popcorn went through her and gathered in a pile on the seat. I'd have to ask her later how that worked and why I couldn't see the popcorn after it was inside her. More and more strange ghost rules.

I glanced around to see if anyone was watching or sitting close. We were in luck. This movie was a real dog and there were only five other people in the theater.

After every preview she leaned over and whispered that she wanted to see that movie, just like she had always done. And, as when she was alive, the thought made me shudder, but now for different reasons.

I spent most of the movie trying to work out plans of escape. I even thought of just going out of the theater and walking away. But I didn't have the guts to do that. Besides, eventually the police would find the car and her body and I would get caught. The life of a fugitive just wasn't one for me.

When the movie ended she sighed. "I really love movies."

"No kidding," I said under my breath and luckily she ignored me. I sat still, watching the credits and waiting until the other people left before standing.

"Too bad you couldn't just stay here."

Again she sighed. "That would be wonderful."

We headed out the back door near the screen in silence and it wasn't until I was at the car that I had realized what I had seen.

The multiplex theater's back door was right beside the screen. Under the screen, like in old theaters, was a stage, only this stage was fake, just used to get the screen up in the air. A maintenance man, or someone, must have left the access door open to the area under the stage, revealing rough planking on the floor spaced evenly over hard packed dirt.

There was nothing else under there and no reason for anyone to ever go under there.

"You really want to stay here?" I asked as she settled into her seat.

She looked at me with that questioning look, meaning she didn't understand. I always had liked that look because it meant she didn't understand something about me. She always took such pride in knowing everything about me, so that look had always cheered me up and tonight was no exception.

I pointed back at the closed door. "Go back through there and take a look under the stage."

"But—"

"Just do it." I loved having the upper hand.

She shrugged and floated/walked/moved toward the closed metal theater door and then through it like it was the surface of a lake.

A full minute later she was back, excited. "I see what you are thinking. You could bury my body under the stage and I could see all the movies I wanted."

I nodded and she tried to hug me, which failed totally. But I suppose it was the thought that counted.

We went home, got my gloves and a shovel, and I tossed in my Wizards book just in case I might need it. We were back to the theater in less than an hour. I backed the car right up to the closest place I could get near the stage door and we waited until the next show ended and the people were leaving.

She went inside and stood guard and when she motioned that the coast was clear, I blocked the door open. As the credits were playing I got her body from the car and under the stage.

While she watched the movie again with eight live people, I buried her. I had to be real quiet, especially taking out and replacing the flooring planks. But I got it done, finishing the digging during the noisy love scene in the middle and then putting back the flooring during the loud chase scene at the end.

I did a quick Wizard invisibility blessing over her grave, then left the shovel in the back corner, as if it had been left by a workman. I went out behind the last movie-goer of the last show.

She met me in the car, smiling. "Thanks," she said.

I think that was the first time in years she had said that to me. I was taken aback. "My pleasure," was all I could think to say.

"Would you come tomorrow night and see a movie with me?"

"Sure," I said.

She clapped her hands together like a kid. "Great. You can buy me some popcorn."

"I'd be glad to," I said. And I really meant it. Since then I went to the movies there about once a week. No one ever talked about the ghost of the twelve-plex theater, except to complain about rude noises from empty seats behind them.

No one ever found her body.

I bought her popcorn every week and we never fought again. She seemed totally contented.

But after a few years I noticed she had this yellow tinge about her. I tried a Wizard curse to help her, but it did no good. I figured it was just too much yellow oil build-up.

Call Me Unfixable

A Bryant Street Story

Dean Wesley Smith

Act One

I sat in my brand-new green Lexus on the hot pavement of Bryant Street and stared at the front door of my home across the lush and expensive green lawn, always perfectly kept, of course.

The car's engine idled almost silently and the air conditioning blew cold.

Before any rough day in court, as a major trial lawyer, I always sat in my car and made sure I was completely in character. The worst thing I could do in a courtroom was to have sudden doubts, or fall out of my belief system.

I thought of it as going on stage. I had to be completely in my character, completely submerged in the part I needed to play.

And that's what I had to do now. I had to stay in the part, in character. I couldn't let a stray thought break my concentration.

I again stared at the house. Right now the state-of-the-art sprinkler system was giving the lawn "just a taste" to keep it fresh looking even in the August heat. Most of the watering was done at night.

That stupid piece of green lawn had been taken out and replaced four times because Salina, my wife, wanted it to look better. Four different times it had been carefully rolled into place, carefully cut, carefully everything. And "carefully" meant expensive.

The brick planters along the front of the house always had to be perfect as well, present the perfect picture to the world of a happy, perfect home in our little subdivision. The perfect flowers had to be planted carefully in each planter for each of Portland, Oregon's seasons. Those flowers got replaced every two months, even if some of the old ones were still blooming.

And even worse, I had spent more money than I could ever imagine on slug poison because Salina had read an article about how slugs were bad in this part of the country.

Our lawn and planters, plus parts of the garage and the basement, were pure death to any poor slug that happened to wander into the yard. And who knew what all that poison was doing to other animals unlucky enough to venture across the line into Salina's perfect point-four acres in the suburbs.

Salina had loved her home, her yard, her plants, her furniture, her clothes, her dishes, her kitchen, everything she touched. She had tried to make everything perfect.

Even me.

But I was the one thing she could never make perfect, or convince to spend enough of my own money on myself to become what she considered perfect.

I was the one flaw in her perfectly ordered and maintained life.

She could spend my money on everything else, but I had drawn the line with changing myself.

And that had become our biggest problem. I just didn't care enough to be perfect. I kind of liked myself the way I was. I stood six-two, worked out so I had no excess weight at thirty-three, unlike most of my friends and co-workers in the law firm. And I had a smile that many said lit up a room.

But Salina said my nose was crooked and it needed to be fixed. It was crooked, slightly, because of a skiing accident up on Mount Hood when I was twenty-four, a year after I married Salina. But I liked it. I thought it gave my face character.

Salina saw it as an imperfection.

And she was big into yoga, but no chance in hell I was going to do that. I ran in the gym down near the office and played golf in the summer and skied in the winter. No way I was going to sit and try to get my damned leg over my head.

Salina was into fine wines and had me spend a fortune for a wine cellar dug under the house. That cellar had been one of our biggest fights. Of course, she won.

The wine cellar was tighter than most bank vaults and controlled with its own environmental system. Expensive didn't begin to describe that room.

I hated most wines. I liked a good micro-brew and had a fridge in the perfectly clean garage that kept my beer.

And she had wanted me to learn to like the cultural stuff around Portland, but all I had wanted to attend was a University of Oregon Ducks football game.

So after years of marriage, I had become an abomination to Salina. She wouldn't allow me to touch her and she seldom talked to me unless she wanted something from me or wanted to criticize something I was doing, eating, or watching.

So today, as planned, I would end it.

If the plan worked as set out, Salina's little perfect world would come crashing down around her head.

I was in perfect form, ready to go on stage and play my part. It felt good to do this preparation time again.

I glanced up the street at the deep-blue convertible Cadillac parked like it belonged to the house three doors away. But Jimmy, my private detective and best friend, told me it belonged to Percy Samuels.

Salina and Percy.

Such a perfect-sounding couple.

Percy owned what seemed like a swank health spa in the Pearl District downtown, but Jimmy told me he was completely broke. Percy lived in a sloppy apartment littered with Coors beer cans and was within one month of having that fancy blue car repossessed.

On top of that, the IRS had liens on his business and were about to strike, a source told me.

That source, of course, was Jimmy.

Everything I knew about Salina and Percy came though Jimmy.

Jimmy and I had been friends since college and he knew how to dig out information in both legal and illegal ways. We skied together in the winter and played golf together every Saturday.

And now, with everything, we spent almost all our time together.

He only stood five-four, but was the most powerful small man I had ever met. I might be ten inches taller and weigh more, but not a chance in the world would I ever want to take him on in a fight.

Jimmy often found me information for a client I couldn't legally use, but that illegal information usually pointed to something I could use.

Way back when I asked him to look into what Salina was doing, all he did was laugh. Then he said, "I was wondering when the sex was going to turn bad and you were going to grow a pair in dealing with her."

So Jimmy did his best and found all sorts of information that would allow me to kick Salina down the road and not pay her a cent.

Salina and Percy had been lovers now for six months. Usually in the afternoons when they knew I was going to be in court.

I had to admit, that was smart.

Of course, that backfired on them, all their careful planning.

And Salina had been stashing some cash away, which I had managed to make vanish out of her accounts.

Jimmy managed to get all our joint accounts locked down tight and all her credit cards cancelled.

Salina was as broke as her lover Percy.

I looked out over the perfect green lawn saturated in snail bait. It was time for me to play this game, walk on this stage, and go into that house once again. I already had a wonderful condominium downtown, only blocks from my office. And I liked it, had furnished it the way I wanted a place furnished, including the biggest screen one of the rooms could handle.

Percy and Salina were in their perfect world. They just didn't know it.

I almost felt sorry for him. Her, I never would have a moment's regret.

My cell phone in my pocket was on and open, connected to my best friend. "You there, Jimmy?"

"Waiting just around the corner as usual, Craig," Jimmy's deep voice came back strong. "Just leave the line open and I'll make sure I get everything. I'll come running if there is an ounce of trouble."

"Thanks, buddy," I said.

Jimmy played his part in our little play perfectly. You couldn't ask for a better friend.

Leaving the connection open in my pocket so that Jimmy could hear, I moved from the car and out into the sun.

For Portland, the day was warm, promising to top out in the mid-nineties.

Taking a deep breath to steady my nerves, just as I did when going into court, I moved up my front walk, my leather dress shoes making faint clicking sounds on the concrete that sounded like it echoed up and down the street.

I wasn't actually sure they made any sound, but I sure hoped they did, at least a little. In this play, I wanted them to make the noise.

Then, moving as silently as I could, I went through the front door and stood just inside. It felt like I was sweating slightly in the sudden coolness of the air. I wasn't sure if I actually was or if I just wanted to believe I was.

I had done it. I was inside.

I stayed very still to try to discover what I could hear.

Of course, there was nothing. I had done so much build-up to this, like planning a major court case, my nerves were almost out of control.

It made me feel alive, which I loved.

"You okay, Craig?" Jimmy's voice came faintly from my phone in my pocket.

I whispered. "Inside the house. Give me a minute."

The play continued.

I started down the hallway toward our master bedroom, working hard to make as little noise as possible.

No one there.

The huge room was in perfect condition, the bed made, the blinds open, the summer light filling the pink and orange space that was Salina's idea of a perfect master bedroom.

I felt dizzy, so I made myself take a couple deep breaths until the swirling passed. I couldn't let the images of anything but today come into my mind. I had to stay firmly in character or this would not work yet again.

After a moment, I went back to the game of searching for my wife and her lover, making sure I stayed right on the script Jimmy and I had worked out.

That was critical.

Of course I found nothing.

The house was empty.

I carefully opened a cabinet and took one of my old coffee mugs out and placed it on the counter, just where it wasn't supposed to be.

I stared at it for a moment, almost stunned, but again working to keep myself in character, acting as if what I had just done was perfectly normal.

Salina would have never allowed that to happen. It was something out of place, something not perfect, so if I left the mug there, she would have cleaned it up.

And then I would have heard about it for an hour.

"A place for everything and everything in its place," she would repeat over and over.

I tended to agree with that now for her.

I stared at the mug for a moment longer, savoring the victory.

Then I walked through the house again, looking in all four bedrooms, in my study, in her private room. Then I went down the narrow flight of stairs and into the wine cellar, making sure that I covered everything.

I had come to love the wine cellar and actually stood for a short time with one hand on the wine racks and just smiled at all the wine I had bought Salina that now she would never drink.

Then, as if I did the action every day, I took some slug bait from a trap in a back corner and spread it into the small wall heater. Then I turned on the wall heater.

It started to crackle. Perfect.

It worked.

I had managed to do at least that much this year.

I caught myself and made myself stay in perfect character for the play.

I continued my search.

No one.

The house had a feel of emptiness to it, and now that I was looking around again, I could see faint signs of dust in certain places.

The cleaning services were clearly not doing a good job.

I moved into the kitchen area and looked out over the living room. A very empty place, even though it was full of very expensive furniture.

I talked in the direction of my shirt pocket. "Jimmy, no one home."

"Be right there, buddy," he said and hung up.

I stood there on the edge of the living room staring around at the empty house with all the perfect furniture that had never felt like a home to me.

The play needed to continue.

Every detail needed to be perfect if this was to work. So I headed down the hall to make the motion of checking for her car. I had to stay on stage. That's what kept me grounded.

It was the only thing that mattered.

As I expected, her car was still parked there.

I went back to the dark granite kitchen counter as Jimmy came through the front door and moved over beside me.

He had a very worried look on his face.

I gave him a thumbs up and pointed to the mug.

"So where are they?" I asked him, indicating the empty room, continuing the script we had set up.

"Damn," Jimmy said. "I was so hoping that this year you would remember."

"Remember what?" I asked.

Jimmy started into his part of the script.

"Three years ago Salina and Percy figured out that you were going to kick her down the road. So they tried to poison you with slug bait."

I shook my head. I needed to pretend I had no memory of any of that. "What happened?"

"You managed to fight them off and get outside and call me and I managed to get you to a hospital. You were in a coma for almost four months."

I said nothing since I had no lines in this play and Jimmy went on talking, telling me a fantastic story that I knew wasn't possible.

Yet part of me wanted to believe it was possible, because it was such a nice story. A lot better than the truth I wanted to believe.

And a ton better than the real truth.

"When Salina and Percy realized you were going to live and they were going to be arrested, they made a run for Mexico. They didn't make it. She's still in jail in California for some crime they did down there and will be for another ten years before coming back up here to face charges for trying to kill you."

Jimmy could really tell a wild story and he had this one very well practiced after the years of telling it to me.

Again I said nothing, staying in the part of a person who couldn't remember anything that happened.

"When you woke up," Jimmy said, "you had only half your stomach left and no memory of anything. You were convinced instead that you and Salina were divorced and that she's completely gone. You just won't seem to believe anything else."

I would have never thought it would have been possible for Salina to try to kill me. I would have never thought the perfect woman in the perfect house with the perfect life had that sort of thing in her. Yet, in the real world, she got rid of everything that wasn't perfect or fixed it, so getting rid of me would have seemed logical to her.

It sure made for a great story for Jimmy to feed me to keep me on stage and solidly in this play.

Jimmy just went on telling me the story that he told me every year at this point. "You've kept this house perfect, just as Salina would have wanted it, even though you never come here except today. Every year, on this day, you come back here to tell her you are kicking her out. And I come with you to help."

I honestly loved this play. It was so real.

And Jimmy made his part of the story very convincing.

"And it happens like this every year?" I asked.

"Every damn year," Jimmy said, answering my question.

He was standing beside me, looking very worried.

"I think I'm going to be all right. The memories of the last few years seem to be coming back."

"Seriously?" Jimmy asked, his square face set in frown lines.

"Yup, I think I remember now," I said. "At least most of it. Still some foggy places."

Jimmy's large brown eyes just looked even more worried.

"So what do you remember?" Jimmy asked. "Everything. Run me through it."

And so the second act of our little play started.

Act Two

"I don't remember Salina serving me the slug bait," I said.

Again, this was just like being in a courtroom defending a client. My beliefs needed to be distant from my actions. I could never allow any belief but the belief I needed that day in court to come to the surface.

And that's the way I was playing this.

"I do remember a doctor telling me that the kind of coma I had gone into can cause some brain damage, especially to memory."

Jimmy nodded, staying on his part of the script and I could feel all this becoming solid and very real.

I smiled at my friend. "I remember you and I were planning on coming here later in the week to catch Salina and Percy doing the bed-sheet mambo and kick them out. But it never happened. Right?"

Jimmy nodded and said nothing.

I looked around the perfectly decorated big house.

And just like I was supposed to do in this part of the story, I did not mention to my best friend that Salina and Percy were behind the shelves in the wine cellar. That was the script. So I went along with the game he and I were playing to bring me back to the world.

We had tried this same game for the last couple years. Same game every year. Same script. We were getting better at it.

This very well might be the year.

"I have no memory of Salina being in jail however. Didn't she and Percy just vanish?"

"They did." Jimmy shrugged. "I've thought that they were better off gone from the start."

"But I do like the story of her being in jail," I said and Jimmy smiled.

If I really had memory issues.

As I did every year at this point in our little play, I asked the question once more. "Any idea where they are?"

Jimmy shook his head.

I looked around. "So why do I keep this place?"

Jimmy shrugged and said his lines perfectly. "Maybe it's because you think Salina and Percy might return if you keep it."

"That's just flat silly," I said, smiling at my friend and getting a smile in return.

I knew for a fact that they had never left.

"So you are making progress," Jimmy said.

"Real progress," I said.

I picked up the mug and put it back in the cabinet.

A place for everything and everything in its place.

Jimmy just nodded and smiled.

Salina and Percy were drinking wine naked the day I walked in on them, four days before I drank the slug poison to cover for me killing them, making people believe they had tried to kill me instead. She loved her wine cellar so much. She and her lover are now happy together down there.

A place for everything and everything in its place.

The wine cellar is a little smaller than it was originally designed, but I doubt anyone will notice.

"That's a hell of a story you tell me every year," I said to Jimmy, pretending I now remembered how much of a story it really was.

"I'll do anything to help," he said.

"Oh, you do help," I said.

And thus started the third act of our little play as we walked out into the afternoon sunshine.

Act Three

Salina and Percy were sitting there, in my car, Percy behind the steering wheel.

Right on schedule, as they always were. Salina did not believe in being late for anything.

I was now in perfect courtroom mode. I was deep in the belief of the case, knew what I had to believe and had tossed out all other beliefs. The ability to do that, stay completely submerged into the play in the courtroom, was why I had won so many cases.

After a moment Salina and Percy got out and started up the walk toward the front door, neither saying a word to the other.

Clearly the sex was going bad between them and poor old Percy was starting to understand what kind of woman he had gotten hooked up with.

Jimmy and I stepped to one side and let them pass, then followed them back into the house.

We had done the same thing every year, but this year I hoped things would be different.

I made myself stop and not think that way. I needed to stay solidly on the script.

"So how come we just don't sell this place?" Percy asked. "We could sure use the money."

I was stunned. They had gone through most of my money and insurance in just three years. That was a lot of money.

I pushed that thought down as well and got back into my belief system.

Salina turned to him and gave him that nasty look she used to give me. "And have someone discover the bodies in the wine cellar?"

"That would be nice," I said.

Jimmy laughed.

Of course Salina and Percy didn't hear me. They just headed for the wine cellar.

Percy pulled the door open and said, "Wow, that's a smell."

Jimmy glanced at me and smiled. He knew at that moment that I had managed to get the slug bait on the heater and turn it on.

"It's in your head," Salina said, pushing past him and going down the stairs. "The bodies can't smell, you fool. We wrapped them up too tightly in layers of plastic and they are behind a very solid wall, remember?"

"How could I ever forget," Percy said, following her.

They went down the narrow stairs to check on where they had buried me and Jimmy behind the wine racks after killing us three years ago today.

I turned to my best friend. "I seemed to have left the door to the wine cellar open in my check of the house."

"Better close it," he said. "You know there are expensive bottles of wine down there you wouldn't want stolen."

So as if I was still playing the game of looking for Salina and her lover, I moved to the wine cellar door, pushed it closed, and locked it.

Everything in its place.

Then I turned off the lights and went to the breaker box and flipped the breaker switch, leaving the breaker for the heater down there on.

Jimmy just cheered beside me.

"Holy crap, we did it!" he shouted, jumping up and down in his excitement.

Actually, I was pretty stunned as well.

I could feel myself smiling and smiling.

The two people who had killed Jimmy and me were now locked with our bodies in the wine cellar in the dark.

And they were breathing very poison air.

A moment later I could hear Percy banging on the door shouting to be let out. His voice did not sound like he was much in control.

Behind him I heard Salina coughing. Then she said, "Idiot! Why did you pull the door closed behind you?"

"I didn't," Percy said, his voice a couple octaves higher than normal.

Salina coughed a few more times, then said, "Break it down, you fool."

The door pounded hard, but I remembered that when we had that wine cellar built, Salina wanted the best material and the best locks since we were going to have a lot of expensive wine down there.

She had said that many, many times to me during construction and in the arguments leading up to construction.

So the door held and then after a moment there was a loud crashing sound as two bodies tumbled back down the stairs.

And then it was silent.

"I'll be," Jimmy said, laughing. "We did it! We actually did it!"

I could feel this immense sense of satisfaction. Three years of practicing the scripts to make sure I felt connected to the real world. Three years of returning here to this house I hated on the day she had killed me and my best friend. We had caught her making love to Percy, but we didn't expect the gun she had bought and had in the drawer beside her.

And I didn't know about her trips to the gun range to learn how to use the thing.

Three years waiting for revenge.

And now it was here.

Outside I could hear the faint sounds of a siren headed this way.

"She got off a 911 call," Jimmy said, suddenly looking worried again.

"They won't be alive by the time the police find them," I said, smiling at my best friend.

"I hope you are right," he said.

"I am," I said. "Head back to your waiting spot for a minute, would you? We need to start the play over just one more time. I want to make sure they find our bodies as well."

He looked puzzled, but just nodded and then vanished.

A moment later his voice came over my phone inside my suit coat. "I'm here if you need me."

I said in the general direction of my pocket, "Listen and enjoy."

I put myself back in the courtroom, back in the belief that I was alive and could actually move physical objects without thinking about it.

I believed it more than I had ever believed in a case.

I was here to look for Salina and Percy in bed together.

I looked around the home I hated, then moved over to the front door and opened it and left it standing open for Jimmy to come in. Just in case I had trouble when I found Salina and Percy in bed together.

Staying solidly in my belief of where and when I was, I went back through the house, looking for Salina and her boyfriend. Making sure that with every thought, every belief, I would find them alive and making love.

Of course, I didn't find them.

As I finished my search of the back bedrooms, I heard a call from the front door. "Police! Anyone here?"

I had heard no sounds at all from the wine cellar in almost five minutes. So on the way toward the front I clicked back on the breaker lights for the wine cellar.

Then focusing as hard as I could to stay in the act of our little play and not get caught for murdering my wife and her lover and putting their bodies behind the wine racks, I went forward to greet the police.

I had to play this one perfectly. Just like a summary statement in front of a jury.

I had done it a thousand times. Once more, with flourish this time.

"Hello," I said and two young cops both turned to me.

Wow, they were making patrol officers young these days. Both looked like they were right out of college, if that. One even had a face of pimples.

I pointed at the door just off the kitchen. "My wife and her boyfriend are dead down there in the wine cellar."

They both just looked at me, clearly stunned and trying to process what I had just said. Then the one with the bad skin said, "Did you do it?"

What a stupid question for a policeman to ask, but I was glad he did. He played right into my plan perfectly.

"Of course I did," I said. "I killed them. But there are two bodies behind one of the wine racks that she killed. Make sure you take care of those as well."

Then, while they stood there stunned, I walked for the last time out the front door of the house Salina built and I had come to hate.

"Hey, wait a minute!" one cop said behind me and turned to follow.

But I was gone.

"Where did he go?" the one cop asked.

Quickly they went in different directions around the house, looking for me while calling in for backup.

But they would never find me, at least this part of me. I hoped they found my body down there behind the wine rack.

But this part of me was back in my reality. I was off stage, out of the belief that I had needed to touch the few things I had needed to touch. I knew and believed now that I was only a ghost.

And beside me, Jimmy was laughing.

"Well played," he said. "Who knew you could act like that."

"I'm a trial lawyer, remember," I said. "I can believe anything if I really need to."

"Oh, yeah," he said. "Who would have thought as a ghost I would need a lawyer."

Laughing, we turned and walked down Bryant Street.

I had no idea where we were going, but anywhere was better than staying in that home with that woman.

I Killed Jessie Took

Dean Wesley Smith

One

I take out human garbage. It's what I do.

Since my former employer decided that I needed to be taken out as garbage as well, I have gone freelance. It was never difficult for me to go freelance, since I had saved almost every penny of all the millions I had earned from all my garbage runs for them. My former employer never really ever knew who I was or where I was or where I was based.

I had always made sure of that.

My real name is long lost in the past. As are my real looks.

I only had contact with my former employer from a distance when getting an assignment and when reporting in that the garbage was removed. I was always paid through accounts that only existed for each job and then vanished and could not be traced back to me or any business associated with me.

My former employer didn't even know what I looked like exactly. I had made sure of that with changing looks for every assignment.

I could do little about my six-foot height, but I changed hair color, facial features, walk, and other features with simple disguises and a vast amount of training.

I am also an expert in the modern computer age. I can make an identity appear and disappear at will. I can change identities easily, and study my targets carefully.

Before being a freelance human garbage collector, I never felt any need to record my job. It was just a job, after all.

But now, as a freelancer, I have decided to record these events in a case-by-case nature.

And since my first official case on my own had actually been my last for my former employer, I have recorded it under the case title "I Killed Adam Chaser."

Granted, my former employer did transfer my standard four-point-one million to my accounts after the initial job was finished, but I considered that a freelance fee in killing the agent they sent to kill me. Seemed only a fair trade.

I unofficially call my little business "I Killed..." I could think of no name that suited "Garbage Man for Human Waste" that I liked. So simply "I Killed..." But no one would ever be able to track it under that name or any other name.

I am that good.

This, my first job after becoming a freelance human garbage man, taking out the human waste of society, I will call "I Killed Jessie Took."

The reason for that, I decided, was to track easily what each case is about. The target's original name is Jessie Took, but he went by Joe Harley in Portland, Oregon.

And I know for a fact that this case will also involve my former employer. It must.

It is the nature of my former employee, to leave nothing unfinished. I am a very unfinished business they cannot leave open.

I must be killed. I must be taken to the curb.

I welcome their involvement.

And they have presented me this Jessie Took, my first freelance case, like it's tied up in a bow, a bow they know I will not resist.

They believe that sometimes garbage men must be taken to the curb as well.

I've killed other garbage men in the past; I can do it again if they force my hand.

Which, of course, they will do.

Two

Unlike when I worked for my former employer, I am fed no information on which garbage needs to be taken out. So over the last year, since the Adam Chaser case, I developed a method of searching for unsolved crimes, of criminals going free for various reasons, of simple "talk" about a person.

One series of unsolved teenage girl disappearances came to light, seeming to string across the country from Michigan to Oregon. They did not seem to be related and each remained active cases in their local areas.

But since I was looking at patterns as my former employer knew I would, the cases came together for me fairly clearly. Each girl was sixteen, each brunette, each had slight problems in school, often with minor drugs and boys.

And each had brown eyes.

Seven missing teenage girls in seven years. A trail leading to Portland, Oregon, like a neon arrow as far as I was concerned.

Right back to the same town of my first freelance case, my last working assignment that became "I Killed Adam Chaser."

That seemed to tell me that more than likely my former employer had set this up, made it clear, to attract me like a bee to a flower.

It would not matter. They could keep sending agents and I would keep helping them remove that agent from their workforce.

But before I could have that looked-forward-to meeting with another garbage man or woman, I needed to find who was taking the girls and why. I was sure my former employer already knew.

So for each girl's disappearance, I searched for the one common denominator that held that trail together. That took me almost four months of searching from my Las Vegas home near the University of Nevada.

Of course, my research could not be traced in any fashion.

I spotted a few attempts to backtrack on my traces, but they were blocked easily.

What became the clear connection in all the disappearances was a yard maintenance man who went under a different name in every town. He seemed about twenty-five, had short brown hair, a slight moustache, and dark eyes that seemed to see everything. And they looked hungry.

I could find no picture of him in any fashion where he was smiling. Even in security camera footage, stoplight security cameras, and so on.

He never smiled.

He worked for different yard maintenance firms in every city, always under different names, and always quit early in the fall to move on. Always a month before a girl disappeared.

He had been born and raised under the name Jessie Ben Took in Lansing, Michigan. Right out of high school he had started working yard maintenance and he had left two months before a popular girl from his former high school had gone missing. The reports of her disappearance never mentioned his name in any way since he was already out of town and living outside of Madison, Wisconsin.

Every fall he moved on. A month or so later a girl went missing from his former town.

It was a trail I could not miss.

And my former employers would know that if I remained freelance, I would not miss it.

So I went back to Portland, Oregon, changing identities as I traveled and setting up escape routes.

The day I finally settled into Portland was a warm early-summer day, the leaves green, and the air smelling of open restaurants baking bread. The apartment I found was in the Northwest section of Portland with a slight view down the street of the river and one of the many bridges.

The apartment had large windows and too much light. It was on the second floor of an old Victorian that had been divided into four apartments, plus a manager's apartment on the main floor.

I went in under the name Nick Benson, an engineer from Idaho brought in to work on a new building down on the riverfront. I told the woman with large sixties' gray hair who was the landlord that I would be in and out of town a great deal and not to worry. I paid her four months in advance, which she liked.

The apartment was directly across the tree-shaded street from Jessie's apartment in a small ten-apartment complex that had been built in the mid 1960s out of cinder blocks and concrete stairs.

I bugged his small two-bedroom apartment one afternoon when he was at work, filled his walls with tiny cameras that looked like fly specks so there was no place in the apartment I couldn't see.

Then I put a few cameras in my apartment as well and rented another house a quick train-ride and identity change away. The second apartment was in a complex similar to Jessie's and the apartment had a very clear method of entry that required me to climb a flight of stairs.

The cameras in Jessie's walls any agent from my former employer would recognize. They would know I was here.

The ones in my apartment in the old Victorian were far better hidden and the signals could not be traced in any fashion. I wanted to know when my former employer's agent came snooping around my apartment.

But I knew they were already here. This had been a set-up, of that there was no doubt. They were well-trained in situational death, otherwise one of them would have attempted to kill me the first moment they realized who I was.

But as I said, they would work to cover their tracks. It was the nature of the business they worked for.

I doubted my employer had yet to realize I no longer needed to follow those same rules.

In my second apartment, as one more level of protection, I rented under a corporation name the empty apartment under my second apartment. That had a number of varied exits through a back door and a couple windows. I cut a hidden escape hatch through the closet floor of my second apartment to the third apartment's closet.

Then, protected with a number of back-up plans, I went about the business of making sure that Jessie Ben Took, maintenance man from Lansing, Michigan, really was responsible for all of the disappearances of the girls.

It became clear in very short order that he was human garbage that really, really needed to be taken out. He had a notebook hidden in his apartment of pictures of all the girls. All of them were nude and he was posing with all of them.

Typical of sick humans like him, he kept trophies.

All of them were the old Kodak-style prints. And I found an old camera in his apartment as well.

I captured each of the images, then spent the next day checking that none of them had been faked, that the locations and times were accurate. I did not put it past my former employer to set up an innocent man.

But with very little research, it became clear that Jessie was far from innocent. He spent a night a week poring over that notebook and reliving sexual acts he must have performed on each girl.

So I was the major target in this game and he was just a bonus.

So I spent the next few days tracing back through his employment in a new town, searching for where the girl's body would be buried. It made sense that since he worked yard maintenance and landscape work, he would bury the girl when he was finished with her in one of his projects.

He clearly had no young girl in his apartment across from my Victorian apartment, so I started tracing him. His last victim had been a girl from Boise. I doubted she would still be alive since it had been six months since she had been taken, but there might be a chance.

I found in a quick search, under his mother's maiden name, a storage locker that had been rented outside of Portland off of I-84.

I watched the rental for a few days to make sure it was not a trap by my former employers. They were not there and he did not visit the unit at all.

So after two days I moved in so that no security camera could see me and I opened the storage unit.

She was there.

In a large wooden crate inside the unit, with high levels of soundproofing covering the inside. She wasn't dead, but she might as well have been. She would be in another day at most. He had left her tied up and gagged to starve to death.

Now I was very, very angry at my former employee. They were willing to let this young girl die just to get me.

This had to end, and end now.

Three

I left, locked everything back up, and made sure I was not seen when leaving.

Then, from a secure phone, I called the police and told them where they would find the poor young girl from Boise and who she was. She would survive.

That left me only a few hours at most. Jessie wasn't good at covering his tracks and clearly would be identified and quickly arrested. So I needed to move fast and take care of my former employer's agents.

I went back to my Victorian apartment and made sure no one had been in. I knew no one would be, but better to be safe. My former employer had sat this trap up a long time in advance.

I had to admit, it was a well-done trap. And if I hadn't been expecting it, I would have walked right into it.

I set the signal to self-destruct all my cameras in Jessie's apartment and the Victorian apartment.

On the way out, carrying a suitcase with everything I would need to make my escape clean, I knocked on my landlord's door and told her that I would be gone for a few weeks on a trip to Boise.

To any other agent, that would be the signal that I was leaving and she had to act and act fast.

"I've got a package that came for you today," she said, turning away from me.

She should have been ready for me. Sloppy work.

I put a bullet in the back of her head.

Actually, she should have shot me the first moment she saw me. But my former employer had taught all its agents, including me, to play out the scene and cover tracks. She had lived, and now died, by that rule.

I glanced around. No one had seen.

My sound-suppresser was good and the shot had not been heard.

I quickly pushed her body back inside and closed the door. Her computer had cameras all over the building next door. And as I had suspected, the young guy in the apartment next to Jessie's apartment was the second agent on this job.

He was asleep in his apartment.

I sent a coded message from her computer to my former employer that said simply, "The garbage has been taken out."

That was a signal that she should be paid.

That I was dead.

I gave them an account number as was standard.

I made sure that the ten million and change she was paid was moved out of that account quickly and shuttled around so that it couldn't be traced. It would eventually land in accounts I controlled, but could not be traced back to me in Las Vegas.

She would have instantly moved the money as well if she had been a good agent.

She had been far higher paid than I had ever been. That meant she was in charge of this entire hunt for me. And that meant that more than likely there was more than just a second agent. Otherwise her pay would not have been so high.

I hadn't expected to make any money on this job, but a few extra million would make up for the extra mess I was being forced to cause.

Then I triggered her computer to self-destruct and destroy all her cameras in both buildings.

As I turned to leave, I could see that the mask over her face had been blown partially off her face by my shot. She had been far more beautiful than her disguise had played.

And far younger.

The local police were going to have a field day with this one. I wonder what happened to the actual landlady of this building.

I walked across the street and up to the location of Jessie's apartment. I knew for a fact the other agent was asleep. The two agents slept in shifts as they had been trained.

Just to be sure, I planted a few small explosive charges along the staircase. Blinding charges. In case I missed a third agent, I didn't want to be surprised and caught without a defense in this hallway.

I entered the second agent's small apartment very silently and put two bullets in him before he could even roll over.

Then I went to his computer and sent the same coded message to my former employer.

"The garbage has been taken out."

I moved another four million that was his payment to my accounts, then set his computer to self-destruct, along with all the cameras he had set up from that computer.

Two down, one to go. This was a lot of trips to the curb.

A lot of human garbage to haul.

As I stepped into the hallway, I saw Jessie coming up the stairs.

And my little voice rang out clearly.

My former employer had already killed Jessie and had replaced him with a disguised agent as bait.

Of course.

This Jessie was smiling. The original Jessie never smiled.

And this agent was pulling out a gun as he saw me.

The tiny button in my left hand instantly triggered the string explosives across the stairs and I dropped to the concrete entrance floor.

The small, but bright and violent, explosion sent the agent back as he fired and tried to catch his balance at the same time.

His shots went over me and into the old wood siding behind me. I put two in his chest and another between his eyes before he could get off a third shot.

He was dead before he hit the bottom of the stairs.

My small explosions were also designed to start a heavy-smoke fire.

I went down the stairs quickly, moving through the smoke and out into the street, my gun now hidden in my suit-coat pocket, but my hand on it.

The day was warming up by the moment and the heat on the street was more than I had noticed the first time across.

I pretended to cough and stagger to the far side of the street and the mowed lawns there, keeping my head down as neighbors came running.

"Fire," I said, pointing at the smoke now pouring out of the staircase of the building while keeping my head down and then again pretending to cough.

I had to be really, really careful in case there was a fourth agent close by.

Around me a dozen people were on their cell phones and two men were running at the building while another man was banging on apartment doors on the ground floor.

The fire I had set wouldn't spread, but they didn't know that.

"You all right, mister?" a woman asked.

I didn't want to look up, but I had to.

I stood and nodded, taking a deep breath of the warm Portland afternoon air.

The woman had a cell phone against her ear and as I looked at her and nodded, I saw a flicker of recognition cross her eyes.

She was young and I had surprised her. She did not expect to be talking with me.

Her hand went for her jacket pocket and I put one shot through my jacket pocket into her forehead.

She slumped and I caught her, pulling her over toward the shade of a nearby tree, talking to her as if she had just grown faint from the heat.

The wound in her forehead wasn't bleeding much, so I pulled her medium length hair from her wig down over her forehead and sat her down on a bus stop bench and posed her with her head between her knees, talking with her all the time as if I was trying to calm her.

I quickly slipped her gun from her pocket and put it in mine.

Then I pointed to a young guy about twenty feet away standing watching the fire, holding his bike that he clearly had been riding.

"She fainted," I shouted. "She's going to be all right. I'm going to get her meds for her. Watch her, would you?"

The guy nodded, looking at her as I turned and went toward the Victorian house with my apartment in it.

Walking quickly and still carrying my case, as if I was in a hurry to get her meds, I went inside and then through and into a back corridor. There I lost the coat and the brown hair and the slacks, switching them out for a pair of jeans and a light Levi jacket.

When I ambled out the back door I had long blonde hair flowing out of the back of a Oregon Ducks baseball cap. Any sign of Nick Benson, the former engineer from Boise, was gone.

I unlocked a used Jeep I had bought and parked a dozen blocks away as the sounds of police and fire sirens filled the afternoon air. I drove it to a Mongolian restaurant in Tigard, Oregon, about five miles outside of Portland.

I parked the Jeep down the street from the restaurant near some suburban homes and behind a new Dodge minivan that I had bought as well under yet a different name.

Then in the bathroom of the restaurant, I lost the Levi jacket and the long blonde hair and replaced it with gray hair pulled back under a plain gray baseball cap, different color contacts for my eyes, and padded shoulders in a sports jacket over the jeans.

I collapsed the small suitcase I had been carrying and put it inside a brown backpack.

I sat and ate, then paid with the credit card of my new name, Dan Curtis. After an amazingly good meal, I climbed into the mini-van and headed for Salt Lake City, going through Bend, Oregon, and across the desert.

Salt Lake was where the identity of Dan Curtis was from.

Two days later, Dan vanished there, never to be seen or heard of again.

Driving my three-year-old Cadillac, I headed back to Las Vegas and my teaching job at the university. I was a tenured professor in prelaw and law enforcement.

And I was a garbage man on the side, between semesters.

I took out the human garbage.

And sometimes that included other garbage men.

The Road Back

A Doc Hill Story

Dean Wesley Smith

When you are short-stacked in poker,
and in life, the road back
to being in contention
often has a very sudden end.

ONE

"Do we have any idea where he might be?" I asked Annie over my shoulder.

She had crouched down behind my chair at the no-limit ring game I had joined a few hours before at the Bellagio. I was almost a thousand up and had been enjoying the game as a warm-up for a series of poker tournaments coming later in the week to the Bellagio.

I seldom played regular ring games anymore, only tournaments. But at times it felt right to just sit and play for a time. This hot September afternoon was one of those times to relax in the air-conditioned poker room and drink iced tea and win a little money in the process.

"Not a clue," she said. "Dad's got all the information."

Annie had her long brown hair pulled back and the white blouse and dark slacks she wore accented her perfect body. She was the best-looking *former* Las Vegas detective I had ever met, with brown eyes that could stare through to your soul. Actually, she was one of the best-looking women I had ever met, and also one of most deadly poker players in the modern game.

In the year we had been together, she had taken down a dozen tournaments and won two World Series of Poker bracelets for two different events.

Now she wanted my help to find some guy her dad thought was missing. Actually, her dad, Detective Bayard Lott, also a former Las Vegas police detective, wanted her help and she was asking if I would help out as well.

"You want me to deal you in, Doc?" the dealer asked.

"No, thanks, Al," I said, pushing back from the table as Annie stood and stepped back. I flipped him a twenty-five dollar chip and he tapped it and nodded thanks before slipping it into his tip slot.

I turned and nodded to Ben, the brush in charge of the room at the moment who was headed my way from the poker room desk.

"Cash you out?" he asked.

I flipped him a twenty-five dollar chip as well and said, "Thanks. Just add it to the account."

I had had a running account at the Bellagio for almost ten years now. Made it easier than hauling racks of chips to the cage all the time. And after the two tips, I had five hundred in starting money in my stack and another eight hundred and fifty in winnings.

My chip vanished into Ben's pocket and he worked to rack the rest as I turned and headed with Annie out of the poker room and into the noise and bells of customers filling the slots.

"Dinner?" I asked, realizing I was starting to get hungry as we turned toward the front of the casino.

"Dad's meeting us in the Café Bellagio," she said.

I laughed, taking her hand. "You were pretty sure I was going to help you, huh?"

"Not really," she said, smiling at me as we wound our way through the people toward the restaurant. "I would have gotten the information from Dad and told you later if you were really interested in staying in the game."

"It was enough warm-up," I said. "More than enough, actually."

"Lucky for those guys at the table," she said, laughing. "You warm-up much more and they would have been broke."

"That's the point, isn't it?" I asked.

She agreed and then waved at her father sitting at a semi-private four-person table off to one side of the café where it looked out over the pool. The smell of hamburgers and steaks drifted from the direction of the kitchen and my stomach rumbled. I really was hungrier than I had realized.

I liked her dad a great deal. He looked pretty sharp for his sixty-three years with short-cut white hair, broad shoulders, and only a hint of a gut around his stomach. He had a wicked sense of humor and his laugh could start an entire room laughing with him.

He and a bunch of his retired detective friends played poker every week in the basement of his house and worked to solve cold cases for the Las Vegas Police Department on the side. They called themselves the Cold Poker Gang. Annie and I helped them when we could.

But from what Annie said, this didn't sound like a cold case. More like a missing person problem. And in Vegas, there were always a lot of those.

For all sorts of reasons.

Two

I was into my rib steak and onion rings, Annie was picking at her hamburger, and her dad was about halfway done with his French Dip before Annie finally broached the subject.

"So who is missing and why are you involved, Dad?"

"Steve Benson Junior," he said between bites.

Both Annie and I glanced at him.

Finally Annie asked exactly what I was thinking. "The son of Chief of Police Steven Benson?"

"One and the same," her dad said. "Chief Benson called me, asked if I would look into it for him."

"He thinks his son is in trouble?" I asked.

Annie's dad shook his head. "Not that kind of trouble. He's a good kid, graduate student at UNLV focusing on Nevada history. But his dad this morning went to meet him for breakfast and Steve didn't show up. Steve's best friend hasn't seen him either."

"And his dad's worried?" Annie asked.

"I would be too," her father said, smiling at her. "Steve is like you in that he calls when he has to cancel something."

"He have a car?" I asked.

"Red Jeep SUV," he said. "About a year old. It's missing as well."

"So he went somewhere and hasn't returned yet," Annie said. "More than likely he's fine."

Her dad nodded. "That's what the Chief thinks as well, but he's still worried. Steve's cell isn't picking up. I think that's really why the Chief called me. He doesn't want this out yet, so he's just calling in personal favors at the moment."

I sat back munching on a crisp onion ring, thinking. My little voice was telling me that something was wrong with this kid. I didn't know him and I didn't know his father, but this felt wrong for some reason I couldn't put my finger on.

However, when at a poker table, I had learned to trust that little voice when it told me something was wrong with a play another player made. And in life I had also learned to trust that voice. And right now the very same voice was telling me we needed to move on this and fast.

I finished the onion ring and leaned forward toward Annie's dad. "Could you call the chief and ask him if Steve is back yet? And if not, could we go look at his apartment?"

Detective Lott slid the key across the table at me, smiling. "Steve wasn't back five minutes before you two showed up, and I got this key from the Chief before coming over here."

I just shook my head and grinned as Annie patted her father's arm, smiling. It was no wonder the guy had been such a great detective in his day. He was a half step ahead of everything.

Three

Steve's apartment near the university seemed far neater than I would have expected a grad student's apartment to be. And it was clear with only a quick look that there was nothing at all out of place.

Nothing.

The apartment had one bedroom with a living room with only a couch and chair and a large desk in it. A small, clean dining room table with four chairs sat near the open kitchen. There was a bathroom off the bedroom.

There was no sign at all of any woman's touch in here. Everything was standard apartment except the large computer on an L-shaped desk on the left side of the living room and large wall of books on the right side, mostly textbooks that at a glance I was glad I never would have to read. My college days were a long ways behind me now.

However, one full shelf was full of books on various aspects of Nevada history that looked very interesting, from the gold rush towns to railroad history to the founding of Las Vegas.

All of them in perfect order by author.

Annie was looking through Steve's desk. There were a couple of books open on the desk on Nevada place names and another on lost mines of Nevada.

"Can you access that computer?" I asked Annie. "See what he was researching before he left?"

"If it's not password protected," she said, sitting down in the chair and moving the wireless keyboard closer toward her.

Her father came out of the bathroom shaking his head. "This kid is the cleanest kid I have ever seen. Nothing out of place, no sign that anyone else but him even visited here. Not even a hair on his comb."

"He folds his socks and underwear," I said. "His bed is made, even though he slept in it recently. And he washed his breakfast dishes before he left, more than likely yesterday morning, since the dishes are completely dry as is the dish towel."

Annie brought the computer up and then shook her head. "Protected."

"He's going to have a password book," I said. "Upper drawer on the left."

She opened the drawer and pulled out a small notebook, shaking her head. "How did you know that?"

"Someone like Steve is completely predictable. Every move, every detail. It's how his mind works. He has no choice."

"Easy pickings on a poker table," Annie said.

"He'd never sit down at one," I said. "He wouldn't be able to handle the uncertainty that comes naturally with the game."

"Obsessive-compulsive?" Annie's dad asked.

"Borderline," Annie said, nodding. "It goes toward hoarding or being neat freaks."

"We know which way Steve goes," I said.

As Annie worked on the computer and bringing up the history, I went back into the small apartment bedroom. Steve had his shoes lined up perfectly along the bottom of his closet, from dress shoes through tennis shoes to boots. There was an empty spot between a pair of tennis shoes and a heavy pair of boots. That's where he would put his hiking boots.

His shirts were lined up hanging in his closet and there was a clear opening where a light casual shirt had clearly hung. More than likely brown from the patterns of the colors.

I went into the bathroom and opened the medicine chest. There was an empty spot where a tube of suntan lotion would have sat right between a small jar of Vaseline and a tube of blister cream.

I closed the cabinet and went back into the living room with the desk and books. "He's gone into the desert. More than likely yesterday morning. My guess is he was planning on returning before dark last night and something happened."

Annie's dad looked around at the apartment. "I can see why the Chief was worried, now."

"Got it," Annie said, moving back through the history of what Steve had last looked at on his computer.

The very last thing was a map of an area of the Nevada desert to the north and west of Las Vegas along Highway 95.

"Skeleton Mountains," Annie said, hitting a button to print up the map just as I was sure Steve had done.

One of the books open on the desk referred to the area as well, and I picked it up as Annie kept going back through the history on the computer.

Seems the Skeleton Mountains were a group of rocky peaks sticking up out of the desert about ten miles to the west of the highway. The article said that no one knew exactly how it got its name. From what I could tell in the book, the rocky peaks had just always been named that.

And they weren't that big, with the largest being not more than six or seven hundred feet off the desert. Compared to the mountains I spent the summer in every year in central Idaho, guiding rafts on the River of No Return, these Skeleton Mountains were nothing more than large piles of rocks.

"He was researching some old patented mining claims in those mountains," Annie said, again hitting the print button. "All of them are long dormant and never produced anything of real value."

"So we know where he went," Annie's father said, nodding.

"Get a search team set up from the Chief," I said to him as Annie printed a second copy of the map of the small group of mountains.

"Where are you going?" Annie's dad asked, as he pulled out his phone.

"Fleet's in town and he loves testing out his new helicopter," I said, and Annie laughed. "He'll get us up there and we'll see what we can see from the air, see if we can spot his car before you and the Chief get there."

I was on the phone to my best friend and business partner, Fleet, and Annie's father was talking with the Chief of Police as we headed out into the hot early evening air and Annie pulled the door to the apartment closed behind us.

FOUR

Fleet lived in Boise with his family. Annie and I had a house there as well, but unlike Fleet, we were seldom in Boise. Fleet had a wonderful wife and two kids there, but at the moment they were all here, letting the kids have one last vacation before school started up again.

Fleet had decided that our company needed a helicopter to go along with our own private jet. It seemed that over the years, his investments of my poker winnings had made us, as he said, stupidly rich. We gave millions away to charity every year and spent what we wanted and somehow just managed to get richer.

Fleet was that good with business and investments.

My father's death a year ago had just added more millions than I wanted to think about into the picture.

When Fleet bought the jet helicopter for the company, he had decided he wanted to fly it, much to his wife's horror. And in the last year he had become a very good pilot.

On the phone I told him what was going on and he almost beat us to the airport, even though we had a shorter distance to go. Any excuse to take out the helicopter was a great idea as far as he was concerned.

Within forty minutes after leaving Steve's apartment, we were airborne and headed for the Skeleton Mountains, the loud drone of the chopper a constant noise around us.

"So what do you think we're going to find?" Fleet asked through the communications links we all wore.

Annie was in the co-pilot chair because she had taken a few lessons with the chopper last year. I was behind them, strapped in tight. I wasn't afraid of flying, but I had to admit having my friend from childhood doing the flying didn't instill great confidence, even though he had a lot of hours in the air already.

"Besides rocks and snakes?" Annie asked.

She moved slightly so I could see the wink she gave me.

I smiled. Fleet was deathly afraid of snakes. Any kind and size of snake, actually. And everyone knew it.

"Not funny," he said.

"If we have to land, you can stay in the chopper," I said. "There will be snakes."

Fleet shook his head. "You two sure know how to kill a good flight."

Less than fifteen minutes after leaving the Las Vegas airport, the mountains sort of rose from the rolling desert floor in front of us. They were sure nothing to look at. Mostly rocks and scattered open areas covered in scrub brush. I hadn't been kidding Fleet. Those rocks would be infested with snakes, since it was clear the area got little or no attention by humans at all.

"Come in from Highway 95," I said to Fleet. "See if you can spot a road into those mountains."

Fleet nodded and slowed until Annie pointed ahead.

A bare excuse of a dirt road left the highway and wound toward the mountains.

Fleet banked over it and followed the road, moving slowly as we all studied the area.

There was no place to hide below us at all. Just open desert and scrub.

Up ahead the road started to wind up a small canyon and then seemed to break out into an open flat area before going back into another canyon and deeper into the piles of rocks laughingly called mountains.

Nothing but huge rocks and scrub brush.

"On the right," Annie said, pointing.

It took me a moment, but finally I saw what she was pointing at. A glint of the sun reflected off some metal. At closer look I could see hints of a red car hidden beside a rock and covered with scrub brush. Someone had spent a lot of time in the task of hiding the car and had the car off the road so it couldn't be seen by anyone driving in.

"Someone really wanted that hidden," Fleet said, shaking his head.

My stomach was twisting like my rib steak was suddenly not agreeing with me.

"Same speed," I said to Fleet. "Just keep going straight and off into the desert on the other side of the mountains."

"Like we're on Fleet's tour of the desert," he said and did as he was told.

Annie had her cell phone to her ear as all of us watched the ground below. To the right of our flight path I could see a trail going up to what looked to be an old mine entrance. There was no sign of anyone there, but that meant nothing.

Then, near where the dirt road came out the other side of another rock canyon and started across the desert, I spotted an old pickup truck parked under a rock outcropping. It was brown and clearly dusty and blended in perfectly with the rocks.

"Truck on the right," I said as we went past and out into the desert just as if we were a sightseeing chopper doing nothing unusual.

"Get us away from these rocks and turn back toward Vegas until we are completely out of sight," I said to Fleet.

"Looks like the kid found some real problems he didn't expect in there," Fleet said.

"Dad," Annie said into her cell. "We found Steve's car, but looks like he's in trouble with someone living in an old mine in the Skeleton Mountains."

She waited for a second. "They hid his car," she said. "Spent a lot of time doing so, actually."

Again a pause as her father said something on the other side of the conversation that I couldn't hear.

"There is," Annie said. "A brown pickup, dirty, also hidden. We've moved away from the mountains to not spook anyone in there."

Then she gave a description of the truck to her father.

This one-sided conversation was driving me crazy. I had a hunch that the longer we delayed, the less chance Steve was going to make it. He had clearly walked into something ugly. You don't go to that much trouble to hide a person's car if you ever plan on letting them leave.

She nodded for a long minute, then she glanced at me, her brown eyes big. Then she said, simply, "Shit."

Then she hung up.

Fleet had the chopper flying low over the desert and had turned back for Vegas. We were out of both hearing and sight of the mountains.

"Dad and the Chief and a bunch of Vegas police and the State Police are all coming hard and silent from all directions. They are going to button up all ways in and out of that group of mountains."

"What did he say?" Fleet asked just before I could.

"A brown truck matching the description of the one back there has been connected to a string of disappearances. Maybe up to a dozen women going back years."

Now the steak in my stomach was really twisting around. Steve really had stumbled into something far, far bigger than he could handle.

"Take us back up to where the road into the mountains hits Highway 95," I said to Fleet. "Drop us off there and then make a wide circle out and around the rocks to the other side and out of sight and watch the road on that side. We don't want this guy getting away before the police get here."

Fleet nodded and two minutes later had us on the ground next to the highway. Then he lifted off and swung back to Vegas, climbing and moving fast.

I had tossed in an older twenty-two Remington saddle rifle from my car in case we needed to take out a couple of snakes and Annie had brought along her revolver. We had both grabbed bottles of water.

The air around us was hot, and there were very few cars passing by on the highway. The sun was low on the horizon, but not low enough to cut off the heat. It would be dark in less than two hours.

As Fleet vanished and the sound of the chopper faded off, Annie pulled out her phone to call her dad.

She told him what we had done and then asked how far out they were. As she listened to the answer, she shook her head.

"They are still a good fifteen minutes out," she told me. "And it will be thirty minutes or longer before they can have the entire place locked down from all sides.

I glanced at the half mile of road between us and the first edge of the rocks they called Skeleton Mountains. I wasn't sure that Steve had that long. If the guy had a police scanner, he would know the police were on the way.

I glanced at Annie and she could read my mind. She nodded and then said to her dad. "We're going in on foot. Warn everyone we're in there. And don't put that on the scanner."

Then before her father could object, she clicked off the phone and tucked it in her pants pocket.

"Up for a jog?" I asked.

"Why not?" she said, smiling as she made sure the clip in her gun was in place and ready. "Seems like a perfect evening for some exercise."

I knew there was a reason I loved this woman.

FIVE

It took us less than five minutes to run the length of the dirt road to the edge of the first rock canyon. It was a tough and hot run since we both had to keep looking ahead and also down at our feet to watch ruts and rocks that could twist an ankle.

We slowed as we entered the shadows of the canyon and walked, both of us drinking from our water bottles.

The rocks towered a good hundred feet over the road that ran up a wash. Annie watched the left side, I watched the right.

And I had been right about snakes. A couple nasty Speckled Rattlesnakes lay on rocks. As we approached, they slipped down into the brush. Both of them were large, far larger than I had seen in some time, actually.

In Idaho, as a guide on the summer rafting trips on the River of No Return, I warned people away from climbing the rocks near the river. The rattlers there were much smaller, but could still ruin a good rafting trip if you cornered them or got too close.

The road came out of the rocks and opened up through an open area a quarter mile across before ducking back into the rocks on the other side. Steve's Jeep was hidden to the right about a hundred yards into that canyon ahead.

We stopped, still in the shadows and both took another long drink. Then we left the bottles beside the road. I had a hunch we were going to need our hands free from here on out.

I glanced at my watch. Eight minutes had passed since we left the highway.

"You ready?" I asked?

She nodded.

Running low, bent over, we headed out into the sun and across the open area. I kept expecting to hear a shot or something, but we made it quickly to the shade of the other canyon, both of us panting.

From there we slowed to a walk, Annie again watching the right walls of rock while I watched the left.

As we got even with where Steve's Jeep was hidden, Annie pointed it out. No one would have ever seen it simply driving this dirt path up this narrow canyon between all the rocks.

We kept moving up the road and within a minute we were at the place where the path left the road through some scrub and up a narrow cut in the rocks toward what looked to be an open mine.

"Got any ideas?" Annie asked as we stopped in the shadows and studied the path.

"Nothing," I said. "Trying to climb these snake-infested rocks to get up there another way would be suicidal."

"Going up that trail won't be very healthy, either," Annie said, studying the trail up to the mine opening a hundred feet above us. "It would be like shooting ducks in a pond for anyone above."

We both stood there, with not an idea in the world between us. The heat of the day had really baked the rocks around us and even though we were in the shade, everything was just radiating heat. I would have bet the temperature was a good hundred and twenty and there wasn't a breath of wind. Sweat dried so fast it left my skin feeling coated in dust and salt.

Annie took out her cell phone, then shook her head and put it back.

Then an idea hit me. "Car alarm."

Annie glanced at me, puzzled and listening. There was no sound at all out here in the desert in these rocks.

"Steve's car," I said. "I'm going to go back and see if I can set off that car alarm. If the guy up there doesn't know anyone is on the way to look for him, he's going to come out thinking a snake set it off or something."

"Good idea," she said.

"Don't let him get back in that cave or Steve is dead."

She nodded and glanced around for a place to hide. I started back down the road and behind me she whispered, "Watch out for snakes."

"You too," I whispered back.

Actually, snakes were my biggest concern with this entire plan. With brush all over that Jeep, there could be a dozen rattlers in there already, both in the car, in the engine, and under it. The car formed a perfect snake cave and I wasn't looking forward at all to wading in there.

I spotted a long piece of brush in the ditch beside the road and grabbed it. It was a good six feet long and sturdy. A rattler needed to get within four feet to strike, maybe more if they were big ones like we had seen coming in.

I glanced at my watch as I neared the Jeep's hiding place beside the road. Annie's dad and the State Police would be almost into position. If this guy ran, and Annie couldn't stop him, they would.

I just hoped Steve would still be alive if the guy did run.

I took a deep breath of the warm afternoon air and started off the road toward the red Jeep buried in the brush. Then, before I had taken two steps, I heard Annie's clear voice ring out through the rocks.

"Stop! Police. Let him go and put your hands up!"

Then two shots filled the air.

Running low and silently, I headed back up the road, not allowing myself to think about Annie getting hurt.

As I neared a corner in the road that would allow me to see the road ahead and the area where the trail left the road to the mine, I slowed.

Annie somehow had gone up the trail a dozen steps and then climbed into some rocks. Somehow she had managed to stay hidden as the guy holding Steve had come down the trail to the road. He must have had a scanner and finally clued to the fact that they were coming for him.

She now had him basically pinned on the road using Steve as a shield.

Steve looked tired and scared out of his wits in his tan slacks, hiking boots, and tan shirt. The guy holding him was short, about five-four, and wore jeans and a light green T-shirt that was stained by sweat. His face looked like it had a five-day growth of beard and his dark hair looked like it hadn't seen a comb in days.

He had a large pistol pressed against Steve's temple and was holding it as if he knew what to do with it.

Annie saw me and nodded.

"Police!" I shouted. "You are surrounded!"

The guy spun in my direction, trying to drag Steve with him, but Steve tripped. The guy's gun left the side of Steve's head as he fought to get his hostage back into position. In doing so he gave Annie a clear shot.

And she took it.

The guy spun from the impact and smacked back into the rocks and brush in the shallow ditch beside the dirt road. His gun flew away from him to the left.

Steve spun the other way, tumbling to the ground in the middle of the road.

I came in fast and Annie was almost faster down the trail, both of us watching for any movement in the guy. Annie had gotten him in the right shoulder. He had been holding his gun in his right hand. It didn't look like the wound would be fatal. There was blood, but not enough to cause him any danger.

A huge rattlesnake came out of the brush under him and struck at the guy's left arm. Clearly the snake wasn't happy about some guy landing on him.

The kidnapper moaned and jerked away.

All I could do was laugh.

"That's going to make his recovery a little longer," Annie said, laughing and shaking her head as she turned to help Steve to his feet.

"You all right?" she asked the son of the Las Vegas Chief of Police.

Steve nodded and didn't say anything. He was clearly in shock.

"You dad will be here shortly," Annie said, patting Steve's shoulder. "Is there anyone else up there in that mine?"

Steve shook his head. "No one alive."

Then he dropped to the road and buried his head in his hands and just sobbed. The guy in the ditch moaned and the large rattler slithered off down the ditch, clearly not happy, as I glanced at Annie.

She looked up at the mine entrance and shook her head.

I had a slight desire to see what was in there, but my better judgment quickly got control.

Some things were better just left unseen.

SIX

I had managed to go up the dirt road a short distance and get a clear enough phone signal to get word out that it was clear.

Then I called Fleet and told him it was clear and to meet us back at the intersection on Highway 95. But I told him that it might be awhile. He might have to transport Steve to the hospital with his dad before he could take us. We had some paperwork to fill out and a story to tell before we would be released, of that I had no doubt.

By the time I got back to Annie, I could hear two Las Vegas Police cars powering up the road.

They slid to a stop just short of us in a cloud of dust and Annie's dad and Steven's dad both piled out.

"You two all right?" Annie's dad asked.

"Had to put a bullet in his shoulder," she said, pointing to the guy in the ditch.

"And then a snake helped keep him down as well," I added, smiling.

Annie's father just shook his head and studied the moaning man for a moment before turning back to us.

The Chief helped his son to his feet and eased him back toward the patrol car as a number of State Police officers arrived on the scene sending up even more clouds of dust into the hot evening air.

As we watched, two Nevada State Police officers carefully worked to extract the guy from the ditch and made sure he didn't have any other guns on him. Then they flipped him over on his face in the dirt and handcuffed him in the middle of the road, not seeming to care at all that he had been shot and snake bitten.

I moved over to the tall State Police officer who seemed to be in charge and pointed up the trail. "From what the Chief's son said, that cave up there isn't pretty. More than likely a major crime scene."

The guy nodded. "Which one of you put the bullet in this guy?"

"I did," Annie said, coming up and handing him her gun. "Retired Detective Annie Lott."

"Thank you, Detective," the officer said, handing the gun to one officer to put away. He didn't seem to care at all about the rifle in my hand.

Then he motioned for two other officers to follow him up the hill.

Annie's dad, Annie, and I moved into a deep area of shade and stood watching as the three State Police officers went into the cave while another stood near the prisoner in the road.

A short minute later one came out, moved to the edge of the mine entrance, and threw up.

"That can't be good," I said.

Both Annie and her father just shook their heads. In their days I was sure they had seen things I flat didn't want to know about.

A few minutes later the other two came out and came back down the trail, a haunted look in all of their eyes.

The Chief climbed out of the patrol car where he had been sitting with his son.

"Your son is going to need counseling help after what he saw up there," the officer said. "He's going to have a long road back to normal."

"That bad?" the Chief asked.

"Worse," the officer said. "This is going to solve a lot of missing persons' cases. More than either of us care to think about."

I had never seen a police officer look so haunted in his eyes. He also was going to have some trouble dealing with whatever horrors were in that old mine.

Then the State Police officer walked over to the guy lying handcuffed face-down in the dirt and kicked him square in the side of the stomach.

After that, the officer turned and walked away down the road past the patrol cars, leaving the desert silence and heat closing in around all of us.

At that moment I was so glad I had resisted the slight temptation to go up to the mine opening.

The Chief glanced over at us, a look of relief in his eyes. Then he said simply, "Thanks."

"You are more than welcome," Annie said as her father put his arm around her.

"Just take care of Steve," I said.

The Chief nodded and went back to the car to sit with his son.

As the door to the patrol car closed, I turned to Annie's father. "Think all the good feelings will cut down some on the paperwork for us?"

Both Annie and her father laughed, as did the state cop standing near the prisoner on the ground.

"Not a chance," Annie's father said between laughs.

Annie stepped over and kissed me. "You always were a dreamer."

Newsletter sign-up

Be the first to know!

Please sign up for the Kristine Kathryn Rusch and Dean Wesley Smith newsletters, and receive exclusive content, keep up with the latest news, releases and so much more—even the occasional giveaway.

So, what are you waiting for?
To sign up for Kristine Kathryn Rusch's newsletter go to kristinekathrynrusch.com.
To sign up for Dean Wesley Smith's newsletter go to deanwesleysmith.com.

But wait! There's more. Sign up for the WMG Publishing newsletter, too, and get the latest news and releases from all of the WMG authors and lines, including Kristine Grayson, Kris Nelscott, Dean Wesley Smith, *Fiction River, Smith's Monthly, Pulphouse Fiction Magazine* and so much more.

To sign up go to wmgpublishing.com.

About the Author

New York Times bestselling author Kristine Kathryn Rusch writes in almost every genre. Generally, she uses her real name (Rusch) for most of her writing. Under that name, she publishes bestselling science fiction and fantasy, award-winning mysteries, acclaimed mainstream fiction, controversial nonfiction, and the occasional romance. Her novels have made bestseller lists around the world and her short fiction has appeared in eighteen best of the year collections. She has won more than twenty-five awards for her fiction, including the Hugo, *Le Prix Imaginales*, the *Asimov's* Readers Choice award, and the *Ellery Queen Mystery Magazine* Readers Choice Award.

Publications from *The Chicago Tribune* to *Booklist* have included her Kris Nelscott mystery novels in their top-ten-best mystery novels of the year. The Nelscott books have received nominations for almost every award in the mystery field, including the best novel Edgar Award, and the Shamus Award.

She writes goofy romance novels as award-winner Kristine Grayson.

She also edits. Beginning with work at the innovative publishing company, Pulphouse, followed by her award-winning tenure at *The Magazine of Fantasy & Science Fiction*, she took fifteen years off before returning to editing with the original anthology series *Fiction River*, published by WMG Publishing.

To keep up with everything she does, go to kriswrites.com and sign up for her newsletter. To track her many pen names and series, see their individual websites (krisnelscott.com, kristinegrayson.com, retrievalartist.com, divingintothewreck.com, pulphouse.com).

About the Author

Considered one of the most prolific writers working in modern fiction, *USA Today* bestselling writer Dean Wesley Smith published far more than a hundred novels in forty years, and hundreds of short stories across many genres.

At the moment he produces novels in several major series, including the time travel Thunder Mountain novels set in the Old West, the galaxy-spanning Seeders Universe series, the urban fantasy Ghost of a Chance series, a superhero series starring Poker Boy, and a mystery series featuring the retired detectives of the Cold Poker Gang.

His monthly magazine, *Smith's Monthly*, which consists of only his own fiction, premiered in October 2013 and offers readers more than 70,000 words per issue, including a new and original novel every month.

During his career, Dean also wrote a couple dozen *Star Trek* novels, the only two original *Men in Black* novels, Spider-Man and X-Men novels, plus novels set in gaming and television worlds. Writing with his wife Kristine Kathryn Rusch under the name Kathryn Wesley, he wrote the novel for the NBC miniseries The Tenth Kingdom and other books for *Hallmark Hall of Fame* movies.

Dean also worked as a fiction editor off and on, starting at Pulphouse Publishing, then at *VB Tech Journal*, then Pocket Books, and now at WMG Publishing, where he is the editor of *Pulphouse Fiction Magazine*.

For more information about Dean's books and ongoing projects, please visit his website at www.deanwesleysmith.com and sign up for his newsletter.

Also from WMG Publishing

FICTION RIVER

Kristine Kathryn Rusch & Dean Wesley Smith, series editors

Doorways to Enchantment
Edited by Dayle A. Dermatis

Stolen
Edited by Leah Cutter

Chances
Edited by Kristine Grayson

Passions
Edited by Kristine Kathryn Rusch

Broken Dreams
Edited by Kristine Kathryn Rusch

Missed a previously published volume? No problem. Buy individual volumes anytime from your favorite bookseller.

Unnatural Worlds
Edited by Dean Wesley Smith & Kristine Kathryn Rusch

How to Save the World
Edited by John Helfers

Time Streams
Edited by Dean Wesley Smith

Christmas Ghosts
Edited by Kristine Grayson

Hex in the City
Edited by Kerrie L. Hughes

Moonscapes
Edited by Dean Wesley Smith

Special Edition: Crime
Edited by Kristine Kathryn Rusch

Fantasy Adrift
Edited by Kristine Kathryn Rusch

Universe Between
Edited by Dean Wesley Smith

Fantastic Detectives
Edited by Kristine Kathryn Rusch

Past Crime
Edited by Kristine Kathryn Rusch

Pulse Pounders
Edited by Kevin J. Anderson

Risk Takers
Edited by Dean Wesley Smith

Alchemy & Steam
Edited by Kerrie L. Hughes

Valor
Edited by Lee Allred

Recycled Pulp
Edited by John Helfers

Hidden in Crime
Edited by Kristine Kathryn Rusch

Sparks
Edited by Rebecca Moesta

Visions of the Apocalypse
Edited by John Helfers

Haunted
Edited by Kerrie L. Hughes

Last Stand
Edited by Dean Wesley Smith & Felicia Fredlund

Tavern Tales
Edited by Kerrie L. Hughes

No Humans Allowed
Edited by John Helfers

Editor's Choice
Edited by Mark Leslie

Pulse Pounders: Adrenaline
Edited by Kevin J. Anderson

Feel the Fear
Edited by Mark Leslie

Superpowers
Edited by Rebecca Moesta

Justice
Edited by Kristine Kathryn Rusch

Wishes
Edited by Rebecca Moesta

Pulse Pounders: Countdown
Edited by Kevin J. Anderson

Hard Choices
Edited by Dean Wesley Smith

Feel the Love
Edited by Mark Leslie

Special Edition: Spies
Edited by Kristine Kathryn Rusch

Special Edition: Summer Sizzles
Edited by Kristine Kathryn Rusch

Superstitious
Edited by Mark Leslie

Fiction River Presents
Allyson Longueira, Series Editor

Fiction River's line of reprint anthologies.

Fiction River has published more than 400 amazing stories by more than 100 talented authors since its inception, from *New York Times* bestsellers to debut authors. So, WMG Publishing decided to start bringing back some of the earlier stories in new compilations.

VOLUMES:

Debut Authors
The Unexpected
Darker Realms
Racing the Clock
Legacies
Readers' Choice
Writers Without Borders
Among the Stars
Sorcery & Steam
Cats!
Mysterious Women
Time Travelers

Pulphouse Fiction Magazine

Pulphouse Fiction Magazine, edited by Dean Wesley Smith, made its return in 2018, twenty years after its last issue. Each new issue contains about 70,000 words of short fiction. This reincarnation mixes some of the stories from the old *Pulphouse* days with brand-new fiction. The magazine has an attitude, as did the first run. No genre limitations, but high-quality writing and strangeness.

EXPANDED COPYRIGHT INFORMATION

Expanded Copyright Information

Expanded Copyright Information

Expanded Copyright Information

Expanded Copyright Information

CPSIA information can be obtained
at www.ICGtesting.com
Printed in the USA
LVHW091156150422
716296LV00027B/1580